BROTHER TO DRAGONS

David Hartnett was born in 1952 and read English at Exeter College, Oxford. He has published four previous collections of poetry and one novel, *Black Milk*. He is married with two children and lives in Sussex.

David Hartnett

BROTHER TO DRAGONS

VINTAGE

Published by Vintage 1999

2 4 6 8 10 9 7 5 3 1

Copyright © David Hartnett 1998

First published in Great Britain in 1998
by Jonathan Cape

Vintage
Random House, 20 Vauxhall Bridge Road,
London SW1V 2SA

Random House Australia (Pty) Limited
20 Alfred Street, Milsons Point, Sydney
New South Wales 2061, Australia

Random House New Zealand Limited
18 Poland Road, Glenfield, Auckland 10, New Zealand

Random House South Africa (Pty) Limited
Endulini, 5A Jubilee Road, Parktown 2193, South Africa

Random House UK Limited Reg. No. 954009

A CIP catalogue record for this book
is available from the British Library

ISBN 0 09 977811 4

Printed and bound in Great Britain by
Cox & Wyman Limited, Reading, Berkshire

When I looked for good, then evil came unto me: and when I waited for light, there came darkness. . . I am a brother to dragons, and a companion to owls. My skin is black upon me, and my bones are burned with heat.

These wars have been so great, they are forgotten
Like the Egyptian Dynasts. . .

Note

All the people in this story are imaginary; so are many of the places. My 'Chalkhampton Chums' regiment is, likewise, an invention. Nevertheless it could be said to typify the many volunteer units – Kitchener's 'New Army' – raised all over the United Kingdom during the first months of the Great War and 'baptised', two years later, on the first day of the Somme. My regiment's Second Battalion finds itself deployed in part of a sector occupied on that morning by units of the 4th and 29th Divisions. Needless to say, what happens to my battalion – or rather, what the Captain of one of its front line companies remembers to have happened – must remain a necessary fiction.

The epigraphs are from Job 30: 29–30 and Louis Simpson's poem 'I Dreamed that in a City Dark as Paris'.

Contents

1. On Thundersbarrow

April – August 1914

In those days a branch line ran almost as far as the village, forking away from the main line out of Chalkhampton terminus to creep north up the flood plain of the Rother. Squeezed between the river's senile loops and the serpentine ridge of the Downs, the railway ran on top of a raised dyke until, arriving at a gap eroded in the hills towards the end of the last Ice Age, it turned sharply west and melted into the mauve haze of the weald. At this intersection of chalk, water and clay, where the frozen waves of downland plunged into a foamy woodland trough, lay Ecclesden Halt. Named after the manor whose yellow slated roof and black peacock weather vane could distantly be glimpsed through thick strata of beech, chestnut and oak, this isolated platform seemed at once a gateway and a barrier, inviting the traveller to pause yet urging him in the end to hurry past to more overtly welcoming destinations. Here the north-facing escarpment of the Downs rose steeply, surging up from the track between the ticket office and the stationmaster's house towards the distant conical summit of Thundersbarrow. It was the presence of this hill, rooted in earth yet haunted, in its vertical sweep and lift, by a dream of ancient seas, which gave to Ecclesden Halt its air of self-reliant if baffled solitude. At this period Thundersbarrow itself was a stark wilderness, the monotonous grey-green of its flanks relieved here and there with dirty white flakes of sheep or the darker smudges of wind-moulded hawthorn. Other marks which, when seen from the station platform, seemed no more than shadows running in confused streaks and arcs this way and that along the surface of the hill, revealed themselves on a closer inspection to be the gouged and heaped up remnants of prehistoric workings. What these slumped embankments and silted ditches might once have guarded or imprisoned few nowadays were bothered to consider. Yet their silent witness to an age of furious embattled action was not as anachronistic as it seemed. The wilderness had long since been invaded.

As far back as anybody could remember, so far back that the very fact had accrued a canonic permanence, the hill had been quarried for chalk. South-east of the station, in a combe hidden from direct view of the railway, a tiered succession of pits climbed up the side of the hill, their white scars spreading nearly to the top of Thundersbarrow itself. Even when they did not say it, people felt this place harboured the real heart of the hill. Everything seemed naked here, exposed. The chalk, hidden or weathered elsewhere, was always new in the quarry, its tones, passing from white to grey to green, always fresh and gleaming. Here could be traced the secret history of the hill: its strange and difficult birth in water, its long sojourn in the darkness of oceans, its gradual rise into light as those oceans receded. The quarry was Thundersbarrow's secret chronicle.

It was also an arena of work and noise and danger. If the pits seemed as old nowadays as the slumped earthworks upon which they were gradually encroaching, the men who presided over their kingdom, ensuring that lime would always be available for field and wall, appeared no less rooted and essential. It was the quarrymen who clambered up the sheer blocks of the chalk cliff-faces to pour the black grains of lyddite into a prepared borehole. It was the quarrymen who set the detonators and slithered back to the safety of corrugated sheds to wait for the explosion. They loosened the blocks with augers, then took pickaxes to break them up, carting the fragments away to be pulverised in the steam-driven crushing mill. It was quarrymen too who served the three great flint-faced lime kilns that rose out of the scree at the back of Lower Pit like carvings of pagan gods, their features eroded to a sinister anonymity. Setting beech and ash branches to smoulder in the grated fire chamber, the limeburner would pack the neck of the flue with chalk then keep vigil for weeks, an alchemist presiding over the mysterious transformation of rock into lime. Afterwards, the soft corrosive powder

4

would be shovelled on to trucks and driven down a funicular that ran south round the summit of Thundersbarrow to a wharf beside the river. If the quarry was the hill's stronghold, the quarrymen were its garrison.

They were also a race apart. Far from the somnolent deep-laned world of farm and field, that wealden kingdom presided over by manor, church and school, the quarrymen lived with their families in a muddle of hovels along either side of a valley whose sides still bore the striated traces of glacial melt waters. The quarryfolks' permanent presence was also an exile. Without a conventional god (their church a corrugated hut in an abandoned pit where, unmediated by a priest, worshippers would speak spontaneously in tongues); without morals (some quarrymen were known to take more than one wife); without prosperity (lime, so the saying went, never bought anyone a feather bed); the people who worked the chalk were condemned not to escape it. Their children irregularly attended the village school despite the blandishments of vicar and governors. Though they drank in the Limeburner's Arms the actual limeburners hardly mixed with those who worked the land or served up at the big house. There was an apartness about the quarryfolk which put them beyond the ordinary. They were touched some said; one or two of their women had the second sight. And indeed if a stranger were to glance at one of the leather-aproned men bent over cairn or rockface, he might see in the eyes or the set of the face something both furtive and noble which he would forever afterwards associate with the grey and orange patina of a flint or the dry shudder of an explosion.

For the quarryfolk this internal exile had come to be a part of the pattern of things, handed down and almost ordained. So that when, on one famous occasion, the vicar had been heard to pronounce that at least one tribe had eluded God's Wrath and escaped the flood, he was instantly understood. That Good Friday in Lady Tremain's drawing room after morning service, it was obvious to the scatter of guests that the Reverend Langridge had had one sherry too many. Yet no one demurred. The Tremain family owned the quarry. That too was an inheritance of centuries. They did not love what they owned. For generations now the pits and their ever-spreading slum in Quarry Bottom had been a source of conflict and difficulty: labour disputes, standoffs, even the odd riot. Latterly too the business had begun to lose money, closing down two of the three kilns until further notice. Yet, if the huddle of dowagers and ex-servicemen turned briefly from the ruby-faced vicar to glance at their hostess's ivory imperturbability, it was not to communicate any sense of compassion. For just as the quarrymen had always worked the hill; so the Tremains had always owned the quarry. This too was a part of whatever divine plan vicars and the second-sighted had been put on earth to receive and expound. The Reverend Langridge's intimation of some primal fault, some ancient turning aside from the paths of righteousness, embraced both hill and village, quarry and manor. And Lady Tremain, who might have been expected to allow the merest hair crack to appear just this once in her ivory mask, merely gestured to Simmons to refill the Reverend's glass.

Outside the wind was getting up. It shook the clipped screen of box on the terrace and raised little swirls of grey dust in front of the French windows. Chalk. Even here it penetrated, a slow tide creeping into every corner, furring every surface with its arid and futile memory of water. Each morning down at Ecclesden Halt a boy with a broom moved along the platform in a white cloud. Yet by noon the stationmaster's carefully tended barrels of flowers would be covered with a fresh skin of dust. Even his fossil ammonite, bought for a chew of tobacco from Mucky Gurl the crushing mill foreman and set into the wall of the waiting room, was speckled with the very substance that had helped preserve it. Ecclesden, so the legend went, would last until the dragon under Thundersbarrow awoke and, famished after his long sleep, bit a hole in the side of the hill, thus allowing the sea to flood down Quarry Bottom. Every day the quarrymen woke the dragon with gunpowder. Every day the landscape was flooded. Lady Tremain turned back to her guests. The vicar had moved on to the subject of German expansionism and the Kaiser, another race born out of darkness and fated to return thither. It was time for the lunch gong. On the terrace the wind summoned up yet more brief ammonites from the dust.

That blustery Good Friday afternoon, when the four o'clock from Chalkhampton drew up at Ecclesden Halt, only two passengers stepped down into the wind. The first, a bent old man, wearing knee breeches and a stiff smock, was Joseph the superannuated homefarm shepherd. He had been into Chalkhampton on a visit to his sister who was in service at one of the big seafront hotels. Under his arm he carried a brown paper parcel badged with smears of sealing wax. The stationmaster turned from watering one of his half barrels of wallflowers. Setting down his can he stood with arms folded, blocking old Joseph's way.

– Home is the sailor, home from the sea, eh Joseph? – said the stationmaster and laughed, for he would have liked to have been appreciated for his literary allusions, however inapposite, and had long since learnt that the most enthusiastic audience was himself. For reply the shepherd who, in his youth had joined up with the Chalkhampton Territorials and seen active service in the trenches before Sevastopol, made a short retching sound and sent a yellow arc of phlegm hurtling towards the nearest flower tub. The bright clots of wallflowers shivered a disconsolate welcome. The stationmaster averted his gaze. But he was still inclined to banter.

– What's that under your arm then, Joe? A new dicky for the Fair?

– 'Taint none of your business stationmaster, not now nor when the world ends neither. Now fuck off out my way. There's a skirt coming behind me. Get paddling with her.

Joseph spat again, this time on to the track, as the stationmaster executed a curious half jig to let him past, winking all the while, out of pious shock perhaps, or a purer physical disgust. Then he turned the full beam of his attention on the 'skirt' Joseph had mentioned. It was carrying a cardboard gladstone bag tied round with an exiguous strip of violet ribbon. The stationmaster prepared to be gallant, leaning forward as if to take the burden on himself but was rebuffed by a dark-eyed stare.

– I'm to be met here I think. By a brougham.

The stationmaster, who was inclined to become condescending where young ladies were concerned, raised one eyebrow and repeated

– A brougham, – as if only he, in his maleness, could comprehend the unfathomable implications of such a word. The wind was tugging at the young woman's trilby so that a strand of black hair escaped, whipping across her rather thin-lipped mouth. She raised a gloved hand and hooked it out of the way. She was stern.

– Yes, a brougham. Mrs Eddles gave me to believe . . .

But her other words were carried away on the wind, if indeed there were any other words. The young woman's confidence, so strong at the outset would often falter in this way. But the stationmaster was relieved.

– Ah! Mrs Eddles, – he exclaimed, delighted to find he was suddenly able to incorporate this hitherto troublesome phantom into the orderly furniture of things. – Then you must be the new assistant teacher. Mr Noone's replacement – I hope you'll forgive so mechanical a sobriquet Miss, er Miss . . . – There was a terrible silence during which the stationmaster sought relief in contemplating the oily eye of water inside his watering-can. It was as if his question had suddenly confronted this woman with an imponderable conundrum. Then at last her name did return to her, out of the wind or the hill or the ferocious shivering chorus of wallflowers.

– Miss Lumley, – she replied, setting down her bag with a sigh and looking past the stationmaster into the windy afternoon. She was pale he noticed but with blotches of colour on either cheek. And a full figure under that raglan coat. He liked a full figure even on a shortish woman. He felt inclined to grow expansive.

– Poor Noone, it was so sudden. And such a help to Mrs Eddles. Dug the garden for her. Planted it up. Though he could never quite achieve the quality of wallflower that I . . .

– I take it you *have* received my luggage. I went to the trouble of arranging to have it sent on from Chalkhampton this morning.

Wrenched back from his dream of horticultural gold the stationmaster winced, as though he were personally to blame for the trouble of Miss Lumley's arrangement. Which in her eyes he was. Only an assistant teacher but as uppity as a Tremain. He felt it incumbent to indulge in a hollow cough. He did not like to be made to feel defensive.

8

– Of course madam, of course. I sent it on this lunchtime. By the post van. As for the brougham. Mrs Eddles, I'm afraid, can be a little vague. There's only one in the whole village and that belongs to the manor. – The stationmaster smiled as if recollecting a particularly good joke. – I could telephone them if you like. Since you're stranded.

– She's not stranded. Wren was due to pick her up. In the dobbin cart. I heard it from the missus. But his kiln's been playing up lately. And he's not been so well.

The stationmaster resented the return of the shepherd more violently than he resented Miss Lumley's diffident hauteur. He rounded on Joseph, kicking over the watering-can so that it leaked a dark thread on to the swirling platform.

– What do you know Joe? You and that sheep's head or whatever it is under your arm. And as for that Wren and his so-called turns. He's probably lying inebriated outside the Limeburner's at this very moment.

– You and your fancy words. You know damn well Wren's took the pledge. Like his dad before him. And . . . – But here the shepherd's reply trailed away. He had seen something in the pretty stranger's face. A dream or the residue of a dream. And heard something too. A voice whispering out of bottomless suffering *All this because of her* which had woken him stark upright last night in that rundown boarding house up Orion Parade run by that ponce type Birkett. Now he approached closer as if trying to see through or behind her skin. Miss Lumley stiffened.

– You could take the shortcut over Thundersbarrow, missy. I'd come along if it weren't for this here parcel. Sheep's head he calls it, the pegging idiot, if you'll pardon my French.

And the stationmaster, who had begun to take a rather refined pleasure in the spectacle of Miss Lumley's discomfited arrival, suddenly saw his initiative slipping away. The assistant schoolteacher was leaning attentively to Joseph. Her sternness had melted into something more innocent though no less reserved. A brief smile had already pardoned the shepherd's French. The stationmaster coughed again.

9

– Permit me. We have a waiting room and a fire. I'm sure the Tremains will oblige. Lady Tremain is one of the school governors after all. A brougham you said so a brougham it must be. This way please. Permit me.

But the shepherd and the schoolteacher went on leaning together, as if supported by the wind, discovering a mutual warmth in the fierce red and brown embers of wallflowers.

– Yes missy, over the hill. You see that little bit of rail what brings the lime down to the wharf? Follow that until you reach a hollow way what forks left and dribbles all the way up over Five Lords Burgh where there's three old sticky pines (some call them the Whispering Knights) then down again past the quarry and then you can see Ecclesden itself. There's an iron paycock on the roof that Sir Colin had forged, and next door's the schoolhouse. I've done it in twenty minutes and you might in half an hour. Seeing as how you're a healthy wench.

The stationmaster coughed for one last time. He had resolved to be superior but firm. The situation was becoming most irregular.

– Really, Joseph. What is all this nonsense about hills and hollow ways. The lady does not want to be walking in this weather. It'll be raining soon I'll be bound. Look at that sky. And the quarry. And that dreadful Bottom. You can't seriously suggest that a lady . . .

For a moment Joseph appeared to have forgotten the company he was keeping. He spat directly on to the platform and shook a veinous fist under the stationmaster's nose.

– Bugger off, you old goat's turd. What do you know about rain. Go water your gillyflowers.

Surely now this sullen bitch would be brought to her senses. Surely she would see who was to be trusted and who reviled. Then he heard it, high, thin, borne away on the blustery wind. The new assistant schoolteacher was laughing. At him.

– I'm not a porcelain doll you know. I have walked before. – Then turning to Joseph, whose nose was running in the wind. – Thank you, Joseph. I'm sure it will be a tonic after that stuffy carriage. This man with the dobbin cart?

– Eric. Eric Wren. – The stationmaster listened to his own voice small and flattened in defeat.

– Thank you. This Eric Wren. Well perhaps his delay or his illness or whatever was fortuitous after all.

Crestfallen, the stationmaster nodded vigorously, making a mental note to employ fortuitous more frequently in his own vocabulary. The medals of the wallflowers were quivering with a malignant vivacity that would have earned his hatred if he hadn't himself raised them from seed. Joseph and the schoolteacher were already walking off down the platform towards the wicket gate in the palings that opened directly on to the windy flank of Thundersbarrow.

Beatrice Lumley was weary after her journey. Not one to admit fatigue, she stifled a yawn by pausing just inside the fence on the far side of Station Road and taking out a handkerchief to dab her forehead. As she had intended, Joseph, who was standing a little way down the road to make sure she took the correct path, did not notice. Waving his parcel in the air which, he had confided to her after they had left the platform, contained a rope for the bank holiday tug o'war (*stationmaster's jealous see, being referee and all*) he shouted something which the wind immediately snatched away and fragmented, so that his mouth went on working uselessly in his face like a frantic sea anemone. Pretending to understand Beatrice waved back with her handkerchief then turned to begin her climb.

The hill rose above her, its smooth metallic dome brushed by the brief racing shadows of clouds. She could not deny she was excited, she who in any public place would mount a rigorous guard on all inconvenient inner feelings. Yet the excitement had a heavy rooted feel, as if its source lay far beneath, hidden at the hill's core. So Beatrice climbed, traversing the short turfed slope on a track whose chalk ruts had been deep when carts travelled down them loaded with grain for export to Rome, and as she climbed the wind grew steadily stronger. Soon it was whipping at her hat and coat, stinging her eyes and pouring into her mouth with a thick fleshlike solidity. Gulping for breath, holding on to her trilby with one hand, while with the other she felt her cheap fibre gladstone bag buck and dance as if it wanted to become a leaf, Beatrice felt that the wind too was a part of the hill, that its invasive animal stealth had as much to do with the chalk under her feet as with the torn dirty white ribbons of sky which flapped and shifted restlessly over what remained of the afternoon. Beneath her the landscape flowed away into a haze of woodland and hamlet. She could make out the silvery streak of the river which the train had followed on the tedious journey out of Chalkhampton; the huddle of huts by the wharf where the lime was loaded on to the barges; the Halt where even now the stationmaster bowed to his tyrannical blooms. How far and small everything had become, filtered by the element of wind, as through a smeared glass. While on the bank at the side of the track, shivering clumps of some fur-leaved plant grew monstrous in their proximity, revealing to the breathless climber whorls of dirty cream flowers. So she went climbing upward, past the encampments of what she would one day learn to identify as Dead Nettle, then turning left as she had been advised into a narrow path between two high banks. As if reluctant to enter on what might prove to be an endless tunnel, the wind dropped away to a remote flamelike murmuring. Freed of its possessive attentions, Beatrice began to walk more calmly, unbuttoning her coat to allow the stiller quieter airs of the hollow way to soak up her sweaty perturbation.

The thickset bowler-hatted figure climbed briskly up the wooden ladder leaning against the greenish marl of the lower cliff-face. At the top he climbed out on to the outer ledge of Middle Pit and turned right. The sun, sinking in a cauldron of ragged clouds out beyond Chanctonbury, caught something bright and small on the man's dust-white leather jerkin. Briefly, he shielded his eyes, scanning the horizon for some sign, then moved forward to the edge of the shelf. A few inches below him, like the neck of a giant prehistoric storage jar, the flue of number three kiln, Nebuchadnezzar or old Neb as the quarrymen called it, gaped its dark mouth. Lying on his stomach, the man extended his arm to its full stretch and let his hand pass quickly over the kiln's mouth. A thin but steady stream of acrid smoke rose from the layers of small chalk and coal packed just below the rim of the mouth. The heat here was intense so that, as the man withdrew his hand, he took the time to wipe the back of it across his sweating forehead. Then he stood up, climbed back down the ladder and walked to where, an orifice in the kiln's flint-lined belly, the firing tunnel led back to the charging chamber. Crouching into the tunnel the man crawled forward to a wooden door wedged half shut against the chamber itself. He stared briefly then, shaking his head and muttering a repetitive self-deprecatory falsely refined *What a silly arse I be*, yanked the door savagely towards him. *Green am I Dadger? Forgot to sparge did I? Made Bucks? Made Blues?* As he spoke a blast of fierce heat escaped from the chamber beyond, followed by a coiling hank of smoke and some serpent-like sparks. But the man was oblivious to the threat of conflagration and busied himself with wedging the door into its new position. He went on muttering but in a high-pitched voice that seemed designed to parody some unseen enemy. *Too much small chalk on top. Let the fire go out sometimes. More straw in between. More straw boy.* The litany ended in a chuckle of self-congratulation. *Now you'll see. Saccy Horwood must be turning in his grave.* Then he turned back down the tunnel, emerging to straighten up with a satisfied groan and feel for the flint lighter which had reflected the dying sun some minutes before. Soon the cupped Woodbine took light. But however relaxed the man now seemed, the tense absorption which had enveloped him did not evaporate; it merely shifted further back inside him. And waited.

– Lob! Come out of it there. Come out I say.

The man had stood up. His spent cigarette spiralled into the windy evening, flaring briefly as he called again.

– Out you bugger!

There was an answering bark and, from the shadows under the hay-barn, a black and tanned terrier came hurtling bandy-legged with a mouth full of cobwebs. Eric Wren squatted and let the dog snuffle and nip round his three days' growth of beard. Then deftly he caught Lob's snout in one hand and with the other went picking through the wiry fur for fleas. One rose up to the surface like a shiny jet black water insect. Then it dived again. Eric Wren cursed goodnaturedly. The dog struggled and whined and finally broke free. He sat with his head on one side while his master addressed him.

– You old flea bag. What'll Charlie say, eh, when he comes home? He won't let the little bitch near you. Nor Nimrod neither. Will he? No, 'course he won't. 'That cur of yours,' he'll say. 'I won't have my beauties defiled by a cur.' Eh, eh? – The dog barked happily more for the tone than the content of the man's speech. He could tell his master was in one of his rare contented moods and was determined to make the most of its short life. Eric Wren stood up.

– It's a good burn if you ask me. That soap Pedgell pulled out of the top pit isn't half bad. No. It'll make best quicklime. Tod Dadger will have to eat his hat.

Almost before the wind had engulfed these words he turned and sent a meteor shower of phlegm arcing across the pit. He was shaking now, shaking and shouting.

– And I don't bloody well care, do you hear me. About the tapes or your bloody dead old man or anything. I don't care Charlie, for it's mine. It is. It's mine.

Lob cowered away, intending to lose himself in another ratting session. The man's voice was frayed and taut. It might have snapped altogether if, at that moment, the hill itself hadn't risen up, a gigantic beast pressing in upon him, hotly, without mercy. So that the tears came. As they always did.

– I'm sorry Charlie, so sorry.

He sank down on the ground, his head between his knees. The beast was still there, in the place where his skull should be, both light and heavy. Oh so light and so heavy. The limeburner groaned and then went very still. The pressure in his ears was growing. They would come now, as they always did, echoing through him as if he were a tunnel, which he was, probably, whispering and shouting, cursing and laughing. But it was not the right place. Not now, not here. Not with the lime burning so well. He could hear Lob as if on a distant peak, whimpering and squealing after a rat. He must summon him before he disappeared down some impossibly narrow tunnel. Except that he himself was the tunnel, down which everything had already disappeared, in preparation for the voices. But Eric could not move. The air felt very still and sharp. He could hear the ants tickling with shiny black antennae through their endless mazes. He could see the birds ruffling out their feathers in the hawthorn. He could feel the weight of every block of chalk in the entire hill. He was the dragon eating it all up, swallowing the darkness and spitting it back as light. There were footsteps too. He smelt the shyness and nobility of the stranger who was coming towards him through the dark light of the hill. Shyness, nobility and something else. A mischievousness almost. Like a curse. If he could only lift his head.

The hollow way had died out; to her right the three Scots pines loomed up. Beneath them, at an angle, stood a small wooden cross. She might have gone over to it and attempted to decipher the scratchy inscription if, into the corner of her eye, there hadn't intruded the faintest glimmer of white. Directly ahead lay a grassy mound in the rough shape of a bell which she guessed immediately must be the 'burgh' Joseph had mentioned. Beside it, appearing to hover above an area of mounds and hollows choked with thistles, nettles and sheep dung, was the whiteness which had caught her attention. Drawing nearer, she soon realised that what had appeared to be a continuous sheet was in fact a complex net of ribbons. The ribbons were made of cotton and knotted tightly to pickets driven down into the turf. In the fading light it looked as though someone might have been trying to stop a section of the hill from rising explosively into the air or, more strangely, to mark the place where something falling from the windy air might settle and burrow down into the chalk. The tapes fluttered and hissed in the wind, making a thin mournful sound. Then all at once, as if the sound of the ribbons were its prelude (and indeed, long afterwards, she would associate the two noises, as if they had arisen simultaneously out of the depths of the hill), there came a cry. Though high-pitched and wordless, it was unmistakably human, which only made the shivering in Beatrice's body the more disturbing. Now as the cry subsided the fire rose up, brief and distant like a tongue. Leaving the mysterious tapes behind her, Beatrice came to what seemed like a great trench or mouth of darkness. There was the fiery tongue again, flickering out from the mouth which, as her eyes adjusted, became a pit. At the bottom of the pit, beside what looked like a huge carved torso, a man was crouching in a posture of worship or exhaustion. Suddenly the man sat up. His body, she saw, wavered, as if under some constant unseen bombardment. Then the cry again, wordless as before but coagulating to words in a foam of bloodstreaked saliva,

    – ever for Lord the of house the in dwell will I and life my of days the all me follow shall mercy and kindness loving they . . . But white city white city white city

She knew then that she should turn, turn and run, back down to the Halt, into her old life. But remained standing on the lip of the crater until he looked up, wiping the bloody flecks from his cheeks and fumbling for the bowler hat that had rolled away against a cairn of chalk. It was too late now to do anything but speak as calmly as possible out of whatever it was she had lost, in her new nakedness of exile.

    – I'm looking for the schoolhouse. They said I could reach it from this direction. But I'm lost. I think.

How small and cold her words sounded, as if she were no higher than the turf-covered molehills with their beaded caps of rabbit dung. The man, who might have been a fragment from the carved torso which, she now saw, was a sort of massive flint bottle, staggered upright and lifted his hands to his ears. The bowler hat was back on his head now, the tilted trademark of some demented music-hall star. The thought would have made her laugh if she hadn't been so frightened. For some reason the arena of hissing tapes came back into her mind. Somehow she must go forward. She resolved to be stern.

    – I say. My man. Down there. I must reach the schoolhouse by nightfall. Mrs Eddles expects me. I can pay. Look.

And he who had surrendered as the vicious and ungainsayable tongues lapped at the edge of his mind; he who had borne their terrible withdrawal and must now bear the still more terrible hole of their absence; saw through his flayed eyes and heard through his violated ears the woman who had come to Ecclesden.

– It's you then. They said it would be you. Yes.

Beatrice Lumley, who was nothing if not down to earth, so she averred, laughed a small laugh into the blind eye of the kiln.

– Of course it's me. Who else should it be? The Great Whore of Babylon?

Why she had chosen these words and why she didn't immediately blush for shame, she couldn't afterwards quite remember. But thought it might have had something to do with the man's sudden radiant smile which seemed to announce his full recovery from whatever possession had been inflicting him. *He's not been well lately. And as for Wren's so-called fits.* She had come down now to where he stood at the base of the kiln. And peered at him curiously.

– And you must be Mr Wren. Down at the Halt they . . .

But her words were drowned in his long guffaw.

– That's what I'd forgotten. That's what I was trying to remember. And you took it upon yourself. Right over the hill. – He laughed again and scratched the back of his head. A dog was barking somewhere near.

– Lob. New schoolteacher's come. We forgot to fetch her in the dobbin cart. Won't Mrs Eddles be hopping? Quick now. The lady's cold. – Then more quietly, offering her his hand to climb up into the wobbly three-wheeled wagon which stood near the head of the funicular, harnessed to an ageing piebald pony, – Yes you've come all right. You've come just when I wasn't expecting. – And Beatrice, who had never had much time for riddles, supposed that this guardian of the kiln was indeed a trifle touched as the stationmaster had implied. Which he was. But not in any way she might yet have understood.

Beatrice Lumley, who had never had the occasion to travel in a three-wheeled trap before, especially not one caked with powder of lime, attempted a grim composure. Straightbacked, the gladstone bag on her knees, she tried not to register the vehicle's vicious joltings as it limped down the rough flint track out of the quarry, nor the sulphurous halitosis of the terrier Lob who would insist on standing with his forepaws on the back of her wooden seat, his head resting against her shoulder. Her driver too was quite unlike any she had so far encountered, humming tunelessly the words of a hymn, then breaking out in a shout of abrasive laughter which he would as quickly cut off in order to whisper into the ears of the horse (who would keep veering toward any grass on the steep banks), or to the dog who, it appeared, was quite within his rights to intimidate, not to mention suffocate, their captive passenger. To make her still more uneasy, the limeburner did not talk to her directly but, when the road or horse allowed, would study her face and figure in darting sideways glances that made her feel he was reacquainting himself with someone he had met before. The track had broadened out now and they were passing between dark buildings set at random in the sides of the trench-like banks. Somewhere a dog barked making Lob growl so that the hair on Beatrice's neck stood on end. There were lights here and there, in uncurtained and roughly framed windows, illuminating bare interiors where shadows huddled to blackened flue-pipes or gnawed chunks of bread and dripping at scrubbed tables. A woman's scream drifted across from one of the buildings higher up the valley. A door banged. Eric Wren had passed on to another hymn.

Christian dost thou see them
    On the holy ground . . .

Lob's whiskers were tickling her neck. She felt an intolerable urge to scream back at the now muffled, or strangled, screaming woman. Her voice when it came was high-pitched, thin.

– Is this the village?

– *How the troops of Midian.* No. *Prowl and prowl.* Quarry Bottom. *Prowl and prowl.* Eh Lob? *Prowl around.*

For answer Lob yapped three sharp barks that quite deafened

Beatrice for a moment. How far away the Halt seemed now and her mood of exaltation as she had climbed the hill. What dark interior was this man taking her to, past the hovels of the people who lived for chalk? Would he have taken her this way if he had come to the station as Mrs Eddles had evidently planned? At any other time such careless indifference to her feelings would have stung Beatrice Lumley to the quick. But tonight she had travelled beyond the boundaries of aggrieved self-worth. She felt empty and afraid. Yet alert. They were turning out of Quarry Bottom. She looked back at its dusky depths.

– Do the quarry children attend the school?

Eric Wren had lapsed into silence. He looked up and grinned, a ghostly guide spotted with lime.

– Some do. When they can be spared. Book-learning doesn't make lime. That's what my dad used to say.

Beatrice shivered for a lost gentility. But the shiver soon passed. She felt Lob's tongue flicker across her left ear lobe. And laughed despite herself. Eric Wren studied her for a moment.

– I can see you won't be against us, Miss Lumley. I can see that much at least.

If his words had been intended to reassure, their intimation of suppressed conflict made her stomach knot nervously for a second. She remembered she was due on this weekend. Up ahead the darkness seemed to be gathering in thick pools at the base of a new cliff. But what rock could billow like that, parting to reveal a long drive at the end of which stood a lit vessel of a house, moored under Thundersbarrow as if waiting for calmer weather? The cliffs of rhododendrons and camellias were spotted with cones and pleated medallions of blossom that the darkness had drained of colour. They might have been sea creatures abandoned by daylight's tide: clots of barnacles, sea anemones, lava fronds, enduring the suffocation of night.

– What do you call that house beyond the big shrubs? Ecclesden Manor?

She had answered herself so that Eric Wren merely spat, though

19

whether to confirm or curse or simply to mark another stage of their descent, it was impossible to say. Briefly, an uncurtained window in the manor's upper storey revealed the silhouette of a figure against its orange glow. Then the curtains were drawn or a shrub intruded, harried by the wind. So Beatrice Lumley arrived at her destination on the evening of the last Good Friday before the war, in a dobbin cart with a limeburner and his dog.

Two days previously, Beatrice Lumley had left the Surrey town where she had hitherto spent almost all her life, to journey south to the coast. From the moment Aunt Millicent had craned up to the carriage window to bestow one of those frigid pecks on the cheek which passed in her world for a kiss, to the encounter with Joseph and the stationmaster, the journey had been stunningly uneventful. The only out of the ordinary incident had occurred during the evening of her overnight stop at the Terminus Hotel in Chalkhampton, when she had witnessed a drunken commercial traveller being evicted from the lounge for bad language. *Snot me sat bloody Kraut* he kept shouting as he was hustled through the revolving door, an occult chant which the embarrassed night porter elucidated as referring to some domestic dispute involving a Hamburg butcher recently settled in the town. But to Beatrice, alone and away from home for the first time, every incident, every setting for every incident took on a colouring that seemed to precipitate her towards dream even as she felt herself plunged in a world more solid, more grainy, than anything she had ever known before. The world seemed at once very fast and very slow. As in nights of childhood fever, objects could be both far and near. One moment she would be staring at open pores the size of lunar craters on the nasal wings of a ticket collector, the next she would be looking down on the entire town of Chalkhampton, its maze of hilly streets, its ruinous Roman fort (now housing a hospital), its pier like a black horizontal trunk sending out aerial roots of girders into the grey Channel. Then that vision too was gone, shrinking to another stuffy railway carriage, carrying her north-west this time, towards a range of hills that seemed higher than they ought to be. Beyond this barrier lay her final destination. But whenever she tried to put flesh on the fact, knowledge darkened and she was obliged to stare blankly at a glass-framed advertisement for Thermogene ('Defeats Rheumatism') on the partition opposite.

Beatrice Lumley had longed for this moment again and again during the last six months. But now that it had finally arrived she felt inadequate to concentrate on what she fancied must be its essence. A solitary, somewhat solemn girl, she was inclined to spend much time on abstract notions and had even dipped into a dog-eared translation of *Also Sprach Zarathustra* which her aunt had inappropriately inherited from a second cousin who had studied at Heidelberg. Beatrice's mother and father were both dead, her father in a railway accident during the South African War where he had served as a senior stores clerk; her mother of a long consumption. She could barely remember either of them, having been adopted at three by her mother's one unmarried sister and taken from Ealing to live in Surrey. Her Aunt Millicent, a proper, somewhat humourless vegetarian, entirely untainted by Fabianism, had brought Beatrice up to be self-sufficient yet diffident. Unloving but fanatically devoted to duty, she had ensured her niece had an untroubled if dull childhood. Then, when her charge had reached the age of twelve, she issued the standard minatory instructions about the dire consequences of allowing yourself to be touched by men, skirted all mention of the menses and indulged in a long disquisition on the evils of dyspepsia. Beatrice had not been brought up to eschew meat since, with the logic of a genuine fanatic, her aunt believed that true conversion could only come from within. A false light at fourteen exposed her to the withered defecations of her aunt's nut cutlets after which she gratefully returned to the no less arid parade of pork chop and sausage. By the time she was fifteen, having sought through school friends and reading to fill in some of the woeful gaps which her aunt had deliberately left in her rather fragile ramparts, Beatrice had realised that reserve and watchfulness could protect as well as alienate. By seventeen she had shed altogether any shreds of childhood levity and was known to her schoolmates as a swot, ever willing to withdraw into the library, terminally reluctant to trade secrets or exchange visits. Then at eighteen had come the opportunity to study for the National Certificate. Vigilant and undemonstrative as ever, Beatrice embraced her chance with a fervent self-disciplined energy that would only have been recognised as passion by the most minutely particular observer. For beneath her reserve, Beatrice longed for some intimacy she did not have the knowledge either to define or name and, in the sitting of an exam that would qualify her to teach, saw the chance to move, or sidle, towards her goal. How galling then to find, once the results had come through and the congratulations been received, that she must resign herself to working in the very school from which she had hoped to escape, a student teacher labouring under the despotic and inconsistent rule of Mr Nelligan. Beatrice had despaired then, in the Winter of '13, walking home through wet twilit streets towards the comfortless comfort of her aunt's house, where she would lie for hours in her bedroom staring at the outline of a hook-nosed ghoul in the cracked plaster ceiling, a half-read and never finished copy of *Middlemarch* by her side, while downstairs her aunt and two fellow altar decorators knitted to the accompaniment of murmured platitudes. Sometimes she would touch herself gently, almost sorrowfully, between the thighs, then flinch away, terrified by the puritanical lusts of youth. At such moments she was visited by a self-hatred that was almost physical. *Why me why me why me* she would moan, unable to root the grandiosity of her self-pity in any recognisably appropriate cause. Gingerly sniffing the salts on her forefinger she would weep for the world she wanted yet loathed for wanting, since want was a measure of ignorance.

Then, soon after Christmas, another dismal affair unenlightened by the visit of one of her father's brothers and his noisy family, Mr Nelligan had summoned her to his study and told her the news. Down on the south coast, near Chalkhampton, Mrs Eddles, his old colleague at the College, was in desperate need, now that Mr Noone, so long her right-hand man at the village school, had taken himself off to a sanatorium at Leukerbad. Could Mr Nelligan be of service, for old time's sake? It would be a temporary post of course since Noone was a Christian and bound to recover, but a post ideally suited to a student. Mr Nelligan had looked up and, deep within the distorting prism of his pebble glasses, Beatrice had detected that familiar blend of amusement and contempt with which her headmaster treated all old pupils. He would be glad to see her go, with her reserve and her watchful, almost aggrieved silences, even though Mrs Eddles's letter had implicitly anticipated a male. So, one bright frosty January day, Beatrice travelled down to Chalkhampton to be interviewed by the Board of Governors. The setting was an office next to the town hall. Nervous enough to trip as she negotiated the steps to the front door, Beatrice had recovered to deliver an impression of self-containment which had overridden any lingering doubts in the governors' minds about the village and its press-ganged contingents of quarry children. Beatrice seemed, that chilly afternoon, to be almost sexless and certainly beyond the frailties commonly attributed to her sex. That she was bleeding profusely at the time and had had to retire just before the interview to stuff yet another napkin into an already overloaded pair of drawers, only made her more icily determined. So she was offered the post, despite the absence of the governor closest to the business, Lady Tremain herself, who, nevertheless, wrote a week later, approving the appointment. Beatrice had been so excited that she had actually embraced her aunt on her return, a gesture that had as much to do with guilt as thankfulness. But Aunt Millicent had been primly practical as ever and Beatrice's mood soon settled back into a familiar unforgiving watchfulness.

The sound was unearthly yet of the earth. Subtly, her dawn dream made way for the invasion, if such it was and not some gentler more terrible beckoning and prayer. So that the stationmaster, who had been condescendingly showing her through a door into the barrow on the hill, suddenly sprouted wings, leaping up on to the top of the mound to shout again and again the same staccato phrase *Come sleeps four sleeps four come sleeps four sleeps four* followed by a high-pitched miaowing wail that had Lob the terrier running toward the barrow, a knot of white worms wriggling in his mouth. These he seemed to want to bury in the mound but now the stationmaster, who had lost his wings and turned into a soldier with the face of Eric Wren, threw himself on the dog and began firing down towards the quarry. She wanted to hide inside the mound but had grown too big for the door. The sky grew darker. Objects were falling out of it, raising up the chalk in dense billowy clouds. She crouched in the ditch naked and grew aware of a tall figure leaning towards her. The figure, whose face she could not see, filled her with dread and longing. It leant towards her, blindly. She woke with the one insistent thought *white city we must get back to white city*. In the greyness of the morning the voices of her dream hovered for a moment then died back into distant inhuman cries.

– Peacocks, – Mrs Eddles replied curtly when the new assistant teacher enquired, drowsily perched on her chair in the clammy steam-filled kitchen of the schoolhouse. Beatrice, who had slept with great difficulty despite her fatigue, burdened on her new hard bed by the almost mineral density of some boiled mutton which her landlady had reluctantly supplied on her arrival yawned, yet attempted to demonstrate an interest.

– Are they wild? I thought they only lived in the Himalayas.

Mrs Eddles, strands of whose thin carroty hair had straggled from her mobcap and lay plastered on her forehead like poisonous vegetation, did not look up from the range where she was trying to excavate a gurgling saucepan with a spoon.

– Wild! Good gracious me, no. Pets. That's what they are. Or were. When Sir Colin was alive.

The spoon must have encountered something solid, for suddenly she withdrew it, staring down into the pit of the saucepan with a look of outraged amazement. Beatrice yawned and felt her mouth filling again with the rotten fumes of the night.

– Are they as close as that, then, at the big house?

Mrs Eddles had dug to her satisfaction and was heaving the

saucepan on to the table. Ladling out the grey mortar of porridge she did not bother to conceal her dissatisfied sighs at having to serve the woman who was supposed, in a sense, to serve her. But today was Easter Saturday and her usual help had not been willing to sacrifice a precious holiday.

– Sir Colin loved them. Used to feed them every morning on the terrace and call them all by name and goodness knows what else. But Lady Katherine, she's not at all enamoured. It's the noise you see. And the damage. She keeps them penned up now. I don't blame her. If you want my opinion they're a damned nuisance. But then – and here Beatrice noticed that the headmistress's eyes glimmered with a malign glee – Sir Colin left a lot of things for others to sort out. He was that kind of man.

Beatrice went on sipping unenthusiastically at the tip of her spoon. Her stomach was cramping again. Tomorrow it would be. Or tonight. She had already had a show. The Curse, Aunt had called it. Eve's curse. After she ate of the tree of knowledge.

– Damage? To what?

Mrs Eddles sighed, evidently disappointed that her new charge had not succumbed to her temptation to gossip.

– Plants of course. They're perfect demons for all sorts of buds and flowers.

But Mrs Eddles, who had little patience even at the best of times, was growing tired of this small talk if only because it reminded her too keenly of a life she would never be able to attain. She heaved up the saucepan.

– Now polish off that breakfast, Miss Lumley and we'll begin our tour of duty. The classrooms first. And Miss Lumley – here she placed the saucepan back on the table and leant forward so that Beatrice glimpsed down a funnel of nightgown two wrinkled swinging breasts – One word of advice. Don't concern yourself overmuch with the manor. Like last night when, between you and me, you said things that were better left unsaid. It's always awkward and seldom profitable, concerning oneself with those who are fated always to be above one's own station in life.

And Mrs Eddles smiled the complacent smile of one who has just delivered the very admonishment she herself would never dream of heeding. Beatrice stifled another yawn and carried her half-empty plate to the sink in the scullery. Far off yet near at hand the peacocks wailed again.

To Beatrice the night before seemed more dreamlike than her dawn visit to the barrow with the door. And truly she had been closer to sleep then, jolting on Eric Wren's cart and watching the cone of light made by his horn lantern slide in great arcs along the bushes at the side of the road. The limeburner had grown quiet passing the manor, as if he feared his hymn-singing might alert something or someone, perhaps the very person who had shown himself so briefly at that upstairs window. But now, in the lane leading to the schoolhouse he struck up in a pulsing baritone.

From Greenland's icy mountains
From Afric's coral strand . . .

The evergreen shrubs were so sheer at this point that Beatrice felt she had entered a tunnel deeper and longer than the hollow way on the hill. Down here the wind subsided to a far surf. Eric Wren's evocation of remote vistas and geographies only served to heighten her sense of suffocated nearness. She was entering a world where to cross a single five-acre field might have as much significance as an expedition to the Pole. The schoolhouse, a timber-framed building with a brick extension at one end, rose up in a gap among the rhododendrons. Startled by the movement, a grey form froze in the light of the swinging lantern. Its eyes glowed red. The terrier was crouching low on the footboard.

And only man is vile.

– Later Lob, later. Now I am about my father's business.

Beatrice barely had time to consider this aside for a figure was standing in the lighted doorway, beckoning with short violent jerks of the arm. Whoever it was clearly deplored their lingering outside and wanted the door closed as quickly as possible. Lob jumped down from the cart and barked but did not move closer to the schoolhouse. Eric Wren held out his hand for the new arrival to alight. As she did so he gave her arm a sudden squeeze, whether to encourage or warn she could not tell. Later, at the mirror in her little attic bedroom she would discover the pressure of his fingers still outlined in faint pink on the white flesh above her elbow.

If Beatrice Lumley had expected a conventional welcome after her long journey she was disappointed. Mrs Eddles seemed unaware of her new assistant's proffered hand, looking past her to where the limeburner was tethering the horse to an elder bush.

– Nothing for me then, Master Wren. Nothing for your old teacher?

The limeburner finished the slip knot in the rein and looked back down the tunnel of lane.

– I've other customers besides you, Mrs Eddles. And it's Easter.

– Martha, you mean. What do you get in return I wonder. Anybody would think you favoured them at the manor. That you liked them.

In answer Eric Wren cleared his throat but did not spit. He came up the path and stood just behind Beatrice who felt like a ghost, invisible and unheeded.

– Martha's just the undercook. Rabbits aren't as plentiful this year. And the new keeper's a sharp-eyed little runt. I'll get you your Easter Sunday dinner, Mrs Eddles. Miss Lumley here looks as though she could do with a good plump Ecclesden rabbit.

Grateful to be acknowledged, Beatrice smiled up at Eric. Mrs Eddles moved forward, seeming to notice her guest for the first time.

– You're late so there's nothing hot. I assume you ate along the way.

Taken aback by her sudden inclusion in this windswept secret world, Beatrice nodded furiously, though in fact she hadn't eaten since that morning. Eric Wren touched her shoulder briefly.

– Give her something to eat and I'll be off to see about them rabbits, Mrs Eddles.

The headmistress frowned. By rights this newcomer should have no more status than a pupil.

– A late arrival isn't a good start but I expect we can learn to do

27

better. Come in and leave your coat on the stand. Your trunks are here already. Eric here will take them upstairs.

Torn between resentment at the ease with which Mrs Eddles had blamed her for lateness and gratitude to the limeburner for appearing to consider her welfare, Beatrice busied herself removing her raglan in the narrow hall where tea chests and cairns of exercise books combined to exude a sickly odour of gas or rotting vegetables. Next to the coat stand a mirror reflected the limeburner and the teacher, the one burly and dark the other pale and scrawny. With a little shock of insight that had her instantly blushing, Beatrice saw, in that reversed world, who was the more vulnerable of the two and pitied Eric Wren for the quizzing he must endure.

– So if it's almost exhausted why don't you apply for permission to dig elsewhere?

– Dragon Pit you mean. Like in Dad's day?

– Why not? There's good soap up there, as you well know.

– And some bad bones. And the beginning of the end of one man's life. You oughtn't to say these things, Mrs E.

The headmistress laughed.

– Oh, oughtn't I? Then who else is going to say them? Your father would have wanted it. And if you can persuade the others. If you can knock it into their thick heads, Pedgell, Tod Dadger and the rest, you can *be* your father.

Silence. The wind fluttering round the house in nervous gusts. Mrs Eddles moving closer to the limeburner.

– He's back by the way. Your old friend. Or is it enemy? I never could tell. Anyway he's back a day early.

So the voices rose and fell in the glistening well of the mirror. And Beatrice on the far side of that silvery ambiguous world felt a sudden urgency to plunge in at whatever cost.

– Is that what the white tapes are for? Up on the hill? Near that cross? Is that where you'll be digging, Mr Wren?

At first the mirror people seemed frozen by her words. Or else they were too deep within their own world to hear. Then slowly the limeburner turned to her. He seemed diminished somehow, older.

– Tapes you say, Miss Lumley? On the hill?

She nodded diffidently, as if confessing to some shameful act. Eric Wren made a curious contorted movement with both his hands. They ended up being clasped together, though not in prayer.

– You saw them today? When you walked over?

She was frightened now of whatever it was she had helped to summon through the ruined arch of the limeburner's hands. Mrs Eddles was watching Eric Wren with a kind of vengeful tenderness. She was the true go-between forever excluded from the lives she moved among and fed off. Beatrice nodded, then turned back to the mirror and her rather unkempt hair. There was after all nothing else she could do. Mrs Eddles had turned away too.

– Don't forget the cases, Eric. Miss Lumley, come into the scullery and I'll serve you a cold collation. It really is very late.

Beatrice could tell her words had disturbed the pool of the mirror, perhaps forever. But already the only person who might have been willing to explain why this should be was stamping upstairs, carrying all her worldly possessions toward some unseen room.

– I've applied for more but the governors have their budget and won't be budged.

Beatrice glanced swiftly at her superior, wondering if she had noticed her own pun. She hadn't. They were standing in front of a tall bookcase in the second of the two classrooms which St George's could boast. The dusty shelves were scattered with a few dog-eared copies of Meckeljohn and Gill; some spelling primers and elementary tables books. Otherwise the cupboard seemed more regularly used for the storage of wood. There were stacks of cordage and neatly bundled faggots stuffed into every available space. An archive of timber. Yet there was no stove in the room. Beatrice experienced a wave of depression. Was this the freedom she had craved when living in her aunt's house? A tilting cupboard in a grimy room in a grimier house under a dark hill.

– What *are* the tapes for that I saw yesterday?

Her voice could not survive the icy breath of low spirits. It died on her lips and Mrs Eddles continued the guided tour.

– This will be your class. The fives to eights. Quarry and farm about equal. They come in rotas. When the harvest's on you'll have half a room of quarry. And during the winter when there's nothing doing on the land the quarry urchins will be off in the pits.

The desks faced her like mute ranks of headstones. There were no pictures on the yellow walls, merely a sampler invoking Our Lord and a small cotton Union Jack suspended from a scroll emblazoned with the rubric *Empire Day*. Beatrice moved down the aisle between the tombs of desks letting her fingers trickle over their wood and bolted iron, their surfaces like ancient tablets gouged with a palimpsest of curses, promises, desires. Here the semi-literate heirs of field and hill had established their claims and dynasties. *C is a shit. E hates M. Quarry 103 all out. Farm 104 for 2.* At home, for she found she suddenly had need of that vanished word however jarring it was to her memory, Beatrice had come across such inscriptions. But here they seemed more of a piece, more interlocked, less random. It was as if their semi-innocent codes mirrored a darker adult world. She looked up just as a shaft of sunlight escaped the morning's thick weight of cloud and came tilting down the room. It fell at her feet in a faint penumbra of warm days. Outside, against a high brick wall, the white blossom of cherry trees foamed. Dislodged by yesterday's wind, some of the petals had gathered in adhesive swarms on the dusty glass of a skylight. This was what she had chosen. This was the arena of her new life. Circumscribed, violent, inconsolable, the emotions of this place were to be hers too. So be it. She looked up at Mrs Eddles and smiled. Mrs Eddles did not respond. A sharp urinous smell warned Beatrice that the jakes were near at hand.

I don't believe you.

You don't believe me. You will.

I won't. You're just lying. Liar liar pants on fire.

You will, you will, believe me.

Where is it, where is it then? We could play in the kilns. We could play the battle of the kilns.

It's in the old pit. It's astounding. You'll see.

We haven't played kiln battle for ages. Look there's lightning over there. One. Two. Three.

Just up here in Dragon Pit.

It's coming nearer. Cripes look at that.

Bugger me. Like a blue knife. But all twisted. And another.

Eric I'm scared. And you shouldn't swear. Mater says.

C'mon it's just up here. You said you'd come. Let's count together. One two. C'mon.

It's louder in here. Like it's coming from underground. Is that where the thunder comes from, Eric?

How should I know. You're the one gets all the schooling.

Miss Jupp doesn't teach me anything I want to know. Just boring things. How I wish I was at big school.

I like Miss Jupp. She's got big jugs. You know what I'd like to do to Miss Jupp?

Stop it.

Well . . .

Stop it.

I'd like to get her in here alone with no clothes on and . . .

Not listening not listening not listening. Hic haec hoc hunc hanc hoc.

Jesus was a brasher. Right overhead. It made the chalk come down. Look, Charlie.

Is it safe? Are you sure?

C'mon Let's go right inside. It's starting to piss down.

And old Joseph found it?

When he was knocking in hurdles before shearing. Didn't know it was a cave. Just a 'ole in the ground he said.

And we're the only ones that know in the whole wide world. Isn't it exciting?

The only ones. And we'll have feasts here. And wars. Lots of wars. We'll fight to the last man. You and me. In this cave.

The storm's still around.

Yes, a storm over Thundersbarrow always strikes twice. That's what Dad says.

My pater and your dad don't like each other. If they knew we were up here.

But they don't, do they? Look here's the lantern I borrowed. Let's light it with a flint.

It's not just one cave. It's lots. Look at the way the light shines on them. And there's marks too. Like someone's been here.

Not any more.

And we're not to tell anyone.

We're going to swear on it. With blood.

I don't know whether I want . . .

You promised, Charlie.

You know what I think?

What?

I think this was made before the Romans. By the stonemen. I've been reading about them in Meckeljohn.

What for? To live in?

Maybe.

Dad says we're nothing but stonemen. Born with a flint instead of a heart. That's what Dad says.

Your dad doesn't like my pater.

Look how far back they go, right into the darkness, like tunnels. Perhaps the stonemen are still down there. Let's call them. Hey, hey, stonemen, stonemen.

Shh Eric stop stop I don't I feel I can't breathe Eric. I can't . . .

All right, all right, but you promised to swear the oath. You can't wriggle out of that, Charlie Tremain.

The thunder's back. Will it hurt, Eric?

Na. Hold your arm up. I'll do mine first. Then yours. Then we hold them together. So it all mixes together.

Ready?

Ready.

Say after me, We are blood brothers for evermore.

Listen to that thunder.

Say it.

We are bloodbrothers for evermore.

Sworn to help each other in every way.

Sworn. I say Eric, this isn't blasphemy is it?

Soldiers do it. And the Indians. All the tough fellows do it. All the real friends. C'mon Charlie. I've got to be back before dusk. Dad's not well.

Sworn to help each other in every way. There. I've said it. Quickly now. Oh OW.

There. Didn't hurt did it?

No, didn't hurt.

And now this cave is ours forever. In Dragon Pit on the side of Thundersbarrow. And we promise to defend it to the last man. For the honour of our tribe, Amen.

Amen.

That's a good cutter that black flint.

Where did you find it?

Over there. It's like it was made especially. With all those flakes sliced off. I'm going to keep it.

Isn't blood funny when it starts to dry. Not red at all.

No, more orangey. Like rust. Here, your rash looks bad again, Charlie. Does it itch?

Sometimes. C'mon Eric, the storm's going away again. It won't strike three times. Not even on Thundersbarrow.

She was lying in her grey attic room with its two slant windows, the one overlooking Thundersbarrow and the other a sloping pasture leading down to the Wild Brooks. She had been unable to manage any lunch, nauseated already by the grease-encrusted deposits that had passed for breakfast in the kitchen. Soon the queasiness would condense into a spiral in the pit of her groin, the spiral give birth to a red wheel that would somehow find its way by many secret tunnels up to the point behind her forehead just above her left eye. It was the old trouble, her Affliction as Aunt had termed it, which began just before she was due and would often be accompanied by nosebleeds and palpitations.

So she lay now, the cold flannel on her pulsing forehead while the peacocks next door ran through their gamut of cries, from a sad long-drawn-out miaow to a series of stabbing high-pitched wails. As she drifted through the first vertigos of semi-conciousness, the dream of the morning seemed about to continue where it had left off. Once more she found herself on the hill near the barrow. Once more the people of that country began to move round her. But suddenly from deep within or beyond her sleep, a long thunderous percussion seemed, if not to disperse the dream entirely, then to carry it out into the afternoon. All at once she found herself standing up. Through one window she could make out Mrs Eddles, hooded in a dirty green gaberdine, struggling to carry the recalcitrant frame of a mangle into the house. A couple of crumpled sheets lay nearby on the ground. Briefly, savagely, the headmistress looked up at the window, as if to throw a barb of resentment at a headache she both disbelieved in and wanted to worsen, then returned to her dark struggle. Now, through the other window Beatrice noticed that a grey mist had descended on Thundersbarrow, so that the hill appeared to wear a swollen fungal crown that had battened on its chalk skull. It was from deep within this mist that the explosion had come. Half-expecting to witness some terrible disaster, Beatrice pressed her face like a child against the cold rain-blurred glass. But there was nothing to be seen. Only, down in the front garden where a path ran between straggling lavender bushes, someone was running away hunched, his back turned, flinching at the decayed ripples of shock waves, intent at all costs on escape. At that moment she knew she had seen the faceless person of her dreams, the one who had stood in the manor window the night before, the one for whom Eric Wren lowered his voice. The rain was hardening. In the window-pane an old tin ventilator whirred with melancholic irregularity. Dead flies lay along the windowsill in dry pyramids. She felt a loosening in her groin and then, as if in sympathy, blood dripped from her nose. With head tilted back, pinching her nostrils, she let the stream tickle down her throat in a salty ribbon. The figure below had dissolved into the rain. Her spiralling headache slowed to a quiet throb.

That Easter Sunday, to Beatrice's delight and trepidation, a lawn fête was held in the grounds of Ecclesden Manor. Mrs Eddles announced this news over a breakfast whose elements, as if to reflect the benign influence of their neighbours, were both dry and light: oat cakes, a couple of speckled brown marans' eggs. Spooning out the yoke Beatrice felt emboldened to attempt a certain intimacy. Even her pains were quieter now.

– Will Mr Wren be going?

The harshness of the woman's laugh mocked both her question and its presumption of casualness. Beatrice's eyes clouded.

– To the fête? Him! The last time a Wren was invited to Ecclesden was when old Eric was alive, after the riot. And that was more a command than an invitation.

Mrs Eddles allowed a thick rope of egg-white to slide from her spoon to her bluish lips. Beatrice felt reprimanded. Yet detected in her new employer a barely controlled compulsion to talk.

– There was a wooden cross up on the hill. I've been wondering . . .

Mrs Eddles laid down her spoon and sighed.

– Well you *have* hit the nail on the head. And I suppose someone else will tell you if I don't. He asked to be buried up there, you see. In his last illness.

– Who?

– Old Eric of course. Young Eric's father. After his disgrace.

– In unconsecrated ground?

– Consecrated as far as the quarryfolk are concerned. You may as well accept that they are a race apart, Miss Lumley. Here Mrs Eddles glanced at the clock. – Goodness, we'll be late for church. Hurry now.

The questions which jostled to be answered would have to wait. Beatrice stood up, hugging within herself a child's unquenched capacity to be amazed as well as frightened. Or so she hoped. For there was little else to protect her in this place.

The fête was due to begin directly after Sunday morning service. At a quarter past twelve, still wearing her church hat and shawl, Beatrice accompanied Mrs Eddles down the rhododendron alley that led from the schoolhouse grounds to a gate in the wall of the manor gardens. Here and there beneath the great winged purple and crimson and mustard yellow shrubs that had so disturbed her on her arrival in the dobbin cart, Beatrice could make out a first foam of bluebells. The rain had passed over. The earth breathed a warm dampness.

– A perfect morning, Miss Lumley. As I always say, the sun shines on the manor now that Lady Katherine is in charge.

Mrs Eddles leant forward as if some ancient script were floating before her, with its raft of graven absolutes. Remembering a wild-haired hag wrestling in the rain with a cast iron juggernaut, Beatrice nodded non-committally. To her the rhododendron alley seemed both threatening and alluring. She could not bear to hear the sound of her own voice at such a moment. In the little church under the hill she had been disappointed not to see any of the Tremains. *They often attend evening service, it's more select you might say*, Mrs Eddles had whispered. So Beatrice had found herself looking beyond the swarm of strange faces to the fragmentary wall paintings which, according to the headmistress, some self-appointed local antiquary had uncovered the previous year. Though as far as Mrs Eddles was concerned it was a mystery why he had bothered, they were so old and bitty and what you could see was almost pagan it was quite revolting all that nakedness in a house of God she wondered the vicar allowed it. But as the querulous voice subsided into disapproving silence and the vicar slid with sublime ease from Asquith and Kaiser to death and resurrection, Beatrice found herself plunging deeper and deeper into a submarine kingdom of flickering jades and ochres. The wall paintings had poured into the church as sea pours into a newly breached cave in a cliff. The building had been transformed forever. The reflected reefs and rocks of masonry were softened yet deepened by the paint which rippled across them. Over the chancel arch a Christ in Judgment had been enthroned, a cold blue deity of shell-banks in some drowned city of marble. Beneath him Adam and Eve were being expelled from a garden whose leafy trees waved like crinoids brushed by shoals of fish. Their naked flesh had a slippery sheen that did not belong to creatures of the land. So they entered their exile, watched by an angel long-haired and silver-scaled as any mermaid. Meanwhile the vicar intoned and the people sat on, unaware of these oceanic mysteries overhead. And suddenly to Beatrice, sitting there in her own exile, the blood leaking out of her in jellied clots, it did not matter that the Tremains were absent. She had claimed this place for her own. What happened now would be a consequence of her own deliberate act. The sea-serpent grinned down at her, streams of bubbles escaping from his lips. The artist who had painted these forms knew the stories of which the Bible was just a recent redaction. He had stood on Thundersbarrow Hill and seen the powers of the world spread out beneath him. Offering a silent prayer to the maker of these images Beatrice knew that she would suffer in this place. Yet embraced that suffering, as Eve may have, floating out of her charmed reef garden for the first and last time.

The rhododendron alley had melted into an expanse of lawn that ran down past the east wing of the manor to the marshy edge of the Wild Brooks, where a line of pollarded willows already showed the rust of their spring leaves. On the clipped lawn stood the ranks of the stalls. People were moving there, in the wet afterlight of the overnight rain, arranging their goods or bowing to select. There were flower stalls and stalls of early vegetables, radish, spring cabbage, lettuce. A bookstall spilt its dusty spines on to the grass next to a table on which someone had arranged a whole army of clockwork mice. Off to one side of the fête, the Reverend Langridge had set up his model railway, to the delight of some local children who had been selected by invitation. On the terrace behind the low box hedge Lady Tremain sat with some attentive house guests discussing the merits of fund-raising for the Red Cross. Beatrice moved on across the open space of lawn. At her side Mrs Eddles carried a trug of tomato seedlings. What was she doing here with this woman, walking in front of a house whose facade suggested spaces too large to be properly lived in, yet too small to be abandoned or shut up? She felt the eyes of the whole multitude upon her and heard, above the general murmur, the bright harsh lilt of the owner.

– Oh that must be the new teacher. Pert little thing, isn't she?

– Don't let Charles catch her. Eh?

– Oh Charles, he's quite out of temper about the digging business. He won't be bothered by little chits like that.

Wearying of the subject the voices drawled lazily away. But Beatrice took care to put Mrs Eddles between her and the terrace until they arrived at the schoolhouse stall. Here she could at least sit down under the awning and stare into the translucent green stems of tiny tomato plants.

– Well may we labour still to dress this garden, still to tend plant, herb and flower.

He stood before her, his back against the sun, his boater fringed by a dim fire. The peacocks were calling again, but more quietly, two long dying falls, like meteors of sound curving earthward. She was hastily repotting one of the seedlings which she had knocked over in her surprise. The white bristled roots tickled her palm. Loam crumbled on her sleeve.

– Aren't you going to ask me who said that?

– I . . . I thought you did . . . I mean. – She pressed the seedling too firmly. Its stem collapsed, bruisedly.

– I say, you shouldn't be so rough. Old Eddles will be mad.

– Who then? Who said it?

She was hot with her error and his mockery. The wilting plant dropped from her thumb and forefinger. She noticed that his neck above its stiff wing collar was welted and red. A skin irritation of some kind. But she had no intention of showing compassion.

– Eve in her garden. Before she misbehaved.

– Like I have. – She wanted to appeal to his sympathy despite her irritation. He smiled.

– An accident with one of that old battle-axe's plants is hardly analogous to the original sin. Here, let me help.

Then he was brushing up the spilt compost with a hand whose back bore the same weltings as his neck. He looked up almost quizzically.

– I'd thought you'd recognise the quote, being a schoolteacher.

She blushed and bent down to rid herself of the offending plant. When she came up again, as if for air, he was signalling to someone or something at one of the windows. So the manor would always claim him at decisive moments in his life. He turned back, no longer seeming inclined to banter.

– Poor Oenone. She'd love to join in.

Beatrice suffered a brief envious vision of a glamorous girl, some cousin perhaps.

– Why don't you fetch her then?

He laughed.

– There'd be chaos if I did. Overturned stalls and screaming children. She's an excitable bitch.

– A bitch? Oh, I see.

It was her turn to laugh, if only to cover the embarrassment of so revealing a mistake.

–Yes, a retriever. She's still quite young. Mother hates her. Says she chewed up a pair of her satin slippers. Still, she's got old Nimrod for company. He's a retriever too. But I say, I owe you an apology.

– An apology?

How she hated her tendency to echo, as if she had no thoughts of her own.

– Yes, quoting at you like that. I haven't even read all of it, *Paradise Lost* I mean. Actually, I was almost certainly trying to impress you.

A woman with a large feather boa pushed forward and stared critically at Beatrice's stall.

– Are these Harbingers?

– No. They're tomato seedlings.

She had not meant to say so terrible a thing. The woman

39

withdrew affronted. The young man in the boater spluttered approval.

– Oh well done, you. I've always wanted to say something to her but never dared. But listen, this won't do. We haven't even gone in for introductions. I'm

– Charles Tremain. And you don't like walking in the rain.

He arched sandy eyebrows. He was prepared to be ingenuous.

– How do you know that?

– I saw you from the window at the schoolhouse. She decided not to mention the explosion.

A shadow passed across his face. The cloud overhead was swift moving.

– Oh, of course, yesterday. I'd gone to retrieve a book. So you were there watching. Quite the little spy, aren't we?

His irony imperfectly concealed a tremor of anxiety she was keen not to intensify.

– And how did you know who I was?

She was rolling a pellet of compost between forefinger and thumb.

– Oh, I've heard all about you from Eric Wren the limeburner. To be frank I fancy he's half in love with you already. But we'll have to put a stop to that. He's my best friend, Eric. Has been since we were so high. And of course we hate each other thoroughly.

This time she managed to retrieve the pot before the seedling came away. Yet she was assailed with a longing to go back, to be again in a time when she needn't be told and needn't understand. This land, half water and half earth, half underground and half among clouds, where words were whispers and whispers often curses, was claiming her too quickly and too completely. Yet standing in front of Charles Tremain she knew she could not go back again. She looked the heir of Ecclesden full in the face.

– I've heard the peacocks from the schoolhouse. I'd so like to see them. Look, here's Mrs Eddles. She can hold the fort for half an hour.

And Charles, watching with a certain disgruntled ennui as the headmistress moved toward them, seemed glad of the diversion. But was able to remember other more solemn duties.

– But you must meet my mother first.

Up on the terrace Lady Tremain still affected a languid vagueness, letting slim fingers drown in the opalescence of a triple rope of pearls. Yet if Beatrice had already guessed this woman was vehemently vigilant where her older son was concerned, she was soon to detect a dismissiveness in the way she spoke to him, suggesting expectations too low to be disappointed. This contradiction transferred itself to Charles, so that he seemed at once desperate to go and hopelessly entangled in his mother's pearly deeps.

– Really, Charles, I don't see why this dig or whatever you call it is so important. After all they're digging up Thundersbarrow all the time. It looks horrible enough already.

She turned to a grey-haired smiling man nervously fingering a camellia buttonhole.

– What do you think, Samuel? Should my son be allowed to dig or shouldn't he? His father was just the same. Always ranting on about what might lie under the hill.

The nervous Samuel gaped his mouth but nothing emerged. Charles was flushing unaccountably. Beatrice noticed the rash on his neck turning ruby. She could not bear the tension between them. And blurted

– I saw the tapes when I walked from the Halt. I told Eric Wren. I . . .

Slowly, magisterially, Lady Tremain turned a flickering lorgnette on the new arrival. The introductions had already been made. But might not have been. Charles was quivering.

– Pater knew Pitt Rivers. They were both convinced there must be some sort of Stone Age mine up there. One's been found in Norfolk. Only this year. If I could dig. Jessup would come out and supervise. He'd help me write up the report. I could use it to support my scholarship entrance. Don't you see, mother.

Samuel was still gaping silently. The lorgnette was swivelling back to Beatrice.

– And what did Master Wren say when you told him about the tapes?

Beatrice flushed herself now. Quite a crowd had gathered on the terrace.

– He . . . nothing . . . he didn't say anything.

– That's because he ripped them up and I put them back. Yesterday evening on my way over from Tongdean. Now he says there'll be all kinds of trouble. A strike even. Can't the damned fools see it won't affect them? Might even earn them a bit of extra cash if they agree to help.

Again Beatrice felt herself swayed between currents whose source she did not know.

– They're superstitious, the quarryfolk. – Samuel had spoken. – It was the same in your father's day. Oh yes.

– If you ask me they've got something hidden up there. Some contraband – another man's voice interposed.

– Smuggling? How exciting – a brittle woman's voice chipped in.

– Or else it's their courting ground. Where they go to . . .

Lady Tremain held up a finger transparent with light.

– I'm sure this is all very interesting. But Charles – and here she turned her silvery blue eyes on her son – we don't want a repetition of what happened in your poor father's day, do we? Now I must be seeing about the tombola.

In the wake of Lady Tremain's departure, Beatrice realised that, while the exchanges were taking place, she had picked up and nibbled a sponge cake like any awestruck child. She put the remnants back on the table and nudged Charles.

– You won't forget your promise, will you?

He turned and shivered, as though recovering from a bad dream.

They were standing in front of the peacocks' run, a structure of wire netting and wooden struts roofed over with more netting to prevent the birds flying away. She noticed that the rash on Charles's neck had stayed livid since the exchanges on the terrace and decided it was best not to probe.

– What are they doing now?

– Oh that's the mating dance. Look I'm sorry about mater you know. She improves on knowing. It was she who tipped the committee in your favour by the way.

Beatrice nodded but decided to concentrate on the scene in front of her. There were six peacocks altogether, four males and two females. The males shook out their great bronze and green tails with a hissing sound then, their blue serpent-like necks arched, their beaks slightly open, pattered slowly round the females. The females, speckled grey and brown but with phosphorescently green necks, pretended to ignore this exercise in engulfment altogether, eyeing the ground critically.

– Why are there more males than females?

– Father wouldn't cull them. And now I suppose no one has the heart.

– But are more males hatched out?

– Oh yes. It's nature. The same with chickens. And us. They'll be fighting soon, too.

Suddenly one of the males let out a series of staccato cries so deafening as to make her cover her ears, laughing.

– I can understand why your mother doesn't like them.

– I'm afraid animals are a part of creation she could do without. Excepting horses. How did Eric seem when you told him you'd seen the tapes up on the hill?

The sudden change of subject made her let go of the wire so that it twanged. Deep in its throat a peacock clicked a repeated warning: *Too close. Too close.*

– He seemed . . . I don't know . . . angry . . . but pleased. There I've said it. – But the admission did not lessen her sense of foolishness. She looked up. Charles to her surprise was smiling. He gestured toward the back of the run where a small temple stood among conifers. Beneath the slender Corinthian columns the steps were spattered with grey and white droppings.

– It's a model of a temple in Rome. But you're laughing. May I share the joke?

– It's nothing, it's just that oh, I don't know, birds in a temple. He was grave now, a scholar.

– It's not so peculiar. They are Juno's birds after all. Have you been to Rome, Miss Lumley?

If she had been flattered by his assumption of intellectual equality in quoting Milton, she was insulted now by his easy condescension. He knew damned well where a woman on seven pounds a month had and hadn't been.

– On the pier you mean. In Chalkhampton. The diorama?

He didn't mean but blushed at his own naivety.

– I . . . thought you were from Surrey way.

– I have travelled as far as the coast once or twice. For a treat.

He blushed again then launched back into his theme.

– Rome. Herculaneum. Ostia. Whole cities brought back to life. You can look down into rooms that haven't been entered for two thousand years. There are bodies, too, fossilised in lava.

The peacocks were rustling and dipping. She ran her hand along the wire.

– Is that why you want to dig on the hill? Is that what you hope to discover?

Brought back from the cicada-hush of his ruined cities, Charles Tremain seemed for a moment transparent and ill at ease, as if two contending forces were struggling for his identity.

– Yes, of course, in a way.

– But the superstitious quarryfolk won't allow it. They won't allow the heir of Ecclesden Manor, who owns the quarry, to dig on what he owns. – She listened to her gentle mockery in a rapture of horror.

– It's not just that. It's . . . I'm frightened of what I might find. Or not find. Oh it's too complicated. It was a wish my father had. A dying wish. So I . . . But you've seen how mother . . .

He stopped and looked away. There were tears in his eyes.

– And the limeburner, the friend you hate. – Another layer to be cauterised, stripped away.

Suddenly Charles seemed to recover himself.

– Oh Eric. He's not all there you know.

– You mean his fits.

How different their conversation was from her guarded exchanges with Mrs Eddles. Charles Tremain seemed able to create an atmosphere of ease and freedom at will. Or so she would have liked to believe.

– You know about them too? What don't you know, oh sybilline one. But yes it's true. It's in the family. And goes with something else. A sort of spontaneous speech. I believe it's known as glossolalia.

– Like at Pentecost? – Old Sunday School readings came to mind.

– I suppose so. His grandmother had it too, apparently, and was a big influence on the quarry religion. Came from up north somewhere. Eric's grandfather met her when he was working on a tunnel they were hoping to dig under the Channel. Anyway, she was from some kind of strict Baptist sect and almost singlehandedly took over the running of the chapel they have up there.

Beatrice remembered the muttering figure by the kiln and shivered. Charles seemed terribly eager to continue.

– Anyway, what I was going to say was they're what old Langridge would call godless antimonians.

– Anti?

– They believe in the Second Coming. A time of destruction. Apocalypse. And there's some old legend about the hill. If you dig out the top there'll be a second flood.

Always earth and water, water and earth. The limeburner was crouching in front of his kiln as if it were a heathen idol.

– So Eric Wren would want you to dig. He would want the second flood if it meant the second coming.

– Yes and no. He's like me. I suppose that's why we've been friends for so long. And why we quarrel. – Charles paused and she sensed, a little resentfully, that he felt he had said too much. Then once again the cloud passed and he was taking her familiarly by the arm. – But let's forget all this. You probably think we're all mad enough already, with our peacocks in temples. Come with me. There's something else I'd like you to see.

Together in the little room's scented twilight, they stood before a glass-topped cabinet. She had only once been inside a house as grand as this, on an open day at an Elizabethan grange near her hometown. For the moment the cabinet was not commanding her attention. She had followed Charles Tremain through a tiled hall from which stairs fled away in affronted silence. Pictures had glared down at her as if greedy to interrogate. Now she gazed at the carved figures on either side of the oak fireplace. They were watching her too. Everything seemed conspiring to exclude and diminish this invasion by an assistant nineteen-year-old schoolteacher. Yet all the while she had a strangely confident feeling that she had been here before, that what she would do next had already been done. His hand lay on the rolled canvas sheet which protected whatever lay in the glass cabinet from the depredations of light. She brushed it with hers and felt a subdued fever pass between them. That too had been prepared for.

– This is what I wanted to show you. Miss Lumley?

– I, I was miles away.

– 'Gone out' as they say in the quarry.

Then he was rolling the canvas sheet up. Inside the cabinet, butterflies and moths had been arranged in ranks on pads of cotton wool, their thoraxes perforated by pins, their wings outspread. There were Swallowtails, Fritillaries, Purple Emperors and among the moths a single Deathshead. But the eyes that had smouldered red against windows opening on to vanished dusks had long since guttered to ash. Here and there wings had crumbled, spotting the cotton wool with a rusty powder. Beatrice felt cold after the brief flare of contact with Charles's hand.

– It's too sad. They can't fly and their colours have all faded.

He didn't grow angry as she had expected and half-hoped. But looked suddenly serious.

– I used to think so too, as a child. Mater says she found me in here once trying to unlock the cabinet. I wanted them all to fly again.

Once more she noticed tears gathering on the rims of his eyes. What cause had this privileged and protected scion to lean so frequently toward lamentation? She looked away, the desire not to intrude cut across by an almost equal sense of being drawn into things against her will.

– And your father, he collected these?

It was something to say. After all, he might just be prone to self-pity.

– And his father before him. Our family has something of a fascination with dead things, I'm afraid. – His voice was still thick with some unnamed melancholy. – I think it's termed necrophilia.

– Oh look at this one. Now this one is still beautiful.

She would not give in too quickly but attempt a visitor's interest.

– Yes, that's a Chalkhill Blue. I've seen them up on Thundersbarrow. They live in ants' nests. As caterpillars that is. The ants bring them food.

– I should like to see one. Then she was looking up, suddenly happy, bathed in the radiance of a summer day brushed by butterfly wings, although both the day and the butterfly would never perhaps exist. – I'm so glad I came here.

– I'm glad you're glad. To tell you the truth those birds rather depress me.

– Oh not just here to this room. To Ecclesden. From where I lived.

He coughed awkwardly and the echo fled away into the maze of its forebears. There was a muffled faraway bark.

– All right Oenone, the fête won't last much longer, thank goodness.

Beatrice realised she had ventured too much and felt flattened.

Outside in the bright unforgiving air a child, one of the privileged few who had been allowed in to look at the vicar's train, ran up to them. Bubbles of snot burst from his nostrils. Beatrice would be teaching him soon. Her gloom deepened.

– Are you going to on Monday? Are you sir? Mucky said you weren't.

Charles too seemed downcast, deflated by too much talk about himself and his life.

– We never win do we?

– You might this year. You could bring your lady friend.

Charles looked at Beatrice and laughed. Her embarrassment spilt over into annoyance.

– Well I'd better go back to Mrs Eddles, since this conversation doesn't include me.

Charles's hand was on her shoulder.

– Wait. Miss Lumley. Perhaps you could come.

– To what? You seem to forget . . . No, everybody here seems to forget that I am a complete stranger, an outsider. I don't belong and I don't want to. No, you needn't tell me. What happens here is none of my concern. Now I shall be going.

The bubble-nostriled boy looked on in wonder. He would recount all this later, with embellishments.

– Forgive me. You're quite right. But it's easy to forget you're new here. You seem to observe and remember so much.

Despite herself, Beatrice did not walk off. Charles continued.

– It's a tug o'war. We have one every year on Easter Monday in the quarry. Ecclesden versus the quarry. I'm our team's anchorman. But we always lose, don't we Jake?

– Eric sees to that. He's like a giant Eric is.

– No wonder you hate each other.

She was being drawn back in. Charles was looking at her again, hard.

– But you could come. Would you come, accompany me, be my guest? There that's more formal isn't it? You might bring me good luck. And if we do win I can insist on a prize. That's the unwritten law. Can you guess what that prize would be?

She could not and blushed, confusedly recalling stories of medieval knights winning damsels in jousts.

– Why, to dig Thundersbarrow, silly. Wouldn't that be marvellous?

She agreed it would be but turned away nevertheless in self-reproach.

– And you might even see a Chalkhill Blue. No you wouldn't, it's too early in the year. But I could show you where I've seen them.

– Hurrah. He's going to do the tug, he's going to!

– Do say yes. It would be awfully jolly.

So that Beatrice, pretending to be more interested in watching the child running off across the lawn to where his mates were rolling wooden eggs down a slope, assented distantly. The fête was drawing to a close. Over by the stalls Mrs Eddles waved a gloved hand for assistance.

He sat facing her in the twilight of the lean-to shack which had been built against one side of Old Neb. The heat from the kiln made the atmosphere suffocatingly close. Although stripped to vest and pants the limeburner sweated profusely. She however could afford no such luxury and sat swathed in her raglan, like a mummy whose unguents have escaped their swaddling. Again, she felt the absurdity of her position, its essential fragility. She dabbed at her cheeks with a handkerchief and peered though the gloom. In the far wall, a grate whose fire must be fed directly from the furnace, breathed a dull crimson. Eric Wren scratched a luxuriantly tufted armpit.

– Maybe it ain't our quarry, Miss. But we're the ones that dig it so we must have our say. And we say not on top. Not where He is. More s'hots?

A massive stone jar stood between them on the scored wooden table. At its rim, pickled shallots glowed a luminous yellow-green in their thick pool of vinegar. She had taken one out of politeness. But recoiled at the tart heat, still crinkling at the back of her throat. She shook her head.

– They're going a bit soft-like now. Last of the crop. The new crop's already in the ground.

He leant forward, fished out a handful, made short chopping stabs with a bone knife and dropped the glistening half moons on to a cratered plateau of bread littered with yellowish knobs of cheese. Lifting the thick stratified block to his mouth, he chawed at it noisily, the vinegar running down his chin, while breadgrains and splinters of cheese sprayed out to stick among the whorled hairs that had escaped his stained grey vest. She did not want to look yet looked. The kiln was flaring less than a few feet away, turning rock to dust. She coughed as if this scene of heat and appetite would steal her very words, regurgitating them as ash.

– Charles says you and he have been friendly since you were boys.

Eric Wren looked at her round either side of the violent molten implosion occurring in the middle of his face.

– Um um thince boyg.

A shower of wet crumbs spattered over her and she was suddenly filled with despair. Why had she come here to this hot cave on the side of a cold hill? After the febrile excitement and fascination of her meeting with Charles Tremain that afternoon, Beatrice had walked back to the schoolhouse with her superior, helping to carry the several trays of unsold seedlings. In the shadowy rhododendron alley and later in front of the kitchen fire, toasting crumpets that she had bought at the fête out of her own month's advance, she had babbled like a schoolgirl. Mrs Eddles's disapproving silence made no impression. Bathed as she still was with the promise of summer and something closer, more intimate, which she could not or dared not define, Beatrice felt driven to speak. Until, during a particularly voluble encomium of the Ecclesden heir's culture and knowledge, Mrs Eddles had slammed down a fender she was polishing and said sharply,

– Lady Katherine has had the devil's own job to do anything with that boy. Always picking up one thing and dropping it for another. They didn't want him at Tongdean let alone Oxford. But he scrapes through everywhere in the end.

– But I think it's marvellous that he wants to find Stone Age things up there. He's interested in the whole panorama of history not just the here and now, getting and spending . . .

– His own whims more like. But you're young so he would say those things. And it isn't so marvellous, this digging. It opens old wounds. And divides people.

– Eric Wren, you mean.

The butter was dripping from the honeycomb of the crumpet on to the parquet. She placed a hurried foot over the stain.

50

– Eric Wren had more natural gifts as a lad than all the Tremains put together. With the exception of Lady Katherine of course. But then she's only one of them by marriage. But Eric Wren is his father's child. He won't go anywhere now.

– He loves Charles.

Mrs Eddles screeched in that way she had, her chest quivering.

– Love! What do you know of love?

– I can see it in others, I . . .

Mrs Eddles banged the fender back into place. She looked at Beatrice.

– Another holiday tomorrow and then it's back to work. You must help me clear the classrooms from top to bottom. I hear you're going to watch the tug o'war.

Beatrice nodded, wishing she could outflank if not defeat her opponent.

– Don't believe everything he tells you. Not every word. And Miss Lumley, – here Mrs Eddles moved crab-like toward the scullery – the stain on your sheets has sunk through to the mattress. I hope you'll be more careful in future.

Beatrice had sat on holding the uneaten crumpet in a paralysis of anger and shame.

And now she was in the quarry. It had been that final gibe that had goaded her, linking her always vulnerable womanhood with the object of the afternoon's admiration. As if her womb's bleeding and her mind's worship were somehow indissoluble, born, in Mrs Eddles's opinion, of the same gullibility. Very well then, if she were to be humiliated as well as browbeaten she would plunge more deeply into her error. To her, Charles Tremain's desire to dig on Thundersbarrow still seemed a noble vision, shining out in a world gone murky with chalk dust, suspicion and envy. She would say as much again to anyone, even Eric Wren. So she had gone out, into an evening where the wind was beginning to rise once more, stripping yet more petals off the cherries, so that they lay heaped round the tree trunks like pale cast-off clothing. That her body should have lead her inexorably to an elder-arched trackway running up the flank of the hill; that she should have turned away before reaching open downland into the pit on the left; that she should have come to the ruinous hovel in the shadow of Old Neb where an invisible terrier yapped continuously at a stranger's approach; that she should have done all these things, was not perhaps part of a conscious plan; yet underneath it all she felt driven to justify the vision she had encountered that afternoon and in doing so to justify her own precipitate, guilty, unexpressed offering of love.

– Go on then you old cur, have it.

The voice and the growling which accompanied it brought her back to the unassailable fact that she was now in the very den of the person she had dreaded yet determined to see. There was no escape. Lob had withdrawn into a corner to gnaw at a crust of bread. Eric Wren was picking his teeth with the tip of the knife blade. She peered round in the rippling stuffy air. From the wooden ceiling carcases of salted rabbit and hams hung from hooks. On top of a meat safe by the window lay a thick battered leatherbound Bible. Between the far wall and the flint flue of the oven a dishevelled bed lay, its tumuli of blankets and trousers suggesting that the terrier slept there too. The floor was bare chalk, the walls limewashed. There were no ornaments or pictures. The hut could hardly be a darker and more indigent contrast to the house where she had lived with her aunt, yet compared with the whispering corridors of Ecclesden or the cold order of the schoolhouse it felt familiar, comfortable even. Struggling not to recognise this inconvenient sensation Beatrice shifted ground.

– And have you always lived here, Mr Wren?

She realised the absurdity of the question almost before she had spoken. Yet the limeburner smiled.

– Since Dad died. I moved up here from the Bottom. It helps to be near Old Neb. He's got a temper he has. Here I can feel it through the wall. Oh, we're quite old friends now. Even Dadger admits I know the blighter better nor he did.

– And your mother?

– She's gone too.

She sighed. There could be no escaping their strange affinity. But when she attempted to point it out he surprised with a swift rebuff.

– No Miss, we're not alike. I could see that when you rode on the dobbin. It's Charlie you understand. I said so that first night and now you've come here to remind me. Lob! Let that boot alone.

– I must admit to being frightened when I think we're actually talking like this. Do you really consider I could understand Charles?

Beatrice blushed even in this hot place.

– I used to think I did. But he's gone beyond me. – Eric Wren shook his head sadly. – That's why I can't abide this digging business. It upsets everybody so. Especially after what happened when the old man . . . No this isn't right. And you aren't right either, Miss Lumley, to come badgering me about the hill.

– I'm not badgering you. I'm just asking you to look at it like an old friend.

– I admit I helped him stake it all out but then I had second thoughts. Even his mother agrees with us. Take chalk from the sides but not the top. That's what Dad always used to say. – He stopped and rubbed knuckles into tired eyes. She stood up.

– Do you want to be friends with me, Mr Wren?

He stopped rubbing and looked up. She had not meant to say this but could not somehow stop herself. As if the clamorous heat were fuelling her mind.

– Because I knew it was right that first night. I mean that I should meet you first. You were like a . . . a – she looked round for inspiration – a doorkeeper, yes with your flues and your kiln, waiting for me to cross your threshold. The threshold into Thundersbarrow and Ecclesden. Well I'm here now and I won't simply be cast out.

She sank back and despite herself, plopped a whole viridian shallot into her mouth. She found now that it did not taste so acrid. Eric Wren was humming softly to himself,

From Greenland's icy mountains

– I think we can be friends, yes, Miss Lumley. But it won't be easy not when . . . there now, who's this?

Lob was barking at the door on his hind legs. Beatrice suddenly grasped the ambiguity of her position and shrank into the hot shadows. But the visitor did not enter. One day she would know why. But for now she was only relieved that she had not had to encounter a third. And that Eric Wren, despite his battiness (Charles's word), was well on the way to becoming her ally in a confusing land. On the way out she even bent down to pat Lob, who responded by jumping up and nuzzling her ear with a relish that only confirmed her uneasiness among animals. But that night in her stained bed at the schoolhouse, she woke once to hear herself laughing, *Lob, don't don't*, though what Lob had actually been doing she did not in the morning care to remember.

Some said it was the heron flying over Five Lords Burgh; others that it was the mobbing of the heron by several jackdaws, wheeling up from Ecclesden Hanger; still others said it was neither the heron nor the mobbing but the way a flock of starlings, which had been gathering for hours in the branches of an ash near the Halt, suddenly rose in a black swarm, causing the sun to ripple and fade as if sheeted by smoke. Then there were those less prone to take comfort from shifting natural signatures, who merely pointed to the inevitability of odds (since the quarry team that year lacked both Gaffer Wright and Padger, both injured in a rockfall); or to an error of judgment on the part of the anchor; or to the simple fact that men, in the end, grow tired. One observer, not much listened to at the time (his loose teeth made his spittly speech almost incomprehensible), muttered something about the new arrival and how he'd thought as much when he saw her lifting up her skirts to cross Thundersbarrow in the gloaming. But by the time the explosions, for which the single blast that had so frightened Charles and puzzled Beatrice two days before had been a mere rehearsal, were over (three carefully spaced detonations in the work-face of Upper Pit, which simultaneously sucked in and expelled the air with a pure percussive violence), most of the crowd had lost interest in seeking a cause for the quarry team's defeat. What concerned them now was the eerie novelty of having to fulfil the wish of the victor. It had been so many years since an Ecclesden side had won, that people had forgotten the quarry teams' inevitable firkin was a choice and not a tradition. But slowly, after the last echoes of explosion had rippled into quietness, here and there one or two older quarryfolk began to remember. When the tug o'war had been instituted in old Wren's time there had indeed been an unwritten agreement that the victor might request his prize, as long as it was not unreasonable. What dark fate this year had decreed that not only should Eric Wren slip at the vital moment, but that the heir of Ecclesden should be obsessed with a plan to dig near Five Lords Burgh. No one, from Tod Dadger down, could be said to have anticipated Charles's request that the right to dig be his prize. But, their nostrils, mouths and ears still filled with the black alchemy of lyddite, all the members of that seething crowd sensed the disaster looming. Threatened by the undercutting tactics of the larger pits down Lewes way, its better quality soap almost exhausted, Thundersbarrow quarry was already in serious decline. Defeat at the hands of an inferior tug o'war team seemed at that moment to have a symbolic resonance. Nothing now would be the same again. This was the first of a series of defeats which would bring the already antiquated industry to its knees. Indeed, not many years later, after the quarry had been abandoned and the few remaining inhabitants of the Bottom hovels scratched a living by poaching and taking in washing, the day Charles Tremain requested the right to dig could only be mentioned if at all with a gesture warding off the evil eye. Those who were left could see how, from the depths of Lower Pit, invisible ribbons began, tracing a path that led for many to the low chalk slopes of the Somme. The defeat of the quarrymen was their entry, premature, unlooked for, into a world of war. And if Charles Tremain was their conqueror, Eric Wren too had played a part. What happened later between him and the heir of Ecclesden Manor would be grimly linked to the moment when Beatrice Lumley stepped forward into the flint arena and did what she did. By that time the heron had disappeared, along with the jackdaws and the starlings. But the shadow remained, casting before the crowd an image of wings, coldly beating, slow, deliberate.

Beatrice had been nervous about going to the event, still more nervous about being accompanied by Charles Tremain, with whom she did not want to be seen walking out, however innocent the walk might be. Worse still was her dawning intimation of the mistake she had made by visiting the limeburner's shed the previous night. It had been a secretive underhand meeting, of the kind that this place seemed to encourage, and though nothing had come of it (what indeed had she expected would come of it?), she felt a dread of what might happen next. Then, inevitably, there was Mrs Eddles's disapproval. This had become so regular a thing that Beatrice, for all her timidities, might have been expected to shrug, if not laugh it off. But her headmistress had a knack of shifting her position so as to undermine that of any opponent. Critical of Charles Tremain the day before, she did not appear, this morning, to regard him as an unsuitable companion. Indeed, she seemed to have anticipated and accepted the fact. It was Eric Wren who concerned her now. This former paragon of virtue, this unsung village Milton, had for some reason fallen off his pedestal. This morning he was vacillating and easily led. He would spoil a sheep for a happorth of tar and blame another. He was in short the kind of holy fool who does more harm than good.

– He likes you, Miss Lumley. Anyone can see that. Don't abuse that trust.

It was almost as though Mrs Eddles knew about the meeting in the shadow of the kiln.

On top of all this a sleepless night, made the more gruelling by her having twice to get out of bed and change blood-sodden towels (she was determined from now on not to leak on to any schoolhouse mattress), had left Beatrice feeling dizzy and on edge. Even so, when at last she saw him, standing on the path with a lavender shoot in his blazer buttonhole, accompanied by two dogs and a small boy in a sailor suit astride a pole with a wheel at one end and a papier-mâché dragon's head at the other, all her doubts evaporated. Whatever would happen would happen. She was still an outsider, with no influence over events. Or so she thought.

– My dragon'll bite you, look – the small boy shouted, catching sight of the strange new young woman. And indeed, as she diffidently approached (here were more dogs to be negotiated), the red and green dragon's mouth did appear to open, revealing greyish fangs.

– Oenone. Down. This is the bitch I told you about. And here's old Nim. – Oenone panted, one paw in Beatrice's trembling hand, while the older Nimrod looked on dispassionately. Charles turned to the small boy. – Here Robert, I'll trounce you. What do you say to the lady?

Shamefacedly, Robert let the string which controlled the monstrous mouth go slack. – How do you do, Miss – Then, brightening up. – Are you really going to watch Charlie in the tug o'war?

Beatrice glanced at Charles who smiled back at her. Meanwhile the dogs ambled off to examine the lavender bushes.

– Of course. Now I'm invited.

– He won't win, you know. There's a girl he's sweet on and she spoils his . . . his . . .

Looking down at a lavender bush for the word he either could not remember or pronounce, Robert almost fell prey to Charles's sudden lunge. But in the end he, or the dragon, was too quick and went bounding off along the path.

– Sweet on Maud! Sweet on Maud!

With a stifled groan Charles took up the pursuit only to abandon it almost immediately, turning back to display what Beatrice noticed was a deeper than usual flush where his neck and open collar met.

– Out of the mouths of babes and sucklings.

She was determined to be amused.

– Oh, it's too silly of him. He must have been listening to the housekeeper again. – Then, seeing her raised eyebrows – He's my brother by the way. Robert. Tongdean would dampen his mischief-making but he's, how can I put it, a little backward. And has to wait another year.

– Backward or forward? I never had a brother or a sister. He seems normal to me, speaking as a teacher I mean.

There was a pause during which the unmentioned name of Maud seemed to echo in the hum of a bee out early among some flowering heathers. Oenone was rolling on a patch of grass, her fur glistening. Nimrod went idly lifting a leg here and there. Then Charles hastened to fill what Beatrice would have preferred leaving as a void.

– As for Maud. She's just a cousin. We haven't met for ages. The usual understairs myth-making. – Then, turning to where Robert was beating the side of a cherry tree with his dragon's pole. – You won't come if you do that.

Now it was Beatrice's turn to flush.

– Robert is coming too? – She had assumed Charles's younger brother was simply accompanying him to the schoolhouse.

Charles sighed.

– He was quite insistent, the little brute. Says he's old enough this year. But it wouldn't have been possible without you, of course. I must say mother was quite taken with my proposal.

She had turned away, her vision darkening, her head filled with the muffled thudding of Robert's dragon against the shiny bark of the cherry. At each new blow white petals fell in shoals to the ground.

– So I am to be the chaperone. Or wet nurse. They start early it seems, my teaching duties.

She had not wanted to sound so dryly bitter. He flushed again.

– I say, I didn't mean. I mean I had the idea of inviting you before . . . It was mater's idea really, if you must know. She didn't like the idea of us two, you know, alone.

His words trailed away. The petals were still falling. Suddenly she could not bear the sight.

– What's he doing to that poor tree. Oh do make him stop it, Charles.

Glad of an opportunity to conceal still further embarrassment under the cloak of physical action, Charles bounded down the path and fetched his brother a sharp slap across the back of the head.

Oenone barked in approval or apprehension. Then the older brother dragged the younger whimpering back. She winced yet felt a tremor of excitement. Charles was panting.

– Loveliest of trees. Evidently you haven't come across that line yet. Perhaps Miss Lumley here (who's kindly consented to look after you today, so behave) will teach you the rest of the poem. – Charles looked up at Beatrice who managed a smile of consent which did not reveal her ignorance of the quotation's source.

The pit was dark with people. They swarmed over its ledges and lay on the roof of the hayloft; they stood in line beside the tracks of the funicular and sat three deep up the steps of the foreman's office. Some had even dared to shin up the flint belly of Old Neb and perched precariously on the rim of its mouth, their eyes streaming for the smoke that rose up there, as if from some entrance to the underworld. Yet despite all the noise and bustle, the cries of greeting or threat, the shoving and elbowing for position, the great double arena of the quarry gave to this human gathering an air of stillness and waiting. It was as though the event which they had come here to witness were not a part of their communal life at all, but an emanation from the scar of the pit itself. On every side its jagged walls rose up, jade-green at the base then passing through many shades of grey to the blinding creams and bluey whites of the upper levels. Here and there old auger holes bled an iron rust which fanned out down the face of the chalk like the scab of a wound. There were platforms too which, balanced against the work-face by means of pulleys and ropes, suggested the presence of some race who had no need of steps or ladders, a race that lived suspended in air, moving surefootedly back and forth across sheer chasms. Casting shadow on the people below the quarry walls seemed to cut off the outside world so that it was easy to believe there was nothing at all beyond them, no Ecclesden, no England, no earth. The crowd waited.

In the midst of this floating world, on top of a block of chalk whose deep parallel grooves suggested it might be the drum of a pillar from some ancient temple of chalk, a temple perhaps dedicated

to the brooding and violent deity now long since walled up in Old
Neb's infernal belly, Beatrice Lumley sat, her raglan open on a white
muslin dress. Nearby on another chalk drum, Robert chipped idly at
some protrusion with a pocket knife, sending up little puffs of dust
which Oenone idly snapped at. Nimrod lay further down, in the
shade. A few quarry workers, glancing over at the stranger from their
vantage point by the rail of the crushing mill, whispered together and
gestured. The words *teacher* and *knee trembler* merged with the action
of one man who appeared to make his forearm stand involuntarily
erect by pressing the inside elbow. The brief spluttering hymn of
laughter which followed might have been both an expression of
delight and a cry of black anxiety. So the stranger sat on, worshipped
or reviled but always careful to smooth down her skirts at even the
slightest threat from an unruly April breeze.

In the middle of the Lower Pit floor a circle had been constructed
using small fragments of flint and marl. This compound, perhaps
more ancient than the now ruinous temple which housed Beatrice
and her charge, was severed across its diameter by a thick red line
daubed with sheep-marking paint. Outside the circle, like a
kingstone, a thick wooden post and crossbar had been set up, the
crossbar bearing a bell on one side and a pocked brass gong on the
other. Beside this structure a man stood to attention, holding in his
right hand a crook such as old Joseph might have used and in his left
a sponge still dripping from the galvanised bucket that stood at the
base of the post. His military bearing was somewhat offset by the
smock which covered him from head to foot and seemed at a
distance to be covered with planetary signs. That these were
probably stains of mould and mud did not detract from the
onlooker's sense that he was in the presence of some pagan high
priest. Beatrice thought she recognised this figure as that of the
condescending stationmaster. But when he turned briefly in her
direction, she was confronted with a mask covered in lamb's-wool
which completely hid the face.

Now, out of the seething mass of spectators another man came
forward. He seemed at first to be labouring in the grip of some

underwater serpent, whose tight braided coils ringed his entire torso and thighs. Staggering towards the compound of flint he fought with this laocoon of the quarry until gradually, one by one, the suffocating rings loosened and fell away at his feet. Meanwhile, heads were turning, as the centre of the crowd's attention shifted from the magic circle in front of Old Neb to a point halfway up the cliff. Here a series of steps cut in the chalk led to a ledge which ran back to a wooden door braced with iron. As Beatrice watched with the rest of the crowd, this door suddenly opened and a line of men emerged, blinking. Each man was stripped to the waist and already bore, like flagellation stripes, the red marks of practice ropes on hands and sides. They waved as they jogged jauntily down the steps. Some smiled. One even blew a kiss at what people presumed was his sweetheart.

Lastly, arm in arm, came Charles Tremain and Eric Wren, walking slowly down the steps as if to delay the trial they must now endure. Their black hose tights, leather jerkins and thick hobnail boots proclaimed that they were both to be anchormen. Beatrice looked then looked away. She had seen the mauve tattoos floating beneath Eric Wren's roiling chest hair. She had seen the hairless small nippled and eczema-scarred chest of his friend and rival. *We hate each other.* Lower down, the bulge of Eric Wren's groin contrasted strangely with the girl-like declivities of Charles's thighs. How could there be a contest between two such ill-matched figures? Yet both held her attention and loyalty. The damned troop were milling in front of the cross now, limbering up, shivering, grinning sheepishly at friend or foe. Only the two anchormen seemed composed, squatting to rub hands in a pile of lime and spread it in swathes across belly and chest. How vulnerable Charles looked, his goosepimpled areoles as small as a terrier's. Yet he had a kind of liquid power which the thickly set and earthbound Eric Wren might not easily master. In her dark fascination Beatrice swayed a little then turned to Robert for relief. Her charge was still working at the chalk with his knife.

– You shouldn't do that Robert. It's destructive.

– It's a fossil. I'm trying to get it out. The way I've been told to. Do you know what it is? – Robert was suddenly solemn, a privileged interrogator. She leant forward, not wishing to be taught.

– An oyster? It's a seashell of some sort, anyway.

– It's a devil's toenail.

– That's vulgar, Robert. And almost blasphemous. – Her voice sounded lame. When she closed her eyes she could see the naked flesh of Charles and Eric imposed upon one another, as in a double exposure on a photographic plate.

– That's what it's called. And there's another one, long and thin and pointy, that's called a devil's thunderbolt.

– So many devils. I'm sure no one in this day and age would call them that.

– He does. – Robert was not to be thwarted.

– Who does, Robert?

– Eric of course.

– Ah. But why the devil?

– Because he made them. He wants to be God you see. And every thousand years God comes down and destroys all the evil creatures made by the devil and puts them in the rock. He's going to do it again soon, God is. There's going to be a great flood. And then a great battle. Eric told me. Sort of.

Robert was holding up the scalloped shell fragment. Under the chalk matrix a faint pink glimmered. Flesh. Oh flesh. She shivered and shifted her buttocks on the cold chalk drum. The mad wizard was rattling the bell with his crook. It was time.

So the two teams, each with tin flashes stuck on their right shoulders, blue for quarry, black for Ecclesden, moved into the ring of flints and left the pit behind. They were exiles now and could not be reached by any ordinary means of communication. Their eyes seemed hooded, their bodies moving as in some dream of ardour, impervious to the shouts of encouragement and mockery from the world beyond. Dismayed and wondering, Beatrice turned away from Robert's tales of divine vengeance to see how the rope, simultaneously taken up by twelve pairs of hands, drew energy from the

contact, writhing and squeaking back into life, then coiling round
the two anchormen in a gesture of cunning compliance. Already
singing along its length, this new incarnation seemed to want to
persuade the shuffling snorting humans to join and merge with it,
making a beast twice as strong and twice as deadly as before. From
her vantage point, still sniggered at or invoked by the three crushing
mill novices, Beatrice realised that the contest would take place not
only between men but between men and rope also. So they hung
there on the rope, like drops of water on a washing-line, preparing
to evaporate or gleam. The bell rang.

– First Round. Take up the slack. Take the strain. Heave.

The stationmaster's voice, muffled by the mask, rose for a moment
in the thickly expectant air then became irrelevant and died. No one
was paying any attention to him. All that mattered was the stone
circle where the two teams had suddenly gone absolutely still,
floating with their rope in a space that had no up or down. No one
spoke, no one moved. Even the teams themselves barely grunted.
Then it seemed to everyone that it was not twelve bodies pitted
against one another in two groups of six, but one body pitted against
the rope, which threatened now to tear in two, leaving a hole in the
day for darkness to flood through. This the tug o'war teams were
sworn to resist, working with sweating concentration to keep the
rope whole and within the circle. If this meant moving one way or
the other then so be it. The danger only came when the two teams
tugged in opposite directions. So, responding to the tiniest shift of
things, the dislodgement of a chalk nodule, the shedding of a single
hair, both teams began to move left toward the quarry's home-
ground. The middle of the rope crossed the reddle line. A great
cheer went up. The gong echoed.

– First round, the quarry. Prepare for round two.

Beatrice turned away, not wanting to watch, not wanting either
side to win, yet feeling that if Eric Wren's team were triumphant
some underlying darkness would be unleashed. Again she saw him
sitting opposite her in the hot twilight of his hovel. Why had she
gone? Why had she said those things? It had only made him the

more determined to humiliate Charles. She felt the fragment of oyster in her palm. She had been gripping it so hard its impression had burrowed into her skin.

So the second round began and once more the rope seemed bound to escape its captors. Beatrice added her flutey voice to the small number of Ecclesden supporters who had dared venture up to the quarry. Some said the teacher should keep quiet. Others agreed that she was a spirited wench to support the losing side like that. Then, when the second round looked like becoming a reversal of the first, with Charles and his team beginning to drag quarry back the other way (how hot Charles looked, the rash on his neck now spilling down over his shoulders), some said that the teacher must have the evil eye and spat thoughtfully. The gong resounded for a second time.

– One all and everything to play for.

Now the tension in the quarry was like a membrane stifling the air. The kiln smoked. Shadows gathered in the remoter corners. The wind was up. Yet in their charmed circle the two teams stood facing one another, the rope between them, a mocking spirit. Then it was that the first of the three terrible things happened, the things that changed the world of quarry forever. Suddenly the new school-teacher left her charge and ran or rather skipped down to the teams. There, bold as brass, she went up to the heir of Ecclesden and kissed him full on the lips. Next, turning to the limeburner, she planted a peck on his cheek which had him rubbing dazedly at the spot like a young boy. She showed them something, too, which she was holding in her hand, a locket maybe, though it could have been a spell and then laughed in that glittery way of hers. People were nonplussed. Some began to mutter about how it was bad luck for an onlooker to step into the flints. Others said it was even worse if it was a woman, especially if she had the flux too. It would all end badly, if not now then later. A few even shouted *Let's abandon the whole fucking business*. But then Tod Dadger the foreman stepped in. Ever so slowly he went up to the schoolmistress and shook her by the hand. That was the signal for general applause. Afterwards some said the little bitch must have put a hex on him too. But others were more philosophical. How was he to know what was to happen next? He was just extending the hospitality of the quarry to strangers, as he ought. So everybody settled down, the schoolmistress went back to her place and the stationmaster rang the bell for a third time.

Back on her perch Beatrice felt elated by what she had done. Yet puzzled. It was as if the quarry had made her do it. Or what the quarry contained. Perhaps then her visit to Eric's hovel hadn't been so awful an error. Perhaps she might influence events in this place after all. Charles's lips had been dry and cracked; Eric's cheek was bristly and cool. Robert stared at her dispassionately.

– Are you like Maud, then?

– She could not help smiling.

– I don't even know who Maud was. Or is. I'm not like anybody. I'm me. And don't be impertinent.

– I bet you're going to be like Maud. She did things like that. I didn't want her to. I wanted her to be my friend. But she did and then she went away.

Beatrice would have asked questions. But there was no time except to whisper,

– I think Charles may win today. Then he could obtain permission to dig. Won't that be exciting?

– He'll never win. Can I have my devil's toenail back?

And at first it seemed that Charles's disaffected younger brother was right, as the Ecclesden team slid inexorably toward the reddle line whose width and darkness made it seem a bloody trench into which they must fall. Then to Beatrice's absolute delight the process was reversed. As if sensing some slackening of will on his opponents' part and remembering, perhaps, the brush of her lips on his, Charles seemed suddenly to pull the quarry team singlehandedly a full two feet across the ring. At that moment the heron flapped slowly overhead, followed by its wake of jackdaws. Beatrice was standing up now and screaming through hollowed hands. The dogs were barking. Eric had fallen. A catastrophe. Oh come on. This was no contest. But a war for souls. And only she could decide. So she stood there on her chalk block or altar, black against the thin disc of a daylight moon. Come on Charles, come on. Then strangeness of strangeness. There was Eric Wren sliding on his haunches like the rest of his team towards ignominy and defeat. And he was laughing. Laughing like a maniac or a child. Years later many who had been there remembered that laugh and shivered. But at the time it only provoked dismayed shouts of encouragement and lament. *C'mon Eric boy, you can't let them, not now.* But gradually the cries diminished. The crowd went quiet as it dawned on them that the unthinkable was indeed happening. Quarry was losing. At last, with one final heave, the entire Ecclesden team fell backwards, dragging the ribboned centre of the rope across the fatal rubicon. It was all over.

Then, before anybody had the time to think or act, the heir of Ecclesden ran across to the chalk block, jumped up and standing beside the schoolmistress made his request.

At first everyone was too stunned to absorb the words. They hung in the air, mysteriously. Soon however the sense of the words floated down and people began to understand. There was shame in the quarry then. And anger. And a bitter resignation. But now the last of the three terrible things happened and this stirred the crowd's emotions into an unstable mixture that threatened to explode. For, wrongfooting Tod Dadger, who even now was beginning to come forward to respond, Eric Wren broke free of those who were binding up his grazes and himself leapt on to the rock.

– We'll help you, Charlie. It was a fair fight.

Too late now for the foreman to come up with objections and compromises; too late for the quarry to defend itself. The anchor himself, old Eric's only son, had pledged his word. The quarry was committed to its own inevitable destruction. Stopped in his tracks, Tod raised a hand to his forehead then turned back to the office with a gesture suggesting he washed his hands of the whole business. One of the three crushing mill apprentices flung a flint that thumped against the side of the rock. There were shouts of *Shame* and *Unfair*. Despite their acceptance of his words, the crowd might still turn ugly and Eric gestured urgently to the dobbin cart. So began what many remembered afterwards as the Flight down the Elder Path. The dobbin cart groaned under the weight of its load, for aside from the four humans, Nimrod had been joined by Lob, Oenone having chosen to run on ahead. At first all was quiet. Then out of the gathering twilight came a few shied flints. These were followed by cries and soon a whole rabble of the younger quarry folk could be made out in the distance like a grey ghostly army. Beatrice clutched Robert who was sobbing over his lost shell. Charles, swaying beside her, with Nimrod's head on his knee, kept casting nervous glances over his shoulder. Only Eric, with Lob beside him, seemed to enjoy what he had raised up, and hummed loudly.

Christian, dost thou see them

– It's too bad, Eric. We've a lady here. And my brother.

– They'll calm down.

– And the way you laughed when we pulled you all across the line. What were you about, man?

But the limeburner did not answer. Suddenly, from the direction of the quarry came a low rumbling. Then, as if foam were breaking out of the hill's frozen sea, three columns of smoke rose and broke in the sky. The dobbin cart was bombarded by a scattering of small chalk nodules.

– They're trying to kill us, – Charles shouted, out of the jolting sombre dream in which they were enveloped.

– No lad. – Eric replied, turning round. – Three explosions means quarry's lost. It hasn't happened this twenty year. It had to happen today.

Charles stirred but did not speak. It was as if the long-hoped-for victory had terrified him.

Beatrice looked back and saw where the moon had risen above the smoke, grey, pitted and old. Below it darkness oozed out of the side of Thundersbarrow like blood from a wound.

Sunday May 10 – Dear Aunt Millicent, Thank you for the bed jacket and the drop scones. Yes, I am well though I had a sniffle about a week ago. I hope this finds you in the pink. The work here is rewarding and I don't have time to be lonely. I . . .

She looked up from the little desk in her sloping room. Down in the alley the rhododendrons had smouldered away to a dense dull jade of leaves. There was no more cherry blossom. The lines of a poem learned long ago floated idly through her mind:

Out of the day and night
A joy has taken flight.

She sighed and bent back to her letter of duty.

The days were long and the nights longer. She was utterly alone. How different things had been even on the night of the tug o'war, even during the headlong flight downhill when, despite the fear and the speed she had found herself laughing into the wind that flowed up to greet them from the rich darkness of the weald. What a distance she had travelled since. Yet everything she was now had come into being that night. At the moment when the stationmaster had announced that the Ecclesden team had won, her present misery had been born.

Charles had wanted to take Beatrice straight back to the schoolhouse. Even in the lurch and buck of the dobbin cart she could tell his mind had turned away from her and was hovering restlessly about some other magnet. Eric looked back briefly from his seat.

– No, to the manor. Some might try to follow.

Charles had shrugged and started to whistle 'She was only a bird in a gilded cage'. This too was a covert way of separating himself from her. The elation she had expected to encounter in his face was nowhere to be seen. Something had gone wrong.

It was wrong still when they swung into the little cobbled yard at the side of the manor and entered by the kitchens. Robert was still whimpering, though more quietly. Charles stood stiffly to attention as she walked through, then followed, letting the door swing shut on Eric who would be obliged to open it for himself. In the soft flare of the gas lamp Beatrice could see that Charles's lips were pale and compressed. Flakier than ever. He motioned to the undercook to attend to Robert (who they now realised had cut his hand clambering down off the chalk block), and make hot chocolate for the schoolmistress. Then he was gone, up into those whispering regions where perhaps he truly belonged. So much for the victory of his team. So much for Eric Wren's generous offer of men to help him dig the sacred summit of the hill. So much in the end for her selfless attempts to assist and influence. Mrs Eddles had been right. It was better not to meddle. But worse was to come.

It started as a low murmur of voices behind a door with a small wire grille set in its panelling. Robert and the undercook had long gone. Eric had never actually appeared (she had assumed he was still tending to the overtaxed horse), and the kitchens were quite deserted. She sat listening by the range, a shawl over her shoulders, the steaming cup half empty in her lap. The voices rose higher.

– *How can you say that? How can you honestly expect me to believe that? You deliberately lost. You fell on purpose. It was a humiliation.*

– *I fell 'cause I had to. I knew 'twere right to do so. After Miss Lumley . . .*

– *Miss Lumley. What has she to do with it? Good God, man, am I to be the laughing stock of the whole county?*

– *Miss Lumley showed me like in a picture. That you had to dig. That I had to help you. I knew it when she came over the hill. The voices said so. I didn't lose. You won.*

– *By a dirty trick. That's what they'll say. And now I have to face these people. It's too much to bear.*

– *I told you. They'll calm down. I'll calm them down. They know we're near the end. The dragon has come to have his bite. Then the flood and the last battle. And then . . .*

– *Oh sod off, you illiterate bloody fool. Who wants your old wives' tales? Nobody goes to that apology for a chapel anyway. What about me, that's what I want to know. What about me?*

The pantry must have had two doors. First Eric Wren had gone in looking for some bread and dripping. Then, after changing into ordinary clothes, Charles had come down for a Bass and encountered his friend. They had completely forgotten about Beatrice, except as a pawn in their argument. They faced each other under the hung pheasants in the gelid blue light, their faces prematurely lined, as if they had already endured some suffering that still lay far ahead of them in the unformed future. They looked up simultaneously.

– Why, Miss Lumley, why? I would have dug anyway. We would have worked out some compromise. We always do. But now because of your blasted interference I'm in one hell of a pickle.

– Charlie, she meant well, you know it.

But Beatrice had already recoiled, clawing back the kiss which she had so recently bestowed.

– Oh never mind me, either of you. I'm just an interloper. And now, being an interloper I'll leave.

– Yes! Leave, why don't you. We don't need you. Why don't you go back to Essex or whatever provincial hole it is you came from?

– Charlie! – Eric Wren was hissing. – You've had enough, you have.

As she turned a bottle smashed on the stone floor and someone began to weep. Through the sobbing she heard,

– *Don't you see I always lose. Especially when he lets me win. I can't win. Ever. I wish I were dead sometimes by crikey I do.*

Then she was running, out into the cobbled yard to be met by the faces of the gathered quarrymen silhouetted in the flares of their brands. No one spoke as she passed through. Somewhere towards the back of that sullen parting crush, at the dead bottom of the night into which she must plunge, she understood now, because of her naivety and arrogance, she watched hands loop tight round a speckled white cockerel's neck and twist. Then the knife came, letting out the black blood for the thin moonlight to drink as an offering to whatever powers the terrible profanity of the dig would offend. Tod Dadger was there and Joseph and the stationmaster. And deep in the shadow, under the high flint wall, Mrs Eddles, her peacock mask awry, clicking, *Too close. Too close.* And lastly, as she gained the protection of the schoolhouse garden (where was Charles, her protector, now?) Eric Wren himself appeared, barring her entrance and winking, *Just a little kiss now. I kept my part of the bargain.* So that she must scream and scream then wake sweating in her solitary bed.

Then had followed her exile. During the next few days she had lived on the hope of some word, either directly from Charles or through Eric as his shamefaced intermediary. Surely he hadn't meant all he had said back there in that larder reeking of feathers and suet and spilt sour beer. Or if he had meant those things surely he regretted them and would say so. But no word came and her hopes died. One afternoon in the schoolhouse, while she was busy scrubbing desks, Mrs Eddles had come in and announced that Eric Wren had been demoted to the rank of junior crushing mill operator because of his foolish part in the tug o'war business.

– But he meant the offer as a gesture of reconciliation.

– Reconciliation! Pah! If you knew what his father had been through at the hands of Sir Colin you wouldn't be so free and easy with your reconciliations. His family on the breadline. Him unable to work. If it hadn't been for Lady Tremain's soups I don't know what would have happened to them.

– Then why did he do it? Why did he make that offer in front of the whole quarry?

Mrs Eddles had looked at her then grimaced.

– You need more bleach on that desk. One of the Gurl twins vomited in it last term. He'd been trying to eat toadstools. Remember that, Miss Lumley, the next time you seek to descend from your angelic heights. Toadstools. The quarry may well close before the year's out.

So it was all her fault. That Eric had been disgraced. That Charles had been humiliated. And now no one would come near her. The following week Charles went back to Tongdean and her own schoolwork began. Isolated among the children who were alternately surly and aggressive, Beatrice could have been permitted to feel she had plunged into a bleak region from which there was no escape. Even on her walks she was not allowed to forget. People would stop and stare. Or worse still, avoid. Once, turning a bend in the elder path she came upon a man unbuttoning himself. Normally she would have averted her gaze and hurried on. But today that was not possible. He barred her way and slowly drew out a thick-veined member. For what seemed hours she was forced to watch as he urinated copiously like a horse, the acrid liquid foaming into a ditch where violets grew. Long afterwards the bristly brown tube would come pushing towards her out of the night seeking both solace and revenge.

Then came the desertion of the quarry children. It happened slowly at first with two empty desks one Monday morning. But over the next few days the gaps in the class increased until by the following Friday Beatrice could hardly muster half a dozen pupils. The peace which reigned at this time made her reluctant to tell her superior. But, as it happened, there was no need. That evening just as Beatrice was clearing up the detritus of a nature lesson (broad beans on blotting paper; the different shapes of leaves) Mrs Eddles came in herself and announced that they were wanted at the manor.

Tall and pale, Lady Tremain glided between the pierglass and the walnut table. Her rings flashed out an occasional agate or ruby shard. Beyond this light the translucency of her skin gave her an almost posthumous feel, as if she were practising to join those shades which, so local gossip averred, she evoked every night in her late husband's study, left as it had been at the moment of his death. That that death had not been mourned as profoundly as his surviving wife would have people believe, that her table-rapping in the upper reaches of the manor might have had more to do with another man, also dead, who had lived close by, only served to make Lady Tremain seem, in the eyes of those who did not know her well (and who did?), both more formidable and more vulnerable than ever. Although not a Tremain, as slavish flatterers like Mrs Eddles liked to assert, she had become as rooted in the manor as the quarryfolk were in the hill. But something she had brought from outside that world, some instability of judgment or will, threatened at times to take the upper hand. So now, having summoned the two teachers to her drawing room, she grew by turns irate and petulant, thinking of the inconvenience to herself, much as her son had done when he realised that his vision had been realised by sleight of hand.

– Ah good Mrs Eddles. And your assistant. Come in both.

Seeing her superior simper forward, Beatrice lingered in the door. Behind her the maid's departing footsteps echoed back, as if looking for something they had left behind. Ecclesden was a house of echoes. All of them unsatisfied.

– Still so cold and gloomy. For May.

A kimono'd arm gestured vaguely at a window half obscured by the leaden cones of wisteria blossoms. Then the rings flashed out, mercilessly.

– Miss Lumley, do stop skulking on the threshold.

So in the tinkling room where glass gave back to glass the same shared secret much smoothed by time and always titteringly opaque to the puzzled guest, Lady Tremain drew Beatrice into the shallows of polite enquiry where Mrs Eddles was already wallowing. Until the first shoal should be encountered.

– This business of the truants. It's too vexing.

Mrs Eddles had warned Beatrice that this was behind their summons on the way over. Although she had not said so, she made it plain that she regarded Beatrice as partly to blame and would intimate as much to Lady Tremain. Never had Beatrice so longed to run away. But followed meekly, only looking up when, down the gravel drive at the front of the house, she heard the crunch of retreating footsteps. The figure was too far away to make out as it shrank along the peristyle of limes, but she was certain the broad back belonged to Eric Wren. So he too had been summoned.

– There's six from her class and the two from mine. But I can assure your Ladyship that I warned her when she arrived. Don't meddle I said, just don't meddle.

Lady Tremain closed her eyes to discover the source of an imminent migraine. When she opened them again Mrs Eddles might as well have not been there.

– And how do you find my son, Miss Lumley? Speaking as a professional of course.

Beatrice, who had been expecting yet not expecting this sally, drew her glove off and on, seeking guidance from the condescending room. Which gave none, unless it were a starburst of ruby reflections in the pierglass. Though this would only seem to have confirmed her defeat. She was on enemy soil. But must speak.

– He seems, – she paused, not wanting to look directly at the rather equine face of her interrogator. – He seems very interested in history, – she said in a rush which included in compressed miniature love, rejection, Robert's bleeding cheek, the smile of Eric Wren, even the quarrel in the stinking pantry. Then gulped hopelessly at the thin perfumed air.

Lady Tremain laughed. Or whinnied. Then smiled.

– He thinks the Romans defeated Harold at Hastings. Tongdean will be a hard place unless he learns to buckle down.

Perhaps Beatrice had gulped too readily at the violet-scented atmosphere. Deluded into thinking this a game she felt obliged to defend.

– But he seems to know so much. He's told me all about the barrow. Five Lords I think it's called. And I still think it's wonderful he wants to dig up there despite all that's happened. I . . .

Again her interrogator laughed but more artificially.

– Of course, you mean Charles. Doesn't she, Mrs Eddles? Which is only natural in a girl of her age. He seems like a god, doesn't he dear? But no, I mean Robert, little Robert, which is only natural since he is my youngest.

Beatrice felt her left eyelid flicker uncontrollably. She had been caught out and ambushed, forced gently to reveal more than she had intended. Yet Lady Tremain, all shantung and smoothness, affected not to notice.

– Ah youth, don't you say so, Mrs Eddles?

Mrs Eddles did say so. With bitter emphasis.

– But there is still the question of the children. Charles, despite all his virtues, and I can see that Miss Lumley is conversant with several already, can be a little wayward. His plan to dig was one thing. But then to go and involve a complete stranger.

Beatrice opened her mouth to speak, to justify. But the words would not come. Lady Tremain held up a hand.

– Still all that's a *fait accompli*. And I have been able to make certain, shall we say, concessions where the quarry is concerned. But the children. They will not let us have the children unless you, Miss Lumley, go up the hill and fetch them publicly tomorrow morning.

At the other end of the *chaise-longue* Mrs Eddles stirred with a spasm of violent delight. Beatrice stared so hard at the purple cones of wisteria they began blurring to serpent heads, the beaks of peacocks, dragonish tails. Was this what Eric had come to the manor about, her public humiliation?

– Now you must understand, Miss Lumley. This is not a personal matter. Our reputation as a Church of England school is at stake. And I, as one of the governors who offered you a contract of employment after poor Mr Noone was obliged to retire, must insist that the duty is carried out.

Again Mrs Eddles stirred and made a clicking sound in her throat. *Too close. Too close.*

– And if the duty is carried out. Well then . . .

Lady Tremain allowed a number of unspoken possibilities to trail with her kimono sleeve down the arm of her winged chair.

What now? Must she be lead away, trussed, a sacrifice?

– Mrs Eddles of course will accompany you.

Of course.

– And thus the slate will be wiped clean.

Where to look? Where to go? How to be? The wisteria blooms were swelling to the dreadful heaviness of lead. Was there to be no assistance? On the mantelpiece opposite, three gilt frames held the Tremains in sepia traction. Here Sir Colin, a short, rather effete-looking man, stood to attention behind his wife who was seated on a bench in an arbour. Here the same bench held husband and wife, while their two sons stood on either side. Charles would have been about fourteen Beatrice reckoned. Even at that age he had had what she now knew was the Tremain look, at once condescending and unassailable. How could she ever have hoped to be on intimate terms with such a look. Miserably, she studied the third frame. Smaller than the others and at an angle, as though it had been recently moved, it held a tall pale-haired girl in a reefer jacket and calf-length dress. Unlike the people in the other frames, the eyes of this girl seemed intent on outfacing whatever reality might be offered down the aperture of the lens. She was perhaps thirteen and, understanding everything, winced at the knowledge with an estranged self-deprecating humour. So Beatrice thought to herself, suddenly transported from that clever unforgiving drawing room to a bower of shadowy confidences. The chestnuts in flower behind the girl's head suggested Ecclesden Park. *I should like to meet her*, Beatrice heard herself murmuring, a little too loudly, out of her distress and humiliation. Then more quietly, *I wonder who she is?*

– Well I think that is all. Yes. All I have to impart.

But Lady Tremain had noticed Beatrice's intensity of gaze. Following it back to its source she tutted and stood up, letting the kimono ripple over her willowy form.

– He's put it back, the scoundrel. – Beatrice heard her hostess mutter, before the frame was swept up and placed glass downwards on a rolltop bureau.

Yes I should like to meet you, whoever you are, however you came to be here, in this mocking echoey place.

The fair-haired young girl's teeth had been somewhat irregular. So were Beatrice's, a fact she had often deplored. Now she let her tongue explore those irregularities with a certain shy confidence. It seemed to suggest a bond of sorts. If they were ever to meet, she knew they would have no difficulty in sharing secrets.

Here Nimrod, catch it.

He throws the ashstick high into the autumnal blue of the sky. It lands near the barrow among the soughing Scots pines. Once he had been afraid of their voices as he had been afraid of Eric, during the foaming fits. Now he knows better. Even the explosions didn't worry him as they did last holiday when he had gone running to Miss Jupp screaming airbang airbang. Oh he is older now. And knows a heap of things.

That's it, Nimboy, bring it here.

The retriever comes sleeking back to lay a wet forepaw in his master's hand. Nimrod's great grandmother was bred by pater. He looks up, liquidly.

Be off tomorrow, won't I, boy? Won't see you again till Christmas.

With a sudden catch of breath that is part excitement part fear he bends down and lays his cheek on the dog's damp forehead.

Yes off tomorrow to Tongdean. It'll be swell.

Silence in the abandoned pit, Dragon Pit they call it. He hates going this way back but it's a kind of short cut and darkness is falling. Nimrod has bounded on ahead as he always does, sensing home. Once he and Eric had had a hideout here, a sort of cave where they'd pretended to be outlaws fighting on the side of some dispossessed king. Now there are brambles everywhere. He couldn't find the cave if he tried. A good thing in a way. He'd always felt nervous underground. In the dark. So many years ago. And now even Eric is distant, abrupt even when he tries to tell him his worries about the new school, busy about the quarry in the shadow of his bullying father whom pater wants to be shut of. Time is money, he keeps saying nowadays to which Charles always replies, – I don't need to work. I own this quarry, – which isn't exactly true but sounds good. And makes Eric walk away with clenched fists and a brooding look such as he used to get before the fits started.

The great tangles of thorn bushes are rustling as if an animal is trapped inside. Or an army. The darkness clotted here seems to slow his pace. Nimrod is nowhere to be seen. There are voices too, deep in the bushes, a stifled laugh, a cry. And so they are on him, the quarry boys led by no one or a ghost. Brandishing flint axes tied to sticks with knotted grasses. A tribe from before the flood. He is running, at first ever more slowly, then falling as his ankle twists in a rabbit hole toward a void of blows and kicks and scratches.

Let's be friends!

Naow! Hurt him, Mucky. That's right Tod.

Please let's . . .

No. Give him one in the bollocks, Razzell.

Silence. Pain. A time too broken to be time. Then more silence. The pain filling up all the empty places inside him. Then out of the heart of pain, like an angel standing in the sun, this dark figure leaning over him, weeping.

77

I tried to tell them no. I said not the boss's son.

He is lying on a sort of trellis in the underkitchen against the range. Vesta the linnet is singing in her brass cage against the black light. It is Eric leaning over him, his green teeth faintly luminescent in the gloom.

Why didn't you fight Charlie? Why didn't you fight back?

Because you didn't want me to. Did you?

Here, I've the vinegar compress for that lip. Don't want them seeing that at Tongdean, do we Master Charles? And as for that calf, that's a nasty gash and no mistake. We'll have to bind it tight.

The housekeeper moving forward with a steaming enamel bowl and a towel embroidered with dirty cream flowers. Dead nettle.

Here Eric, my lad, go back to the quarry and tell them there'll be trouble now.

Already is Miss, between my Dad and the master.

Is that why you did it, Eric? Is that why you ambushed me? Because of them?

Not me, Charlie. I was up by Old Neb.

Then both of them crying together, crying for the end of childhood, locked in a bond deeper than any bloodmingling: the bond of betrayal in which cowardice masquerades as strength, tenderness as cruelty. The bond that will kill them both in the end.

A child on either side, Tod Dadger's girl holding her left hand, the grubby paw of Razzell Bushnell's hare-lipped son in the other, she walked down the steep ravine that wound through the Bottom hovels. Ahead of her Mucky Gurl's son capered, banging a small drum made from a dustbin lid. Behind, the other children bunched together, shouting at the tops of their voices a song about The Worm of the Hill. The day shone. Sun smoked the dew off the hovel roofs and made the puddles beneath her feet glint and quiver. People came out from behind hovel outhouses, or through rickety doors or higher up over the ridge which divided the Bottom from the quarry. Women clutching scrubbing brushes; a man with an axe slung over his shoulder; a girl with a baby at her hip. All were smiling, waving, laughing, wishing her and her troop the best of luck on their way down to Ecclesden. The song had changed now at her behest. As she led the quarry children in a slightly garbled version of 'All Things Bright and Beautiful', Lob burst out from under a wheeled henhouse and bounded beside her yapping. She greeted him fulsomely and on an instinct looked up. There against the skyline stood Lob's master. He too was waving, his bowler hat in his hand. So she walked on, the woman who had traced the evil piper back to his lair in the side of the hill and plucked these children from his cave. Lob barked, Eric waved, the children sang. She could not restrain her tears, her happiness.

How had it happened? How had the day which had dawned so cold and misty, produced this ecstatic morning? After the interview with Lady Tremain the night before she had returned to the schoolhouse with an aching heart. She had sensed the woman's disapproval not only of her involvement with the business of the dig, but more importantly of her friendship, however tenuous, with her eldest son. Then in the rhododendron alley, which she had come to dread as a place of oppressive revelation, Mrs Eddles had gripped her by the arm and whispered,

– You know she hates him, don't you? Sir Colin's favourite. And I don't blame her. He reminds her of him. He was his father's favourite. Oh yes.

And Beatrice, still smarting from the knowledge that she must do public penance for her sin of innocent interference, had burst out,

– Do you think I care? I don't care about any of you. Not any more. – And run off into the cold schoolhouse slamming the door.

Then had come the restless night when she had dreamed over and over again that she was trying to push at a door which wouldn't open until her aunt came along and showed her that she must pull. In the morning, dense with a fog that poured down the side of Thundersbarrow in clammy billows, Mrs Eddles had announced with a satisfied look that Beatrice must set out on this particular journey alone. This had caused her such panic that she had resorted to abject entreaty. But the more she begged and promised the more her superior hardened. So that in the end Beatrice did have to go alone, her stomach knotting, into the kingdom of the enemy.

Halfway up the elder path she realised she had no idea where she was going or what she should do. The memory of her previous visit convinced her she should try and find Eric Wren, who would no doubt be working at his new menial job in the crushing mill. But almost before she had entered the Lower Pit, in the shadow of Old Neb which seemed, in its flint solidity, to have registered the surrounding perturbation with as much sensitivity as a cliff will register the nesting and squabbling of birds, she was confronted by one of the very children she must humiliate herself to retrieve. Tod Dadger's daughter had been sitting in wait on a wheelbarrow by Eric's hovel and jumped down to waylay her.

– Miss must come up to Dragon Pit.

So it had all been arranged, down to the very arena of her disgrace. She bowed her head, her stomach clenching more fiercely than ever and followed the limping girl round the side of the kiln. Here a path snaked upwards in long coils, crossing a vast cone of chalk that seemed to have foamed like water out of a gap in the cliffs above. As they ascended, dislodged flints clattered down from time to time, colliding with a hollow ringing sound against the flues below. It was a desolate place, permanently in shadow from the overhanging cliffs, so that the scree's grey whiteness might have been glacial. Beatrice began to shiver.

Ahead of her, despite her limp, the girl scrambled like a goat. Then suddenly she was gone, as if the icy cone had opened to swallow her. Toiling below, Beatrice called in alarm but received no response other than her own echo. Far off, on the face of Lower Pit, two men with augers turned their heads briefly from where they were working on a platform. Then the girl reappeared and beckoned Beatrice to hurry. The assistant schoolmistress, trained as much in the art of obedience as the science of command, struggled to obey.

But at the top of the scree everything changed. Suddenly they were out of the shadow and bathed in warm sunlight. Turning to look back at her climb, Beatrice saw where the mist lay in pools at the base of the hill, snagged by the branches of the Hanger trees or trapped in hollows around the manor. Further off, beyond the Wild

Brooks, the weald rose in a series of blue-grey strata, each representing a further distance, field overlain by coppice, coppice by wood, wood by ridge, ridge by cloud, cloud by clear sky and all glistening, all restored to a pristine clarity now that the mist had wiped the air of night's dregs. Panting from her climb, Beatrice felt briefly at peace, the purpose of her visit forgotten. Even when she turned to survey what lay in the other direction, her mood stayed bouyant. Dragon Pit had long since been abandoned. Its once stark outlines were softened now by years of growth. Hawthorn trees rose from the old work-faces, their roots splayed over the rifted blocks like wizened crabs. Brambles and elder lay dense in the floor of the pit. The remains of a funicular wagon supported a leaning ash. Feeling the sun on her back, Beatrice closed her eyes. In one of the higher cliffs a pair of kestrels was busy building a nest, their voices rising and falling in bubbly high-pitched chatter.

– This way, Miss.

She opened her eyes. The girl was gesturing towards the back of the pit. Here a V-shaped cleft led to a further smaller hollow in which stood a large shed made entirely of corrugated iron. At one end a rusty door creaked on its hinges. At the other a tin chimney tilted. The shed looked deserted and Beatrice was struck with paralysing fear. She would have gone no further if the unaccompanied voices of many people hadn't risen up muffled out of that iron den. It was a hymn. 'Jerusalem'. This then was the chapel which Charles had so slightingly referred to. Over the rusty door, a spidery inscription read: *He Brings Down the Fire from the Skies*. What had Charles said? A breakaway sect. Primitive Baptists. Eric's grandmother. From the north. Hartlepool. The limeburner would be here. He at least was not an enemy. Or so she hoped.

To begin with, it seemed as if no one in that packed muggy shed was concerned about her presence. Sitting down on a low bench at the very back of the congregation, Beatrice was surprised to see that, in contrast to the parishioners in the valley, no one turned to enquire who the new arrival might be. It was as if they were used to people appearing casually at any moment and indeed, as she sat there in the silence that followed the hymn, she noticed one man, Tod Dadger himself, exit by a side door. Still the silence continued and she realised, with a little shock of alarm and excitement, that no single person presided over this meeting. All were equal here, each waiting to see upon whom the spirit would descend. The silence intensified. The kestrels were squabbling distantly. One or two people murmured as if in a trance. Then at the very front there was a sudden commotion and a figure rose facing them. His mouth was flecked with foam. His eyes blank.

– Nebuchadnezzar the king made an image of gold whose height was threescore cubits and the breadth thereof six cubits.

There were murmurs of assent.

– Ah he did.

The limeburner stared as if into a pit of the distant past. Or the looming imminent future.

– And whoso falleth not down and worshippeth shall the same hour be cast into the fiery furnace.

Again the same stirring, as if the congregation were a field of wheat being crossed by contrary breezes.

– If it be so, our God whom we serve is able to deliver us from the burning fiery furnace and he will deliver us out of thine hand O king.

– Deliver us, yes.

One man had fallen on his knees. An old woman was swaying back and forth. Beatrice felt obscurely that this seemingly spontaneous spectacle had somehow been contrived for her. That the ancient story of exile and miraculous escape was sending out tentacles to include her. Was her humiliation to occur here, in this stark and pitiless shed?

– He answered and said, Lo, I see four men loose walking in the midst of the fire and they have no hurt and the form of the fourth is like the son of God.

Eric Wren staggered and almost pitched forward into the congregation but at the last moment righted himself. The murmurings were dying down. The old woman had stopped swaying.

– And if it wasn't for her we would be in the midst of the fire without God's protection.

– In the midst.

– And the form of the fourth.

– Come forward, Miss Lumley.

So she stood in front of the congregation of the quarry chapel, waiting for the moment of her humiliation and realising through her tears that that humiliation had somehow miraculously been transformed into a triumph. *And they have no hurt.* Eric Wren had wiped the foam from his mouth and was no longer speaking from that place where the words gathered when he was not himself. *Gone out the quarry folk call it.* With growing delight she realised that he was praising her for having intervened, for having convinced him that Charles Tremain's dig must go ahead. For only through her had he, Eric Wren, managed to secure Lady Tremain's promise of more cash to reopen Dragon Pit. And when the pit was in operation again, as it had been in his father's time (some cheered, some shouted Amen), the chapel would be a memorial to her bravery and foresight. (More cheers; a solitary hallelujah.) Then the congregation was standing up and crowding round her, patting her on the back, shaking her hand. One even leant forward to kiss her but Eric Wren would not allow such profanity in a place of worship.

– But I only came to collect the children, – she said weakly through her tearful smiles.

– They're waiting for you, Miss Lumley. In Quarry Bottom.

The air still and heavy in Dragon Pit. Dusty light coagulating under the brambles. A ewe glances over the lip of the pit, chewing. They are lunging through. He does not want to, not again. He is frightened to be up here after the fight a year ago. He longs for Tongdean. Escape. But the coiling brambles snag him too. His friend, back bent, dark-stained at the armpits, moves forward on all fours through the bramble tunnels. An underworld guide.

– We're not going back to that old cave again? Are we?

No reply.

– I have to be home by four, pater said.

No reply.

– Is it true your Dad's planning to reopen Dragon Pit?

No reply.

– Eric, is there going to thunder?

For he has seen where the flying ants have emerged, spilling over the scattered chalk blocks in lace-black rivers, the worker ants beside them, scribbling their manic zigzags.

Eric? Eric? Why don't you answer me Eric?

Gone. Into the cave. Where I must follow.

The afternoon grown old. Thunder now near, now far. No rain. Behind him, the cave recedes into a darkness he has small desire to explore. Eric is sitting on the old chalk altar leafing through an outdated Tit Bits *which he found stuffed behind the stove in the foreman's office. He looks up.*

– Charlie, do you ever get, you know, hard?

He should say yes but shakes his head.

– I could show you how, if you want. It's the feeling when you do certain things, you know, rub and that.

Motionless in the sticky darkness of the cave he sees his friend pulling roughly, almost apologetically, at his groin then taking out what looks like a pigmeat sausage, violet at its acorn tip.

– Come on, you do it too.

And he does but cannot somehow manage the complicated operation flapping at his thin yellowish member until the foreskin blurs.

– No, like this.

Eric understands. He has the mechanical skill. And something else. A kind of daring. A surrender. Like when the voices come. Is that it? Is all this to do with the voices which come into you from the hill?

– Sometimes . . . I . . . look at the pictures . . . you know . . . stuff comes out . . . Oh . . . it's coming out now . . . Oh . . . it's coming . . . I think . . .

The pearl arc of a subterranean meteor's tail splashing hotly on the photogravured bodice of a music hall singer. Charles still limp, seeing against the marbled mauve sky the marriage flight of ants spiralling ever upwards in gross transparent winged loveliness. Always he is the weaker. Always he knows less, understands less. Yet later in the privacy of the gardener's earth closet behind the blistered green slatted door, he will achieve what Eric achieved, though more slowly and without the triumphant gush, staring at a flying ant lying half-dead at his feet, its wings sogged in a pool of urine, as he raises the pinprick globule of cloudy white to his trembling outraged humiliated tongue.

So, by the brilliant and unexpected striking of his bargain with Lady Tremain, Eric Wren, the hero who had lost, perhaps deliberately, in the Eastertide tug o'war was reinstated in the quarry. In addition to allowing him to take up his old job as limeburner, Tod Dadger appointed him foreman of the Dragon Pit dig. There were still memories of the disaster which had occurred the last time the pit was opened, for which the scree, slanting up behind the kilns, was a chilly memorial. But along with these memories ran other more importunate feelings: the desire to clear the name of Eric Wren's father, a great man who had tried to outface Sir Colin and perished in the attempt; the no less urgent need for some return from an ever more impoverished operation, which at times during that year had seemed about to collapse altogether. Then too there was the sheer excitement of tapping another source leading into the hill's mysterious white core. So that for all the anxieties he had aroused, Eric Wren was generally felt to have righted a wrong, even to have thrown the towel back down into Ecclesden courtyard. People began to talk about helping the young Tremain with his excavation come the slack days in August. That the limeburner's coup had roots in some old gossip about Lady Tremain and his father, was recognised but not closely examined. Even the assistant school-teacher's ambiguous involvement in the business was for the moment overlooked. In their new-found expectation of prosperity (the 'soap' in Dragon Pit was rumoured to be better even than the famed 'snow' at Lewes quarry), people were prepared to be indulgent. Perhaps, they whispered, Eric Wren was a little in love with the pert bitch. Certainly he went past the schoolhouse more often these days, though nobody could say that he had actually walked out with Miss Lumley.

For Beatrice the gladly brilliant visit to the chapel began to tarnish after a few days. It was true she had brought the children back singlehanded, for which Mrs Eddles and Lady Tremain herself (waiting in the schoolroom) were forced to express their gratitude. Indeed Lady Tremain was seen almost to soften towards Beatrice, a phenomenon which, in the life of that sheened and jewelled idol, was believed to be almost unique. Mrs Eddles, brooding on this turn of events, had even abjured her customary lecture about not having ideas above your station. Her assistant, she realised bitterly, might turn out to command a species of regard in certain quarters which would make it imperative to have her as a friend. But Beatrice suspected that once again the attitudes of the people of this place towards her were controlled by currents whose strength she could neither gauge nor predict. If Lady Tremain spoke approvingly of her to Mrs Eddles, even allowing herself to touch the young woman's shoulder with a gloved hand, she did so because of Eric Wren's visit to the manor. What had happened at that interview remained dark, except in relation to the decision to allow the reopening of Dragon Pit (such decisions being the only areas now in which the Tremain family directly interfered in quarry affairs), but the darkness bled over into Beatrice's daily life. She did not trust Lady Tremain. And despite everything, she did not trust Eric Wren. That bowler-hatted shadow would smile through the window when he passed the schoolhouse on the way to the Limeburner's Arms. Once he even turned up at the class with a particularly persistent truant and lingered as if enjoying the sound of her teaching voice. Yet she could sense that his actions had not been prompted by pure friendship. It was as if everything that had occurred between her and the limeburner (even down to the embarrassing never to be repeated moment of the attempted kiss), had to do with Charles Tremain. Here, with a little sinking sadness Beatrice, whether teaching in the classroom or walking in the small schoolhouse garden (she still disliked going further afield, even though the few quarryfolk she met now were unfailingly polite), realised that the heart of her disillusion had been reached. The estrangement from Charles had been so sudden and violent that it had numbed her at first. Then, when she had been able to reconsider it in detail, she had asked herself why it should matter. Indeed how could so grand a word as estrangement be made to sit on so fragile and transient an acquaintance? They had only talked two or three times and it was quite evident (even if his mother hadn't taken it upon herself to hint as much in various asides), that they were not out of the same drawer, socially or intellectually. Yet even as she admitted these things, Beatrice knew that estrangement was the right word, that the affinities they had uncovered could not easily be buried again. So she blamed herself; then Eric Wren; then the world and finally Charles Tremain who would go off the deep end and might at least have been expected to write.

The days and nights wore on. May faded and the pink climbing rose on Mrs Eddles's front porch began to unfold. There were explosions in the quarry almost every day now. Chalk dust lay thick in road and hedgerow. The reopening of Dragon Pit which, she reminded herself with a certain warm satisfaction, she had helped bring into being, was gathering momentum. The children chattered about it in the classroom if they could. They told how Eric Wren was working like three men. How there had been a small rockfall but a deal of good soap so that they were thinking of firing up the defunct second kiln. And also about how one warm afternoon Lady Tremain herself had been seen near the edge of the pit, riding sidesaddle on her gelding. Beatrice noted all this but said nothing. Elsewhere in a world she could not imagine, Charles was no doubt getting wind of what was happening. Did he think of her ever, lonely in her slant-ceilinged room? She hoped he did yet almost immediately dismissed the thought with a wry self-protective smile. He thought of his coming dig that was for sure. And of his mother. And of Eric Wren, the friend he affected to hate. And of Robert. And Nimrod. And Oenone. But her? The flowery cipher which she had been doodling in the back of an exercise book slowly developed into a full-blown line-drawing of a rose in which the initials C and T were thoroughly expunged.

Then one day towards the second week in June, in the garden where the real rose blossoms were unfolding, the man who had both too much and too little influence over her life in that mysterious kingdom appeared covered in white dust. School was over for the day and, exhausted as usual with the beginnings of a migraine, she had attempted to empty her mind in the presence of many bees. But the explosions up on the hill would keep intruding, reminding her of that fateful dusk when she had fled back down to Ecclesden with Charles. Then she had believed things were beginning. How naive she had been. And arrogant. Now she simply existed. Until the phantom stood before her, his smile creasing the caking of chalk dust like a mask. Unless his face itself was the mask, on which a second had been placed, slightly awry.

– Hoped to find you here. We're that busy I haven't had the time I'd have liked.

His jerkin was open to the third button. She glimpsed chalk-encrusted curls. But was inclined not to be moved.

– I'm busy too. And don't hope at all.

Immediately she regretted the self-exposure. But gave up any attempt to recover lost ground in the red shadow of migraine. Eric Wren brushed back a white shock of hair.

– He's written. Replying to me. He comes home for half term soon. He knows all about the pit and you fetching the children.

Despite herself she granted her stomach a slight lurch.

– Does he mention his insupportable rudeness, his self-absorption, his puerile temper?

Eric Wren scratched his head, a puzzled phantom. She noticed that one of his jerkin pockets was moving.

– Charlie's forgiven me the tug o'war. He says we'll have another bout in the summer. When the dig's done with. He's over the moon about Dragon Pit.

Again that glitter in the dark eyes, as if registering the shock waves of some remote violence. She shivered despite the sun's warmth. And resolved not to capitulate.

– Well God's in his heaven and all's right with the world. You'll be saying he forgives *me* next.

– He does, I mean, – and here the limeburner squatted down in front of her, – he wants you to forgive him.

– Why doesn't he write then? Why does he go through you? Perhaps he wouldn't if I told him you tried to kiss me.

Eric Wren looked down at the path. Then smiled unexpectedly.

– Out of friendship. I never had a sister. And you coming here. I knew you'd come here. Before it happened.

– Your voices, you mean?

She hoped she sounded suitably contemptuous. For reply he delved suddenly into his jerkin pocket.

– I wondered if you could do anything with this?

His hand opened on what looked like a ball of soot. But feathered. And absurdly long-legged. Beatrice the townee looked down in fascinated disgust.

– What on earth is it?

– A moorhen chick. Lob did for the henbird before I could get to him. I wondered if you'd like to try mothering it.

She almost reared away, so great was her amazement and horror. Yet took the frail and feathered warmth in her palm.

– Why Eric, you do think of some odd things.

And returned the kiss he had invited on that dark night a month back. The kiss of one orphan for another. Chastely severe.

Lying in a box of cotton wool in her room the chick had little strength and died during the evening, despite Beatrice's fumbling attempts to feed it on the corn which Eric Wren had given her. She might have taken this as an ill omen if, behind it, there hadn't lain what seemed to her a genuine innocence of impulse. Perhaps she could be friendly with the savage and taciturn limeburner after all. Then too, he had come especially, despite the demands of the quarry work, to tell her that Charles had written. Perhaps she could even dare to look forward to the coming half term. Carefully she carried the tiny corpse down to the garden and buried it under the climbing rose. From the flint of the wall, a long last breath of the day's warmth wafted up. She hugged it to herself, like some rich all-enveloping garment.

That night Beatrice was woken by a low howling. It could not have carried over from her dream for that had been dully unremarkable. Nor were the manor peacocks able to produce such a sound. The moon had risen in a windless starry sky. Down in the alleyway between the schoolhouse and Ecclesden something stirred against the glossy darkness of rhododendrons. Slowly a figure began to peel away from the background. It was staring up at the manor where, as usual, a light burned in Lady Tremain's bedroom. Something fluttered at the figure's side, writhing to be free. But the grip in which it was held must have tightened for, after a sudden convulsive twist, the creature hung still. Then, as if to gain a clearer view of the manor, the figure turned slightly, allowing moonlight to spread across face and shoulders. Beatrice had already guessed it must be Eric Wren. But instead of confirming her guess, the moonlight actually seemed to cast doubt on the matter. It was as if the cold illumination blurred the limeburner's familiar features, depriving them of any recognisable mark or characteristic. This then was not the man with whom she had talked in the schoolhouse garden that afternoon; still less the man who had plucked the tiny moorhen chick out of his jerkin. Someone else had come down from Thundersbarrow inside the limeburner's body, someone who, by what rite or incantation it was impossible to tell, had discovered the emptiness beneath all faces and wore it like a bone-white mask. The figure shifted again and the moonlight slid away along the ground as if relieved to be free of the duty to fall on such a terrible void. Beatrice too was inclined to leave the window for, with pounding heart and sweat beads on her forehead, she knew that the man she had just seen standing in the rhododendron alley was already dead.

Below them the pit swarmed with figures. She had witnessed a similar scene on the fateful day of the tug o'war but now there was one important difference. Before, the figures had been motivated merely by the promise of spectacle and entertainment; this hot June afternoon no one was inside the quarry who did not have a specific task to perform. That Easter Monday people had moved of their own free will, bunching together or thinning out as the fancy took them, sitting or standing on whatever vantage point offered itself. Today the patterns the figures made against the whiteness of chalk were all variations on a central design: the opening of Dragon Pit. Fanned out in long wavering lines hunched women bore away baskets of spoil or 'brits' from the cliff-face towards the scree. Further back men stood in circles round fallen blocks of chalk, each circle raising and lowering sledgehammers in blurred unison. Against the cliff-face itself ladders rose up like the dead stalks of gigantic plants. Higher still, on suspended platforms, men knelt and levered, in some rite or difficult devotion. Beside the cleft which held the chapel, flames were being kindled under a massive flint slab by two men who capered in front of it like devils, waiting for the moment when they could fissure the heated surface with a sluice of cold water. The noise in the reopened pit was of a piece with this concentrated and complex activity. A psalm of many interlocked melodies it contained in its higher registers the metallic ping of metal on flint, descending via the darker keys of hammer and auger to the bass pulse of chalk blocks in collision with the pit floor. And round all these notes human voices wove. Crying out, laughing, cursing but above all murmuring, a constant surf of murmuring which suggested that the sea which had once toiled here had risen up once more to add its sounds to the day.

The hub of this performance, the core from which the various details of the pattern emerged, like ripples from a stone dropped in water, was a man sitting on a chair set between two blocks of chalk over which, in accidental imitation of a trilithon, a spar of wood had been laid. If the long auger which he held in his hand gave him the look, now of a prehistoric chief surveying his clan, now of an archpriest intent on some sacred dance, the fact that he was stripped to the waist and covered in chalkdust and bloody scratches made him seem more slave than master, a victim rather than a lord. So he sat there, on his wooden throne, bellowing out encouragements or warnings. Until the work in the pit took on a dreamlike inevitability. Or so it seemed to the two observers, high up on the lip of the crater, as they peered down through rippling skeins of heat.

– Well he's got what he wanted. I shouldn't be surprised if that wasn't his plan all along.

Charles Tremain aimed a riding boot at an outcrop of chalk on the crater's edge. It skittered away down the cliff. Issuing a new set of orders to two men carrying a rope-handled box of lyddite, Eric Wren turned on his podium or pulpit and squinted into the sun. His hand went up to wave. He shouted something unintelligible.

– Well said, old mole. You know sometimes he's the spitting image of his father. I don't know what pater would have said.

Beatrice, who had been sitting on a molehill overgrown by turf, stood up and stretched.

– I must say I liked the place better when it was full of brambles. Is it true your father forbade any digging in Dragon Pit? Mrs Eddles told me . . .

Charles grimaced.

– And twisted the truth in the process no doubt. But yes it is true. I can't say I'm happy about this – and here he extended an arm to take in the pit.

– But you've got what you wanted. Their cooperation when you open up the flint mine.

Charles smiled, the sun doubled in his irises, two silver moons.

– Yes, I've got what I want. Come let's go up there. Right to the top. I'll race you.

– What was your father like, Charles? Was he stern?

– Oh, stern and kind by turns. Aren't all fathers?

– I can't remember mine. Come on. But I want a head start.

He had returned two days before at the beginning of his half term and stood shamefaced in the schoolhouse hall, clutching in one hand a small paper parcel and in the other a complexity of rods and gauges. Coming down the stairs (Mrs Eddles had shouted through her customary 'Front door, Miss Lumley') Beatrice had noticed that, in the dim light filtering through the glass fan in the porch, Charles's face had taken on a yellow hue. Certainly his abject look had all the intensity of some physical illness, so that she swallowed the words of reproach that had been lying like bile in her system all these weeks and ushered him through to the dampish-smelling front parlour, a little-used room with a portrait of Victoria over the mantelpiece and starched antimacassars on every leather armchair. The institutional atmosphere helped perhaps to ease the constraint both felt. It was as if the heir of Ecclesden had come to visit the inmate of some exclusive asylum or retreat.

– I brought you this. It's in translation of course. Rossetti.

Later she would remember that *La Vita Nuova* recorded Dante's spiritual love for a girl named Beatrice. But now, glancing from Charles to the brown-edged tongues of an aspidistra which had somehow managed to survive in a ceramic pot by the fireplace, she could only recall the extreme youth of the poet's muse. The thought kindled something, part memory, part apprehension. *She has the same teeth as me. But her hair is finer. And she is slimmer too. Taller. Not dumpy. The cusp of womanhood.* She handed the book back.

– I should have thought there were other more appropriate recipients. The girl in the photograph on your mother's bureau for instance.

How she hated her tone at such moments. An affronted primness armoured in abstraction. Yet he laughed.

– You mean mother's been showing you our rogues' gallery? You must have come across that old picture of my cousin. When she used to stay at the manor, oh seven, eight years ago.

The realisation that the girl in the photograph had long since grown up left Beatrice feeling nonplussed. Yet no less threatened. Charles was placing the book on the arm of the chair. He would make her receive his gift. In the end.

– We never hear from her now. Maud that is. There was some scandal. Something to do with the Pankhursts. You aren't a suffragist by any chance are you, Miss Lumley?

She forbore to answer, recalling instead the taunts of his younger brother and something else, a mention of the name Maud through a wall of the Off Sales at the Limeburner's Arms where she had gone one Sunday to fetch a draught of stout for Mrs Eddles who said it did wonders for her rheumatism. Her hand lay on the book. An ideal love flowering in the summer of the world. Who was she to concern herself with long-lost Tremain cousins? She looked up and smiled her thanks. For the moment they were reconciled.

The arena of Stone Age labour was far below them. They stood panting and laughing on the cratered summit of Five Lords Burgh, Oenone bounding in circles round them, her saliva flying out in ropes on the warm breeze. She was so puffed she said she had to lie down and did so, shielding her face both from the blue flare of sky and what might be more unbearable, the presence of his body beside hers. Inside the hollowed-out top of the barrow, created by some forgotten and fruitless search for treasure, the wind dropped to a faint susurrus. Yet when she turned her head to look at him, the grass-stalk in his mouth wavered against the skyline, a needle tremulous in the shock waves of distant storms.

– When I was little I used to pretend that it wasn't the clouds moving at all but me, lying up here on this barrow or under the pines over there where they buried Eric's dad. I used to pretend I was looking down from the hull of a ship into a blue sea. And the clouds were, well, like underwater reefs, coral and so forth, which I was sailing over. Does that sound silly?

– No, – she murmured, letting the harsh blue soften to red on her closed eyelids. – I imagined something similar myself.

Which was not true but might serve as a makeshift bridge to the moment she knew was coming, when his shadow must arch above her and she would feel for the second time the pressure and texture of his dry lips on hers. When that moment did come, she found she was not as prepared as she would have liked. And flinched away from the flicker of his tongue as it sought unbidden entry into her mouth. Then, when his hand rested a moment too long below the shirred waist of her jacket, she sat up sharply, smoothing and smoothing at her skirt, as if to remove invisible creases. So Beatrice realised that her girlhood dreams of a vaporous intimacy could no longer suffice. The man sitting up beside her, was as gauche, as

94

importunate, as selfish in his way as she. But he was also as warm, as solid. Trying to hide her confusion, she stared down into the blue strata of the weald, where the heat made the landscape almost glassy. Perhaps it was for the best, this death of an impossible ideal. Looking south now, towards the distant Channel, she saw how clouds had gathered, isolating the sunlight in molten pools on the sea's surface. Her intense disappointment of a moment ago was beginning to evaporate. He had kissed her and that was more than any ideal lover could manage. Standing up, she pointed to where the white cotton tapes still tried to keep the earth in place, binding the turf as if it were wounded flesh.

– Wasn't I going to help you with your survey, Charles? Wasn't I to hold something while you looked at it through your machine?

And Charles Tremain, who perhaps had not intended to kiss the assistant schoolteacher, having resolved in advance to make the occasion of their walk on Thundersbarrow a pretext for confessions of friendship, not love, seemed filled with immense gladness and shouted into the wind,

– Of course you can help, of course, – keeping his back turned until the inconvenient erection should fade.

And indeed the work, which had so strangely brought them together on Beatrice's arrival, might have seen them through that afternoon to the moment outside the schoolhouse when they must again wrestle with the embarrassment of physical proximity. Instead, there came a certain shudder, a shift in the arrangement of what had appeared to be immutable things. At the moment it happened, Beatrice was holding the calibrated staff in the middle of the jumble of hollows below the barrow, while Charles busied himself with his theodolite under the pines near old Wren's grave. All at once it seemed to Beatrice that she rose up and he fell; then that he rose up and she fell. A second later and they were both where they were. Except that there was a certain silence. And the larks had switched to a thinner, more cautious melody. Charles came running across.

– What was it? I felt the ground move.

She was holding him for a moment, out of animal fear.

– Can'st work i' the ground so fast? – He seemed delighted. But it was a delight she knew instinctively she could not share. – As I predicted. As pater predicted. It's weak you see. That side of the hill. They've had a rockfall.

– Oh, I do hope Eric is not hurt.

Immediately she regretted this remark. Yet felt a certain obstinate pride.

– I'm glad now I pushed the date for the excavation forward to the beginning of August. There may still be something of the hill left by then.

Beatrice listened again. There were distant shouts and some kind of bell clanging. Was this the price that Eric Wren would exact for defeat in the tug o'war. The second flood. The destruction of the quarry itself. But why? Why destroy what you loved? Again she saw the man with the moonlight mask in the rhododendron alley. Again her consciousness of her own role in bringing all this to pass rose up like the foetor of indigestion. *We hate each other*. And now she had been kissed by Charles Tremain.

It had only been a small rockslide. Not even a cliff-face. People were clearing up, dragging out some damaged panniers. Eric Wren was on the side of the pit looking down. If Charles had been elated, he was sombre. This too Beatrice had not expected. Nor the way he studied her hard, as if searching for some mark, some indication of what had happened on Five Lords Burgh. As if, in this place of delicately balanced darknesses, the touching of two mouths could cause catastrophe.

– We may find the old cave at this rate, eh Charlie? Then we can go into the old galleries the flint men used without having to dig down at all.

At which it was Charles's turn to stare hard for a sign or the absence of a sign. But only at the ground, whose palimpsest of chalk and turf and mud had long since been trampled and tamped into illegibility.

The conservatory was still and warmly wet. Ferns lifted their jade straps from a wall that had been built to resemble a low cliff. Streams of water trickled down the side of the miniature cliff into a basin where moustached orange fish glimmered. A smell of damp peat and leafmould wafted past. Instinctively lifting her dress to avoid the hem being dirtied or soaked, Beatrice negotiated the fibrous aerial roots of some leathery-leaved tropical plant and came face to face with Lady Tremain, dressed in a flowered housecoat and carrying a small brass watering-can. The older woman sighed.

– Now I must water the philodendron. It's always the same. If you want a job done properly do it yourself. Look at all those dead-heads. I've been here since nine.

She waved a loosely clad arm in the general direction of a small basket in which some withered geranium flowers lay, then busied herself over a standpipe. The chilly sound of the gushing water made Beatrice long to quench a hitherto unnoticed thirst. She swallowed to create saliva.

– I believe you wanted to see me, Lady Tremain.

She had feared this second interview almost more than the first. Lady Tremain was bound to have discovered something about her walks with Charles or worse, to have assembled hard and fast evidence about that solitary kiss, so ill-advised, so hasty and so brooded over. The summons to go to the manor had come soon after Charles had returned to Tongdean for the remainder of the summer term. Although he had visited the schoolhouse to say farewell and had even brought her a copy of some poorly translated guidebook to the ruins of Pompeii as (in his words) *a sort of keepsake*, their manner with one another had been constrained, falsely jovial even. Indeed, at one point, when she had been quizzing him about the school in Chalkhampton, she had actually caught him surrepti-tiously glancing at the clock in Mrs Eddles's seething and malodor-ous kitchen. So that the gloom which had descended on her when he had finally gone, a gloom compounded by the increasing surliness of her headteacher and a general disillusion with her own work, had only deepened when she discovered that yet again she must confront the idol of the manor. That this second interview was to be conducted in the shadow of an artificially constructed primeval forest, only added to her sense of discomfiture. By the time Lady Tremain had deposited her watering-can, Beatrice was miserably aware of the acrid stains beginning to spread outwards from the armpits of her blouse. She would faint if she did not sit down soon. But her hostess did not intend to sit down. She was tutting now over a fountain-shaped plant whose central cone had sprouted something pink and swollen on a stalk. Beatrice longed to look away.

– There, what did I tell you. The stem should be full of water at all times. It's that new maid. – She turned in the steamy air as if the offender might be lurking like a primitive tribeswoman behind a convenient trunk. Then recollected.

– Yes. I wanted to see you. Of course. Now Miss Lumley, don't you think it's time we had a chat?

Here then was her nemesis. Beatrice put out an arm to steady herself and encountered something sharp.

– Don't touch those thorns, they'll give you a rash. Here, come this way.

In the conservatory's inner sanctum the air was stiller and thicker than ever. A plant with flowers like clots of blood drooped menacingly over Beatrice's head. But at least she was sitting down. She determined not to raise her arms and reveal her sweat-stains.

– He's ready now, you know. It's time you and he got going.

Beatrice was so dizzy with apprehension that she forgot from moment to moment what she ought to be saying or doing. Her arm went up to adjust her hat and the terrible stains were revealed. Lady Tremain grimaced.

– Well, girl, have you a tongue in your head or haven't you?

– I don't think we're ready at all. I don't believe . . .

Lady Tremain drew out a fan from her sleeve and opened it with a snap.

– He has all the books. And as you know, Mrs Eddles has agreed not to let your room for the summer.

Beatrice felt as if her entire body was leaking, sending runnels of salty juice coursing down every available path and cleft. What a little fool she had been not to look out over the parapet at the greater world. No one in this place was interested in a kiss, still less in an assistant schoolteacher's feelings about that kiss. Here, in this conservatory, no less than anywhere else at Ecclesden, she was merely another kind of servant. To be used and paid and dismissed. As on her previous visit, the subject was Robert, not Charles. She had already been approached about coaching him during the holidays. What a little fool. That once, towards dusk, looking down from the summit of Thundersbarrow, she had felt this place might welcome her as an equal, only added to the bitterness of the draught. Keeping her arms firmly by her side Beatrice looked up at her employer whose face stayed partially eclipsed by the fan.

– I meant I need a little more time to prepare some exercises. But by next month when the schoolhouse is quieter. Shall we say the last Monday in July?

The fan dropped. Its folds she now saw, bore a pattern of splayed peacock tails. *Too close. Too close.*

– Sooner. When term ends. It is imperative Robert goes to Tongdean this autumn. His governess was very remiss in many ways. He has fallen behind according to Mr Jessup, who would coach him himself if he had the time.

Beatrice sensed that the interview was drawing to a close. And wanted somehow to risk the intrusion, however covert, of her feelings for Charles.

– Is that the same Mr Jessup who will be supervising the dig?

But Lady Tremain didn't seem to hear. And Beatrice, who might have gone on to mention Eric Wren and the opening up of Dragon Pit, found herself being led back through the tentacular maze of the conservatory by a maid especially summoned for the purpose. At the doorway the colder air made her gulp shallowly for breath. The peacocks were calling in the garden but more mutedly now after the fury of spring. She would be back here in a few weeks' time. Charles would be too. The dark cave of the future seemed suddenly to open and glow. By the conservatory door a mound of old newspapers lay waiting to be spread out under the tropical plants as a mulch. On the topmost paper dated Friday the twenty-eighth of June (that would make it four days old she remembered thinking afterwards), there was a small report about some assassination in a remote European state. At the time she could hardly have registered the headline, yet years later it seemed to Beatrice that no detail of that moment had in fact been lost, from the cool trickle of sweat trapped in her cleavage, to a chaffinch's insistent *You did you did you did* deep inside a creamy flowering clematis smelling of vanilla. Then, in that future time, when the glowing cave had opened on to a windswept and cratered plateau, the words Archduke and Serbia would indeed seem to float at the heart of this day, like fragments of some ancient inscription glimpsed at the bottom of a lake. Except that in the hiatuses between the surviving letters other words had intruded, modern words, private words, words of accusation, betrayal and loss.

– A letter came while you were out. It's on the hall table.

Beatrice stopped in the kitchen doorway, uncertain whether to pretend indifference or not. Word from him coming so soon after the elation she had felt in the conservatory at Ecclesden could only be interpreted as a double blessing. Yet she feared to encounter the envelope, the handwriting she had never yet seen, the turns of phrase mere speech would never attempt. At that moment she seriously doubted her ability to bear the burden of such a document. Or confession. Mrs Eddles looked up from where she was beating a slab of streaked raw meat with a wooden spoon.

– Well, aren't you going to fetch it? I've set the Dadger girl a hundred lines. They say Dragon Pit's almost collapsing. Wren's going round like a savage apparently, harrying and worrying them to take out as much soap as possible. It'll be his downfall. And the quarry's. And the Tremains'.

Slap slap. Slap slap. The spoon dripped blood. The meat, apparently, deserved a good drubbing.

But Beatrice was already moving in a dream of fronded intimacies towards the porch. What had Mrs Eddles's bitter prognostications to do with the fernlike unfurling of her love for Charles. She could hear the peacocks again but muffled. *Too close. Too close.* She swept the envelope up without looking at it and rushed upstairs.

My Dear Beatrice. Please forgive this hurried missive but I'm to set out for Chalkhampton tomorrow. Dr Blake has finally insisted that I spend a month down on the coast. He's arranged for a room in the sanatorium attached to the Roman Fort hospital where I stayed once before, perhaps you remember, the one with the lovely gardens. Now don't be alarmed, dear. All in all my heart is bearing up. But Doctor thinks that a month of sea air might do the trick and set me up for the winter. If not, and we will have to discuss this dear, when we meet, he hints that I might be obliged to househunt down there. Now what do you think of that? Perhaps you might find a more permanent post in the town and come and care for me. That would be a marvellous comfort, especially since Dr Blake is moving down himself soon, to take over the running of the hospital. But this is all as they say in the lap of the gods. I will be staying at the Grand Hotel for a few days until my room at the sanatorium is ready. Send word to me there saying when you can come out to visit, your ever loving Aunt Millicent.

Beatrice let the thin blue paper drop to her table and stared dully at the window framing Thundersbarrow. Coming back through the alleyway from her interview with Lady Tremain she had walked straight into a spiralling cloud of gnats. Excited, careless, she had brushed the fluttering veil aside. Now the gauzy many-particled film seemed to return and blur her vision. These were not the words she had expected to read. In their banality and self-absorption they dragged her back to the reality of the day. He had not written. Soon, perhaps sooner than she realised, she would be leaving this land behind the hills, never to return except as someone else, someone older, for whom the young woman sitting in the schoolhouse attic would be a dim and no doubt inaccurate memory. The gnats danced before her, a curtain draped across an enchanted doorway that continually withdrew when approached. He had not bothered to write. He had probably not even thought of her. Her aunt's crabbed tremulous script mocked her misapprehension. Indeed it was almost as if he had written it, wearing the mask of an elderly egotistical and ailing woman to mock and deride her. Beyond the mirage of the gnats Thundersbarrow lay sealed in the heat haze of late afternoon. Up there Eric Wren was working like a savage, bringing about the end of things. And here Charles Tremain, ventriloquising from inside a valetudinarian's brain, paraded his true nature. She was glad then that she had not put down roots but drifted between the schoolhouse, the manor and the hill. Soon she would be gone, leaving these people to live out their own conflicts and terrors. She would live in Chalkhampton and look after her aunt and teach in the national school. *Oh Charles*, she gulped, *why didn't you write*? And screwed the blue lavender-scented notepaper into a ball.

The sound coming from A form was rhythmical and hollow. Sharp intakes of breath followed by a gulping sigh. It was growing dark. Mrs Eddles had long since gone out to visit the vicar's wife. Beatrice tugged at the door which had always been stiff. There was a flurry of movement in the twilight then silence. Then the rhythmical hissing and gulping again. Her candle drew a hunched back and head into its penumbra.

– Molly? Molly Dadger. Is that you? Are you still here?

She moved forward and the figure hunched over the desk flinched slightly. A scatter of papers lay on the desk.

– I can't . . . do . . . anymore . . . my hand . . . won't . . . hold . . . pen . . . I hate . . . her . . . I . . .

The words struggled up out of a pulsing centre of misery and resentment. Beatrice felt a stab of pity.

– You should have finished hours ago, Molly. It's nearly dark.

But for now Molly Dadger was not living in a world of time and place. She had entered a cave where only hatred and revenge dwelt, like savage ancestral ghosts.

– I . . . hate . . . her . . . she . . . said . . . she . . . she . . . said . . .

And Beatrice, who had herself only recently been hurt by what people said and didn't say, set the candle down and took Molly's cold hand in hers.

– It doesn't matter what she said, dear. You must go home. I'll take you home.

But it did matter and Molly was not to be so easily pacified.

– She said he isn't right in the head. She said his dad wasn't either. Which was why he did it with Lady . . . Did it with Lady. Which is why Eric got permission to dig . . . because Lady . . . because Lady . . . because she's frightened of it getting out . . . And I said it isn't true. Because I love him, Miss Lumley. And one day we'll be married. And then she pulled my hair and said I was a dirty girl and I cried and she pulled it again and she liked pulling it, Miss Lumley, look some of it came away, all because I love Eric Wren.

Then Beatrice was holding the frail weeping wraith and saying it didn't matter because that was all you could say when things did matter. And she was weeping too, not only over the poor innocent love of this girl for Eric Wren, but also over her own poor innocent love, if that was what it was, weeping and stroking the violated head and knowing all the time it was her own head that she stroked.

Flimpy too? That makes four.

Will we go on looking?

Too dangerous that scree. It might move. Ma, where's young Eric?

Still out. Said he wanted to see it. Or said they said. You know. His friends.

Inside him, you mean.

His grandma heard them too. Don't forget that.

His grandma was a moon calf.

Don't speak ill of the dead. If it weren't for her we'd have no religion in the quarry.

The quarry needs work, not religion. And if you want religion why don't you go down to the parish church?

That's not religion. They don't bow before the spirit. They don't hear.

And now the spirit has told him to go into Dragon Pit. It's the danger, Ma. He might go too near. It only happened yesterday.

He'll be all right.

His Nibs isn't half angry.

Why should I care?

He won't let you dig there again.

We needed the soap, Razzell. It's good soap in Dragon Pit.

He says you knew the risk. And didn't tell him.

There's always a risk.

True, Eric, true. But he says you didn't tell him.

About what, you old bastard, about what?

The tunnels. All that.

But I did. I told him everything when he said he wanted to dig up the Five Lords. Said some archywhatyoumacallem put him up to it. And did he listen? Not Colin Tremain. The old legends about the dragon could go hang as far as he was concerned. And now we've disturbed the dragon in an honest search for good soap, he can't hear anything else. It's all on account of me refusing to help him dig for gold up there. Now are you satisfied, Razzell Bushnell!

It don't look good for you. That's all I'm saying.

Eric boy, is that you?

The horn lantern's light. A circle where they sat. His dad and Razzell Bushnell. Ma in the wash-house, sighing.

It's gone, Dad. It's gone.

What lad?

My cave. The one I used to play in.

We can't be thinking about your games now, lad. The whole cliff's gone. And four men underneath. All because we have to go digging in dangerous places now those damned Tremains won't put cash into the pit. Isn't that right, Razzell?

If you say so it is.

Remember that, Eric. Remember it was the Tremains woke the dragon not me.

(Remember.)

And don't go up that way again.

Charlie'll be sad.

What did you say?

Nothing, Dad.

(Remember.)

You can see the belt, can't you, boy?

Yes, Dad.

On the wall. On that hook.

Yes, Dad.

You know what happens when certain particular names are mentioned.

Yes, Dad.

What happens?

The belt turns into a snake and comes down off the wall. And I have to have pain because I don't listen to my elders I listen to my voices which is a great sin and I am truly repentant Amen.

Stop whimpering, boy.

Yes, Dad.

(Remember. Remember. Remember.)

The train was slowing down, negotiating a curve that lead directly into the great hangar of Chalkhampton terminus. Taking her coat from the rack Beatrice felt a strange apartness. A few months ago she would have thought nothing of leaving Thundersbarrow and Ecclesden behind her. In the first days of homesickness she might even have felt relieved, greeting the sight of the Channel and Chalkhampton's narrow streets with the sharpened senses of a newly recovered invalid. But now it was the outside world that seemed unreal while the world of Thundersbarrow, a diminishing blue ridge in her mind's eye, claimed all her memory, all her attention. It was not that she had found peace of mind there, nor even a measure of contentment. As she readied herself for climbing down out of the carriage into the salty cold air of the terminus the people whom she had encountered in that land behind the hills rose up darkly one by one, rebuking, cajoling turning away. There was Lady Tremain in her hot conservatory, only prepared to be nice as long as Beatrice undertook to coach her backward youngest; Mrs Eddles in her seething kitchen, cruel and servile by turns; but always cold, coldly reluctant to allow her underling a day off to see her aunt. Then Eric Wren rose up out of the primeval fastness of Thundersbarrow, hugging his secrets and revenges as if they were druidical spells. And lastly Charles who could not write; who would not write; who thought only of himself. Yet as she swivelled the carriage handle and stepped down it was these shadows, thin and insubstantial as they so often seemed, which thronged around her, pushing out the hundreds who surged hither and thither through the station. For better or worse she was wedded to Ecclesden. To come away now was to leave part of herself behind.

Even as she boarded the tram that would take her to her aunt's sanatorium she could not forget. Once again Molly stood with a tears-stained mask of a face by the door of the schoolhouse waiting to be escorted home. For Beatrice had felt obliged to accompany her pupil at least as far as the top of the elder path. From there the hovels of the Bottom were only a stone's throw away, on the far side of Lower Pit. As they had walked up the rankly close footpath, Molly still snivelling a little, Beatrice increasingly numbed by the disappointment of the wrong letter, something had come out of the darkness at her, brushing briefly against her cheek then floating away. Despite herself she had cried out, raising her hand to her cheek as if it had been burnt. Molly was laughing.

– That's good luck, that is!

– What was it, Molly? I've gone all shivery.

– A goatsucker. – Then seeing her schoolteacher's evident incomprehension, – A kind of bird. Some call them churn-owls. On account of they're supposed to sip milk from the dugs of cows. Lucky in love if anyone's touched like you was. On the cheek.

Which would have been all if, at that very moment there hadn't come a shout of laughter from the shadows clustering around the trunk of Old Neb.

– You're only telling her the good news, Moll.

At which, with a little squeal, Tod Dadger's daughter had run forward. Eric Wren was shovelling lime from a wheelbarrow into a truck on the funicular. Lit by the fire inside the tunnel of the kiln, he looked like a cinder afloat on some molten pool. Molly was keening.

– Eric, when will we go to the fair like you promised. The one in Saddlescombe.

– Every valley shall be exalted. And every mountain shall be made low. That's when, Moll. Good even, Miss Lumley. I saw you up near the grave with Charles measuring for the dig.

At another time Beatrice might have paused and shared confidences. But not this evening with this infernal figure. He knew about the kiss. And as if to demonstrate the fact, bowed down in an embrace which threatened to swallow Molly up. The girl emerged gasping but flushed. That was the way to kiss. So Beatrice had turned away, the touch of the nightjar still searing her cheek like a brand. Looking back she saw both Eric and Molly disappearing into his furnace of a hovel beside the kiln.

Sitting in a wicker chair on the sanatorium terrace, Aunt Millicent seemed to have shrunk since their farewell at Easter, shrunk and grown transparent. A shawl over her shoulders and several medicine bottles on a chair at her elbow, she looked out on the gardens with unseeing cloudy eyes. Her ignorance of what her niece had encountered and suffered over the last three months set a gulf between them which the younger woman had no desire now to cross. Yet, nibbling at a McVitie's on a chair opposite, Beatrice could not resist mentioning the darkly enchanted names. Even their sounds had the power in that grey place, with its smells of disinfectant and boiled cabbage, to make new and transform. So she talked with a feeling of delicious guilt about the heir of Ecclesden and his plans to excavate on Thundersbarrow Hill until she could almost feel the wind in her hair or his hand resting on her shoulder.

– Is that Charles Tremain?

Her aunt's sudden sallies of interest could be unnervingly direct.

– Yes, aunt. He has so many pursuits and such a future.

– There was some scandal I recollect. His father and an American divorcee. And the manor is close to the school? I didn't realise. Well.

Which meant that if she had known her aunt would not have allowed Beatrice to take up the post. But Beatrice was not about to be divested of her privileged knowledge of that new home.

– Oh, all that's in the past, aunt. Even if it is true. And Charles is going to redeem the family name. I can tell.

– You seem to know a good deal about this Charles.

At which Beatrice blushed, remembering that she had mistaken her aunt's letter for one of his. To think that he was nearby even now, in the school overlooking the cliffs. The thought made her want to cry. Her aunt was sighing.

– I think my afternoon nap beckons. I do hope the Doctor's diagnosis is correct. Perhaps I should live in this town after all. Especially since my niece seems so easily swayed by strangers.

– Oh Aunt! Really!

But Beatrice's pretended protest had little strength if only because, not a few hours before, under the influence of her disappointment about the letter, she had almost welcomed the thought of moving into Chalkhampton to be with her aunt. So now she merely stood up laughing, leant forward to peck the papery cheek and left with a promise to join her for tea.

Without altogether realising the fact, she had been heading towards the pier. The promenade lights were already on, their arcs receding along the shoreline between a succession of blue-green posts, each post having three feet in the shape of dolphins. On the pier itself the domes of the various arcades and theatres were lit up too but with lamps that had been arranged to blink on and off in succession, creating streams of light that tumbled down the roofs into the sea. Beneath her feet, through the slats of the pier, lay a vast girdered emptiness and beneath that the foaming summer waves. There were gulls hovering between the pier and the sea and, looking down at their great white backs, Beatrice felt very high up indeed, higher than Thundersbarrow even, surveying the world. Dimly remembering her one childhood visit, she had bought a candyfloss and held its frizzled pink stickiness in front of her. Gradually her lips melted into the honeycombed cave. People were all around her, laughing and talking. She felt positively lightheaded and giggled to see the woman with a rather thin smile poke her head through a screen on which was painted the bathing-trunked torso of a fat man. Perhaps she should write to Charles. The thought had come from nowhere, when she turned for a moment and caught sight of a seafront window flashing in the late afternoon sun. Yes, she should write. Just then, over the pink ragged moon of candyfloss, she caught sight of a little booth near the tower of the helter skelter. A sign over its curtained door read *Madam Ka. Fortunes Told. Cards of Love.*

Inside the atmosphere was stuffily acrid. Somewhere overhead a gull's cry evoked a muffled savagery that contrasted strangely with the familiar honk and click of peacocks. The fortune-teller was not what Beatrice had expected. Instead of a conventional gipsy costume she wore a hobble skirt, a bolero of some silken material and a rather loose turban. It all looked hastily assembled, indeed improvised, an effect compounded by the straggly blonde hair pushed back carelessly behind her ears. When she spoke her teeth looked yellow and slightly askew.

The voice too sounded peculiar, artificially deep and sonorous, as it explained the different available readings (Beatrice chose the simplest three card spread); asked for cash (*First you must cross my palm with silver*); then bade the client concentrate on her question. The fingers that cut the cards were stained at the tips with nicotine.

– Now c . . . c . . . concentrate, – the fortune-teller repeated, drawing out the hard 'c' in a slight stutter that suggested weariness rather than inspiration.

Beatrice, reminding herself that she had entered the booth on the purest of whims (although she could not deny that she had wanted to do something that would affront Aunt Millicent's severely rationalistic universe), closed her eyes but could not resist another surreptitious glance at the reluctant sybil opposite. How out of place she seemed, at once too sophisticated and woefully lacking in the cynicism that would treat the whole charade as a job. Meanwhile the question on which Beatrice was supposed to be concentrating refused to formulate itself. It was as if the fortune-teller exerted the kind of power which made sortilege impossible. Beatrice waited in some confusion.

The illustration on the first card seemed to consist of a number of swords. Beatrice who, for all her lipservice to the deeper irrational truths, had remained firmly wedded to her aunt's material piety, realised that she had never even seen a tarot pack before. The fortune-teller was making awkward circling movements with her right hand, as if stirring a watery surface. The gesture seemed to Beatrice to be cheaply theatrical.

– This card represents the recent past. There has been conflict. Perhaps associated with a change of some kind.

Beatrice, while realising that she was being milked for specific facts, felt an electric jolt of wonder. It was true. The cards could not lie. That this dreamlike amazement had more to do with the need for a confidante than any occult proof, did not occur to her. Or not until later. For the moment she was happy to mention her new post at Ecclesden and, more circumspectly, the difficult friendships with Eric and Charles. The fortune-teller looked on unblinkingly. She had greenish eyes.

On the next card were a number of cups which reminded Beatrice of communion chalices. Again the fortune-teller performed her curious ritual with the imaginary surface of water.

– This is the present. A calmer time. But not balanced. Your emotions, I mean.

Again Beatrice felt that she must speak and again the fortune-teller looked on. It was the fact that he hadn't written, Beatrice wanted her to understand, the fact that he had sent no word. She might have gone further too, mentioning the kiss on Thundersbarrow or the parting at the schoolhouse, if she hadn't suddenly noticed that the woman opposite was shaking slightly. It was a flicker merely, a subterranean tremor. But there, in the booth, between them. She stopped speaking, feeling apprehensive. With a rapid movement the fortune-teller leant forward and turned over the last card.

Beatrice only glimpsed this third illustration before it was peremptorily whipped away and the whole tarot pack thrust into some hidden drawer under the table. But as she looked up in consternation, feeling a mounting sense of guilt and anger, she thought she could remember the picture on the card, the collapsing building, the figure falling, the ruinous sky. Then the strange woman was standing up and removing her turban, speaking in a lighter, more mellifluous voice.

– Look I'm dying for a drag. – Walking over to the curtained entrance, even as Beatrice tried to formulate her protest.

Outside, in the waning light, Beatrice began again, whilst the blonde-haired woman took long sucks on a hastily lit Navy Cut.

– Look dear, I'll be honest with you. I'm not Madam Ka or whatever she calls herself. I'm doing this for her as a favour so she can visit her daughter at the Fort hospital. I work down there, – here she pointed to a silver-streaming dome set so near the end of the pier that it seemed to rise up out of the sea, – with the pierrots. I'm a variety singer.

– But I wanted to see the last card. – Beatrice felt aggrieved. She had been enjoying talking about herself. The fortune-teller frowned.

– I could see you were bright straightaway. Much too bright to be taken in.

– But it's a game, a diversion. Something to do.

– What you were telling me wasn't a game. I shouldn't have been listening. It wasn't what the usual holidaymakers come up with. Questions about marriage. Or careers. It was serious. And unresolvable.

Beatrice was blushing despite herself. Perhaps she had been too open, with this stranger who seemed so familiar. Yet she continued to protest, if weakly.

– But I wanted to see the last card.

– And have me pronounce on your future? Not likely. – The fortune-teller whirled the cigarette stub over the railing of the pier. She smiled, – Look, dear I'm a fraud, that's the sum of it. Look, here's your money back. And – now she glanced back at Chalkhampton as if its flashing windows might indeed contain one occult secret to which only she was privy, – I wish you good luck. There, isn't that what gipsies are supposed to do. Good luck with the school and the hill and the quarry and the manor. And the man you love. Whoever he is. There, isn't that a sort of fortune-telling? Now here's another customer, with some world-shattering question about warts or varicose veins.

The blonde-haired woman mimicked a tremulous middle-aged woman so well that Beatrice had to laugh. Perhaps in the end a fortune had been told. But as she waved to her confidante and turned away, she had an uneasy feeling that this singer who had filled in for Madam Ka was both more darkly capable than any professional psychic and less able to keep her distance. Her refusal to allow Beatrice to see the card of the falling tower had nothing to do with a fancied superiority on both their parts to the easy legerdemain of parlour sortilege. She had seen in that card something she did and did not want to tell Beatrice, something that involved not only Eric Wren and Charles but herself as well. At that moment, walking back to the sanatorium for tea, Beatrice was convinced that the part-time fortune-teller and the girl in the photograph on Lady Tremain's mantelpiece were one and the same. She had met Maud at last. But Maud in disguise.

Dearest Beatty,

There, I've never used your diminutive before, have I? But it has such a homely ring. I cannot excuse my not writing. It's this school, taking up so much of my time. How I shall bless the day when I'm finally free of it, when I can be my own man, when I can see you.

Are you reading the Dante? Don't you think that final ballade the noblest of things? Read it on the hill one day and think of me.

Well, there are odd stirrings abroad. That assassination in Serbia seems to have got the old buffers terribly worked up. Not that it has anything to do with us. By the way I saw the fleet on manoeuvres out in the Channel recently. A sublime sight. It made one proud to be British. And slightly tearful.

I met that relation of mine in town the other day, at a soirée given by our own dear Walter Birkett, the music teacher who runs the Tongdean Choral Society. Seems she has quite a voice. Now don't be jealous, Beatty. I can hear you beginning to be. For, do you know, we had nothing to say to one another. She's a wild suffragist, for one thing. And for another, quite plain. She goes back to London too in a week or so. To be with the Pankhursts. Much to Birkett's disgust. Seems he wanted her in the choir. Between you and me, I think he's sweet on her.

Well dear. Must dash. There's a house supper tonight. And then I must think seriously about the excavation. Mr Jessup can come. But he insists on bringing one of the boys as a factotum. A silly oick by the name of Frith. You won't like either of them. How's Eric the Viking and his pit? Give Nimrod and Oenone a kiss each for me if you ever see them. As I now give you. But more than one. If I am allowed . . .

There were stars over Thundersbarrow. A powdery flickering. Somewhere in the vicinity of Dragon Pit a light glowed fitfully. She sat for a long time at the window of her attic room, touching the letter, sniffing it (chalk? and something sweeter), pressing it to her face and breast. If Maud entered her mind it was only as a reassuring presence. In a sense Maud had brought this long-deferred joy to pass, down on the windy pier, among the crowds and the barbarous shrieking gulls. For hadn't she given her blessing, wished her luck. That night Beatrice slept more soundly than she ever had at Ecclesden before, with the letter tucked girlishly inside her pillow. Even when, on the verge of sleep, Eric Wren appeared to remind her of the ill omen of the nightjar's wing, she could not keep from floating to an island in the middle of Thundersbarrow where Charles and Maud waited among flowers shaped like chalices and swords.

It should have been nipped in the bud.

I can think of many things that should have been. Annabel Cohen née Prescott for one.

He lies under the honeysuckle at the side of the boathouse. Bees drift there, through the scented yellow-winged reefs. He can hear their voices on the far side of the cladding and imagines how they lie side by side on the canvas loungers, as they do every Sunday afternoon, with the marble table between them on which two tumblers and three decanters have been placed. Now pater is lifting his tumbler to his face, slowly.

To think a son of mine should consort with such riff-raff.

She laughs mirthlessly.

The Cohen woman wasn't exactly refined. That brassy American voice. Those jewels.

At least she had a sense of humour. And her father's family are very highly respected on the East Coast. There was a senator uncle. And the father was, is, an archaeologist. Anyway this is all ancient history. Really, Katherine, you are positively addicted to raking over the ashes.

The glass chinks. They are relishing their mutual hatred. As usual.

Don't we own the quarry? Isn't it right that Charles, who will inherit from you, should come to understand these people a little. Now, Wren . . .

Junior or senior? You certainly seem to have made a big effort to understand the father. Though I gather language wasn't much involved.

Oh don't be so vulgar, Colin. I merely helped out in a time of crisis. When his wife died. A charitable act.

Ah, so that's what you call it.

Ancient history dear, ancient history.

Charles will be corrupted.

Or enlightened.

You always favoured Robert, of course. Ever since the dead twin.

That was my sacrifice. And your victim. Charles's twin died because you betrayed me. With that Cohen bitch.

Monotonous, the voices, droning out into the afternoon, stagnated beneath the thick light of the honeysuckle. Thundersbarrow shimmering with heat. Cobalt dragonflies patrolling the caves of the rhododendrons, swivelling with rapacious swiftness. Helmeted demons. You are right and you are wrong. Wrong but right. Right but wrong. You will never escape this, these words, these sounds of people through walls, invisible, never-ending, never understood.

– In 369 occurred the so-called barbarian conspiracy. In 410 the Roman legions left Britain for good, thus ushering in a period of confusion and anarchy known as the Dark Ages. Towns were sacked; villas burnt to the ground; the people slaughtered. In AD 477 . . . Robert, are you listening?

She put down the book and frowned. Robert was bent double, looking under the table. His shoulders were shaking.

– Pooh. You dirty hound. Nimrod's let off, Miss. Shall I open the window?

There was an answering sigh from the twilit regions round their feet and then the appearance of two feathered hind legs being stretched. Beatrice too sighed.

– It's too bright, Robert, with the blinds up. I wish you wouldn't be so vulgar and I wish you would try to concentrate. Tongdean doesn't tolerate slackers. Now what happened in 369?

– The barbarious consp . . . con something. Anyway I don't care about Tongdean. Anyway, what's so interesting about history. Have you heard the news? There's going to be a war. There's been an assass . . . an assass . . . someone's been killed and Germany and Russia want to fight and anyway I hope it goes on till I'm old enough. I hope I get to fight in Eric's regiment.

She sighed again. The muggy atmosphere was giving her a headache. How she wished she hadn't been obliged to forsake the airy regions of the long gallery. She had held the two previous coaching sessions up there and Robert had made some progress in arithmetic and history. But today they had been told the third floor was out of bounds. Charles would be back soon for the summer holiday and the long gallery was his own personal drawing room. So they had found themselves in the butterfly room where a bluebottle beat against the pane in a furious mockery of the dry corpses under the velvet cloth. The memory of her first visit here should have returned to comfort and inspire her but for some reason, perhaps the aftermath of a particularly heavy period, Beatrice felt tired and on edge. Now Robert was tap-tapping something hard on the table. It drilled at her nerves like that woodpecker earlier among the limes.

– For goodness sake, Robert, will you stop that. There isn't going to be a war. Serbia is hundreds of miles away. And anyway . . . and anyway.

To her dismay Beatrice found that her eyes were filling with tears. It was too ridiculous. As if she were about to go into full mourning for something that had never happened. Then she remembered that Charles had mentioned the Archduke in his letter. The sudden intense and alarming grief she now felt had something to do with this. But why? She rubbed a knuckle across the corner of one eye and attempted to divert Robert's bold and contemptuous stare.

– What's that you're tapping, anyway?

Robert glanced down and with a child's instinctive fear of confiscation quickly thrust it deep into a pocket.

– A Devil's Thunderbolt. And it's mine. Nimrod's done one again, Miss.

Now the room was indeed thick with the dog's gaseous eructations. The smell of rotten game wafted up in sweetly overpowering waves. Beatrice raised a handkerchief to her nose.

– You may open the window now, Robert.

Her tears could at last be blamed on an incipient nausea.

The summer term was still not at an end. Although the troubles with the quarry children had long been solved, Beatrice, spending six or seven hours five days a week in the company of her charges, still found herself sliding between a barely controllable tension and catatonic fatigue. The quarry children were particularly demanding, whether possessive and clinging like Molly Dadger, or suspicious and sceptical like Mucky Gurl's son. Sportsday had come and gone, a confused memory of screaming faces and a red-faced Reverend Langridge awarding prizes after he himself had fallen in the three-legged race with the school janitor as partner. But if Beatrice looked forward to the end of term she also dreaded it. There was to be her coaching of Robert for one thing. These sessions had already begun at weekends and apart from the obdurateness of her pupil, there had been the painful business of reacquainting herself with the interior of the manor, that repository of so many failed dreams, wrong starts and memories. Worse still there was Eric Wren's seemingly permanent withdrawal. After the strange and abrasive encounter at the top of the elder path, Beatrice had not come across him since, except on one occasion. It had been during one of her regular walks to Five Lords Burgh when she had heard his voice on the wind. Peering down into the stripped and flayed crater of Dragon Pit she had seen the crowd and, on top of his dobbin cart (Lob lying with one eye open at his feet), the limeburner. He was preaching on a passage from Revelation. It was apparently a spontaneous act, this discourse on the last things, but it filled Beatrice with a sense of inevitabilities, of destinies wound round each other like snakes. So she had hurried on, his cracked urgent voice ringing in her ears, trying to forget the intimation that he was talking about himself and her and Charles. And lastly there was Charles himself. No more letters had come. This at first had been something of a relief. Then when she found that all her efforts to reply ended up torn or scrunched on the floor, she had begun to hope for a second letter, to plump out and underpin the first. For Beatrice, who had no more confidence than anyone of her age, would have preferred the easy escape through another's more powerful will. That Charles was not made in that image, that he was as weak or perhaps weaker than she, she was only just beginning to comprehend. So she sleepwalked through what for her too were last days, waiting for some release, some sign. The weather grew hotter and muggier. When she walked through the rhododendron alley pairs of blue dragonflies would rise up, their tubes of bodies glued end to end, mating.

The khaki-yellow cover of Gill's *History* swam before her. The window was open now and the curtain hung limply. Robert was writing the answers to her questions in his exercise book. What caused the Romans to lose their hold on Britain? Over and over again the words of an advertisement in one of Mrs Eddles's magazines drummed in her aching head. It was a picture of an ox standing beside a tin of Oxo bearing the legend: *I'm dying to get into this*.

– Do you know what's in that cabinet?

I'm dying, dying to get into this into this.

She shook her head. What would she ever find to say to Charles when he did return? And if he should bend to kiss her or worse, what would she do? What wouldn't she do?

—You know. Where the butterflies are.

– Yes, I know. Butterflies.

– No, you don't. What else I mean. What else is in the cabinet? I know.

– Moths of course.

How faraway her voice sounded. As if it too had died to get into this. Robert was looking at her quizzically.

– Are you feeling well, Miss?

She wasn't but shook her head.

– I'm fine. Your brother showed it to me. The day of the fête. When I was dying to get into . . . No. I mean. Yes. Butterflies and moths collected by your father.

– And by them.

– I don't understand. Now why did the Romans leave Britain?

– By my brother and her. Didn't he tell you? Though she couldn't be bothered with all the pins and the chemicals. She just liked to pull their wings off. Before they were dead.

– Who, Robert? Who are you talking about?

– Maudie, of course. But it's not the insects. It's what's underneath them. Under the cotton wool. Shall I show you, miss? Shall I?

Then she was standing beside him in the aquamarine light watching as, for a second time, the velvet cloth rolled back. Now Robert was raising the glass top too. Then very gently, I'm dying to get into, very slowly, this, he took hold of the cotton wool sheet and folded it back, dying, with the crumbling insect corpses still adhering to it like scabs. Underneath, gouged into the veneer of the cabinet base, Oh dying into this, Beatrice saw the two hearted initials C and M.

The attic stretched away from her, a series of caves in the air or, worse, an aisle between tombs. She had reprimanded Robert for disturbing the butterfly cabinet and he, knowing she had taken a painful delight in leaning over the initials, taunted her with Maud's shadowy presence. In the end, swaying through the velvety choking twilight of the violated room, she had gripped him by the shoulders and yanked his hair down hard until he screamed and screamed again, half-whispering as she did so, *There is no Maud. There is no such person*, to which he sobbed between yanks, *Yes there is yes there is*, finally breaking away to lurch from the room into the accommodating echoes of Ecclesden.

How long she had sat there afterwards in a kind of suspended animation she could not say. Nimrod had soon slunk off. Oenone wandered in and sensing her distress wandered out again. Eventually the five o'clock chiming of a far clock reminded her of her duty. Lady Tremain, who had been out all day in Chalkhampton, would be back in an hour. Any inkling that her favourite had been punished, let alone mistreated, would result in terrible retribution. Suddenly, for all her apprehensions, Beatrice dreaded the possibility of being exiled from this house on the very verge of Charles's holiday. She must find Robert at all costs and make her peace. It had been a silly misunderstanding. She was unwell. She had lost her temper.

He was nowhere on the ground floor. Rather than go upstairs where she had no rights of entry, Beatrice ventured down into the depths where she had overheard Charles and Eric all those weeks ago. Today the basement kitchens and storerooms were quiet and surprisingly cool. To her deliberately impersonal question the housekeeper replied that the young master had taken a cake without permission and gone running off upstairs.

– Been misbehaving, has he, Miss? You ought to have seen the dance he lead that governess. If you ask me he needs . . . Come to think of it the governess looked a bit like you. Not so pretty of course. The attic. That's where he goes. There's a window at the far end. Boys today. I don't know.

She would have called, if the sound of her voice in that cobwebbed space could have been disguised somehow. Instead she simply walked on through bays where old packing cases rose up in tells, over the grey-dry plates of coagulated bats' droppings, past horsehair panels and ancient small bricked chimney stacks which looked like the underground roots of some vast plant, a plant growing down out of the sky. How ironic it was that she who, not a few weeks before, had been comforting a child for having had her hair pulled, must now commiserate with and even apologise to

119

another child whom she herself had punished in the same manner. Robert was an unattractive boy at the best of times. Yet she must retain him as an ally, if only for the sake of Charles.

She found him sitting on a box in a little bay with a window overlooking Thundersbarrow. Instinctively he flinched away, his mouth sticky with stolen jam.

– I came to find you. I came to say sorry. I know she's real. I've met her.

His tongue moved idly over the wet glistening of sugar. A snail.

– You weren't sorry when you pulled my hair. I'll tell mater.

– If you do I'll tell her how poor your work is. I'll show her your exercise books.

He paused in his licking and looked at her.

– She is real. She was here. Then she went away. Eric hated her. But I didn't. Only sometimes. She used to come up to these attics. And Charlie. They had a game of dressing up. I was little. It was just before Miss Bates my governess came. When Daddy died. But I remember. Here. They were going to be married, see. And she said. And she said. When they were married I could go and live with them. But then she went away. She used to sing me a song. So I'd go to sleep. She had a lovely voice. All soft and sleepy. Miss Bates didn't. I hated her. She said Maudie was lying when she said she'd be back one day. But Maudie will come back I know she will.

Lully lullay lully lullay
The falcon hath borne my mate away.

Robert's tremulous tuneless words echoed strangely so near the roof. And Beatrice, who had squatted beside the ungainly and rather ugly child, realised many things. That the maternal love of Lady Tremain was a thin thing, dominant and quixotic. That Sir Colin's death had allowed this love the upper hand at Ecclesden, to the exclusion of more genuine emotions. That Maud, who might and might not be both the woman on the seafront and the cousin in Charles's letter, had appeared here once, bearing a more spontaneous and open love. That both sons had responded to this love in their different ways. And finally that Maud, for a reason she could not yet grasp, had been obliged to leave. Was it then surprising that, as far as Robert was concerned, Beatrice was an enemy? Part of the world that had prevented Maud from fulfilling her promise to return. A world of echoes and deceits and darkness.

– I'm sorry I pulled your hair, Robert. Look here's another one of those cakes. I stole this one. There, that's a secret between us, isn't it? Though I suppose you could tell on me if you wanted. Shall we share it?

So in the long dusty attic, the schoolteacher and the youngest son of Ecclesden Manor shared the stolen cake and came to a sort of understanding. Beatrice told him how she had been frightened of Maud because she did not want to lose Charles. And Robert told her how he knew Maudie and Charlie wouldn't really get married. But that he'd like to see her again and give her the Devil's Thunderbolt he'd found in Dragon Pit.

The noise sounded close enough to be in the garden below, yet remote as if from beyond the horizon. It was long-drawn out too, beginning as a slow rumble then ballooning up into a roar that immediately became several tributaries. By now Beatrice was used to the sound of explosions but this was something different, more fundamental, older. Instinctively, she clutched at Robert who flinched away.

– What is it?

– Something in the quarry. Noises always sound louder up in the attics. That's what Maudie said. Louder and stranger.

There had been a landslide in Dragon Pit. Not as bad as the one in '09. But a sign of things to come. So Mrs Eddles reported that evening, crouched over a plate of urinous kidneys sticking up like sleek boulders from a glutinous pool of gravy.

Snow in the air, flurrying round Dragon Pit, where last night's fall drifts bluely against the dirty white of chalk. A cold north-easterly. Rooks from Ecclesden Hanger buffeted against fast moving grey clouds. He scrabbles once more to the very top of the scree.

Where Flimpy is. And the others. Like the cave swallowed them. Then disappeared itself. The hill's revenge. Oh Dad, why did you?

He scrabbles higher to the ledge which used to lead to the cave but is now only half as long, the remainder buried under tumbled irregular blocks of chalk. The wind is loud up here, moaning and whistling through invisible flues, as if the hill were a complicated many-piped organ. He sits down to get his breath. And sees him. Far below. On the very floor of the pit where the spars of the smashed platform still lie among a scatter of broken lyddite boxes. Nobody will come up here from the quarry. Nobody that is except

Dad. He calls but his voice is swallowed by the wind. And suddenly feels relieved because round the corner of the chapel pit someone else is coming. Someone on a horse.

Have they agreed to meet? And why here, in this cursed place? What are they going to do? I don't want to look. To hear. Oh I don't.

But must. For the wind which stuffed his words back down his throat carries their words clearly upwards, as though his ear is pressed to the shaft of some invisible well. It is Sir Colin speaking, tap-tapping his riding boot with a short crop. Not looking at Dad. Like Dad's a lump of chalk.

First the pit. Now this insurrection. You'll never work again, my bucko. Do you hear?

But if Dad is chalk, Sir Colin is glass. To be stared through.

You and your damned orders. Do you think I care! Do you think so!

His hand on the reins. Snow whirling round them, so many pieces of a broken sky.

I told you that was your last chance. But to come with your men and create a ruckus in our court. Frightening the servants. My son. My wife.

It takes a lot to frighten your wife.

And just what do you mean by that?

What do you mean, Dad? What?

I mean she's not frightened to come up here. When you're off. Visiting the ruins.

Up here, here, what do you mean you insolent ape?

Snow whirling. I know what you mean. I know. You have betrayed me. By going with her. You have betrayed your son. How can I follow you now, Dad? How can I love the hill and hate the Tremains? When you love a

122

Tremain and let the hill collapse. Oh I've seen you. Back in the summer.
Under the three pines. She was on top. I saw. I saw her moving. I saw the
darkness. Up and down up and down. Hair. Hair and darkness. I saw. And
now I must see you humiliated too. By the man you hate. And I won't come
down. I won't. I'll stay on this ledge and watch. In the snow flurries and the
cold. With the rooks whirling their black snowflakes over the pit. Because
now I must love the Tremains too. And that will only make the hate worse.
Yes. Love and hate, Dad. You've mixed them all up in me. I love Charlie
and I hate him. I love the hill and I want to see it destroyed. Like you are
being destroyed now. Down in the pit. His foot on your shoulders pushing
you down. Then the whip across your face again again. A hatching of purple
grooves. And you will never recover. Never.

All day it had threatened rain but no rain fell. All day they had been
together in the empty house and garden, moving it seemed as one
through the long languorous hours. They had eaten raspberries in
the walled kitchen garden, crouching side by side against a cold
frame and she had watched fascinated as a stream of seeded juice
escaped his mouth, bleeding down on to his chin. So that she must
dab the sweet stain with a loving handkerchief. Then later in the
morning they had sat together in the long gallery reciting passages
from Tennyson, the two retrievers dozing under their entwined feet.
Lady Tremain had left yesterday morning for London with Robert
in tow. If she had known Beatrice would be free the following day,
she might not have been so eager to leave her oldest son behind,
despite her Red Cross committee meeting and the appointment to
have Robert fitted for his Tongdean uniform. Things had been
whispered about Charles and the schoolteacher and some of the
whispers had reached Lady Tremain. On the day of Charles's return
from school (a day long-awaited and feared by Beatrice), there had
been a heated exchange about her between mother and son in the
library. His mother's assertions of social incompatibility were
countered by Charles's claim of shared intellectual interests. Eventually, the argument had died down. Beatrice, after all, was doing
wonders with Robert and in any case Charles was quick to point out

that there was no attraction on his side. If Beatrice could have eavesdropped she would have been mortified. Yet when his mother did decide to go to London after all and Charles discovered that Mrs Eddles too had been called away to her sick sister in Chalkhampton, he was swift to appear at the schoolhouse and invite Beatrice to come across to the manor.

— I can show you the coot's nest on the lake. And the place where the kingfisher hunts. Oh and lots more.

She had accepted of course, though not without apprehension. The energies that crackled, albeit intermittently, between them were not born simply out of books. She was unsure if she could trust herself. Let alone Charles. Yet, remembering her encounter with the strange fortune-teller on the pier, the thought of some final ruin rose up to haunt. Perhaps there was little time left to them. So that, in the end, her doubts had to fade, along with the memory of the tug o'war and its aftermath, into the rain-heavy, leaden light.

– I think it's beginning. We must shelter.

He had turned up his palm to receive the first spots. There was a low rumble.

– Is that thunder?

– Eric, more likely. You've heard there's been another slip?

– In Dragon Pit?

– I warned him this would happen. I said it wasn't a good bargain. Not after what happened in his father's time.

Again she saw Eric Wren's face in the hovel by the kiln. His eyes cast down.

My Dad died for this quarry.

– There was some dispute between his father and yours. Is that right, Charles?

They were under the lee of a wall up which pears had been trained over many years, their leaders pruned back again and again, until every branch ended in a swollen black knuckle of wood. The unripe yellowish fruits hung down among the brown-tipped leaves like dim lanterns. Rain drops came spattering past, and made the leaves glisten.

– It is, Beatty. But that's ancient history.

– You and he have a strange friendship. It frightens me sometimes.

– Why?

He was looking at her in the rainy air.

– How it will end I mean.

– Well, Dragon Pit's closed, that's for sure. Those explosions are to bring down a bit of the second slip, and relieve some of the pressure. After that he must keep his side of the bargain and help me on Five Lords Burgh.

– But won't he be humiliated? I remember when I went to fetch the children. He said it was the quarry's last chance. Now he'll be blamed for everything.

Without her realising, Charles had put his arm round her waist. Now he tightened his hold. She flinched away involuntarily.

– Not here, we might be seen. I know what rumour-mongers the people round here are.

– Look it's coming on heavier now. Let's go to the boathouse. And don't worry about Eric. The quarrymen always find their feet. Especially Wrens. Perhaps he'll join the army.

She laughed but felt a heavy sadness. All that she had dreamed of during the term was coming to pass. She was alone with Charles and he wanted her. Yet somehow she could not rouse the spirit of enjoyment. It was as if she had suddenly grown older and left her younger self teetering on the margin of a love that would now remain forever unsatisfied.

In the boathouse he drew her to him as she had expected. Feeling his tongue for a second time seek an entrance to the interior of her mouth, she remembered the sticky seeds of raspberries and found herself imagining a pool of blackbird's excrement on the path through the rhododendrons. He felt her resistance and redoubled his efforts, his right hand stuttering clumsily up and down her stomach.

– What was this boathouse used for?

Having managed to pull away she felt a desperate need to play for time. He stood shuddering slightly, eyes downcast, his cheeks

flushed. Raspberry red. Rain was drumming on the shingled roof.
Then he hugged himself, as if emerging from warm water into
colder air.

– Oh I don't know. Father. He used it. As a den. Look, let's sit
down here, Beatty. It's more comfortable sitting down. Please.

His importunacy found an echo in her mind, seeking out her
younger self who should yield, she told herself, if only because the
masonry of the tower was beginning to crumble and there really
wasn't much time. But when at last she did sit down on the
suggested settee and they were locked together once more in an
embrace that incorporated conflict, distrust and sheer ennui within
its urgent mechanisms, she found the void that lay at the heart of
Ecclesden, the void that she had wanted to enter once. And knew
that it was not for her.

– Put your hand on it Beatty, please.

Which she did, feeling all the time his own hand sliding along her
inner thigh and wanting, not wanting it to stop.

The rain was drumming louder now. That she allowed his palm to
rest between her legs, pressing and pressing cotton drawers against
wetly parted flesh, was a segment of the same dream which enabled
her to loop her forefinger and thumb round the veined and stiffening
tube he had insisted she release from the buttoned-up crotch of his
linen trousers. She thought of nothing then except perhaps the
drench and density of the rain, washing over the gutter in a torn but
continuous silver sheet, then dripping down the panes of the
boathouse window in long threadlike scars. How strange it was, to
be in there, watching the fingers of someone else, some other
woman, a woman you might have been, fluttering about the tip of
this stranger's silky glans. While all the time you were outside, alone
under the assault of the rain, hearing within its splash and souse an
echo of that first flood, in which everything drowned. And stranger
still, to feel yet not feel *his* hand, slipping down now between cotton
and flesh and, encountering hair, pause. While outside the rain
redoubled its strength and you, the other woman, the woman who
was not a part of the shadow-scene inside, felt it passing through

your body, a presage of a flood to come, originating in the earth itself, which men would attempt to contain with strips of ribbon as fragile and white as those which dangled now from the waist of your disarranged and partially lowered drawers.

Then all at once the strange dislocation passed and Beatrice was herself again and must decide how to go on or how to stop. At first she felt she could not stop and shifted slightly, to allow the trembling disembodied hand greater licence, in its blind slide from mound to cleft and back again. Meanwhile her own hand set up a rhythm to which he began to succumb, his eyelids fluttering, his enclosed left hand ceasing altogether to burrow into her flesh. Once she glanced down and, through the dim rain-swept light, wondered afresh at how expertly her looped fingers hooded and unhooded the shaft's moist tip to a static fury. But then she must give her attention to his hand which, having been resuscitated, was twitching like a greedy fish down there in the cave of her belly. So that she too felt her eyelids begin to shiver with an upwelling desire for release, explosion, oh anything but this endless tearing and rooting at one another, as if they had ceased altogether to be people and had turned into blind ghosts endlessly attempting to enact what a former life had denied them.

Suddenly Charles was moving. Lurching up and over, he pressed his body down between her legs, pinning her against the old leather settee. She was afraid then and angry, feeling him pressing into her and tossed this way and that, noticing as in a heightened state of fever, how cauliflowers of stuffing came vomiting from a ragged slit in the settee's arm. Oblivious of her struggle, Charles was tearing at his waistband, then switching his attention to her underthings which he might have torn off if, with one last lunge she hadn't dragged herself out from underneath him and slid to the far end of the settee. There with thighs firmly closed and dress hastily rearranged, she could begin the slow process of recovery, locking herself up again, letting her old self die back into this new older and colder woman, who claimed the privilege of youth and inexperience even as she felt the pangs of middle-aged regret.

– No, Charles. I'm not ready. Can't you see that? Not ready at all.

But Charles had frozen, there in the air beside her, the rain tattooing overhead, his willy or John Thomas or whatever a boy his age would call it, sticking out of the gash in his linen trousers like some yellowish stem blanched for lack of light, an elastic liquid string hanging down from its shrivelled bud to touch the parquet floor.

– Oh Charles, honest to goodness, what did we think we were doing?

And then she was laughing or hearing the person she had become laughing, out of shame for her younger self and derision for the self she must now become, thighs clamped firmly together, thin-lipped, moving through life like a mermaid, all fish below the waist.

– Oh really Charles, I just couldn't. It's too silly.

She heard herself say. And laughed again. And felt horror at doing so. Meanwhile the fish-thing suspended over the settee was beginning to cry in sharp dry heaves.

– But I want you, Beatty. I . . .

So that she must cradle his head now, her hand still sticky from its interrupted work, leaving a slick on his pale hair, her lips resting on the slick and tasting salt through their whisper.

– I know you do. I know you do.

Seeing the blanched stem shrink back into a wrinkled bud as in some reversal of a natural history lesson, the bud guiltily tucked back while she must go on crooning over his bowed tormented head.

– It doesn't matter, Charles, not now.

Although she knew it did matter.

– Listen, the rain's easing. Shall we go outside. Say yes. Please say yes.

So Beatrice who, until this terrible sadness fell with the rain into her mind, had always regarded Charles as her superior, was suddenly confronted by the spectre of her own power. And felt frightened. As they stood up and kissed again, apologetically and without passion, she wondered if Maud had ever felt such power and realised that if she had, she would have used it to the full. But Beatrice could not use it. Or not yet. Outside, the lawns of Ecclesden were smoking in the storm's sunny aftermath.

She had hoped to find him in the vicinity of Old Neb: by the funicular perhaps, or in the hovel where he kept his tools and victuals. But the kiln was no longer alight, its great flint-scaled skin felt cold to her touch, like the body of a dead animal. The funicular too was out of action, the trucks gone, the cables that pulled them motionless and rusted. The door of the hovel banged disconsolately in the breeze. Inside, the table was overturned among a litter of dead rabbits, a pick, some blankets. The bed had disappeared. Stepping outside she knocked her foot against a cracked flagon that had once stood between them, crammed with pickles. The breeze played with her hair. A rat scuttled away behind the kiln.

It was true then. The failure of Dragon Pit had brought about Eric Wren's disgrace. He was gone from here, into exile, a wanderer on the face of the earth. The quarry's last hope, which he had tried heroically to realise, was dead. And like all prophets who risk themselves for the good of others, he had been blamed and mocked and driven out. Beatrice shivered although it was not cold and drew her coat to herself. If Eric Wren was to blame so was she. Without her intervention all that time ago, none of this would have happened. She had already sensed that Charles thought as much. There was a distance again between them, after the disastrous encounter in the boathouse, when so much had seemed possible and so little had actually occurred. Afterwards she had run back to the schoolhouse like some wronged maiden in a melodrama, knowing all the time that the truth was muddier, more composite, less comfortable. She had wanted the encounter as much as he, had contrived it even, once the opportunity had arisen. Yet like Charles she had been betrayed by inexperience and fear and something else not wholly definable, a certain distaste which would harden over the years into a loathing for the body and its peremptory demands. Two days later they had met again and argued, nervously, *sotto voce* in the butterfly room. It had been after another long and gruelling lesson with Robert, who had returned from London full of the news of Russia's mobilisation. *There's going to be a war I know it. And Eric'll join up. While Charlie stays behind to look after the wounded.* Perhaps their words had been clouded by this mixture of political reality and childish fantasy which Robert had left behind him in the room. Certainly they lurched wildly between accusation, lament and sheer unadulterated insult. She accused him of trying to take advantage and he blamed her for coldness. She mocked him for knowing nothing about prophylactics and he countered by calling her an old maid in the making. Maud had come into it too but, since she was unsure as to what the relationship between the cousins had been, Beatrice could not capitalise on her jealousy. So the argument had continued until the distant voice of his mother brought Charles up short. Turning at the door he looked back.

– If you hadn't come here everything would have been all right. I would have been happy. Eric would have kept his reputation. Why did you come, Beatty? Why ever did you come?

There had been tears then, suppressed in the butterfly room but allowed full expression at the schoolhouse. There she had found the copy of the *Vita Nuova* and ripped at it until all the pages lay scattered in a heap at her feet. The page from the school exercise book on which she had doodled his initials all those innocent months ago she tore up as well, this time with her teeth, as if wanting to reabsorb a love that could not find satisfactory self-expression. Finally, she lay on her bed, feeling the first pangs of her monthly delayed, she had no doubt, because of misery and anxiety. Afterwards in the failing light she had had to go downstairs and mime some kind of normality in Mrs Eddles's greasy kitchen. Mrs Eddles had resented her presence during the summer holidays from the very beginning, making it quite plain that she could have let the room for a higher rate to another lodger. But she dare not contradict Lady Tremain and had had to content herself with hurtful remarks directed at Beatrice. Buoyed up by her love, Beatrice had not minded at first. Now she sat dully like a penitent and received each wound over a plate on which two grey chops floated in a swamp of mushy vegetables.

– We should stick to our stations. That's what I say. Don't you agree, Miss Lumley?

Silence.

– It's the same in the big world as it is at home. If those Serb anarchists had accepted their lot and not tried to change things, the nations wouldn't be in such a taking. Don't you agree, Miss Lumley?

Silence.

– You're an assistant teacher. I'm the head. Lady Tremain is Lady Tremain. Her sons are her sons. Nothing changes. And if you try to make it change things go wrong.

Briefly, Beatrice wondered if this hundred-eyed woman knew of the terrible sickly sweet afternoon in the boathouse. But Mrs Eddles was moving on.

– Look at Eric Wren now. If he had accepted his lot and not tried to take responsibility for the quarry he might still be one of the community. As it is he's an outcast. Once the excavation is over, once he has fulfilled his part of the bargain he'll have to go.

Suddenly Beatrice was possessed by a longing to see Eric again. Not as he was, but as he had been, when he had encouraged her in his oblique way, and seemed to hover benignly both over the birth of her love for Charles and her difficult entry into the life of Ecclesden. Surely that Eric wasn't wholly buried, despite the many landslides that had occurred. So the next day she went looking for him, hoping if not for advice then at least for the comfort of a trouble shared.

At the back of Old Neb rose the scree which she had climbed on the glorious morning of the children's return. Today the slumped chalk seemed higher and less easily negotiable. The landslides which had eventually forced the second abandonment of Dragon Pit had evidently added their weight to the original cone of chalk. There was a curious noise too, which at first Beatrice attributed to the wind blowing over Old Neb's funnel. But then she realised that this noise contained undertones whose source lay elsewhere. Something nearby was creaking and groaning as though under unendurable pressure. She thought of a ship, invisibly breasting some Channel storm. Then of a person, his voice greatly magnified, enduring some awful torture. It was cold here too, for between the kiln and the scree there had appeared a white steep-sided trench which almost closed over her head, blocking out the high blue sky.

– You can't go up the old way any more, Miss. You have to go a different road.

It was Molly again. She was carrying a bowl over which a chequered cloth had been draped. She smiled wanly.

– Have you come to see him? He mentions you now and then. Shall I take you?

To Beatrice this figure seemed to have aged over the last few weeks. She was no longer a girl trembling on the edge of womanhood. She had crossed the boundary. Beside her, Beatrice herself felt absurdly young and inexperienced. Molly walked on ahead down the trench and then turned sharply left into a kind of gully that rose upwards in a series of steps. The gully was not straight but zigzagged, so that the two women were never in sight of one another and Molly's words came back over the intervening walls as if disembodied.

– I'm just taking his food up to him. No one wants anything to do with him, of course. My father'd kill me if he knew. He's going off with some of the others to look for work in the Lewes pits. But I don't care. I love him you see, Miss. For all that he doesn't want me. I love him because he's Eric.

And Beatrice, who kept trying and failing to see the figure who was saying these things, felt them as a sort of oracular rebuke. When had she ever been able to say so simply and so deeply of Charles *I love him*. Yet that was what she had fancied herself saying only to find that the words always got mixed up with other feelings that she did not like or understand. Then at last the oppressive gully opened out and she found herself next to Molly on the far side of what had been Dragon Pit, near the entrance to the small hollow where the chapel stood. Molly put down her bowl on a flat block of chalk and sighed.

– He'll be in there praying. He won't want me. Would you go in and tell him his luncheon's out here if you'd be so kind, Miss.

Sensing from the resigned tone of these words that Molly not only suspected a rival but was already preparing to make way for her,

Beatrice felt doubly guilty. She, who was partly responsible for Eric Wren's exile, had come up here not to comfort but to be comforted. For her the disgraced limeburner was only of importance as a childhood friend of Charles. So she walked up to the chapel alone, feeling Molly's unresentful eyes still watching her from the head of the gully.

The chapel was empty. She might have gone back down to Ecclesden there and then if, through the window at the far end, she hadn't caught a glimpse of something moving through a haze of brambles. Outside she found that her eyes had deceived her. The moving thing had only been sunlight, reflected on some kind of heavy tarpaulin sheet. But then the sheet itself moved and Eric Wren stepped out, materialising from the very side of the hill.

She had expected a bowed and chastened man, a man full of reproaches, a man who might accuse; instead he smiled, seeing her, and waved for her to come over. She told him meekly about the food which Molly had taken up.

– That'll be grand. But first let me show you this, Miss Lumley.

Then he was leading her back toward the hill and the mysterious tarpaulin sheet. Lifting it aside he gestured for her to enter a large crevasse in the cliff-face. If she remembered his faceless vigil in the rhododendron alley she was woman enough to dismiss it. Something told her that she must see what he wanted her to see; that it had to do with her and Charles.

It was a cave, smooth chalk walls criss-crossed with seams of black flint. The air smelt musty as if it had been pent up in the hill for centuries. At the back of the cave a dark gash suggested further galleries beyond. She turned in inquiry to Eric who was smiling still but sweat-drenched and curiously pale. She could smell the tart reek of him through his moleskins. Involuntarily she put a hand up to her mouth and nose.

– Don't you see?
– This? I see it. Of course I do.

How dead their voices sounded in this place. And there were the noises too, louder down here and seeming to come from deep underground.

– It was the landslide did it. I found it because of the landslide just as I lost it in the first place. I knew you were right. When you came here in the spring and said those things. I knew you knew.

– I . . . about this . . . how could I?

She was alarmed at his intensity. And puzzled. What was so important about this hole in the ground? But he was singing now. As he always did when aroused in any way. The old hymn.

Christian dost thou see them
On the holy ground

He stopped before what looked like a pile of stones on the tamped grey floor.

– Don't you see? This is where it all began. And this is where it will end. For him. For me. For you too. One day.

– What began? And what will end? I don't understand, Eric. You talk as if you love and hate Charles in one and the same breath.

At which he merely laughed.

How the troops of Midian
Prowl and prowl around

– Oh so right. Always so right. Yes I do. And you do too. Isn't that what you came to tell me? That you love and hate him all at the same time.

– I came here because . . . Oh I don't know why I ever came here. I wish I hadn't that's all.

She turned away back to the sliver of light creeping through the hung tarpaulin. And was flooded by an uncomfortable, almost inconvenient knowledge. This was a cave. Under the hill. She turned back.

– Eric . . . is this . . . is this what he wants to find? Have you found it already? The flint mine?

The limeburner was smiling the slowest of smiles.

– Maybe. Maybe not. But he won't know it's been found, will he?

The question seemed simultaneously to forbid and dare. All at once Beatrice knew that she would not tell Charles of the discovered or rediscovered cave. And experienced a wash of sadness. Which she masked, absurdly, with formal politeness.

– Well, thank you anyway. It's been most instructive. And now I must be going.

He was beside her then, in the acrid gloom, pushing his bowler hat back on his sweating forehead. His hand was on her shoulder. Like a brother.

– I'm sorry I spoke so wildly that way just now. It was the excitement of finding this old place you see. After all these years. Where we played as boys, Charlie and me. We were like bloodbrothers in those days. Yes I think I remember we even cut ourselves and mixed the blood together. Don't shiver, Miss Beatrice. It was only boyish fun. But you see, him and me were friends before ever you came along. And to stand here again makes me remember it all. And then I feel bad. For all that happened after. The way Dad died. The way Charlie took his father's side. And then later the way we sort of grew apart. And now the quarry's gone too. Or near as damn it, if you'll pardon my French. After the dig . . .

– That's what I came to ask you. I came to ask you not to help in Charles's dig. It would be, I don't know, unseemly, as if he were claiming a right. You would be humiliated. And it would be partly my fault.

Eric Wren's mouth was working in the twilight of the cave.

– A bargain is a bargain. And no it wouldn't be your fault. All these things had to happen. Just as my dad had to die of a broken heart. Just as Sir Colin had to leave his wife because of my dad. And now we're going to dig on top of the hill. You made that possible. Because you came here. That had to happen too. Soon there may be a war. The French are up in arms so they say. Next it will be the Germans. Then us. And that too will be as it should be. I can see it all now. Now that I've found the cave again. Masks, a sort of crater, white something, white city, I . . .

With a shock of terror she saw the froth at his lips and felt the grip on her shoulder relax. He would fall next and begin writhing on the floor of the cave that had given him back his voices. She shouted.

– Eric! No! What should I say to Charles? How can I help him?

But it was too late. The fit was on him. The cave closed in and waited.

– And you say he had a fit?

They were standing as they had done on the afternoon of the fête, in the clearing in front of the peacock run. The birds eyed them sideways or flapped short wings that revealed a copper underside. The time for displaying was over. One of the hens had made a nest in a hollow near the steps to the temple. It was full of eggs.

– Charles, I was so frightened. I thought I should run and tell Molly at least. But then I felt I musn't leave him. He might choke. It was Lob who brought him round. Yapping in some tunnel he'd found.

They were reconciled at least for the moment and Beatrice associated this new spirit with her terrible and alarming visit to Eric in the cave. She saw now (he had made her see) that she could not simply abandon Charles and this place. Yet just as clearly there would never be a true understanding between them. Today, she had ventured inside a flint mine. Perhaps the very one he wanted to explore. Yet she would not reveal this fact. Things had been too murky before she arrived. Like the stirred-up bottom of a pond. Now the silt was swirling round their eyes.

– But he says he'll help me? Despite everything? That's a relief. You know, Beatty, I think some of my bad temper has had to do with my fear that the whole shooting match might have been wrecked by the Dragon Pit closure. And so much depends on it. Jessup is intending to send a report to my college. I just hope that this bloody war doesn't break out before we've sunk the shaft.

Again Beatrice remembered kneeling with Eric Wren's hot head in her lap. He had seemed at that moment vulnerable yet remote, a creature living almost simultaneously in the far-off past and some unimaginable future. For him the present seemed to have been leached away by a suffering that had its roots in the days of his father's downfall and its stems in the years to come, when he and Charles (she now felt sure) would bring to a conclusion the conflict that had begun in their childhoods. Then quite suddenly he had opened his eyes and begun calling Lob. It was as if the fit had never been. The next moment Lob had appeared carrying something which his master ordered him to drop. A lump of chalk which she would have ignored, if the man who had originally lead her down to Ecclesden hadn't restrained the terrier with one hand while he examined it. Then taking out a knife he had begun working in the gloom like a prehistoric man. Eventually, the lump was thrown away and he stood up, still sweating slightly. The object he pressed into her hand was amber-coloured, stone-cold and long. One end tapered to a fine point, like a missile. She had seen something similar that day with Robert in the butterfly room.

– It's a Devil's Thunderbolt.

He had laughed.

– Truly, Miss Beatrice, you are one of us now. You even know our words for things. Take it. Take it as a promise like. They bring luck in love they say.

Charles was looking up at the Ecclesden windows.

— I hope mater isn't watching. She's still cutting up a bit rough about me and you. But I'm glad we've had this chat, Beatty. You were right. We weren't ready. Kiss and make up.

Which they did, chastely. And she felt the belemnite cold against her breast in the inside pocket of her reefer. *Lucky in love. As a promise like.*

Leaves from the elder path swirling in little knots and eddies round the base of Old Neb. The autumn gale has found an instrument in the kiln's mouth and breathes through it in long moaning roars. Below, all is darkness except where one light quivers like a star in the bleak cliff-face of the manor. He is out of breath from walking so fast over Thundersbarrow. He glances quickly to right and left. No one. It was worth risking. This short cut. He will be there sooner. He will be there before . . .

Halt! Who goes there?

I . . . I . . . For Christ's sake, Wren. Don't be so bloody insolent.

Laughter, as though from inside the kiln. As though the heathen idol which the kiln commemorates has come back to life. The leaves making dry sizzling sounds against its flint footings. Souls of the sacrificed.

Scared you did I? Still that's nothing new.

The figure detaching itself from the kiln. Emerging from the firing tunnel like a priest who has just sealed up the burial chamber. A mocking priest. Mocking the living.

What you back here for anyway, Charlie? Shouldn't you be at school? Learning how to keep the likes of me down.

Panting still. Unable not to stop. To confront this leering ghost. Though he must get down before . . .

That's your father talking. And look where that got him. A suicide's grave under the pines. Unconsecrated ground . . .

At least he didn't screw Yank bints.

Look, I'm in a hurry. Otherwise I'd knock your teeth out, Eric Wren. What with? Your Mummy's favourite pouf? And it wasn't suicide. He died of a broken heart. I don't mind telling you. Your old man broke it.

I didn't come here to trade insults with you. Pater . . .

Is going to get what he deserves. For doing what he did to my dad. He's dying, Eric, for fuck's sake. Haven't you got any decency left?

Silence. Only the wind answering. And the chorus of withered leaves whirling now, a loose ammonite, at Charles Tremain's feet. Eric Wren moving slowly forward away from the shadow of the kiln.

We used to be friends once, Charlie. What's gone wrong?

You've gone wrong, that's what Eric. You've gone badly badly wrong.

We loved the hill, Charlie. We loved being together on the hill. And now your father's dying. We'll both be fatherless then. Don't you see. We'll both know what each other feels. Like we used to. Won't we, Charlie?

Silence. The first cold sprinkling of rain. Charles Tremain hunching up his collar.

I don't want to know what you feel. Not any more. You're just a slave, Eric Wren. But I'm a master. I'll own the hill when pater, when pater . . .

Turning away into the wind while Eric Wren looks back towards the kiln. Whispering,

But I'll own you. I'll always own you. Won't I, Dad? Won't I?

The wind stronger now, hurling bursts of rain against the window. Iron filings. The leaves of the magnolia grandiflora grating and grating on the brick underneath. I've come, father. I'm not too late. Say I'm not. Sharp smells near the bed. Urine thick and bloody in the chamber pot with the peacock-beaked handles. A metal basin holding something green he turns away from. Why now? So soon after Wren's death? Leaving us alone. Leaving me. I've come, father. Though I had to fight off all the ghosts on Thundersbarrow. I've come to be with you. The wind again. Inside the draped four-poster, the swathed body and pillowed sweating grey face. Not my father. A voice only.

He's waiting for me. He's got a chair. Did you know that? He's sitting in a chair under the hill waiting for me. I . . .

What are you saying, father? Do you want me to hear? I can't hear. This wind!

The hand pulling him down towards the grizzled bristly face, the mouth flecked with yellowish phlegm. That smell of something too sweet to be good.

It's because I killed him. In the pit. After he'd slandered your mother. I killed him and then I found out it was all true. They used to meet in the cave. When we were young. When he was almost my brother. Despite, despite . . .

The coughing fit on him. The handkerchief! Quick! And the slimed dish. The head lolling back, lips gasping.

Our social difference. Yes, a brother. And he betrayed me. And I killed him. And now he's waiting. Can't you see? Look. Over there. The light. He's lit it under the hill. Oh don't let him get me. Don't let . . .

The hand relaxing. The wind dying down a little. Oh father.

But you didn't kill him. He did it to himself. And that light is from Eric's kiln. I went by there not half an hour ago. It's all a bad dream, father. You'll get better just you see. You'll forget the dream.

And after me, you. Promise me you won't be a coward, son. Like I was. Promise me you'll fight him when he comes to take you.

Coughing again, leaning over, hawking a bloodflecked elastic thread into the chamber pot where it ribbons out through cloudy urine. Resting back now on the sweat-stained pillow, the face sucked of flesh. Calmer.

Oh, the old ones. They know. All of them descended from that other race. Cain's tribe. This is an evil place, Charles. Beautiful and evil. Remember that when he comes for you, remember I told you.

Wind again crossing the garden like a tide. I will hate Eric forever. I will hate the hill.

Father, are you asleep. Father?
Remember.

It was Bank Holiday Monday, the day of the dig. Charles had arrived at the schoolhouse some minutes earlier dressed (so Mrs Eddles averred, peering out of the scullery window), *like an Irish navvy* in string vest and moleskins with Nimrod and Oenone at his side. Now he fidgeted restlessly in the hall while Beatrice made last-minute preparations. He was in a voluble mood.

– And there was Eric acting like the works manager saying I would be lucky to have half a dozen diggers.

He was telling her about the previous evening while she rummaged in the settle for her stout ankle-length boots. The account centred on Eric's unannounced arrival at the front door of the manor, behaving for all the world like he was some official guest and demanding to discuss the plans for the morrow.

– You know it was he who insisted we dig today, on a holiday. Said men wouldn't take kindly to being taken off work for a mere schoolboy's whim. A schoolboy's whim, I ask you! And what work? Now that most of them have gone to Lewes anyway.

Beatrice looked up from the stale-smelling coffin of the settle and smiled. For she sensed Charles's dissatisfaction was not wholly genuine. Beneath it bubbled an excitement bordering on hilarity. The dig was finally going to take place. And he would be in charge. In the face of this bright reality even the darkness of the past lost some of its shadows.

– At least he's going to be foreman, Charlie.

But the heir of Ecclesden had not heard, buoyed up on his tide of excitement.

– It was too embarrassing. You know I had old Jessup there. And this little fag from the fifth form whom Jessup swears is his factotum but between you and me – lowering his voice – must be a, you know, passion. Platonic of course.

Still rummaging, Beatrice allowed these words to pass over her. At another time they might have stung, given the eager way in which he had embraced the platonic nature of their own friendship after the dreadful wrestling bout in the boathouse. But today she could not be sad. She had found the boots and sat down on the settle to unlace them.

– But wasn't Jessup meant to be staying at the inn?

Charles, whose neck she noticed was once again welted with rashes, whooped then gradually bent down and rubbed his fingers through his hair.

'But surely, Mr Tremain, you have space in your superb residence.' That's how he speaks. The snob. And that Frith giggling like a monkey. Well I packed them off soon enough, my Plato and his Alcibiades. And told Eric to go down and get himself a ginger beer in the pantry. Once a worker always a worker that's what I say.

She smiled again and looked round for her sun-hat with the magnolia ribbon. Charles's good humour was infectious. Yet she had already been bathed by an anticipated happiness before his arrival. There had been a mist when she awoke, its silvery sea swirling between the Wild Brooks and the base of Thundersbarrow. Piercing that sea, the crowns of willows and chestnuts looked like island reefs. Lazily dressing by the window she could imagine sailing between those trees on their voyage to the hill. Indeed, from the way the mist seemed to percolate out from the clefts and hollows at the foot of Thundersbarrow, it was even possible to pretend that the hill had allowed this vaporous flood to pierce its flanks as real water will pierce a dam. But already the waters were subsiding. Over the crest of Thundersbarrow the sun came trailing the first shimmering skirts of heat haze. Caught in that moment between dawn and day, between the cool flood and the burning light, Beatrice experienced an unfettered elation. It had never occurred before. Ecclesden had not permitted it. Even two days ago such a scene would have filled her with anxiety. Every aspect and feature would have complained: *You are a stranger; you do not belong; you have made far too many errors; you must go away.* Not any more. For now Eric Wren had given her the rock-like cylinder with its sparkling of crystals at the base and she and Charles were reconciled. The object and the event were for her strangely linked and instinctively she placed a finger over the point on her breast where she wore the talisman sown inside her bodice. If Eric and Charles were still somehow in conflict and if that conflict spread its circles outwards to include both the whispering maze of the manor and the white tunnels of the hill she, the unlooked-for and mistrusted stranger, had begun to bring about an enduring peace. At long last Charles was going to excavate and Eric would be his foreman. Even her eleventh hour change of heart in the cave, when she had begged Eric to cancel the dig, was part of the pattern leading to this central triumph. She hugged herself and whistled the first few bars of the overture to *Don Giovanni*. Out in the mist, from an ash whose trunk seemed rooted in a mercury lagoon, four, five, six magpies rose up chattering harshly and flew off in the direction of Thundersbarrow. *One for sorrow; two for mirth; three for a wedding; four for a birth; five for silver; six for gold* . . . Joyfully murmuring the rhyme which Charles had taught her, she saw that the sun had risen above the quarry, sending a shaft across her attic room. Dust motes swirled in the shaft and with a swift warm illumination she remembered how, as a child, she had called the tiny particles angels, until rebuked by Aunt Millicent. Angels they were again today, all dancing the dance of things to come. So she had turned, going over to the cupboard where her two summer dresses hung, their folds already scented with the promise of hours hung lazily between white noon and violet dusk.

– Mrs Eddles, have you seen my sun-hat? The one with the magnolia sash?

– Come on, Beatty, do hurry. We need every hour of daylight.

But Beatrice needed her sun-hat if only because of the way it would cast a becoming freckled shadow across her face. Mrs Eddles stood at the door of the kitchen wiping her hands on a soiled apron.

– In the cupboard I should think. – Then running her tongue round her briefly bared teeth as if to get at some rubbery shred of flesh quietly rotting in a crevice – Why people should be so concerned about their own pleasures at a time like this I can't understand. Haven't you heard about Belgium? Germany's threatening to invade.

Charles turned from where he had already begun to open the door.

– Parliament's meeting this afternoon. Grey will speak. A diplomatic solution will be found, you can be sure, Mrs Eddles.

– Diplomacy. Those people don't know the meaning of the word. And all you're interested in is some old mine on Thundersbarrow.

Beatrice came back from the cupboard carrying her sun-hat. She too wanted to go now, before Mrs Eddles hit her stride. She signalled to Charles to pick up the covered basket in which she had secreted a few refreshments. But Charles was standing with his back to the door. His skin above the string vest looked almost hectic.

– You're a teacher, Mrs Eddles. To learn about the past is to learn about ourselves. If Germany would only look into her past perhaps she wouldn't be so bellicose.

Mrs Eddles had found the blocked crevice in her mouth and was working at it with a cracked nail.

– There's a time for teaching and a time for action, Mister Tremain. You'll see.

By the time they reached Quarry Bottom, the great mere of mist under the hill had shrunk to a few ragged lakes separated by blurred violet swathes of slope and hollow. If this flood had at one time threatened to engulf the whole of Ecclesden, the sun had gradually re-established earth's decent sovereignty. Yet in the very way the land now appeared to free itself from the watery vapours which had threatened to choke it, the flood's ancient power was revealed. For the surface of all things glistened like rock newly risen from the waves. And in that glistening, that smoking as of breath or some primal creative conflagration, grass and tree and hedge, even the very structures raised so recently by men, bore witness to the dark submersion which had occurred before and must surely occur again.

Beatrice had been briefly delighted when, coming out from the schoolhouse into an already sunlit garden, she had glimpsed at the bottom of the path the dobbin cart in which she had ridden down from Thundersbarrow in what now seemed another age. But if the presence of the vehicle added a touch of symmetry to the scene, the absence of its owner contributed a slight note of discord. The cart had been lent of course, so that Charles could bring some of his own tools and equipment up to the summit of the hill. They were piled in the back, a jumble of groundsheets and spades, pickaxes and panniers, theodolite and rule along with a figure whose slumped silhouette parodied the upright limeburner who normally held the reins. It was Joseph, the only homefarm man who would agree to help Charles today, the rest having used the excuse of holiday to shroud a more complex motive in which fear and superstition vied with indifference. The old shepherd rose up now and, seeing Beatrice, waved with a *Good morning, Missy. It's a fair one*, the high-pitched words only accentuating the absence of another. As she came closer Beatrice could smell the sharp tang of spirits and noticed a stone flagon half-concealed under the tarpaulin. So the day breathed its first note of darkness.

But once they were underway (Nimrod once again electing to sit in the cart while Oenone bounded alongside), Beatrice felt a renewed zest. Joseph was inclined to doze, leaving her and Charles to talk by themselves. The fact that Jessup and Frith, or the two Athenians, as Charles now insisted on nicknaming them, had gone on ahead direct from the Limeburner's to the summit of Thunders-barrow, only served to heighten Beatrice's sense of being sealed into a charmed world with the man who, if he didn't exactly love her (when had those words ever crossed his lips?), had chosen her as his bosom companion.

Quarry Bottom had changed since the triumphant day when Beatrice had recovered, some said stolen, the children. Many of the hovels were deserted, their occupants having left for work elsewhere. Although still recognisable as a settlement, this miscellaneous assortment of huts and shacks was already beginning its slow collapse back into an earth from which it had never fully been distinct. Serpent-like clefts had riven some of the rough flint walls, making them look more like natural outcrops than structures shaped by human hands. Where the shingle roofs had not rotted away altogether, emerald clumps of mosses and spotted grey lichen plates vied for supremacy. The little alleys that ran up between these ruins were themselves swiftly losing their old identity, being choked by mounds of rubble from some of the fallen buildings. At the entrance to one such avenue (its course so narrow that it looked more like a tunnel), a lurcher's maggoty corpse lay steaming on a pile of greasy rags. There were broken wooden buckets, a rusty bed frame, some rusted chains in a coiled heap. And everywhere a smell: sweet and sickly by turns, the ripe and soft odour of things long decayed, ungathered, undispersed.

Yet through this rotting slum which, in its recent and incomplete abandonment, seemed more ancient than the unimaginably ancient hill on which it had been founded, Beatrice and Charles rode like visitors to some exotic ruin. If eyes still stared out of some of the hovels; if a foot or an arm was sometimes to be seen disappearing here and there into a doorway, the riders in the dobbin cart gave them as much notice as they might have afforded the unappeased spirits lingering in the courtyards of Herculaneum. Today, for perhaps the last time in their lives, the schoolteacher and the heir of Ecclesden had escaped the common round of things and entered into a pure space which they carried round with them like a sacred ark. Out of that sense of fun mixed with solemnity they sang alternate verses of 'She was only a bird in a gilded cage'. The wrecked city of the hill gazed at them from broken and opaque windows.

It was only when the dobbin cart turned up out of Quarry Bottom (Eric's old mare didn't need to be guided) and entered the Lower Pit almost directly opposite the three kilns, that Beatrice's serene sense of self-containment began to evaporate. She found herself thinking back to that other Bank Holiday when she had come up to the pit in her innocence, to be confronted by a swarming and mysterious spectacle. Today all was different. The kilns were cold. The quarry was lifeless. Only in front of Old Neb itself, a disparate knot of figures stood or sat, seemingly having drifted there by chance and remained for want of anything better to do. Then it was that she saw how insignificant the dig was in the run of things. Eric had proved his prophecy. Of the quarry workers who were left, only three, Mucky Gurl, Piggy Baker and Pedgell Wright had reluctantly agreed to give up their holiday. With them was Molly Dadger, who had insisted on being present out of her devotion to Eric, and a nameless boy who seemed primarily interested in playing with Lob the terrier, a game that suddenly became more complicated and less gentle with the arrival, ahead of the dobbin cart, of Oenone. Gazing at this motley crew in the kiln's shadow, Beatrice thought of a sturdy body full of health withering away to the point of extinction. The contrast worried her more than she would have liked to admit, yet she composed her face, determined to be bright. Charles had already jumped down from the slowing cart and was striding forward, a pickaxe over his white shoulder.

– Where's Wren?

His voice sounded all the more anxious and thin for the resounding reply that echoed from within Old Neb's firing tunnel.

– Here. I haven't abandoned ye. Yet.

Now Molly was running up to greet Beatrice.

– Oh Miss, he's got ever such a sharp auger. And a great silvery-looking spade. Do you think we'll find treasure? I hope we don't dig up the king what's supposed to be under there somewhere. Bolt upright he sits. On a great gold throne.

Beatrice, who had begun to feel the brightness of the morning leach away into darker hollows, felt a stab of impatience.

– Now Molly, this is a scientific business. And you must help rather than chatter. I gather we can't take the cart any higher now that Dragon Pit is closed so here, grab these two baskets. Make haste, girl.

Downcast, Molly obeyed, pausing only to pinch old Joseph who was dozing still on his tarpaulin.

Eric Wren emerged from the kiln wearing a rabbit skin jerkin and massive metalled boots. He seemed in high spirits, too high, Beatrice thought to herself, in her newly darkened mood, slapping Charles on the back so that he staggered and pulling at Nimrod's ears until he squealed. Then, coming up to Beatrice, he shook hands with her formally, as if she were the owner of the place rather than a mere onlooker. Beatrice felt uneasy but said nothing, only pausing to wipe the sweat from the limeburner's palm on the side of her dress. Then the little procession set off, not via the zigzag trench that lead to the chapel but round the other side of the new scree that marked the latest landslide. Once again Beatrice could hear the strange creaks and rustlings which seemed to come from inside the hill. She fancied Charles heard them too, wheezing a little as he struggled to keep up with Eric. But if he did he was saying nothing. Soon the white nudity of chalk gave way to a sloping green. The angle was so steep that it felt at times as if they were crawling rather than walking. Looking back Beatrice was consumed by vertiginous excitement. How small Ecclesden looked. And how insignificant the school-house and the garden.

– Oh Miss Lumley, I can see your calves! – tittered Molly from below, obliging Beatrice to smooth down her dress and concentrate more thoroughly on the climb to the summit.

– I say, Charlie, what's that cross over by the pines? I thought it must be a grave but Jessy says it's unconsecrated ground or something.

The carrot-haired boy in cricket flannels and boater stood over Charles who was kneeling amongst a litter of tools in the ditch of the barrow. Nearby the quarrymen had already begun removing the turf in the pitted area marked by the white tapes. Beatrice was sitting with Molly on the lip of the ditch, tying up her hair. Charles gestured impatiently.

– You're right, it's a grave. Now where's Mr Jessup. I need him to advise me on the way we take out the chalk.

The carrot-haired boy looked down condescendingly at Charles. He had rather heavy freckled features except for the chin which was finely chiselled. The effect was of a pig crossed with a weasel.

– Sometimes I don't think you're glad to see me at all, Charlie. I was saying as much in that filthy inn last night. Wasn't I, Jessy?

The teacher had come up beside his pupil. Jessup was a tall thin man with a tightly clipped beard and a habit of wrinkling up his nose to sniff if something displeased him. It did now. He had seen Beatrice.

– Really Charles, I thought there might have been more manpower. And don't ask me to remember last night, Timmy. It was simply dreadful.

– Just because you didn't like me talking to that interesting labourer. He knew a lot about sheep. And even laughed when I told him the joke about the acrostic and God moving in mysterious ways.

The boy laughed again then stopped.

– You were drunk, Timmy. Too much Vino Tinto.

– Vino Tinto! Old Stingo more like. I hope you remembered the flask, Jessy. I need some jolly old hair of the dog all right. Especially if I've got to sit out here all day.

Charles abruptly stood up.

– There'll be no sitting by anyone. We must set to work. Beatty, I'd be grateful if you could organise Molly and old Joseph with the baskets. There'll have to be a spoil heap.

Frith had protruded a petulant tongue but swiftly withdrew it when Beatrice glanced at him. What could have possessed Charles to invite so bizarre a couple? As she moved away to begin her duties, she heard them giggling her diminutive in mocking repetition. Molly was by her side.

– Don't like them two. Hope they fall in. So I do.

Beatrice rebuked her for this sin but crossed her fingers behind her back just in case.

After two hours the hummocked green hollow full of thistles and nettles had entirely disappeared. In its place a pit, perhaps ten feet in diameter and six or seven feet deep, plunged down into the substance of Thundersbarrow. In a sense this was not a new feature of the landscape at all; for the shaft had lain open once before when a different race had mined here for flint. It was perhaps this recovery of something hidden but not destroyed which gave Charles Tremain's excavation its look of permanence, so that a stranger coming upon it in the distance might have been forgiven for assuming it had always been there. Indeed, had he been standing near the hollow way which Beatrice followed that Good Friday of her arrival, the intervening bulk of Five Lords Burgh would have obscured all but the crater, making it seem the product of some sudden irrevocable catastrophe. Only when he had drawn a little nearer, would he have seen the gleaming spoil heap of chalk (itself already a small satellite to the tumulus's planet), linked to the crater by a line of figures pushing wheelbarrows back and forth. Drawing nearer still, the stranger would then have noticed the evidence both of labour and relaxation: the three spades leant together to form a pyramid, like a picket of soldiers' rifles; the patchwork quilt spread out in the shadow of the three pines on which a covered basket lay; stone flagons at the base of the furthest pine; tarpaulin; ropes; a couple of haversacks. Soon he would have heard the sighs of the wheelbarrowers and seen how they had worn a grey track between the heap and the pit. At the crater's lip a woman in a sun-hat was supervising a young girl and an old man who were engaged in drawing up woven baskets filled with chalk on a pulley and tipping them successively into the barrows. By now, above the squeaking of the pulley wires, the stranger would have heard a rhythmical thudding, as if something inside the hill were trying to break out. But only when he, too, came to the very edge of the shaft, would he have been confronted by the diggers themselves, four quarrymen and their temporary master, labouring to make the hole deeper. Then as their picks rose and fell in blurred arcs, the ancient freshness of the day would have been borne home. Here were people doing what the old ones had done before them, in a time so remote it seemed to date from before the flood. But whereas the dark narrow-skulled stonemen wanted flint for axes and scrapers; these taller better clad modern descendants were engaged in a different hunt. If asked, all of them would have said in their different ways that they were looking for the remains of those first excavators, their antler picks, their chalk oil-lamps, their lost or damaged axes. Yet no one there would have pretended to himself that this was what they were really about, on that last Bank Holiday before the war, overlooking Ecclesden and the weald.

Beatrice, who had only expected to be an onlooker, was finding that she rather enjoyed overseeing the disposal of the spoil. Although the sun was beginning to burn rather than warm, rising metallic and pitiless in a clear blue sky, she hardly noticed the beads of sweat trickling coolly down her face and neck. The business of making sure Molly (who was a strong-armed wench but clumsy) and Joseph (who was inclined to skimp on loads) tip their panniers cleanly and quickly into the wheelbarrows absorbed all her attention. Occasionally, she would glance down into the deepening shaft and admire the way the men worked, particularly Eric and Charles, the one all brute strength and force, the other at once careful and relentless, determined at all costs to reach the floor of the mine where the galleries began. Once he looked up, squinting into the sun and caught her eye. His smile, confiding and grateful, hovered in her mind like a promise.

Then the day's first disaster occurred. Frith, who with Mr Jessup had been taking the spoil away, left his wheelbarrow and came over to the pit. He had been surly when it was suggested he assist and less than wholehearted in his labours, stopping now and again to sip from a silver hip flask which he carried in his blazer pocket. Now, flushed with liquor and sun, he tottered on the edge of the pit and called down to Charles in mock cockney,

– Put your back into it, me old mucker. We're grafting up here we are!

And would have fallen, Beatrice saw, if Molly hadn't dropped her pannier and instinctively reached across to prevent it. So that, as Frith lurched backwards into safety, cursing not his own foolhardiness but the bloody bitch who had dared touch him, Molly herself toppled and fell awkwardly on to a shelf three feet below the level of the surface. There she lay until the diggers could scramble up from below and pull her back to solid ground.

It was not a bad fall but she had twisted an ankle and cut her mouth. She lay now in Beatrice's lap while the others milled rather hopelessly around. Mr Jessup and Frith were arguing fiercely in the background. Molly looked up.

– I shouldn't have wished it on him. The wish always comes back to do the wisher harm. I'm sorry, Mr Tremain. I don't think I can lift no more baskets.

Charles, who was plainly anxious to get on, brushed the apology aside. But glanced at Beatrice in momentary accusation.

– How did this happen? We're few enough as it is. I put you in charge up here, didn't I?

Beatrice bridled. But managed to control herself.

– Someone will have to take Molly home. To bind up that ankle.

– You, Beatty. You go. Then we can bash on.

Again she felt her anger rise. How self-absorbed he could be. Hadn't he noticed Molly would have to be supported, all the way down Thundersbarrow.

– Out of the way. I'll take her.

It was Eric, his back already pink with sunburn. Charles stiffened.

– You're the foreman, Wren. You can't.

– It's Molly. I'll take her.

And Beatrice saw again how, at crucial moments, the limeburner became the stronger of the two, if only because he was less anxious about his own vision of things.

Now Eric had gone down to the Bottom with Molly, the rest of the excavators took what Mucky Gurl called an early nuncheon, during which the quarrymen (along with two women who had come up out of curiosity) sat on Five Lords Burgh passing round bread, cheese and their stone flagon. Meanwhile under the pines, Charles, Beatrice, Mr Jessup and Frith began a more complex meal consisting of some cold lamb and mint sauce with a cucumber and tomato salad. Charles was still sulky, while his teacher and friend kept up a constant flow of gibes aimed largely at one another.

– I don't intend to stay another night. Not with you. Now if it was that nice labouring man down at the Limeburner's . . .

– You'll get yourself killed one of these days, Timmy.

– I'm more likely to die of heatstroke. What do you expect to find down there anyway, Jessy?

And to Beatrice's embarrassment, Mr Jessup, instead of ignoring this taunt began absentmindedly to repeat what he had said to all of them before the dig began, not realising that Frith was waiting for a pause to utter with a sneer,

– No dragon's hoard then. Really Jessy, you are such an old dry stick.

At which he lay flat out on his back pushing his boater over his eyes and allowing his partner to gaze long and lovingly at the bur of red hairs on his calves. Charles gnawed absentmindedly at a slice of lamb. Beatrice could tell he was anxiously awaiting Eric Wren's return.

Five Lords Burgh was far behind her, yet she could still be seen. Hot after the exertion by the pit, she had drunk two glasses of barley water straight off with the result that her bladder ached for release. But on the bare side of Thundersbarrow there was little cover and even this far away she still did not care to squat and lift her dress. So she hurried on, through the hammer-blows of sunlight, not wholly unwilling to admit that she was glad for the time being to be away from the sullen quarrymen, the shrill and nerve-jangling Frith and, above all, Charles, who seemed to have taken Molly's fall as a sign of ill-omen. When she had left them, he and Jessup were arguing about the International Crisis. Sadly she noticed that Charles took a much gloomier view than he had done that morning in the schoolhouse. Indeed, he seemed positively to relish the prospect of war, in a brooding sort of way. Perhaps things would look better when she returned. So she walked on, the heat haze ahead of her making the blue distances of the weald shimmer and dance.

She had not realised she was so close to Dragon Pit. It lay below her now, an empty crucible for the sunlight to blacken and cinder. But at least she would be out of view. Scrambling a little way down the slope she came to where, not a month ago, Eric had presided from his throne like a pagan king. The throne was gone now and she squatted gratefully behind the one remaining chalk block which, she noticed, had been scratched with an erect phallus, its tip bulbous and obscenely dripping. Feeling the hot release and smelling the acridity of her thick yellow urine as it bubbled into the turf, she swivelled slightly on her hips and caught sight of a movement to her left. At first she was inclined to hurry away, standing up and straightening her dress as if no exposure had occurred. But the movement occurred again. Squinting into the shimmering air, she saw that it originated in the hollow behind the chapel where Eric had shown her the cave. Simultaneously, she realised that, having walked in a half circle, she was now almost underneath the site of today's excavation. Indeed, as she crossed the floor of the ill-fated pit, she could hear the faint thud of picks on chalk overhead. They must have started again without her. She drew nearer to the cave. From here she could see the tarpaulin twitching slightly in the breeze. Except that there was no breeze. The cliff slanted above her, warped and glassy in the heat, like a polished blade. By some strange trick of amplification, the diggers' monotonous tattoo seemed now to be coming out of the mouth of the cave itself. Unless it were something else altogether, the sound of lost souls perhaps doomed to dig forever towards the earth's core. She could not help herself. But must move forward. Now her hand was on the tarpaulin, drawing it back. Inside, wherever she looked, the air was a black impenetrable hole. Then slowly, reassembling themselves, things did come into focus. The chair that she had last seen in Dragon Pit. And a figure in front of it kneeling. What was he reciting? Was it The Lord's Prayer? She could not be sure. And was suddenly possessed by an intense irrational terror. Outside the whole of the deserted quarry was a furnace. Up above the damned troop was still hammering. She wanted to clutch at her throat, gasping for breath. Who was in this cave and why? What was that groaning and that other swishing noise? Was this what they were digging towards? She must escape this place and tell Charles. He must stop before it was too late. Before something terrible happened. She did not know what but felt it seeping out of the stagnant cave to drink and obliterate the light.

It had all been a delusion of course, brought on by the heat and indigestion (despite her vigilance, Mrs Eddles had undercooked the lamb) and her own absurd trepidations. Now she sat once more under the pines whose tops soughed slightly in a gentle breeze. A parasol gave her double protection from a sun which seemed today to be in league with the very grass of Thundersbarrow to mislead and mirage. Charles had insisted she sit there, saying she looked pale when she returned and blaming himself for allowing her to work so long beside the lip of the shaft which, she now saw, was deeper than three men. So with a panting Nimrod at her side (Oenone had gone off rabbiting with Lob), she had drowsily sought out the shade. Here, when she closed her eyes, a black-red image of Eric Wren would rise up, hammering with renewed vigour at the crumbling floor of the pit. The sight had both reassured and alarmed her. For, if he had returned before her, he could hardly have been the person who had caused the vision in Dragon Pit. Yet, the way he stared while he worked, as if he too had seen something he did not want to see, only added to her foreboding. So that, all in all, she was glad to be out of view for a while, sipping at a glass of orangeade and idly turning the pages of her crumpled, lovingly rescued *Vita Nuova*, while Nimrod sighed nearby, four legs at full stretch. Up here the muffled percussion of the digging sounded less ominous, as if what was being uncovered had more to do with the upper air than some infernal region deep below their feet. Or so she hoped, hearing the continuous bickering of Frith and Jessup who had turned now to the International Situation, twisting it into a scene from their own private drama of attraction and distaste, the younger man blaming the older for all the sins of the European rulers, the older countering with a diatribe against youth and its lazy self-regard. Slowly, inexorably, the harsh voices persisted, accompanied by the low singing of the two quarry women. Beatrice, nodding in her half sleep, heard them all and heard how they were taken up at last into the endless skein of larksong. *Timmy, you're wrong and that's all there is to it. My father left me an acre of land, ivy, sing ivery. No Jessy, no.* A pure world. High overhead. Rising . . .

— I do hope Charles doesn't overtax himself. So like his poor father. His reach exceeding his grasp. Now, Miss Lumley, I hope you, as the only responsible woman here (I except those two trollops with the flagon over by that heathen grave, really what are they singing?), I hope you at least will keep an eye on him.

The shadow which fell across Beatrice in the brief gap between dozing and waking was a centaur's, come up to oversee the dig from the heart of the forest. Then Lady Tremain materialised in a white riding habit and black thigh-length boots, sitting sidesaddle on her gelding. She smiled at the young woman still rubbing her eyes.

– What does he hope to find down there anyway? Bones, I suppose.

– No mama, a dragon sleeping, guarding his hoard. – Robert was beside her, still red-faced after running across from playing on the spoil heap – Hello, Miss Lumley. I've come to see what's going on. But I can't stay because Mama says I have to go to Tongdean this afternoon. To meet the Dean.

Lady Tremain let a languid hand glide over the horse's neck.

– Don't pull, Gemma. Yes, Miss Lumley, it seems my coaching idea has paid dividends. His test last week was successful. I've come up here, partly to say that, as a mark of my gratitude, I propose paying you a ten pound bonus.

Beatrice, who felt that the more she attempted to distance herself from this place and its people, the more she was subtly tied and restricted, murmured thanks. Then to divert the topic,

– Who told you about the dragon, Robert?

– Eric, of course. And when it wakes there'll be a big battle. There will now anyway, won't there? Between us and the Frogs. Or is it the Krauts?

– Robert, don't be so vulgar. Where did you learn such language? – Lady Tremain shot a glance at Beatrice as if she already regretted the bonus. – And what's that in your hand?

– Look, he even tried to make stars.

– Who did Robert, Eric Wren?

– Old Nobodaddy of course, the evil one.

My father left me an acre of land

I harrowed it with a bramble bush
I reaped it with a pen knife

The two quarry women were still slurredly singing on the barrow. Robert was holding the fossil echinoderm under her face. It did indeed have a five-pointed shape on its pink shell, pinpricked it seemed. Instinctively, her hand rose to her own trophy from the hill's seemingly inexhaustible store. What else would they find down there? Lady Tremain was beginning to swing the horse's head away.

– Robert, you must come back with me now.

– Oh mater!

– And Miss Lumley, I hold you responsible for Charles's welfare. He should rest you know, like you are doing.

Then she was gone, leaving behind her a cairn of horse droppings, like steaming gold stones.

One o'clock. The womenfolk had joined their men at the far end of the pines, near the wooden cross. They lounged together drinking and singing.

I sent it home in a walnut shell
I threshed it with my needle and thread

The voices, now jubilant now meditative rose in their bubbles and foam of stingo above the hill. It was as if they were celebrating the end of something, a release from toil, a departure or a dying. Beatrice listened and wondered. Perhaps the quarry was indeed beyond reclamation. Perhaps, as Mrs Eddles and now Charles himself proclaimed, there would be a war. Perhaps she would leave the village school sooner than she had expected and go to live with her aunt in Chalkhampton in the white sea-light. Suddenly there was an outburst of laughter. A new figure had joined the quarrymen. He was raising the stone jar to his lips, letting the treacly dense liquid runnel over his working lips. Lowering the jar, he glanced back to the barrow ditch. Frith was lying there on his stomach, pert buttocks flannel-clad. Mr Jessup tottered slightly, steadied himself, then raised a tuneless voice above Thundersbarrow.

Oh Mistress Mine where are you roaming?

The object of his attention smiled a secret freckled smile under his boater, then rolled over to rest his head on his hands, exposing shortsleeved armpits furred with an orange blur. Some of the quarrymen guffawed but Mr Jessup appeared not to notice. He was taking another swig now, winking at nothing. The heat and the silence grew fiercer.

Two o'clock. He rose up on a ladder leaning against the side of the pit and came towards her, dark against a sun whose remote blinding furnace now held all Thundersbarrow in thrall. Underneath Mrs Eddles's patchwork quilt the turf itself seemed to ooze heat, sweating out the very energy with which it had been so savagely charged. It was so hot Beatrice found herself shivering as she fanned herself under the parasol. He flung himself down beside her, a particle charged with the terrible cold burning of the hillside.

– Well, we're almost there. Just think of it, Beatty, every foot represents a hundred years. Now we've come to within a couple of centuries of their time. The men who lived and died here. Even Eric's excited. I think.

Again she peered into the receding black holes of air behind the tarpaulin in Dragon Pit. Something moved and bared its teeth. Something else glistened soft and pink. Shivering again she shifted the parasol so that it would shade his reddened chest and face. She held a mauve flowering grass stem between her fingers and tickled his face with it in an attempt to woo merciful oblivion in the style of some popular romance.

– What will you find do you think?

– Oh, treasure without a doubt. The dragon's hoard.

He was smiling up at her, having imitated his brother.

– It was right to do this wasn't it, Charlie?

Treat me less as a stranger she wanted to say. He rolled over on to his stomach revealing a tattoo of grass stems between his shoulder blades as though he had been branded.

– Right? Of course it was right. This place can tell us about our heritage. It can enlighten us about our origins. Where England began. How and Who. And we need to know more than ever today with so many threats from abroad, so much sabre-rattling. Yes it is right, it is a duty even to educate these unlettered men, to show them a fragment of our glorious past. For men were digging up here three thousand years ago. That is how old our civilisation is, that is how far we reach back. Now isn't that something to be proud of, to fight for, all those generations that have gone before us, in this beautiful place?

Moved by his own words, he turned away as if to conceal some overbrimming of tears. And indeed Beatrice, who at any other time might have nagged persistently at the ragged gaps in the multi-coloured quilt of Charles's thinking, was content today to turn with him and stare across the breaking wave of downland towards successive strata of mauve, grey, grey-white and blue. Charles was right. This was a beautiful place and worthy to be defended. Then a certain ache of longing overtook her as if she were not an exile here after all, but someone who had returned from a different life to a land she had always known. And she saw the white pit and the spoil heap and the burgh and the pines and the little skewed cross in a new clear light, purged of the suffocating fires she had sensed down in Dragon Pit. And filled with that new sense of wonder, she turned to him again. Only to find him sitting up, frowning.

– I wish they hadn't come.

He was looking across to where Jessup and Frith were taking a five-minute break, talking abrasively and taking alternate sips from the hip flask.

– You thought Mr Jessup would help you.

– He's a liability. Drinking all the time. And trying to ingratiate himself with the quarrymen. And as for Frith. You know I don't like to say this, Beatty, but he's actually been warned for immoral behaviour. In Chalkhampton. Soliciting.

Then she saw that he was flushing and the sun over the hill seemed more cruelly cold than ever, in its merciless vigil.

– Eric hates them. He has very strict morals.

158

And suddenly Beatrice wanted to tell him about the cave in Dragon Pit but realised it was somehow too late. They were nearly at the floor of the shaft where the galleries began. She could no longer intervene. If, indeed, she had ever wanted to.

She was back at the lip of the crater supervising the ever more delicate task of winching up the spoil. Below her the diggers had receded to half their previous height, as if the shimmering heat in the pit were eating at their very substance. Beatrice had the distinct impression of staring down into still, clear water. Under the water, Eric and Charles moved with the slow deliberateness of divers, feeling their way into the heart of the submerged kingdom. Down in Ecclesden the church clock struck three, its reverberation submarine and muffled. She remembered the long-dead sea creature which Robert had found earlier. It was like a star, he had said. But now she saw a shooting star, a meteorite that plunged down into the ocean, its fires hissing, quenched. Charles's voice floated up to her, furred with invisible bubbles.

– Just a couple of feet. The floor may give way. Go easy.

Go easy. Go very easy. Here in this pit under England. Waiting for some gush and explosion of waters which, as the limeburner had often predicted, would wash away the sins of the world. Even their private sin, one afternoon in the boathouse. Was that Eric speaking now, that finned and scaly thing?

– Pull up the basket, can't you? We're knee deep in spoil.

He glanced up and caught her eyes. Simultaneously, she turned and saw that only Old Joseph remained under her jurisdiction. Frith, who had been working the pulley and Jessup, who had handled the panniers, were both gone, vanished into the mirage of the hill. She gave a little cry of concern as Eric, seemingly without touching the ladder, clambered up the side of the pit. Charles was staring at a point in the shaft floor.

– We're there I think, Wren. Wren, where are you going? I say!

But the limeburner would not or could not hear. He seemed swept along by some tide beyond himself as if he had been possessed by the sudden return of a long-forgotten memory. And Beatrice, feeling that this boiling up of outrage and desire had something to do with her earlier visit to Dragon Pit, would have followed too, if Charles hadn't called up to her out of his own dream which must in the end be hers.

– Oh bugger him, then. Beatty, are you there?

He was shading his eyes as if angelically smitten.

– Come down then, won't you. I want you to be the first. – Then in a coarser harder voice. – Yes. Not Wren. Miss Lumley. Everybody else out.

There was a muttering then from Mucky and Piggy and Pedgell about women bringing bad luck, especially this woman who had already got up to no good during the tug o'war. Only old Joseph, leaning over the edge, called down his encouragement. *That's right. A woman's foot. First over the threshold*, although even this support seemed ominous. Still Beatrice had no choice and, as the three quarrymen went filing up one ladder, she gingerly began her descent down the other. At one point her muslin rucked on the thongs of a rung, so that one leg revealed itself to the pit as high as the back of her knee. She was aware then of several pairs of eyes concentrating on this revelation as if it had been magic writing on the walls of Belshazzar's palace. But with Charles below she could feel no shame. Only a sort of levity tinged by fear. With which she descended into the pit.

– Bend down and go in. Just a little way. You must be the first. I'm certain it will bring good luck.

Ahead of her a black jagged hole in the base of the pit, a down-sloping ramp of flint. Above, the faces at the lip of the crater, looking down. As if this were some test, some primitive ordeal. And now she knew what lay down there. And couldn't say.

– Must I, Charles? Small spaces, I . . .

He was smiling at her still but with a hard edge to his cracked lips. As if he too doubted her worth. The air at the mouth of the little tunnel was sweetish-smelling.

– Think of it. The first person in three thousand years.

But she had smelt that smell only three hours ago.

– Take this. Just a little way. I'll be behind you.

The alabaster milkiness of the horn lantern made the tunnel oddly insubstantial as if its walls were about to melt away. Half sliding half crouching, she moved along the narrow tunnel. Strange that this should be a place she already knew. But she would penetrate its secrets afresh if only for Charles's sake.

– Can you see anything yet?

She felt his hot breath on her neck. The hot nudity of his torso. She knew what was up ahead. Yet attempted wonder.

– It's . . . yes. It's some sort of cave. With tunnels leading off. Where they mined the flint I suppose. And Oh!

Then at last she was truly frightened, encountering the fulfilment of whatever had been set in motion that morning by Eric Wren when he took a detour back from seeing Molly home and visited the cave in Dragon Pit. They were in that cave now. Against the far wall stood a chair. On the chair a slumped figure sat wrapped in some sort of blanket. At its feet another figure lay, swathed in a greatcoat. The horn lantern rippled across masked features. She would have run then, back up into the light if, from somewhere deeper yet, some further recess, a voice hadn't seemed to whisper.

– Welcome. For I am a brother to dragons.

And then all at once it was Charles who was the frightened one, shrinking away, clawing at her, his chest heaving, *Oh Christ Oh Christ you were right father oh you were right*, then more quietly with a terrible quietness, *He has you then just as you said he would he waited for you and now he has you forever oh forever* and at last loudly again, *Oh father I don't want to die*, not even bothering to clutch at her, but letting go, crawling back to save his own skin, not concerned with what the terrible figures might do to her when they woke up, only determined to get away, leaving her there in the cave while the strange words reverberated in her mind and seemed to have a calming effect, so that she found herself going forward not back, as if she were in control of this place, its queen or nurse, forgetting

Charles and his juvenile fears, crossing over to where Jessup sat dead drunk in the chair and Frith lay breathing harshly under Eric's father's greatcoat.

– They don't know the land. I fancied this would happen. Found Jessup wondering around as mad as a hatter in the pit, saying the boy had fallen and was dead. They argued of course, being all boozed up. And whether this one fell or was shoved I'm not about to say. But he's alive. Look. See his breath.

Then Eric Wren, who had come out of the further depths of the cave, held a little mirror to Frith's parted lips and Beatrice saw how it had indeed clouded over. She looked up at him, tears in her eyes.

– Charles was so frightened. He abandoned me here.

– He would.

Then Beatrice realised that Eric Wren had indeed come into his inheritance, even if there was nothing now to inherit. But Charles had entered on his long defeat. From which he would never now be able to turn back. So she cried for her love's innocence and loss and the cowardice that had left her to face the ghosts of the hill alone. Until his hand touched her shoulder.

– It couldn't be helped, Miss Beatrice. His father and mine. We were bound to see it through, him and me. Enemies and friends, all mixed up.

– And I . . . And I . . .

Her chest was heaving, where the belemnite lay, in its soiled pouch.

– You are our fate.

– Oh big words. I tell you I'm sick of them, the big words. I want small ones. Light ones. Not all this heaviness and dark.

Frith was stirring under the greatcoat. Her instinct drew her forward to loosen his collar. Eric looked on.

– The first casualty.

She looked up, wonderingly.

– Casualty? What do you mean?

– The first of many. Many millions. And you, you're the nurse. Then she heard them. Deep in the galleries of the mine. The noises which the hill had been making for weeks. As if the very heart of the hill were suffering and lamenting. Mourning a past that was just about to happen.

It was Eric who lead Beatrice back into the light, rising up out of the hill as though he were the object of the dig, the spirit they had sought to release or quell. Charles had long-since disappeared. But the quarrymen's faces still ringed the crater's lip like a torque. At first this torque was inclined to glitter with a knowing laughter. Old Wren again. Up to his mummery. Making the toffs look stupid. But when they were told about the two in the cave their laughter began to tarnish over. No one wanted a scandal. There had been enough upset already. Molly leaned down, having returned to the scene of her fall.

– Mr Tremain seemed awful upset. He shouldn't have dug the hill should he, Miss?

– No, Molly he shouldn't – Beatrice heard herself say, although in her heart she knew he had had no choice.

So the dig was abandoned and down the smooth blue skyline of Thundersbarrow a procession bore the sheeted stretcher on which Frith lay, as if his body were the remains of someone no longer sacred who must be moved away from the burial place so that the new dead king could lie in state in front of the barrow, before the shaft that had witnessed his end. The sun was beginning to drop down the western sky. A breeze had got up. Sitting in the dobbin cart beside Eric Wren and Molly, Beatrice remembered her arrival. Then too, Charles had not been present except as a silhouette at a window. Now, once again, he was absent. The cart turned into the elder path. Behind them Jessup wept about his terrible error and how he hadn't meant to do it but then the body had disappeared and when he'd woken up he'd thought he was already in prison until he saw the body and knew he was buried alive. So to the chants of a deranged man, the diggers left Thundersbarrow forever. That evening in the schoolhouse Mrs Eddles announced that, just as the ill-advised excavation was abandoned, a general mobilisation had been called.

Why, Charles, why?

He was in the room but his face kept receding. The peacocks were calling.

Why?

She must cut through the veils of hot darkness that seemed to separate them but when she reached for her scissors her hand touched Frith's brow. It was cold. And she awoke, sobbing.

– They say there'll be crowds tonight. In London and all the cities. In Chalkhampton even.

Mrs Eddles was leaning over a dolly tub in which some grey nightdresses writhed like flatfish. Beatrice looked on.

– Why? – Her dream question returned even now to haunt her.

– Because of the ultimatum. Germany must agree to respect Belgian neutrality or she'll find herself at war with England. The ultimatum expires tonight. And people will want to know if there's to be war or not.

Beatrice felt an intense listlessness. Mrs Eddles stopped pummelling the doomed clothing.

– I could have predicted an accident. Master Tremain is hardly skilled at digging. And Eric Wren is well, hardly fit for such work nowadays.

– It had nothing to do with the dig. They had some kind of argument. They'll go back to Chalkhampton today in any case.

– Molly, I was referring to. Who did you mean?

Beatrice stiffened. How easily this place could trip her up. Secrets within secrets. But Mrs Eddles was back on her favourite subject.

– Well, if there is a war it won't do some any harm. Sort out the sheep from the goats. And there's too many idle young men in this country, if you ask me.

Why, Beatrice wanted to ask but bit back the terrible word.

She had hoped Charles would call or at least send word. Last night

Eric had dropped her off at the schoolhouse as on that first evening in April. He was reserved and politely tender, seeming to sense (or so she thought at the time) that his charge had no desire to prolong their goodbye, given what Charles had done. She felt exposed by it somehow, as though her faith in him had been held up to the world as a worthless thing. To leave her in that dark place, prey to who knows what terrors. It was indeed a craven and cowardly thing to do. Yet she pitied him too and, closing the door on Eric, had a sudden vision of Charles lying with his head on her lap, asleep. Perhaps that was how she had always wanted him, passive, a prisoner almost, unable to escape back into the labyrinth of his life away from her. So the night had come with its ceaseless feverish questionings. And at the centre of it all stood Charles and Eric themselves, locked into each other's lives by the wrong done in their fathers' time, incapable of breaking away or coming to a conclusion. How she longed to flee this place that, not a few hours before, had seemed to promise so much.

A fine drizzle had set in when, having waited fruitlessly for word from the manor, Beatrice set off at noon to see how Molly Dadger was coping with her injury. She did not wholly deny to herself that, in going on her errand of mercy, she half-hoped to meet Charles, perhaps returning from the Limeburner's Arms where Frith was being treated clandestinely by the local doctor, before his departure with Jessup from the Halt later that afternoon. Failing that, there was a good chance she might encounter Eric, either on the way to the quarry itself or in the hovel where Molly now lived. Today she felt more able to confront him with demands for reassurance if not explanation.

But by the time she reached the kilns, Beatrice had encountered nobody at all. Suspended between the end of the disastrous excavation and the beginning of a world war, Thundersbarrow had become a desert, that wanted and was wanted by nobody. This new solitude felt more oppressive than the old, since it evoked not peace but a multitude of unsatisfied ghosts. The very emptiness predicated the imminence of countless numbers just beyond the edge of sight, waiting to burst into the scene to overwhelm and engulf it. So that Beatrice found herself hurrying to arrive at Old Neb as if she were being pursued by an army. An army yet to be born. The door opened at her touch.

He lay seemingly asleep on the unmade bed and she would have gone straight out again if some brush of her wet cape against the wall had not caused him to stir and sit up. He looked paler than yesterday. But his neck was still mauve where the eczema nested.

– Beatty, it's you. I wasn't expecting . . .

So he stared blearily at her, like a boy woken from sleep. Or a boy surprised in some illicit act. She flushed.

– Molly. I just came to see Molly.

Not you, she wanted to add. But could not bring herself so quickly to betray her feelings. He was sitting on the bed now.

– I expect you can't forgive me. I can quite understand.

– I was frightened, Charles. Down there. Why did you leave me? He turned suddenly, startling her with his glare.

– Don't ask me such things. I've apologised. Isn't that enough. Now leave me be.

She too had her dignity. But was stopped in the doorway to be spun round and embraced.

– I'm sorry, sorry.

She was stroking his head, not wanting explanations. Not now.

– Poor dear. It was only those two. Didn't you know that? Jessup and the boy. They'd had an argument and Frith had fallen or been hit and Jessup ran away panicking. Then Eric came looking for them and found Frith and dragged him into the cave out of the sun. A bit later he found Jessup too. Or the terrier did. Asleep, drunk. It was a cave. Eric said you and he used to play in it as children. Oh Charles, can't you forget the past? – She held him at arm's length, as if seeking the answer in his face and limbs. But found none. And went on – Through me. If we went away. Oh I don't know . . . – and stopped, ashamed both of the intensity of her emotion and its impracticality. He could not meet her eyes.

– It's too late for all that, Beatty. Much too late. – Then pulling away from her – I can't escape him you know, not now.

– And you abandoned the dig.

– I couldn't go on. And what does it matter now that there's to be a war?

– An ultimatum, yes.

– Followed by a war. A great cleansing, Eric calls it.

– What, like Epsom salts? – She was determined not to be absorbed any further into this darkness between the two men. – Why are you here anyway, Charles? And where is Molly? I wanted to see how she was.

– Here, Miss Lumley. Mr Charles. He can't be disturbed. He's in the chapel. Praying. But he said to me. Tonight. If you'd be so kind, Mr Tremain. Just before eleven.

Beatrice looked at Charles. What new pact was this? Or ultimatum. Charles was shivering. Shivering and grinning.

– If there is a war declared we're going to set off one last charge of lyddite. On the very summit. For old time's sake.

So Charles was still in thrall. And Beatrice could not reach him.

That Tuesday evening the few remaining quarrymen gathered with some of the more resilient villagers in the cobbled yard at Ecclesden. Their horn lanterns made radiating spokes of shadow on the brick and flint of the threshing barn. They were not silent this night. A restless excitement glittered in their eyes. They were held trancelike before the imminence of great events. In front of them on the steps of the machine shed, Charles stood next to his mother and a yawning Robert. He was holding a late edition of the *Chalkhampton Herald*. His voice rose trembling slightly into the starry distances beyond the lights and the sweat of men.

– *The deadline passed at eleven PM GMT or midnight Berlin time. Since no reply has been received regarding her violation of Belgian neutrality we are now officially at war with Germany. God Save the King.*

The hats rose together, a dark constellation blotting out the molten quiver of the real stars. Beatrice watched from the side by a feed hopper. She scanned the crowd but could see no sign of Eric Wren. Then Molly was shouting in her ear.

– Look, Miss Lumley, up on the hill.

Where Thundersbarrow rose up to blot out half the world, an orange comet had woken, inhaling and exhaling its flames as if feeding on something more substantial than air.

– He's lit Old Neb. He's lit him for the last time.

And indeed, it did seem like an ending of things, as if the great beacon which Old Neb had become would swallow up the hill and the quarry and Ecclesden itself. But the hill was in control. Or rather the man who ruled the hill. Tomorrow, in the ashen dawn, the kiln would stand as before, undamaged if a little scorched by the fierce brushwood fire kindled at its heart.

Through the swirling crowd she glanced over at Charles still standing on the steps. He caught her eyes and mouthed something. The words were inaudible but she fancied they had to do with the plan to ignite one last explosion. Then all around her the figures, galvanised by the limeburner's threatening or valedictory beacon, suddenly coalesced into a pattern of couples. An invisible fiddler struck up. So all were dancing and Beatrice could no longer see the steps, let alone Charles.

–Dance, damn you, dance!

Lurching into the whirl and press of people she would have sunk to the floor if leathery hands hadn't raised her, sluicing a thick fire down her mouth from the neck of a bottle.

– C'mon, Missy. Think of what's to come. Think of the war.

Joseph rose up before her and, in the savage dream of that place, seemed to Beatrice to be simultaneously standing on the edge of a platform and a deep crater's lip. She could not do otherwise than obey, forgetting Charles, forgetting Eric, forgetting them all, as she went whirling down a long corridor of hands and jigging feet, a prize or lost possession. Though tearful with the frustration of a love she had neither satisfied nor forsaken, she laughed among her smoky captors, kicking up her heels so as to reveal more than was proper of a schoolmistress's legs. Then, after what seemed an age of violent movement, a thought came into the small still cave that she kept always separate: *I must find them tonight. I must see them together for one last time*, the thought said and would not be dislodged. Now with subtle skill borne of desperation, she wheeled and manoeuvred towards the edge of the crowd where Molly was waiting. Together they slipped away into the darkness, leaving the dance to burn itself out in the red and black-spoked yard.

The two figures stood facing each other in the deserted midnight quarry. The blazing kiln sent showers of sparks into the air and made their faces darkly red. They were standing in the old flint and marl circle. The rope lay at their feet. On some agreed signal both took it up and began the contest. Tonight, without the burden of others, they seemed evenly matched. Yet the equilibrium was shortlived. Soon one figure was being dragged inexorably by the other.

– Mr Charles is losing this time.

Molly Dadger's voice sounded unearthly, coming out of the shadows clustering at the base of Old Neb. Beatrice tried to press herself closer against the hot flint, frightened in case they were seen.

– What are they doing this for? Why here? Again?

– It's the return bout. They shook on it yesterday. After you came to see me.

– What for?

– That I don't know, Miss. Not yet.

Down at Ecclesden the dance in the yard was still raging, its cries and lights reaching here like the rumour of waves breaking against a far shore. The contest continued. Eric was winning but, as always, his triumph contained within itself the seed of defeat, surrender. Now Charles was being pulled out of the circle of stones altogether, lying on his back with his two heels dug into the chalk. *Oh let go*, she whispered, *For pity's sake let go*, seeing Charles's shirt begin to shred on the flint rubble. But he would not let go and went on allowing himself to be pulled along like some beast of prey, a thing to be hunted down, captured and trussed up. Then, to her horror, as Charles's flayed back neared the funicular track and Eric seemed about to drag his victim into the very firing tunnel of the kiln, Beatrice saw that both men were laughing. Slowly this mutual laughter, eerie and unfathomable in that dark arena, spread to their bodies so that they could no longer properly fight. The contest was over. Eric staggered back against the base of the kiln, while Charles lay back on the ground, gasping up at the stars. Beatrice and Molly shrank back together against their protecting wall. Two unwilling witnesses.

– All right, all right. You win. You can have me. We'll go tomorrow. But remember – and here Charles sat up, pointing at his slumped adversary who, suddenly reminded of something, stood smartly to attention – you'll be my servant. I'll have a commission. So no nonsense. And remember to salute an officer at all times.

Then Beatrice saw the hand raised mockingly to Eric Wren's forehead, saw the tremble of laughter again, creeping through both of them like a swift virus; saw them embrace and lean on one another and go quiet. She knew now that this flickering pit was the arena of some love which she would never share. Excluded, alone, she must stand in its shadow forever, a woman. She felt angry and afraid. But would not leave. Or waste the chance of concealing her confusion in a certain wryness.

– There's men for you. You fall for them and they immediately go and join the army. What do you think of that. Eh, Molly?

But Molly, who had no such defences, was already slumped in tears against the flint belly of the kiln. So that Beatrice was obliged to abandon irony for the more conventional gestures of compassion.

Years afterwards, when the quarry was quite overgrown and even the faceless giants of the kilns had begun to flake and crumble, people still remembered that final explosion which heralded the outbreak of the Great War. According to some, the charge was set by Wren and the young Tremain together, though others said only Eric went up into Dragon Pit that night, for Charles, always something of a windy beggar, had volunteered to escort two frightened women who had lost their way in the dark back down to Ecclesden. As for the place where the charge was set, some said it was in the chapel itself, which was found afterwards, on its side and roofless at the top of the great scree; others were more inclined to favour the accursed spot, marked by two great chalk blocks, where Eric's father had had his final quarrel with Sir Colin. In either case it was certain that this last explosion woke, to use the language of the superstitious, the dragon of the hill. More rational observers, who had noticed that the underground noises in the quarry had intensified over the last few months, noted that the shock of so many pounds of lyddite merely finished what the second opening up of Dragon Pit had begun. The result was immediate and irreversible. Dragon Pit itself immediately lost half its depth while the scree leading down to the kilns became twice as wide and penetrated as far as the crushing mill itself, quite submerging the foreman's office and the haybarn on its way. Many hovels in Quarry Bottom collapsed on the spot. That there were no casualties (if we except a terrier who had been up in the pit with Wren), could be attributed to the fact that the quarry was already on the verge of dereliction.

The next day the heir of Ecclesden Manor and the limeburner were seen at Chalkhampton town hall, now a hastily reorganised recruiting station. Some witnesses remarked that one man seemed more than a little the worse for drink. They returned the same evening, disembarking at the Halt. Lady Tremain, it was reported, had adopted a grimly stoical if somewhat proud demeanour. Molly Dadger refused to emerge from the much-damaged hovel by Old Neb for a week, then went away to Chalkhampton to stay with relatives. Some diagnosed a broken heart. Beatrice Lumley, who had always been on the margins of events, yet was paradoxically deemed in some quarters to have played too prominent a part, prepared for the new term, sticking exclusively to the confines of the school-house. No one knew what her opinion of these events might be. Only a rumour did persist, unconfirmed it is true, that she had been heard to laugh on the first Friday afternoon of the war, when Mrs Eddles brought home the news that up at the manor, Sir Colin's old butterfly cabinet had been found mysteriously shattered, its cargo of insects drifting about the room as if in the aftermath of a second unheard explosion.

2. A Queen Of The Night

October – December 1915

A rainy dusk was settling over the squares and salt-blistered seafront hotels of Chalkhampton, fingering its way up the glistening ramps of back to back streets and into the blind sockets of curtained windows. A westerly off the Channel was making the twilight restless, so that it went spuming through dustbins with soft flares of sound or caught at the bodies of late pedestrians, until they were forced to clutch themselves for protection, becoming stiff and motionless as figures in a freize. Up on the cliffs, where the town shrank to a scatter of sheds among allotments, Whitehawk Camp hunched in the darkness of the blackout, a dim stain on the swiftly moving stream of cloud. Behind the thin walls of their nissan huts the soldiers of the Second Battalion, 4th—shire Regiment, the so-called Chalkhampton Chums shivered and grinned. Their year's training was coming to an end. After six months at the Regimental base camp near Newhaven, then a further six months on Salisbury Plain, they had marched back to their hometown a week ago to await the arrival of the First Battalion (who had been training up north), followed by orders for the Regiment's embarkation abroad. The front for which they were bound was still unknown. Some mentioned Egypt; others Suvla Bay or Mesopotamia. However, despite the convincing detail of their recounted rumours, advocators of these destinations were greatly outnumbered by those who insisted that the Regiment was bound immediately for France. Though the likelihood had less supporting evidence, the desire to enter the very core of the conflict was so strong, that even those who had heard the semi-official Middle-Eastern stories grew inclined to discount them, concentrating instead on a fancied last-minute change of plan or a possible rerouting intended to confuse the enemy. But whether the destination was to be Desert or Flanders mud, all who lay that night in the huts of Whitehawk, reading or playing cards or listening to the grate and boom of waves that would soon bear their own transport vessels, believed that having come back to the place where they had volunteered during those first few frantic days fourteen months ago, the Chalkhampton Chums must at last be allowed to do their bit.

All, that is, with the possible exception of one man who stood now near the perimeter fence overlooking the dimmed town. Slowly, with the ease and assurance of one long-used to the vagaries of ignition, he struck a phosphor match then cupped it to his cigarette in such a way that the spark remained unquenched yet invisible. Even in this poor light the face could be seen to be weatherbeaten, the skin drawn tautly over a strong jaw and wide-domed forehead. Yet, there was something else, a flicker in the eyes perhaps, where the cigarette's reflected needlepoint of red guttered out, which suggested an underlying impenetrability, a darkness of purpose. After a year as a soldier, lance corporal Wren of C Section A Company was not likely to be found debating the issue of embarkation with his fellows. No one doubted the intensity of his desire to see action, an intensity which, as a private in his Section remarked, would make him bayonet the swinging sack dummies 'like he knew them personally'; nor could he be said not to have an opinion on where or when the Regiment might set sail. It was simply that, after all this time, the people who trained with Eric Wren no more thought to consult or involve him than they would have done one of the screw pickets which they used to support barbed wire in front of their immaculate practice trenches. In his taciturnity, his unwillingness to be drawn on any subject, his sheer indomitable silences, Eric Wren had come to seem elemental. And like iron or flint, men realised, he must be left alone to endure whatever fate or chance might throw in his way. In the early days when, dressed in civvies and carrying spars of four-by-two for rifles, the battalion had drilled in front of Chalkhampton town hall, Eric

Wren had been regarded as something of a wonder. Towering above his contingent of quarrymen, the limeburner from Ecclesden had seemed, to the city-bred clerks and factory workers who dominated the battalion, both exotic and dangerous. Here was a natural leader who, with the likes of Mucky Gurl and Pedgell Wright, had been brought up from the cradle to wield the very tools which sergeant majors were now obliging the pale hands of clerks to handle perhaps for the first time. It was as if the limeburner and his men arrived in the battalion having already fought and come through a whole war of their own. No wonder then that the true novices in matters of entrenching and revetting turned initially to these old lags, of whom Eric Wren was seemingly the master.

They were soon disabused. Not only was the limeburner savagely reluctant to share banter let alone secrets with anyone; it quickly became obvious that he was an outcast from his own tribe. Although men like Mucky or Piggy Baker were hardly less taciturn than Eric himself, they did let drop some details about the decline of the quarry leading to the entire collapse of Dragon Pit, obscurely hinting at Eric's own baneful role in the business. Learning this and seeing that the limeburner was more often apart from his fellows than among them, recoiling too from his alarmingly primitive religion with its spontaneous hymn-singing and quotation, the city men began to treat him more circumspectly. This approach seemed justified when, after the six months at Newhaven, the quarry contingent received orders for transfer to a sapper company in one of the north country battalions. By some mixture of luck and subterfuge Eric Wren did not go with his former workmates. If at this date a few in his platoon might still have harboured any romantic notions of wronged innocence, they were quickly disillusioned. Mucky, Pedgell and the rest were almost brutally glad to be transferring without the ex-limeburner. And for his part Eric marked the occasion by singing pointedly and at the top of his voice about the troops of Midian as the sappers marched out of the camp.

Then had come the arrival of Captain Charles Tremain. Afterwards, when rumours about what had happened to Charles and Eric filtered back to an exhausted and decimated battalion in bivouacs near Millencourt, a few men remembered how, at the time, the arrival of the heir of Ecclesden and Wren's avoidance of transfer had been instinctively linked. They remembered too that the limeburner and the scholar had joined up together on the outbreak of war and, on the day when Charles Tremain had been transferred to one of the Public School battalions, Eric Wren had been found at night on Newhaven rifle range weeping in bitter anger. Now Charles's reappearance at once intensified the old bond between them and weakened their relationship with the battalion as a whole. Just as Wren was increasingly avoided and left to himself, so Charles from the very beginning failed to fit in. Perceived to be conceited and unapproachable by his fellow officers, he was regarded as windy by his juniors (witness his pathological fear of explosions) and therefore potentially unreliable. Indeed some whispered that if it hadn't been for his mother's connections he would have been unlikely to gain a commission in the first place. So it was that the relationship between the two men, rooted in the obscure events that had led to the death of Thundersbarrow quarry, came to encapsulate many of the contradictions which lay at the heart of the battalion's identity. Jealousies and loyalties, emotional weaknesses and great reserves of courage and endurance: all were present in microcosm when this ill-assorted couple came together. Some even felt that, in the mixture of servility and domination which characterised the relationship on both sides, lurked a clue to the uncertainties and contradictions of the war itself.

Eric Wren had been checking the sentries. Now it was time to report back. Grinding his cigarette butt into the chalky mud, the former limeburner turned away from the perimeter fence, where a sheet of newspaper twitched on the barbs like a shred of grey flesh, and moved off towards the hull-like shadow of the Company Commander's hut. The wind shivered on ahead of him, over the blurred and trampled ground, past the latrine block where a sign reading *Abandon Hope All Ye Who Enter Here* had been chalked up over the entrance. The *Enter* however had long since been replaced by a more excremental verb which in turn had also been expunged. So the joke and the threat were likewise ominously absent. Eric Wren looked up at the mutilated words and grimaced. The air in the little hut was stale and close. Beside a kerosene stove in the far corner lay Oenone, a fuller-fleshed bitch than the one-year-old who had followed her master up on to Thundersbarrow, thumping her tail now for the familiar visitor in the doorway. The Captain, who had been nodding off at his desk, jerked upright and brushed something invisible but tenacious from in front of his face. Eric Wren saluted.

 – Reporting as usual, sir. Nothing. Except the night.

The wind made one last circle of the hut and, finding nothing but a couple of duck-boards to rearrange, sped off towards the rifle range. In the ensuing quietness a clock whirred on a shelf above the desk. The polished 'winklestone' base glimmered with packed fossil gastropods. This same clock had once stood on the mantelpiece in the drawing room at Ecclesden surrounded by framed photographs. Twelve months previously a young woman had stood before it, her eyes passing in wondering anxiety from the dial to its retinue of images, among them the figure of an unknown girl. If she could have seen the empty shelf tonight, she might have fancied that all those images had somehow been sucked into the clock in some act of vindictive erasure. Shakily, the man Beatrice had thought she loved stood up and the clock too was obliterated.

Charles Tremain too had aged in the year since he had fought the ghostly second bout under Old Neb in the presence of Beatrice and Molly Dadger. But whereas his old adversary had grown more dense with time, more mineral and opaque, the heir of Ecclesden seemed softer, more expansive, more transparent. There was a slackness about the corners of his mouth which was not entirely physical. His hair, in its dishevelment, hung down across his forehead, like a pale rag. And the old weltings about the neck seemed, by some trick of the light, to have grown puffier, less distinct. He blinked, facing his batman. Then belched.

 – What would I do without you, Eric. My old mate. What did I ever do. Eh? The bloke I love to hate.

The former limeburner raised one eyebrow but forbore to reply. He was waiting for something, patiently, like a necromancer who labours to control the dead. So Charles Tremain would be controlled in the end, hiccoughing words he had not intended or wished to say, as if they were vomit. Or blood.

– I saw her again you know. Oh yes. We ... – and here he stopped, listening, as if for some unheard permission. – We had a good time. She's been staying at the YWCA but thinks she's landed a lodging. It's with one of my old teachers. – Here his silent inquisitor stirred and Charles managed a squeaky laugh – No. Not that old queen Jessup. A music teacher. Mr Walter Sebastian Amadeus Birkett. There what do you think of that mouthful? You can tell what his parents wanted him to be. Correction. I can tell. Anyway, he's just a teacher. And a randy old sod. But – and here Charles glanced over at Oenone as if she had accused him of something despicable – she can handle him. She can handle any man. And I mean handle.

Charles Tremain had slumped back into his chair, muttering. For a long time there was no other sound in the stuffy hut. Then the Captain suddenly looked up again, his flushed face draining.

– Oh Christ, did I tell you, did I tell you I'd seen her again? Did I?

And again silence. Apart from the muttering which had turned now into a tuneless song,

She was only a bird in a gilded cage.

Eric Wren coughed. His superior looked up for a third time.

– What? Still here? What time is it? Maud. What a goer. Eh? We had Beards with malt chasers. You should try it some time.

– You forget I'm not commissioned, sir. Leave's restricted for the likes of us. And I don't drink.

But Charles was humming now, with blurred eyes. Suddenly he stopped, staring again at the corner where Oenone licked contemplatively at a front paw.

– What? Forget? Never forget. The chair under the hill. Brother to dragons. Only it isn't dragons. It's jackals. Meant to tell him that some time. Take the wind out of his sails. What a goer. Eh?

Then it was as if, without moving, the limeburner made himself huge in the hot membrane of the hut, his shadow rising up to engulf the captain, his voice bellowing so that Oenone whimpered, jerking out of her brief doze.

– She's here you know. Training as a whatdoyoucallem? VAD. Mrs Eddles got old Noone back and now she's here.

The wind had returned, having discovered a pile of gravel which it hurled against the netted window in iron salvoes. Charles Tremain rose wobbling to his feet as if to grope away from the tunnel of shadow which his batman had furled around him.

– For Christ's sake man. I don't want. Not now. Espesh. Eshpesh. – There was a pause during which the Captain might have retched if some antiperistalsis of the soul could have cleared his memory. But evidently not. – I'm older now. We've gone to war. Together. As you wanted. To keep an eye on me. Yes, an evil eye. After that dig. That bloody dig. And she . . . You and your bloody tongues and your chosen few. Just don't give me any more. Maud, that's who. Maud. Not her. Maud.

Maud Maud Maud Maud
They were crying and calling.

– The Leith Police Dismisseth Us.

It was Eric, or the shadow he had become, declaiming the tongue-twister like a curse.

Flushed a dull ruby, Charles's face turned up from its seabed of misery.

– What? What's that you say? Old mole?

– Say it after me, sir. If you can. The Leith Police Dismisseth Us.

So Charles was led through the complexity of sounds like a child or a man who had become a child. But could not speak. Out of the Babel of his humiliation.

– Never go back. Never go back now. Lad and girl stuff. Gone forever. In the boathouse once. Christ. Why? Why was I so weak? Why didn't I just take her? – Then suddenly Charles was shouting, – The leish polith dishmisshish ush. – There I've said it. I've repeated your curse. Haven't I? Say I have, Eric. Please.

And there was no telling what Eric might have said or not said if the night hadn't invented a rapping to which Oenone bounded forward, as if for protection, out of the corner.

– I've been told to give you this, sir. – The private stood in a puddle of rain, cap dripping. One hand went down involuntarily to stroke Oenone. Then he gave a start. – Sorry sir I, I didn't know you had company. – Then under his breath – Bugger me, if he was there or not, that bloody Wren, a fucking ghost if you ask me. – Then, more loudly – Goodnight, sir.

Charles was still standing, the sweat pouring down his cheeks, his fists clenched on the desk to steady himself.

– Now they want me to go down to the fort and doublecheck the TCP order.

The limeburner grinned, saluting to depart.

– Don't forget to give those VADs a good seeing to.

But Charles Tremain had slumped back into his chair, his slack mouth trickling a thin brown ooze of spittle.

Converted from a disused Regency Lodge set inside the ruinous curtain walls belonging to one of the Roman forts of the Saxon Shore, the hospital lay in the centre of the town clearly visible, had it still been light, from the perimeter fence where Eric Wren stood, cupping his cigarette. Two hours earlier, when the blackout blinds were beginning to be drawn down, a huddle of dark-coated and wimpled figures had emerged from a postern gate that had originally formed part of defences designed to repel a barbarous and unpredictable invader. Nowadays the modern door was always open and the massive flint lintel, with its interlayerings of orange tiles had grown to seem, in the roundedness of its erosions, a natural outcrop of the surrounding hills. Even so, the wind tonight had contrived to enter this confined place and howl in such a shrill and mournful way that it might have been lamenting the very wars which the gate no longer embodied. So that, coming out from under the shadow of the battered masonry, the nurses, with trenchcoats whipping round them and the wings of wimples flying, seemed like ghosts attempting to flee a terrible past rather than solid women briefly released from the clutches of a more terrible present. But the ghostliness did not last. With laughter and one or two wind-muffled farewells the unappeased victims of dark age massacre turned back into VADs, tired and hungry after a gruelling shift. Confinement within walls so thick that earlier generations had concluded they must have been built by the devil, represented for them neither mystery nor terror, but a daily bending of the will to an ideal of duty and a reality of toil. So they moved on, separating now to thread their various ways home through the wind and darkness of Chalkhampton.

The first and smallest of the little crowd to plunge back into the world of present suffering headed straight for the nearest tram stop and climbed upstairs on to a waiting vehicle whose destination plaque read Orion Parade. Beatrice Lumley moved no less confidently than she had done over a year ago, stepping down into an April turbulence at Ecclesden Halt. Now however, her confidence had grown more studied, as if she were no longer certain whether confidence would quite do. Over the intervening months her search for a fancied and perhaps illusory equilibrium had not diminished; but the many unexpected difficulties and frustrations had turned her in on herself, so that she dug down rather than forward. These excavations had taken their toll. Tonight the shadows under her eyes had a darker tone than before; her nose, which had always preserved a finely etched sharpness, seemed almost defensively honed; while the mouth had thinned and flattened out, as if under the pressure of a thwarted or feared sensuality. This was not the innocent if watchful girl who had stood with her gladstone bag looking up towards the summit of Thundersbarrow. Her sense of herself had solidified without bringing repose. Narrowing down the possibilities of life and then narrowing them down again, Beatrice had not, as she had hoped, emerged with any clearer sense of direction. So she sat on the top deck of the tram while the wind worried annoyingly at the edges of her green trenchcoat. She was, it seemed, a woman who would always be fretted at by such random passing gusts.

Coming to live and work in Chalkhampton had represented, for this isolated and embattled woman, both a necessary escape and a second more final exile. After the strange weathers and moods of the summer spent under the shadow of Thundersbarrow, autumn had arrived with a sharp clarity that did not so much illuminate events as dissolve them, so that what had appeared to be a partially opaque crystal turned into a transparent pane through which Beatrice looked out on a flat and desolate landscape. She had continued teaching in the schoolhouse, enduring alike the sullenness of the pupils and the ambivalent confidences of Mrs Eddles. In those early months of war, the proximity of the Chums, billeted in digs around Chalkhampton and training in front of the town hall or up on the Downs south of Thundersbarrow, had fed a shy hope that she might continue to see Charles and even that their fated affair might progress to a new, more equable phase. And indeed, that autumn and early winter, whilst the initial euphoria over the regular army's victories in France turned imperceptibly to a more sober estimation, there had been occasions when the heir of Ecclesden had returned home, in civvies at first then later in uniform, but always a hero to the neighbourhood, despite the peculiar circumstances of his joining up. Yet if Beatrice had expected intimacy she was soon to be grievously disappointed. There was, for one thing, the very fact of Charles's new status. To Beatrice's misery this only served to increase the distance between them both, so that all the unspoken promises and half-truths of the summer, all the wrongs and misunderstandings, flooded back into her mind, clamouring for appeasement. Then too it all had to be endured at second hand: with Robert at Tongdean Beatrice could no longer claim any legitimate business at the manor while Charles, swept up each time by his mother and the inevitable party of house guests, neither had the time nor inclination to visit the schoolhouse. For a while, Beatrice had wondered if Eric Wren might devote one of his less frequent leaves to a revisiting of old haunts; he at least might act as a bridge, as in the old days. But Molly Dadger, on her first trip back from the town, where she had become an undermaid in one of the seafront hotels, announced that, not only was her engagement with the former limeburner permanently off, but that he himself had damned his old home to hell. He would never return he said, unless he were dead or worse than dead. Soon afterwards it transpired that this definitive curse had been uttered on the very evening of the day that Charles Tremain had been transferred to one of the Public Schools battalions. According to Mrs Eddles, who had had the news from her sister and took a malignant glee in relaying it to Beatrice just before she went upstairs to bed, this would mean even fewer visits home for a man who would soon be commissioned. If Eric Wren had been outraged and lachrymose, Beatrice was numbly resigned. That night a little of her girlhood died.

There was a brief moment of resurrection soon after Christmas when the news filtered back, again through Mrs Eddles, that Charles had returned to his original battalion as a Captain of A Company. But this time even his visits to the manor were evidently to be curtailed. Training was no longer the game it had been in the autumn. Mons and the Marne were ancient history. It was the time of Neuve Chapelle and the first landings at Gallipoli; people dared suggest the war might last another year, perhaps two. Even then, in this grimmer, harsher world Beatrice found herself hoping for a letter, as in the old days when Charles had been at school. But no word came. A month later and the Second Battalion had marched away for the final leg of its English training on Salisbury Plain. Sometimes, walking on Thundersbarrow (but avoiding the site of the ill-fated excavation), Beatrice would wonder if she should not leave Ecclesden altogether.

The first battle of Ypres (though no one then could have had the prescience to place it at the beginning of a sequence that would lead inevitably to Passchendaele), had been and gone; so had Aubers Ridge. The summer term was nearly over, the hot weather reminding Beatrice all too painfully of the excitements surrounding the excavation the previous year. Then two events occurred which, if they did not alter things irrevocably, confirmed what Beatrice had tremulously posed to herself while walking on the hill above the abandoned pits. The first was the arrival of a letter postmarked *Swindon*. Even as she recognised the handwriting and felt her heart execute an almost unfamiliar lurch, Beatrice had the strange sense that she had already read it in some long-distant past. So, as her trembling fingers tore at the envelope, she looked on dispassionately, an observer; and when her mouth whispered the three brief paragraphs aloud, she heard not her voice but the voice of someone already dead. The first paragraph described camp life in general terms; the second apologised for *my caddish behaviour* the previous summer; the third hoped the letter found her well. There was a PS too, hurriedly scrawled, which announced that *Mr Wren suggested I write, if only to release you from a debt which should never have been allowed to accrue.* Beatrice heard a mouth laugh, in long bitter laughter; yet did not know its owner; she saw a hand ball itself into a fist the better to crumple up Charles Tremain's self-serving words, yet did not feel the crumpling. Only that evening, after a long vigil in front of her mirror, when she came downstairs to Mrs Eddles's excited announcement that Mr Noone had made a full recovery and requested his old job back, did she finally re-enter her body. Then, formulating the resolve that had been floating inarticulately in her mind for months, she found she knew who she was once again. That this knowledge was also a kind of oblivion, a letting go of things she had previously believed essential, only stiffened her resolve. Then and there she announced to a Mrs Eddles torn between amazement and delight, that she wished to resign her post. Although she knew the governors normally required a term's notice, she felt sure that they would take the unusual circumstances into account. Listening to her words Beatrice felt as though she was talking to the headmistress through a screen. When Mrs Eddles asked her what she intended to do her reply seemed to float out into the night and hang above Thundersbarrow like a comet: *I intend to go to Chalkhampton and volunteer as a VAD.*

So, numbed yet determined, Beatrice had begun her new life, fully understanding that it involved many small, if marginal, deaths. Yet despite the failure of her hopes, she liked to think that her new role paralleled the more rigorous experiences which the battalion was undergoing on Salisbury Plain. Indeed, beneath her apparent indifference, Beatrice still cherished the dream of a sharing of souls, if only out of respect for the person in her who had died. Living in one room in a lodging-house run by Charles's old music teacher; travelling to and from the Fort hospital where she must struggle to master an entirely new set of weapons and tactics, she too was in 'training'. The hospital was now entirely given over to caring for casualties from the fighting abroad, especially those who had gone through the battle of Ypres earlier that summer when, it was now generally known, gas had first been used. As a novice Beatrice barely got to see, let alone touch these survivors of a conflict into which Charles's own regiment might soon be flung. To this disappointment she soon added the frustrations of the work itself, at once dull and exacting, seemingly more akin to storekeeping than the impossibly romantic ideal of nursing which she had lovingly fostered at Ecclesden. Used to receiving a schoolteacher's wage, Beatrice found she must now fall back on her savings and a small monthly allowance from her aunt; she was often fatigued to the point of trance; and yet compared to the last few months in the schoolhouse, this period of her life offered certain comforts. She was able for the first time since leaving her aunt's house to remain relatively anonymous. At Mr Birkett's 'Superior Rooms' in Orion Parade the other residents were polite and distant. At the hospital she soon established a reputation as a loner, taking her meals on the seafront and refusing to exchange familiarities in corridor and storeroom, with the result that the other trainees gradually began to leave her to herself. It was then that her work took on a new and unexpected meaning. She was past the novitiate stage now; yet remained too inexperienced to be entrusted with anything more complicated than the emptying of bedpans or the swabbing of floors. But whereas in the early days such chores had seemed mere drudgery to be endured for the sake of duty; now they attained a sort of empty perfection akin, at times, to happiness. Allowed more regularly into the wards, even those which contained the very worst cases, Beatrice found she could talk to these seared wraiths with a relaxed insouciance unavailable to her in the old days of peacetime. Although their bodies were scarred and mutilated, their faces inclined to writhe unexpectedly with the memory of where they had been, the figures under the green blankets were still men. So that, exchanging pleasantries with the less seriously wounded or a smile and a nod with the hopeless cases, Beatrice began to understand how unsatisfactory her communication with Charles and Eric had been. In this place of cries and footsteps, where the light filtered down from long windows on to the double ranks of iron bed and suffering flesh, she found fear but not secrecy, endurance but not betrayal. Soon she began to live in her work as if it were a transparent structure balanced on one of the fort's jagged molars of turrets. From this eyrie she fancied she could survey the whole of her life, as well as the life of the world around her, swirling in conflict. When, towards the end of her second month of training, Aunt Millicent visited and raised long-threatened objections about the nature of this sacrifice (as well as the quality of her accommodation), Beatrice argued her case in a radiant storm of eloquence that soon had the older woman nervously capitulating; she even promised to double the monthly allowance, to be paid back *when this ridiculous war finishes and you can return to proper employment, dear.* So Beatrice's aunt had departed (she had begun by now to house-hunt in the neighbourhood), leaving her niece to her bedpans and her liniments, her brief missions of comfort or solace and afterwards, in front of the fire, her lonely evening vigils when, to the muffled accompaniment of Mr Birkett's piano lessons, Charles and Eric and Molly would come to her, voices out of a past she had never perhaps truly lived.

Opening the door with her own latchkey, Beatrice intended to go straight upstairs to her room on the third floor. There she would lie down, fully clothed and stare stupefied at the crack in the ceiling above her bed. Its black fissure had a flowing rhythm which always reminded her of how Eric talked once, in the lean-to against Old Neb, about the way chalk and air borrowed from each other to make the line of the hills: *It joins them you see; but keeps asunder too.* Tonight, however, there was an unfamiliar scent hanging in the dim fanlit hall and, on the hatstand, a strange hat festooned with bunches of glass fruit, grapes mostly. She could hear a voice too, mixing softness and depth: a woman's. Moving forward in the fusty gloom (the unfamiliar perfume had been overwhelmed by a more typical Orion Parade bouquet in which overboiled cabbage fought with the acridity of tom cat for predominance), Beatrice paused to glance at the apparitional white wing of newspaper on the sideboard. 'Gains at Loos' made her pause for a moment, an expression coming over her face that blended solemnity and scepticism. She had seen some of the consequences of those gains, that very day, in Ward Three. Yet, if rumour were to be credited, the Chalkhampton Regiment would soon be going overseas, perhaps into that very sector where, so a sergeant with a missing right hand had told her, *You'd think the bloody air was made of iron.* Last week with a pained excitement, she had read of the Second Battalion's return to the town where it had been raised. Since then, at odd moments, she had found herself glancing in the direction of Whitehawk Camp. If this gesture combined prayer and rebuke in equal measures, it did so less for the circumstances of her abandonment than for the peculiar balance of her nature, in which a tender forgiveness would often rise up unbidden, if scorched, from the flames of humiliation and anger. Now she was about to swivel east once more, when the open parlour door caught her eye and swallowed up everything but the present moment. Years afterwards Beatrice would remember how, on that fateful night, it was not a woman whom she saw first but a woman's reflection. Floating in the flyblown oval mirror over the fireplace, the tall blonde-haired stranger had her back turned to the door. Thus, in that instant preceding contact, Beatrice could see how the woman's full lips parted on front teeth that were not only slightly crooked but yellowish as well. She could see how the restless grey eyes hovered over the lace curtains drawn across the parlour window as if they might be about to tear apart on some unimaginable scene. The hair was evidently long but raked up into a bun. A few strands had escaped to lie plastered on a tulle collar still damp from the rain. Once again Beatrice found herself uneasily remembering something she had experienced before. Then the stranger turned and the reflection was banished forever. Captive but unrooted, free yet burdened by defeat, Maud Egerton had finally entered the life of Beatrice Lumley.

– Ah. Our lodger, the nurse. So early. I didn't expect . . .

It was Mr Birkett, leaping from behind the door, in tight striped trousers like a jester. But this jester was flushed as though he had been caught in some disreputable act which no joke could justify. He resorted instead to ingratiation.

– Miss Lumley. Miss Egerton. Our new lodger to be. Perhaps she will tempt you down from your eyrie once in a blue moon.

When Maud turned at the entrance of a third party, Beatrice had realised that her irises were not really grey at all but close to the colour of emerald. It was as if they needed to be confronted by another person before they could reassemble their true shades from the many false ones which would rise up to offer themselves in moments of solitude. These eyes and their unwitting exposure of a person who only came alive amongst others, coupled with a certain quick way Maud had of gliding her fingers across her hair, convinced Beatrice that what had seemed like a memory of a meeting in another life, had in fact occurred quite recently. But there was no time to quizz the past, nor even solicit Maud's help for now, having shaken hands, the tall woman was staring Mr Birkett up and down, as if he lacked certain vital organs.

– You promised me a phaeton. But it never came. I still haven't dried off. I ask you. The weather down here. God pissing on you from morning till night. But then God would, being a man.

This strange mixture of vulgarity, irreligion and arrogance (whoever heard of a landlord providing his lodger with transport gratis?), excited Beatrice sharply. Not wishing to have this noticed, she lowered her eyes and caught sight of a ring on Maud's right index finger. A white almost liquid stone. When she looked up again Maud was smiling. Her teeth.

– Beatrice, isn't it? I've heard such a bucket about you, haven't I, Walt? In fact you could say I know you already. There, aren't I the oracle?

With this she leant forward and half-tapped, half-cupped Beatrice's shoulder with a slender hand. On any other occasion such familiarity of touch would have made her recoil. But this evening she was surprised to find she felt no such urge. And blushed for it, smiling.

– Nothing deleterious I hope. I'm just a nurse. Not even that really. Not yet I mean.

– What's all this Not and Just and Even? Really dear. Let's try not to be so *diffident*, shall we? – Maud snorted, slumping down into what Beatrice had always assumed was her landlord's favourite armchair, the one with peacocks embroidered on the arm covers, their fanned tails greasy now from the friction of many sleeves. Maud's legs were on the fender, the skirt riding up over mudspattered lace boots to reveal two calves, their barely rounded goosepimpled flesh shockingly white amongst so much dinginess. Mr Birkett seemed to splutter slightly, as if choking. Walt. She called him Walt to his face. Even Mr Birkett's wife dared not use the diminutive.

– I think I will just go and suspend your wet coat over the range, Maud dear.

Maud was taking out a silver cigarette holder from her handbag. She tapped it on the arm of the chair, eyeing it quizzically.

– Do, dear. And bring us both a drink. Hot chocolate would fit the ticket. Cold as a witch's tit tonight, isn't it Beatty?

At which Beatrice began to flounder, in this room whose walls were suddenly melting, whose floor would warp and tear upon the arena of the unknown or the not sufficiently known. To witness her landlord being treated like a servant while hearing herself called by a diminutive not even Charles had used very often and then to be faced with the full glare of an impropriety that seemed both assumed and natural, was more than she deemed herself able to bear. So she stood and wavered.

– And please, Miss Lumley. Do stay and chat. You two must have a chat.

It was less invitation than plea. As if Mr Birkett, unable himself to exist for very long in the blistering fire of this woman's presence, feared that, once left alone, the fire might consume itself. So that he was always flinching away from her yet trying to make sure she could not escape. Maud meanwhile was puffing out a long smoke skein as if it were the exhalation of some long-harboured irritation. Allowing her body to dictate, Beatrice went and knelt on the pouf by Maud's chair. She would not be Mr Birkett's shield. But she might herself venture a little way into the fire.

– I wasn't always a nurse, a VAD. I trained as a teacher. I have my National Certificate. But these times . . .

Maud blew an almost perfect smoke-ring.

– These times are just like any others, only worse. You don't smoke, do you dear? I thought not. Such pretty pale fingers.

Beatrice was shaking her head even though Maud had answered her own question. She had heard another voice speak of history as a speeding towards disaster. She tried to concentrate on ordinary things.

– And you? What do you do?

– Oh. Sing. That's how I met Lothario in there. Or no. Amadeus. That's his middle name. Amadeus. Ridiculous, eh? – She smiled, seeming to initiate Beatrice into a shared secret world. – But – and here her voice seemed to stick on the next syllable as if the word it introduced were too obscene or too true. Where had Beatrice encountered this impediment before? On a day of gulls and loneliness. By the sea. The pier. But again as she was about to join present and past, Maud interrupted. The hurdle had been cleared and now she almost shouted the word that had refused initially to be born. – work! I work in a munitions factory. How are the mighty fallen!

Beatrice must have looked puzzled.

– I mean for an ex-member of the WSPU.

Again Beatrice felt herself going blank and Maud sighed, her full lips working on the tube of her cigarette-holder in tight palpings.

– The Purple White and Green? The Women's Union? You've heard of votes for women I take it? You know we don't have the vote? – Beatrice blushed, even though her inquisitor's sarcasm seemed gently unserious, poking fun at itself as much as any third party. Maud continued, – Yes? No? Well, I can't say I'm surprised either way. Sometimes I forget about the whole shooting match myself. It's as if it never happened. But I was a member, yes and quite an active one. Which is why working in a factory making arms for a war started by men for men seems to me, well, so *risible*. Still even the Pankhursts are doing their bit now. So who am I to question? Jesus wept, what a beauty!

For a second Beatrice wondered whether Maud wasn't referring to one of the suffragette leaders. Then a tabby cat trotted forward, tail erect. Purring loudly, he set about rubbing under the arch of Maud's outstretched legs.

– Who's a wet boy then? Come in from the rain have we? Look at his coat, all sparkly. What's he called, Beatty?

Beatrice, who had long nurtured an instinctive dislike of cats, if only because she had not managed to refute her aunt's labyrinthine theory concerning allergenic reaction, shivered. The cat's rubbing had rucked Maud's skirt up even further, to reveal a brown birthmark behind a surprisingly bulbous not to say sturdy left knee.

– That thing? I don't know. Ulysses, I think.

Maud smoothed down her skirts.

– What a proud name for such a proud tom. Because he wanders I suppose. And who called you that proud name? Was it Wally?

In response the cat jumped up on her lap and, planting both forepaws on her bosom, began a systematic frottage of Maud's face and neck.

– Oh Maud, how can you let him. Look he's dribbling.

With a flush of shame Beatrice realised that she was jealous of Birkett's old mog and had probably given herself away. Maud however seemed oblivious.

– Well I can see we're going to be the best of friends. Will he sleep on my bed? Will he?

The magic circle must be broken. Somehow Beatrice must reassert her fledgling claim.

– Will you be lodging here then?

Maud looked up from tickling Ulysses's muzzle.

– It's either here or the YWCA. And now my job's secure I can afford that skinflint's rent.

– When do you sing? It doesn't, if you'll forgive the presumption, seem to go with making bombs.

Maud laughed, showing a couple of gold-filled molars. Beatrice had the distinct sense that this woman had come down in the world. And was waiting to rise again.

– Well they do call us canaries. But that's because of the colour some of us go. From contact with explosives. Me, I'd probably go that colour anyway. From the amount I smoke. But it helps my chest. I was ill a couple of years back. – She paused waiting for the resurrected stammer to subside. – You were asking?

But before Beatrice had time to repeat her question Mr Birkett reappeared in the doorway. The cat jumped down and ran to him chirruping.

– Not until you catch that mouse in the larder. It's fouling all the cereal. Perhaps Miss Egerton might whisper in your ear.

– I'll need to see the room, Walt.

It was as if the cat and Beatrice were suddenly invisible. Maud fixed the landlord on the needle of her eyebeam. Where he writhed. There was a voice, querulous, from below.

– Walter. Are you there Walter?

Mr Birkett did not know how to proceed. Until Beatrice floated back into his field of vision.

– Perhaps, Miss Lumley, if you were to be so kind. It's the room next to yours in fact. The only one we have free. Here is the key.

Then he was falling towards Maud, inhaling against her face as if he wished to extract some essence from each orifice.

– I can't tell you how glad I am. No. Delighted.

– Go on, Walt. Beatty doesn't want to hear your patter. It ain't edifying. And, as I told you, I won't agree to anything until I see the room. – Her hand lingered briefly on the lapel of his frock coat, then flicked it dismissively. – Your wife's calling.

So the two women went upstairs to look over the empty room. Beatrice returned to the unanswered question and Maud told her how she had been doing a bit of part-time work with the pierrot show on the pier two summers ago when Mr Birkett chanced by and recognised her talent. — Couldn't stay to sing then of course. The war hadn't started and I was still involved with the movement up in London. But then once the fighting began we had to put everything on ice. So I came back down here and now I'm helping the old lecher prepare this charity concert in aid of the regiment going overseas.

Now Beatrice was certain. Maud was the fortune-teller in the booth. And the suffragist — *quite wild* — in Charles's first letter. And, finally the girl in the photograph whom Robert had loved as a substitute mother and Beatrice herself had been drawn to, in a time of self-doubt. Should she say as much? To this woman who seemed at once so open yet reticent about herself, creating long catalogues of former experiences yet forever skirting the issue of what she might or might not have felt. Should she, in short, confront her with the coincidences that united them? As they walked along the landing and Maud continued talking about the coming concert on the pier, — It'll be a mix of classical and modern, with a sort of masque too, but I'm not supposed to mention that. — Beatrice's initial desire to uncover all the subterranean connections between them rapidly waned. What did they matter? Ecclesden lay behind her now, in another age. Whether or not Maud had lived there too was unimportant. Their friendship, if that was what had begun tonight, existed in a pure present. Meanwhile Maud was actually asking Beatrice if she would like to join the female chorus. — We're short of voices and the rehearsals are only once a week. At Tongdean. Walt said you were on a day shift like me.

Dazzled, yet with the uneasy feeling of having been discussed already, Beatrice ushered Maud into the room next to hers. She knew she would not be able to resist the opportunity, so casually offered, to be near this free yet curiously burdened spirit, whatever the consequences. Into the dull round of Chalkhampton days Maud had come, bringing a touch of sandalwood fragrance, a whiff of possibility. She watched as the singing munitions worker moved round the room, seeming to register nothing yet absorbing the tiniest detail with a kind of savage avarice. Suddenly she was at the window with the curtains flung back.

– Thundersbarrow must be over that way. This blackout makes it difficult to get one's bearings.

Beatrice felt a pang of misery. Somewhere she still nurtured the hope that this woman wasn't the girl in the photograph. Robert's voice drifted back down the years. *He's sweet on Maud.* Too late. She must show her cards.

– That was where I taught. Before the war. Do you know the area then? It's very lovely, don't you think?

But once again a kind of gauze had come down in front of whatever Maud might think. She did not appear to be listening.

– It would be wonderful to have you at rehearsals. A proper ally. For we are allies, aren't we Beatty, in this dark old man's world?

And then, despite the unspoken things that lay between them, the two women were embracing beside a window framing a hill swept by silver screes of rain. There was a cry downstairs.

– He's got it. You told him, Maud. He listened.

They descended to the top of the first flight of stairs. Below them, in the dark hallway, among a scatter of newspaper (the latest casualty figures slashed to ribbons), Ulysses sat with a tail hanging limply from his jaws. Without realising it Beatrice came down the last flight of stairs with her hand slipped shyly through Maud's arm.

So Maud Egerton moved from the YWCA to Orion Parade, lodging next to Beatrice in the room with a distant prospect of Thundersbarrow. For Beatrice this event ushered in a short but intense period of mutual sympathy, the first she had ever enjoyed with another woman. They seemed to share everything, from sugar to sanitary protection. About the latter Maud was as downright as Beatrice could have hoped; indeed, looking back on these early days she would remember how for a couple of months her cycle gave hardly any trouble. *Enjoy it*, Maud would say. *Men don't bleed every month so it must be a good thing.* And Beatrice, who had always feared her womb's vindictive power, found herself looking forward to the moment when the dragging pains came on. They were another sign of mutual sympathy.

The days soon took on a pattern. Since their working shifts coincided, the two regularly walked together to and from their tram stops at the bottom of the hill. In the mornings, when Maud's habitual tardiness would have invariably made them both late, a condition which Beatrice suffered with a martyr's contented resignation, never once considering that she might have the freedom to go on ahead without her friend, they barely had time to dash from door to tram, let alone exchange words. On those occasions, her head still dizzy with sleep, Beatrice would rush on through an anxiety which Maud herself seemed to have created, as a sort of test. She could not, she soon realised, aspire to her friend's utter carelessness about time and deadlines; but as she panted towards the last hundred yards of pavement and heard Maud's insouciant laughter and her cajoling goodhumoured cry: *Slow down Beatty, the war won't finish without you, your patients can't run away*, she would often find herself relaxing in a way that would have been unthinkable a month ago. Then she saw that Maud's lethargic indifference to the ways of the world (a man's world she would have glossed) was also a species of brooding power. Tested and found wanting, Beatrice could at least attempt to absorb the lesson.

Their walk back uphill in the evenings was a very different affair. Now both women were tired, their fatigue being mental as well as physical, having as much to do with the endlessly repeated necessity to make sense out of what each was doing, as with the equally repetitious business of getting the job done. It was here that Beatrice came into her own, reversing the morning imbalance to take a dominant role in their exchanges and intimacies. Maud seemed always to have grown taciturn during the day, whilst Beatrice would climb down off the tram bearing a treasure of observations and experiences which she itched to unlock. Noticing her friend's silences she had wondered for a while if Maud was simply uninterested in her work; then, after one rather lurid account of how she had watched Sister Macready packing a wound with gauze, whether the ex-suffragette wasn't a little squeamish; finally she confronted her with the question and found to her astonishment that Maud positively depended on Beatrice's description of her working day. *I love it, Beatty and so look forward to it. Now do go on about the men singing that risqué song. You know the one about the German officers.* It wasn't that Maud lacked her own stock of memories and sights; it was just that Beatrice had a clearer grasp of what she was doing and why. Maud was afloat, adrift even, and relied on Beatrice for anchorage. The long lonely weeks of training had given her a centre and a purpose which Maud, for all her assertiveness, did not possess. Whether, too, the unhappy time the previous summer had not contributed to Beatrice's new-found strength she was reluctant to consider. Nevertheless, she gladly accepted her new role, talking about her work with an easy authority and noticing as they climbed the hill and went upstairs (hoping as always to avoid the serpentine attentions of their landlord), how Maud's taciturnity began to melt. So that by the time they had sat down together to toast crumpets in front of an open fire, her friend had completely recovered and might even launch into hesitant accounts of her own work with detonators and fuses in the acrid skylit factory. Once again, Beatrice realised, it was as if her friend needed someone else to be present before she could come fully alive; sometimes, indeed, she appeared not to believe in her very existence, until it was pointed out to her.

If Maud had difficulty giving shape to her daily experience, she had even fewer words to spare for her past. Beatrice had very soon grasped that what had happened to her friend before she came back to Chalkhampton held the key to her present rootlessness. But whenever she tried to draw Maud on the subject she was gently turned aside. The gentleness she knew was a bluff. If Maud would often stumble over words to describe her days at the factory, her impediment would grow furiously active if she so much as skirted her own history. She did not believe in what she did today; but what she had done or failed to do yesterday was an ever-threatening phantom. Beatrice's intimation, on their first meeting, that Maud was out of a higher social drawer than she was willing to divulge, gained certainty when she noticed an instinctive familiarity with the social calendar, especially now that it had begun to be eroded by the war. She had no direct family (another bond, like their shared exile) but referred obliquely once or twice to a guardian and one or two cousins. The circumstances of her leaving London might or might not have had to do with the Pankhursts. So it went on. And when, unable to resist exploring a mutual connection with places and people still burning at the back of her mind, Beatrice mentioned anything to do with Ecclesden, the ambiguities and sidestepping increased. So that after a while she elected to opt for the present moment. After all, hadn't she engaged in far too much probing the previous summer. Let Maud come from anywhere or nowhere, on a muddy wave inside a shell bobbing under the pier, where the stones grated in the endless folding susurrus of waves. She was here, that was enough, singing as she readied herself for bed, now *La ci darem la mano*, now *Burlington Bertie*, making the swoop from refinement to vulgarity and back again with all the natural finesse of a gull skimming the lights above the promenade.

It could not last. The very tenuousness of its contentment meant that the friendship they had created must change and in changing introduce a conflict. This began unexpectedly and from an unexpected quarter. One evening, after their usual confidences in front of the fire in Beatrice's room, the two women had separated to go to bed. But Beatrice, who was running a slight feverish cold, had been unable to sleep and gone out on to the landing to fetch a glass of water. Passing the alcove where the linen press was stored she had been startled by a movement which made her pause and then rush hurriedly on. Maud had been standing there, in her nightdress, her arms round the neck of her supposedly despised landlord. Thrown into a spasm of embarrassment and confusion, Beatrice had forgotten all about the water and gone straight back to her room. By the time the soft knock at the door came, she had managed to calm herself sufficiently to mouth a parched *come in.* Her own indiscretions in a boathouse were not that remote in time. If Maud had had to make certain compromises in order to escape her past, and if these involved the damp palms of Mr Birkett then who was she to comment? So she waited, preparing to be magnanimous. And found herself confronted by a woman who was neither shamefaced nor apologetic. But elated, as if Beatrice had been witness to some miracle of transfigured love. At which point Beatrice realised that here too was another of Maud's contradictions: she despised men yet fed from them, and in feeding enlarged and solidified her own threatened self-worth. So that when the inevitable embrace occurred and she smelt that familiar sandalwood fragrance, overlain perhaps by a tarter whiff of cologne, she could not be angry, only sad, whispering,

— I don't blame you.

To which Maud, tearing herself away, had responded with a bitter vehemence that made Beatrice blench.

— You naive little goose. Do you think I have to if I don't want to. Do you think I have to do it because a man says so? Forgive? You, forgive? I don't want your piddling forgiveness.

And Beatrice had swayed, kneeling on the bed, her eyes filling with tears, as after the first quarrel with a lover.

They had made it up soon enough. But an undercurrent of tension continued to thread their days and nights. Then had come what Beatrice forever afterwards remembered as the Ecclesden estrangement. This too took place on the landing, one cold morning when they were taking it in turns to use the bathroom. Maud as usual was unconscionably slow and Beatrice, shivering out on the linoleum, had tried to distract herself by drawing a stick man in the condensation on the landing window. Suddenly, in a rush of cistern water and flowing gowns (Maud had a fine collection of silk and lined housecoats; another fact which sat ill with her present circumstances) her friend was beside her, peering.

— Is that Whitehawk? Where the camp is?

Beatrice nodded, sensing the old dim feelings of pride and love and resentment welling up.

— Another bunch waiting their turn at the trough. I hear my old friend Charles Tremain is up there, a Captain apparently.

It was the first time Maud had talked openly about her connection with Ecclesden. The effect on Beatrice was electric, as if her friend had stood up and invoked the dead. She wiped at the wet glass for want of words. Maud peered again.

— I wonder what his mother thinks of it all. Poor Charlie. Always being led by the nose. Wren was behind it, I've no doubt.

Beatrice felt herself falling through the gulf of the window down down into the past. It was as if Maud had suddenly forgotten that they hadn't known each other for years.

— When did you used to stay there, at Ecclesden I mean? I was there. Teaching for a year. I think I told you. And met them all.

Beatrice's face was burning despite the cold. *Beatty, Beatty, red as a beetroot* had been the chant at school. Maud turned from the window.

— They're not my favourite family. We fell out in a manner of speaking. It was ages ago. Ancient history. But you were quite a hit so I heard. Don't shake your head, it's just like my little friend to be so modest. And now Charles is in the Second Battalion. Have you visited them since they came back from Salisbury Plain?

Why here? Why now? After the long weeks when they had built up a careful intimacy based on their shared exile, why did Maud suddenly want to break it all apart by introducing the old names and affections. Yet if her friend was at once annoyingly condescending and hopelessly forward, she was also an adept at divining Beatrice's deeper wishes. Somehow she knew what, until this moment, Beatrice herself had not known or had not had the courage to know. That she wanted to see Charles again, if only to make some peace with him before the final leave-taking. And suddenly on the cold landing, Beatrice saw that that was why Maud had come to her: not as a confidante but as a link back to Charles. And the knowledge made her want to cry, if only for the loss of a companionship so recently forged. Maud had erased the stick man completely. The days of their first innocent intimacy had come to an end. Beatrice looked up, startled by the hissing sound which was beginning to escape Maud's lips. Dully, out of habit, she mumbled interrogatives as to the word which would not be born.

– Foot? Forgive? Feel?

Then at last it rose up, from the same cave where all words are, vomiting out at the air.

– Fucking. That's all they're good for. Men, I mean. Fucking. Don't forget that, Beatty. The only thing a man can do better than a woman is piss into the wind.

I won't allow it. Not down here. Not at Ecclesden.

You! You won't allow it! You got her, didn't you? She's your dirty get.

This is another of your humiliations, isn't it, like the business with Constance. You just want to humiliate me.

Constance has been an excellent and conscientious guardian. Stepping in so swiftly when the grandfather washed his hands of her. As for the matter of humiliation, just what do you think I have had to endure these last ten years? What? Tell me.

The banisters let the light through in long bands then squeeze it as it comes through so that the light has to slant into pillars that repeat each other like pillars of a temple you can't touch. He is lying along the pillars peering down into the hot cave of the house. Be still. Oh be still. But they won't. Ever. Tongues.

And what if she and Charles?

They're children, Colin. Seven and five. Babies. You should have thought of that when you took up with that Yankee tart.

More of a southern belle actually. They were Virginians don't forget. On one side.

Very well. But shop-soiled. She took up with you on the rebound. After Cohen.

This doesn't become you, Katherine, speaking ill of the dead.

As I was saying. The child. Your child. Now I'm not denying I would have preferred the fever or whatever it was . . .

Eclampsia. Dangerously high blood pressure. Leading to convulsions. Leading to cerebral haemorrhage. Am I to be dragged through it all again? Am I?

Don't change the subject, Colin. Now, I'm not denying it would have been better if the child had died with the mother. But she didn't. And we have a duty.

To keep her in England as a torment to my conscience for the rest of my natural life. Exactly.

Oh I feel for you, Colin. How I feel for you. Sometimes you seem to forget that you're the first link in the chain. Taking advantage of young women away from home.

Nonsense, Katherine. You've just put it in your own inimitable way. Annabel was, shall we say, experienced. She knew what she wanted, after that rotten marriage of hers. Just as I knew what I wanted . . .

After your rotten marriage.

There you go again, putting words into my mouth. We've raked it all over countless times. I've nothing more to say. Except that . . .

What?

It's just damnably regrettable I don't fire blanks.

There you go again boasting and pretending it's contrition. Really you are so coarse.

Silence. A moth circling the hall chandelier. If you close your eyes to a slit the pillars of light go thin thinner thinner. But they don't fall over.

I sense a plan behind this visit. Or is it visits?

You know as well as I do that she had money.

Which her solicitor was instructed to put in trust for the child. She was conscious enough to do that at the end. But I still don't see Katherine. It won't come into her hands until she's what? Twenty-one? Why should we take an interest?

We may have to. One day. The quarry.

I've told you I'm going to get rid of him. The fly in the ointment. Or bird.

Bird? What are you talking about, Colin?

Wren. Don't you see. Oh never mind.

It's an insurance policy if you like. By getting to know the child we're

taking out an insurance policy: on the manor, on Charles, even on Robert.
You are her father you know.

Some father. I don't even know what that shrivelled old nun called her.

Constance is forty and neither a nun nor shrivelled. Wrinkled, I grant you.

Silence. The moth suddenly plummeting from its tinkling paradise on to the parquet in a cindering of wings. Outside rooks harshly shouting as they head home for Thundersbarrow hanger.

Don't you remember. Maud. She christened her Maud.

Maud Maud Maud Maud they were crying and calling.

Jupp had read him that. In bed. Last night.

The day of Beatrice's first rehearsal as a singer in one of the two Tongdean Choral Society choirs drew steadily closer. The thought of practising in the assembly hall of a school from which Charles, in those days little more than a lovelorn child, had once written to her, gave Beatrice a certain melancholy pleasure. But this feeling was almost evanescent compared with the tide of excitement that would wash over her whenever she reminded herself that she was about to take her place in a ritual whose potent centre would be Maud Egerton who, despite recent tensions and revelations, remained her best friend and confidante. At such moments all nervousness about her singing abilities would vanish; the painful memory of her audition with Mr Birkett in his basement music room when, to his florid accompaniment, she had staggered through a somewhat flat version of 'Jerusalem' vanished; as did the still more painful recollection of the way Maud had taken the landlord aside and whispered furiously with him until he had turned smiling and pronounced himself well satisfied with Beatrice's voice; at such moments she would stand before the wardrobe mirror and progress through a whole series of mimed stances, with a confidence not wholly underived from the fact that her mouth uttered no sound.

During this fervid prelude Maud continued to take the upper hand in their friendship but with a new subtlety and tact as if she sensed Beatrice's vulnerability. Beatrice in her turn was grateful for the opportunity to admire and perhaps even worship this rising star and consummate artist who would not only take centre stage in a couple of Mozart arias but would be instrumental (much to Mr Birkett's disgust) in introducing a selection of music hall songs which she had learnt on the pier.

– It's for the men, Walt, you old fossil, can't you see that. – Maud said one evening down in the basement where she had reluctantly agreed to spend an hour (*on condition Beatty comes too*), running through some finer points in the scores. – For the soldiers and their sweethearts. Beatty understands. Don't you, Beatty?

And Maud had winked at her companion, making her blush both for the implied complicity and a deeper intimation that Maud was referring however obliquely to her and Charles. Mr Birkett uneasily laid his knobbly fingers on the keyboard.

– I know. But such vulgarity. Such squalor. What is all this low nonsense about drawers and stockings and such things?

A pudency with which Beatrice in former days might have sympathised if it hadn't come from the mouth of so blatant a hypocrite. But tonight her eyes were on Maud who, when she launched into Donna Anna's aria (*I don't need to practise this you know*), seemed to Beatrice to become transfigured, her speech impediment forgotten. Even Mr Birkett soon forgot his quibbles and leant back on the piano stool anticipating, as the astute and daring impresario, a warm bath of second-hand accolades. Afterwards, still flushed from her exertions, Maud had been unusually forthcoming with Beatrice, talking about the holidays she had spent at Ecclesden as a distant and impoverished relation (on the mother's side) and how she and Charles had never really liked each other as children. *One day I dared him to pull up all the gladioli in front of the terrace. He got the blame. He hated me after that. But I didn't care. I was just a poor relation you see.* Then Beatrice had begun timidly to reciprocate, recounting some of her experiences at Ecclesden the previous year. Maud appeared to listen then grew slowly abstracted. Beatrice faltered. It was the old barrier. But after all, she reasoned to herself, a star in the firmament need only shine; its light falls on whoever happens to be underneath.

In the meantime there was the hospital. One afternoon the ward sister, after condemning Beatrice to a gruelling round of floor polishing, sent her all the way down to the stores to see about bed linen. The stores lay underneath the hospital in a maze of tunnels reputedly dug by the Romans and, until a retaining wall had been built, supposed to have been regularly flooded by the sea. Certainly, as you made your way down the iron spiral staircase, there was a sound suggesting a barely contained friction and ricochet. The stores themselves were gathered in the largest of the tunnels, a barrel-vaulted cistern of a place that might once have held prisoners or the dead. Beatrice felt uneasy down here among the tiered shelves, warped with their burden of rolled blankets and starched linens. It was as if this chamber, long-since scoured by the sea of any human decoration, was a direct link between the suffering in the wards above and the remote yet ever-present violence which had caused that suffering. Down here there was a never-ending supply of materials to cover up the dead or dying. Standing under the great tiled dome of the roof and hearing the crash of waves, you felt the war had not only been going on for centuries but had centuries still to run. And there would always be blankets. With a shiver Beatrice handed her message to the storekeeper and turned to climb back into a world she knew.

Long afterwards, Beatrice would remember how, as she turned, the shadow came forward, detaching itself from an alcove in which tins of lint and stone TCP bottles stood ranked like canopic urns in an Egyptian tomb. It was the second of three such encounters with Charles Tremain and all of them would come to seem in retrospect both deliberate and accidental. Certainly, the Company Captain admitted that he had glimpsed Beatrice on odd occasions when army business had brought him to the fort. But the likelihood that he had anticipated so coincidental a meeting seemed improbable. Indeed, the urge to suppose he regretted the encounter was strong, given their long estrangement. Yet when he came forward, out of the embalming darkness, his smile and outstretched hand suggested that the past had somehow been cancelled. He was older she quickly noticed, and not just in body. For there flickered, behind the dark rings under the eyes, the occasional fleck of white in the sandy moustache, the rifting of tiny crow's feet at the eyes' corners, a more general weariness which, had she not known better, Beatrice might have assumed derived from some wrong he had been forced to suffer or endure. Even his eczema, which had so troubled and affronted her younger self, seemed today, when glimpsed beneath the green military collar, to suggest vulnerability rather than defensive anger. Thus, even with his culpability most exposed, Charles Tremain could manage to borrow an air of injured innocence. But when she took his outstretched hand, still cold perhaps from touching the stone of the bottles, some of the old unreasoning excitement rose up unbidden; so that she found it possible to make light of her fatigue and, once her duties at the hospital were discharged, allow him to walk with her through the grey rainswept streets. Eventually, in front of the pier, they came to a Lyons Corner House, its windows briefly defying the blackout with blue and yellow chandeliers aflame against the oncoming dusk.

Desultory, polite, unimpassioned, their conversation might have been that of any two chance acquaintances, blown together in a time of upheaval. In the bustle of nippies, amongst the echoes and the clatter, the steam from their mugs of steeped tea billowed between them as they ranged over all the expected topics, nursing, training, the prospect of service overseas. They were little more than strangers, the VAD and the Captain, passing a few off-duty moments in torpid dialogue. Soon they would leave and go their separate ways, through the wet twilight. Or so it seemed. Yet as the minutes passed and they remained together, facing one another across the mug-ringed linoleum, many long-suppressed currents began to stir, a gathering chain reaction that had both man and woman beginning to gabble, then slowing to an almost mechanical recitative, then launching off again, but each time more incoherently, more vulnerable to emotion. Until eventually, with nothing and every-thing to say they sat still in utter silence, staring at a tarnished geometry of knives and forks. They were strangers no longer; but united by a disharmony that would have driven weaker people far apart.

It was Beatrice who broke the silence, who was perhaps the less able to bear her memories, or more willing to respect them.

– Charles, do you know why I came here? To Chalkhampton I mean. Do you know why I abandoned teaching?

He looked up from where he had been arranging and rearranging the angles of a cutlery rhomboid.

Fucking, that's all they're good for. Remember that, Beatty.

– Know? Of course I know. Just as you know why I joined up.

He had spoken a little too briskly. As if all mysteries were explicable in the end. But Beatrice, who must speak for the girl she had once been, if only to confirm her death, was inclined to be more patient, if less assured.

– You know I'm not talking about the war, Charles. You know I'm talking about us. As we were.

He nodded (*That's all they're good for*) and suddenly the thought that he had deliberately arranged this meeting in order to encourage her to pick at old sores enraged her. So that she wanted to hurt. If only to administer a healing draught afterwards.

– It was that letter you wrote. From Salisbury Plain. How could you be so arrogant, Charles? So unfeeling? But no, you can't answer that question either. And I suppose it made me grow up. I came here to grow up. And if you're expecting me to fall into your arms a second time then you're still as juvenile as ever. Despite that uniform.

She stopped, hoping a few of her words had struck home but wondering at the same time how Maud would have handled the conversation. More savagely no doubt. And with a salt of wit. But Charles was looking up. There were tears in his eyes.

– I was weak, Beatty. And young. But I have grown up too. You must at least allow me that nebulous achievement.

She had not expected to be washed by such an intensity of guilt, if that was what it was, and not some more potent compound of loneliness and yearning. So that she too was close to tears and desperate for a distraction.

– Aren't you going to eat any of that?

The jam rolypoly lay untouched on his plate. But a crimson gore had oozed across the willowware. Blood in the garden. She blushed.

– But you never were much of a trencherman. Remember those raspberries we ate.

– What on Thundersbarrow?

He too wanted to escape the greyness of the hour.

– Yes. But didn't we have them in the garden too, that day your mother went to London with Robert?

The boathouse loomed up, an ark riding the floodwaters of the past. She was skating close to the abyss and both of them knew it. Perhaps there had been something beside failure, in their brief companionship. Or passion. Then their eyes met and they were sharing a knowledge both had long suppressed. So that suddenly they could shed their old innocent and outraged selves and become once more the VAD and the Captain of A Company, Second Battalion Chalkhampton Chums, spending time off in a teashop.

– I'm telling you, when we get out there – Charles was saying between wolfed mouthfuls of rolypoly – I'm telling you, Fritz won't know what's hit him. You should have seen the marches we've been on, the assaults, the trenches. I'm telling you, if I'd known a year ago what I know now about digging holes . . . Oh, blast.

A globule of jam had smeared his breast pocket-flap. She leant forward.

– Here, let me.

Later, in her darkened room, she would sniff the jam on her handkerchief, sifting from its sickly odour the sharper tangs of khaki, Brasso and sweat.

To the left of the pier, at the bottom of a ramp leading down to Undercliff Walk, lay the aquarium. Its lights haloed the drizzle driving in off a slow brown sea.

– Let's go in before the blackout starts. At least we'll be dry.

A grizzled face rose up in a hatchway.

– We're closing in five minutes. Closing for good. This bloody war. I'm telling you . . .

– Mayn't we be the last visitors?

Charles moved forward into the dim light. His buttons flashed.

– Ah. Of course Captain, Sir. I didn't see. Of course you and the missus can go in. Have ten minutes if you like. Is it true you're leaving soon? For the Front? I wish I was going, I really do. I'd like to give them savages what for.

Locked in its thankless task of reconciling resentment and servility, the voice echoed after them, down the draughty tiled tunnel that lead to the tanks. Beatrice whispered,

– Did you hear what he called me? The sauce!

But was pleasantly flustered. For answer Charles squeezed her arm. Then all at once they were in a great circular room that resembled both a temple and a mausoleum. The air breathed damp and warm. Here in their glassfronted tanks the sea creatures lived: irridescent shoals of tiny fish wheeling and spiralling as one; turtles encrusting seaweedy rocks; lobsters and crabs, eels, jellyfish. Beatrice shivered yet felt a curious comfort in the presence of this dumb otherworld, hidden from the war, from people, from their makeshift lives in that wintry town. A feeling that, paradoxically, made her more confident about the ghosts that still haunted her.

– Is he with you still. In the battalion?

Charles nodded then, glancing round

– Ah, now this is what I wanted you to see.

They paused in front of a small tank in which a flint model of the fort rose up from a forest of reeds. A skull with paste jewels for eyes lay outside the postern gate through which, in real life, Beatrice passed twice a day.

– There's nothing there. – She would have liked to return to more private matters and began to move away.

– No. There is. Look.

Then she did see the two creatures, their skins escutcheoned like armour, their tails entwined, bobbing amid a plume of bubbles.

– Oh they look like little dragons. And their eyes. So lovely and soft. Are they mates do you think?

So she allowed herself to become entranced, in the presence of the seahorses. He glanced round at her.

– The last time I went back to Ecclesden you'd gone. I found Noone ensconced in Mrs Eddles's kitchen. I don't mind telling you I went away in tears. I did, Beatty. For being such a cad. And knowing it was too late.

The seahorses were bobbing in their cold embrace. She pressed his hand, surprised to find she hardly cared whether what he said was true or a mere improvisation to suit the moment. For when had he ever bothered visiting the schoolhouse when she was still living there?

— Perhaps it will be different, one day, after all this. I had to join up, Beatty, just as you had to become a nurse. Funny that, isn't it. We kill and you make better. Not that any of us have killed yet. He looked away and she sensed an unwillingness on the part of the untried soldier to face the realities of what war can do. She was superior to him in her knowledge of the consequences of organised violence and, in some faint way, he resented that knowledge.

– Will you be going straight out to France do you think? We've had a big influx from Loos recently, I expect you've heard.

He winced and immediately she regretted her urge to be cruel.

– Oh look, their beaks or mouths or whatever they are. It's like a kiss.

So her forced sentiment drew him away from the shadows that waited ahead. His face brightened.

– Do you know I had a premonition I'd see you today. It should have been Eric who came. Can you believe that?

She could. But the seahorses were moving apart, their eyes stony and dark, their snouts resolutely tucked in. She felt a sudden wave of melancholy. And realised that she had not yet mentioned Maud.

– I'm going to your old school Friday night. A rehearsal for the Chums Concert. I believe you know someone involved with it.

She waited, her heart beating hard. Charles was staring at the seahorses.

– Birkett, yes. He taught me piano for a year but I gave it up at Grade One. Now that's what I wanted to tell you. The male seahorses gestate the young. In special pouches. We had some at Tongdean. Isn't that extraordinary?

– No. Someone else. A sort of cousin I believe. You mentioned her in a letter once.

How her voice quivered as if this banal piece of news were indeed a revelation. Meanwhile Charles was rubbing his sleeve on the glass.

– The temperature's dropped. Someone's opened a door somewhere. Oh, you mean Maud. Yes. I'd heard the old goat had got his hooks in her. Incidentally Beatty, some of us might be performing too. If the regiment stays long enough. Ah here's Mr Sunshine himself.

Beatrice had no time to fathom the tone of this response, nor to work out whether she should be disappointed that he already knew about Maud (did he know too about her friendship?), or glad that he might be present at the concert. The old man in the hatch was beside them, rattling his keys.

– Not much, is there? It's the war. We can't afford to stoke the boiler and the creatures get cold. They're dying off in shoals. We had a dolphin here once. And a sort of monster. Leviathan we called it. Someone found it in one of them quarries up on the Downs. A pegging great shark of a thing with fins as big as your nurse's hat if you'll pardon me, missus.

– You mean they found the bones. The quarrymen often do.

– No no. The whole carcase of it preserved by some magic. But he's not here now. He was spirited away the night Fritz started it and the crowds down here got a bit unruly. Some of them broke in and took him down and went and dropped him off the end of the pier. To see if he'd swim.

– Cans't thou draw out Leviathan with an hook?

Charles turned to Beatrice and winked. He had adopted Eric's prophetic voice.

– Exactly Sir, Captain I should say. – The old man's eyes lit up with yearning for the magical beast. – But come back when the war's finished, or perhaps I should say if the war's ever finished, and we'll have another one just like before.

Out on the promenade dusk had ushered in the blackout and a quenching of lights. The soldier and the nurse hunched shoulders into the drizzle and set off for the tram stop by the hospital. A late gull wheeled shrieking overhead.

The Friday of the rehearsal arrived. By teatime Beatrice had begun to wonder whether the whole idea hadn't been an unrealistic fantasy. The familiar dragging tiredness had set in with a vengeance; and she still had two more hours of solid work ahead of her. But by a stroke of fate the ward sister, normally merciless and unbending when it came to the hours her VADs put in, was called away unexpectedly to help deal with a crisis in one of the operating theatres. Her substitute proved less vigilant, betraying a tendency to wink when certain minor tasks were skipped, and Beatrice found herself free to go home an hour earlier than usual with the prospect of a recuperative bath before the omnibus to Tongdean. If, disembarking from the tram at the bottom of Orion Parade, she experienced a twinge of sadness at not seeing Maud's familiar silhouette webbed by a spiky cage of bare forsythia, the mood soon passed. Even supposing that, by some telepathy of friendship, they had been able to coincide, the old walk up the hill would not have been inevitable. Their routine had become more broken of late, ostensibly because Maud herself was working more flexible hours, but more probably (Beatrice admitted to herself), because both of them needed to escape each other's intensity now and again. So that as she began the walk alone, Beatrice's spirits soon lifted. The October sky was a pure and icy blue. The row of chestnuts on the margins of the little park halfway up the hill were flaming out in a last incandescence of orange. Everything about the world seemed suddenly clean and fresh and pure. She was ready to forget the war and the past. She was ready to forget herself.

The house lay quiet at this time of day, before the influx of lodgers coming in from work. Nevertheless, having elected to whistle the whole Handel chorus and being still in mid flow when she closed the front door, Beatrice might not have heard the sound of voices in the back parlour and gone on her way upstairs. But by some alchemy of chance which seemed suddenly to superimpose this moment on the time when Maud had come to look at her room, she simultaneously smelt sandalwood perfume and saw the paper on the sideboard. As on so many other occasions, Beatrice was assailed by a sense of time flowing toward her from two opposite directions, so that she stopped whistling and stood before the sideboard gazing idly at an account of the latest fighting in the Dardanelles. Then she did hear the voices. Or rather, their tone. It was a tone, she realised instantly, which could only be struck when both voices were together, yet undisturbed. It was intimate yet fierce, abrasive yet tender. Blindly, she put out a hand as if to touch the braille of fascination that had risen up before her in the shadowy hall. Blindly, for the first time, with the very marrow of her being, she touched and absorbed the texture which those two voices shared. Blindly, as if falling down a tunnel of time, she interpreted the secret code which only those two voices could construct. Blindly, she understood what these two people spoke of when they were alone. Blindly, she confronted the entwined voices of Maud Egerton and Charles Tremain.

– I had to, don't you see. I couldn't just keep away.

Fierce Storms in Gallipoli. Much damage to beach-heads. Our lads stand firm . . .

– But here, Charlie. Where I live. I don't like it that's all I'm saying. Why not the Grand, like last time?

Evacuating the wounded. Operation a complete success. All credit is due to . . .

– If I didn't know you better I'd say you had a fancy man hidden in your room. Eh, Maudie, have you? Be honest now.

Turks now low on ammunition. Courage and daring of our brave boys knows no . . .

– Oh fuck off, Charles. You're an Infantry Officer not bloody God Almighty. What if I have? It's none of your sodding business.

At Suvla Bay . . .

– But you can't say you don't like a uniform. Eh, Maudie?

At Suvla . . .

– Well . . . I prefer what's underneath . . .

At . . .

– Crikey, not here. Maudie, I . . .

So Beatrice would have gone on falling forever, down her tunnel of blind seeing, if the hand hadn't suddenly caught her, dragging her back.

– Why, Miss Lumley. So early! This is truly fortuitous. You must come in and meet our esteemed guest. Maud, I mean Miss Egerton, is already with him. What an honour. I have just been downstairs to arrange for tea.

Now that Mr Birkett stood between her and the parlour Beatrice could no longer catch the full force of the voices. They had in any case gone mysteriously quiet. How she would have liked to excuse herself and run upstairs. Yet knew that she must walk past her landlord and allow herself to be ushered into their presence. Mr Birkett, she noticed, had the old desperate look again. Maud was eluding him as usual.

– I have another lodger to introduce.

Standing on the very spot where she had first seen Maud's face reflected in the mirror, Beatrice felt as though she were indeed meeting these two people for the first time. They had changed somehow, by being left alone together, a change that seemed to involve some occult process of reciprocation. For while Maud had borrowed some of Charles's softness, he seemed to have absorbed a little of her vigilant self-regard. They both looked taller too. And colder. Despite the flush in Charles's cheeks and the uncharacteristi-cally flustered way in which Maud moved quickly across to draw the curtains.

– I don't believe you have met. Miss Lumley is also singing at the concert. Miss Lumley, Captain Charles . . .

Taking his hand Beatrice realised with a little shock that Charles had not guessed she lived here. Despite her allusions to Mr Birkett and Maud during their visit to the aquarium, she had never actually mentioned Orion Parade by name. Parting at the tram stop outside the hospital, they had simply arranged to meet again in a week's time on the pier, a neutral setting suitable to her new sense of dignity and self-worth. Nor, obviously, had Maud revealed anything. Evidently recovered from whatever perturbation had been afflicting her, she came back across the room and put her arm through Beatrice's.

– Well now you've rumbled our little secret. What do you think?

Then all further thought was drowned in the chaos of Mr Birkett's ecstasy on realising that they were, in fact, quite well acquainted. Soon all three had sat down to tea and biscuits while the landlord, overwhelmed by this opportunity of being able to entertain both his star performer and the heir of Ecclesden in the same room at the same time, flustered back and forth, alternately offering to fill already brimming cups and absentmindedly stuffing his mouth with biscuits. After the strange intensity of their overheard exchanges, both Maud and Charles seemed remarkably relaxed. Charles, it transpired, had come on behalf of his mother on some business to do with Maud's guardian, to whom Lady Tremain was distantly related. Beatrice, still fascinated by the fragmentary story of Maud's relationship with Ecclesden, would have liked to know more but could see no suitable opening that would not expose in her an indecorous curiosity. In any case, Charles, seeming in Maud's company to be quite purged of sullenness and self-pity, applied himself so assiduously to Beatrice's ease and social entertainment, making her sit in the peacock armchair and tell them all about her day as a VAD, that she quite forgot her lingering doubts and suspicions. Indeed by the end of the tea when Charles, looking at his watch, announced that they would be banging him up in the glasshouse if he didn't return to camp immediately, Beatrice would have been hard put to say whether their meeting that afternoon had been arranged or accidental. Charles even mentioned, to her confusion and delight, their forthcoming meeting on the pier. Only afterwards, in the quiet that followed his departure, when Mr Birkett had taken the tea things downstairs and the two women sat on alone in the gathering dusk, did some of the old jealousies resurface. Then it was that Beatrice caught Maud looking at her in a new way, at once intense and critical. Remembering the fierce and obscure conversation echoing in the hall, she realised that some words, at least, had had nothing to do with family business. Maud was stroking and stroking her hair in that manner she had.

– He likes you, doesn't he? Not that I blame him.

To which Beatrice responded less coolly than she might have hoped, embarking on a flush that had her moving quickly to the door *to take a bath.*

Now, Charles, do come down those stairs. Here's a new playmate especially to see you. Don't be shy. See. A little girl.

(She smells funny. And she's got a funny long nose. Like a horse.)

Maudie dear. Go to Charles and say how do you do. Like I taught you. He's your, Oh what is he Katy would you say?

Second cousin, Constance, of course.

Yes, yes, silly of me. I never was much good about these things. Second cousin, yes.

(He's got bogies coming out of his nose. Bet he eats them. Ugh.)

They're playing nicely now. In the butterfly room.

Sir Colin doesn't approve does he? I could sense it.

Constance, you must know that in these matters Sir Colin . . . Charles! Oh not another paddy. What have you been doing. Where is that governesss. Ring the bell for me, Constance.

She pulled my hair.

He kicked me.

Where did he kick you dear? Is she coming yet? I don't know why we ever employed her.

In the . . . in the . . . I can't say it.

Whisper it to me, dear. I see. Well Charles. I must say that wasn't at all the behaviour of a gentleman.

She pulled my hair because I said she didn't have a pater.

I do I do.

Where is he then?

He's he's . . .

Now that's enough. Both of you. Ah, Miss Jupp. A great absentee in a crisis. Maud here needs a handkerchief. Now. Both of you. Kiss and make up.

(Hate you.)
(Hate you too.)

Lick them. Go on.
  (Wet tiles. Slimy. White.)
  Go on. Dare you. Before old Juppy comes.
  No.
  Scaredy cat. Go on.
  I won't I . . . Oh. Tastes. Tastes . . .
  Oh Charlie, you're such a charlie.
  Quickly, mockingly, she slips from her sheath of a towel. He follows. His hand over his thing. The warm water lies beneath its crust of soap bubbles like dripping under the curdled part. She thrusts out two fuzzy balls of suds instead of hands. White candyfloss.
  Eat this, Charlie.
  Quickly. Mockingly. Until his mouth, buried in that popping airiness finds a finger and clamps.
  You rotter, now I won't show you.
  Don't care. Girls haven't got anything anyway. Their paters chop them off when they're born.
  But I haven't got a pater have I? Cavé!
  Now that's enough, the pair of you. I'm away to see about your tea so no high jinks and no splashing on the floor. You know how your mother complains. Five minutes now.
  (I don't know since that little minx came he's been twice the work. I'll be glad when that woman takes her away again. A real changeling, like old Mrs Wren prophesied. But then she's got the sight.)
  Giggling sitting in the foam that will keep bursting its attempts at rainbows.
  Let me see yours then.
  She has made a foam moustache and a beard that hangs down between her breastless nipples.
  Not likely.
  That's because you haven't got one. Your dad . . .
  I have.

Show me then.

Glancing quickly to check that Jupp. Then standing up. She shrieks.

It's bigger. It's huge.

Squatting again abashed.

Let me feel it.

No.

Her hands fishing. Wriggling. Splashing.

I'll scream. I'll tell Jupp. I'll tell father.

The fish gone quiet.

Would you like to see my bot.

Looking down. Abashed. Nodding.

She turns half-kneeling forward. The warm water-flushed buttocks patched with foam. Her splayed fingers parting the crack. A tiny wrinkled crater or blown violet bud. Outside at the window moths clicking to come in. Red eyes, furred antennae. Softness. Oh softness.

My dad would kill us if he . . .

But he hasn't has he?

No. He hasn't.

No one has. No one.

The voice rose above the silent bowed heads of the choruses, above the heads of the orchestra and Mr Birkett's head with its furze of silver coils. The voice was so strong it seemed it might become visible, a dense molten ball forcing its way higher and higher through the ducts and seams of the air:

I feel my heart aflame with hate and murder.

Death and Destruction blaze around my throne.

Jagged fragments of vengeance and rage, violence and despair thrown out by whatever force drove the voice but transformed in the very act of their ejection into a suspended quivering borealis. Meanwhile the voice continuing to rise, past the quivering spectacle it has created, higher and higher, pursuing something now, in great leaps and dips of coloratura, tracing the flight pattern of some unimaginable prey:

Should you not kill Sarastro as I order,
You are no longer any child of mine.

Up and down and up again, across two octaves, between two worlds, until the pursuit becomes a dance, the dance a celestial track along which the voice glides like a meteor towards top F.

And when the note is reached at last, somewhere up among the dusty rafters of the assembly hall, it is not the end. For still the meteor must continue, following its path out over Chalkhampton and the silent blacked-out camp, over the slumped quarries and cold kilns of Thundersbarrow, over Ecclesden hunched in its quilt of shrubs:

I'll break our ties forever, renouncing you forever,
Abandoning forever, love and care.

And now the meteor is descending, growing dimmer, down down towards the utter deadness of the B flat, not a meteor anymore but a tired bird, then not even a bird but a voice again, a woman's voice while, in another world, the crump and flare of howitzers troubles the unseen horizon:

If you won't kill Sarastro as I order,
Hear, God of Vengeance! Hear a woman's vow!

A vow waiting to be fulfilled, a threat hovering to be carried out. But the voice gone, back into the body that had struggled and fought both to release and contain it, the body empty as if it would only truly come alive again when the voice welled up to be released.

– Good. Very good. But watch that F. And where was the forever in the fifth line. Eh?

Mr Birkett was swaying. He had been pierced by the voice. And bled a misery of unrequital.

– How should I know? Where's the c ... c ... cunt in Scunthorpe for that matter?

There was a stir in the echoey hall. Some who had been inclined to applaud the voice that soared, tutted at the way this other voice had taken over, a voice so bound to the earth it could not without an effort draw together the elements of sound. Others simply giggled or smiled. There she went again, baiting the old fellow. Served him right really. They'd never had a singer like this in the ten years since the Society had been meeting. He should thank his luck rather than cavil. But Beatrice, who had noticed once again how Maud's voice escaped its impediment when riding the molten stream of music, felt a cold foreboding. Maud for a moment had become the Queen of the Night. Meanwhile Mr Birkett was attempting to regain lost ground.

– If only the powers that be hadn't forbidden us the German text. Now if, like me, you had seen Marcella Sembrich at the Met. When was it now, fourteen, no, fifteen years ago.

– Walt, I'm shag-knackered. I don't want your reminiscences.

More giggles. Mr Birkett peered through the murk of his defeat. And decided on an interval.

– You really shouldn't goad him so.

They were leaning together against a huge gurgling radiator. Maud shrugged.

– Listen to that. Just like his bowels. He really should try Epsom Salts. But then that woman's cooking . . .

Beatrice smiled, remembering how they had long ago vowed to eat their main meals in the middle of the day at their places of work. Vowed. They too were entangled in a web of promises, expectations. Not all of them articulated. Beatrice peeped shyly at her friend who was drawing deeply on a Black Cat cigarette.

– What was the family business Charles came to see you about?

The radiator suddenly hissed and Maud drew away, as if scalded. Perhaps she had not heard.

– Anyway, it does him good. He likes to be treated badly. Now. Shall we go outside? I want to get that old hag out of my system. And besides I thought we could take a little look around. I've always wanted to see inside one of these places, haven't you?

Beatrice shook her head, guiltily recalling her innocent attempts to imagine Charles's school life all those months ago. There could be no such innocence now. Maud gestured to where some of the chorus were queuing for soft drinks.

– They're such dull dogs. C'mon, Beatty. Let's go. We might stumble on the showers.

– Oh Maud, how could you!

But Beatrice's cry of girlish outrage was unconvincing, if only because it concealed the shadow of a more violent alarm. She had seen her friend and Charles together. And not for the last time.

It was a cold clear night. Under the full moon the quadrangle lay like a sheet of water. An oak rose up against the stars, its leafless branches suggesting the ironwork of some enormous, empty brazier. Beatrice drew her collar up and squeezed Maud's arm.

– But you sing like a professional, dear. Even Mr Birkett can't believe how good you are.

Her breath rose up in clouds. There would be a frost tonight.

– Wait till you hear my dirty songs. They don't need translating.

So Maud would undermine any edifice founded on too pious an admiration. She, who often did not appear to notice the presence of others, was even less inclined to believe in her own reality. They walked on a little in silence, Beatrice torn between the by now familiar emotions of admiration and disappointment. Hard blue wedges of shadow lay here and there beyond the quadrangle. Figures flitted past, each drained by the moonlight to a flat outline. A clock chimed the half hour with icy clarity. Beatrice pulled up short. All this had surely happened before.

– Shouldn't we be getting back?

Her voice betrayed a quiver of terror but already Maud was dragging her into a dark arch which opened on to a stone-flagged cloister.

– This looks promising. Oh don't be such a wet blanket, Beatty. Don't you want to have an adventure?

They were walking along the flags of the cloister over the black shadows of arches. Beyond they could see an inner quadrangle where the moonlight seemed to have soldified into a luminous lump. The wall of the cloister was hung with portraits of dead Tongdean headmasters, the most recent ones being daguerreotypes, while those that dated back sixty years or more had been done in oils. To Beatrice, peering through the gas-lit gloom, the men in the photographs seemed more ancient than their canvas counterparts. It was as if these newly dead, bearded icons had accrued to themselves a sinister prehistoric magic. She shivered under the scrutiny of their flinty eyes and regretted once again her weakness in following Maud.

– Look at this one, Beatty. Look at the whiskers. Do you think his pubes were as bristly. Imagine kissing that.

But Maud was no longer the Queen of the Night. Her attempted derision sounded almost humble, like a prayer. The ancient priests looked down without emotion. This was not their concern, this invasion of two flibbertigibbets. In their time they had only copulated to make children, mumbling in the scented chancel flakes of a god's transubstantiated body. Now, from death's kingdom, they could hear the thunder of a war they themselves had striven lustily to prepare for. The sound was good. They would listen to that, stopping their ears to those who should be as white hairless statues or better still, hermaphrodites with all their orifices stitched up. Beatrice turned away. This had been where Charles had lived. This had been his world. In a sense it still was. How alien and frightening it all seemed. And Maud who, in her supreme indifference to such power, had once seemed enviably free, now revealed herself to be its not altogether unwilling subject.

The figure was moving towards them, weaving in and out of the cloister arches, unaware of their presence. The hauntings of gothic romance briefly crossed Beatrice's mind only to be dismissed with a sardonic shrug. Not here. Under the flint eyes of the masters.

— Shouldn't little boys like you be in bed by now?

Maud had stepped out of the shadows. She seemed more ghostly than the stranger. Who started. Then allowed a slow smile to flicker in his sallow rather puffy face.

— I know you, don't I? Who's the other one?

Beatrice too felt obliged to reveal herself, as if this were indeed some kind of play. The boy blinked.

– And the schoolteacher! I say! That was a rum do up on the hill, what! Jessy had to retire last Christmas. He always was such a daft old biddy.

There was a dull flash. Timmy Frith had had his teeth capped since the previous summer. They glittered now like cartridge cases. He was fatter too, the shirt protruding tightly between the buttons of a flowered waistcoat. Beatrice felt an overwhelming desire to escape from this presence, whose air of seedy elegance (even now he was rearranging a Wildean silk handkerchief with finnicky exactitude) seemed to be all that had survived from those exhilarating painful days. And hadn't Maud promised such an escape with her irreverences and scatologies. Yet here she was, lingering in front of this dummy as she had lingered under the terrible and empty masters.

– Frith. You and Charlie were quite close once, weren't you? I remember he called you his Alcibiades. How many years ago was that?

The boy sneered, licking his lips nervously. His eyes, Beatrice noticed, were shadowed with kohl. He had grown shaky over the months, and jumped at noises. Now he began rubbing his hands like a latterday Uriah Heep.

– Can't remember, Miss. We fell out that's for sure. That is Charlie went cool me. But I've seen you. Quite recently. Was the apple sauce to your dilec . . . dilectition . . . tation?

That the boy's speech could so easily lose its way in this fashion, suggested to Beatrice that he had for some time now been struggling with a deeper dislocation, his mind knotting round itself in a dream of increasing fear and panic. But Maud had stiffened beside her and her pity guttered. The Stone Age masters looked on.

– I hope I didn't hear what you said.

But she had. And seemed prepared for it. Beatrice was not prepared.

– Shouldn't we be getting back? Maud? Shall I go on ahead?

But these two were sleepwalkers, gliding towards the door in the cloister wall.

She was almost through the arch leading to the main quadrangle when she realised she must have dropped it. The belemnite had been working loose from its pouch in her bodice for some time. Cursing herself for not attending to the matter sooner, she turned back. She had hoped to get clean away from what she assumed would be another of those painful scenes, in which her knowledge of others would be proved wrong or inadequate. She had already witnessed Charles and Maud together. Did she need in addition to listen to Timmy Frith's poisonous commentary? Yet a part of her wondered with fitful curiosity what Maud intended to say to him. It was almost as if the meeting had been prearranged. So she returned swiftly down the tunnel or gauntlet.

The moonlight picked out the belemnite lying on the threshold of the door into which Maud and the boy had disappeared. Bending down to retrieve it she had a brief vision of bookshelves and two figures standing near a billiard table. And would have departed had the words not held her, as they always seemed to do.

– What do you mean you heard? Heard what?

–– I was staying there too, don't forget. With my uncle. For the long weekend. You went up in the lift together. The one the wind blows through. Like a spirit. A bloody ghastly spirit.

– And? It's a hotel isn't it? Why should I care?

– Lady Tremain would care.

– I won't have Charles hurt. Not yet.

– 'You must paint my tummy darling.'

Silence. A rustle. A snapping sound.

– Bitch. Cunt. I'll tell them now. I'll tell them all. Jesus . . . twisted. I'll tell the dumpy one. The teacher. She was warm with him. Till you showed up again. Bleeding bitch that you are.

Another silence. Then her voice. Further away. Near the bookshelves.

– No you won't.

– Oh won't I? Won't I just? You cunt you've gone and twisted . . .

– I expect there isn't a book here that doesn't bear shall we say a certain mark.

The boy tittering now through clenched teeth. The panic worse than the pain. But longed for. Welcomed.

– Wouldn't you like to know.

– Even the Bible.

– Why don't you look for yourself? If you're so interested?

Silence. A flutter of pages.

– Genesis seems to be popular. And Daniel. What about Revelation?

– Never. Unless thou wouldst be cursed.

– Do you assist each other?

– That would be telling.

– You can tell me. Do you?

– Don't come any closer. I'll scream. I can you know.

– I won't. Do you?

Silence.

– Well, yes.

– And shall I assist you now?

Silence.

– Shall I?

– Well . . . If you must . . . I . . .

– But only if you forget something.

– Forget something? Oh. Oh yes. I see. Of course. Yes I'll forget. I forget everything anyway. Even my own name. Yes. I didn't mean it anyway. Or those words. Sorry about the words. I'll forget them. All at once. There.

– 'And I looked, and behold a pale horse: and his name that sat on him was death, and hell followed with him. And power was given unto them over the fourth part of the earth, to kill with sword, and with hunger, and with death, and with the beasts of the earth.'

– Not that. Not those words. Anything but those words.

– But it's the only way to forget Timmy, isn't it? It's the only way to forget the words.

– Oh yes. Oh Jesus Christ yes. Yes it is. Oh the only way. The only . . . Yes yes yes.

Her legs rooted when she tries to run shall I assist you moonlight

226

pure as milk poisonous as mercury the wallhung demons from before the flood stepping down out of their frames to weave low in her pursuit only if you forget great beards of pubic hair draggling the dogtoothed arches you must paint my tummy why Maud why the child who lay in the cave rising up to press his burning ear at a bedroom door why Charles why why must I be betrayed a second time?

– Don't be so squeamish, Miss Lumley. Here. Allow me to demonstrate. There. That's it. Right down. And round. And out. Now. You do it. Let me see you do it.

It isn't my fault. Not my fault.

Beadlets of sweat on his pale, papery forehead. No older than Frith. But with a shaved head. And shaved too where the privates are. Or were. Where her fist moves now, swivelling and gouging the wad of formalin-soaked gauze.

– That's right. Get rid of it. All the matter we don't want. Into the pan.

As the ward sister looks on. Critical. Objective. Cool. The raw purplish crater already filling up again with a thin greenish pus. The pus-saturated pledget slopping down into the cold steel dish.

– Careful of that catheter, nurse.

While in the next bed the sergeant with the shrapnel wound mutters,

– Fuck up his honeymoon. That's it. Bugger his wedding tackle. Go on, why don't you!

And still her hand must invade and violate. And still the boy repeats.

It isn't my fault. Not my fault.

Beatrice looked down as if from a great height on her body as it leant over the suffering soldier. Although she could admire the increasing confidence with which her hands performed the terrible cleansing, she felt at bottom nothing but despair and confusion. How ironic that the ward sister should announce she might be allowed to begin direct supervised nursing on this day of all days. A day squashed between two different but complementary strata. Last night she had witnessed and fled the strange and bitterly obscene confrontation between her friend and the schoolboy. This evening after work she would be meeting Charles for a second time. As her hands passed to the delicate business of plugging what could not be plugged, she thought again about the aftermath of the encounter in the cloisters. The second half of the rehearsal had gone by in frozen unreality. Beatrice could now hardly bear to look at Maud, who sat on one side while the choruses ran through their pieces from the Messiah. Once again Frith had appeared at the centre of a mystery and once again that mystery involved Charles. What had Maud wanted him to forget? What had he said he heard? What did the strange phrase 'paint my tummy' really mean? And what had happened eventually to bring Maud back into the assembly hall looking as calm and beautiful as ever, while Frith watched the proceedings from an upstairs balcony, seeming by his presence to want to remind his tormentor of something. The questions circled in her mind, quite blocking out the by now tedious business of rhythms and notes. Yet when they had travelled back together on the omnibus Beatrice had remained silent, while Maud reminisced about her suffragist days in London when she had actually smashed a window in Oxford Street. Then, after their ritual kiss and embrace on the Orion Parade landing, Maud had held Beatrice at arm's length and laughed,

    – Wasn't it fun bearding the lion in his den? Those portraits! Gruesome. I can't think why you were so anxious to leave. When you'd gone I asked Charles's friend to show me where he used to work in the library. There was a heart carved in the bookshelf. I bet you can't guess the other initials. I mean besides CT?

    Wearied after lurching from the celestial realms of the Queen of the Night to the smoky inferno of the cloister, Beatrice shook her head.

    – Why B L of course, you little goose. Didn't I tell you I guessed he must have been sweet on you. Whatever did you do to put him off?

And Beatrice who at any other time might have told Maud to stop playing the fool, smiled one of her more guileless smiles, if only with relief at not having to ask the unanswerable.

It isn't my fault. Not my fault.

– What you done with his wedding tackle. Give it back. Bitches. Give him back his goolies.

– Nurse. Bring the screens. Quickly now.

The boy with the shot-away privates would be dead by nightfall.

She had waited for over half an hour and he had not come. Below her, through the slatted floor of the pier, a filigree of cast iron girders balanced precariously above the sullenly exploding waves. Nearby, on a bollard, a flapping notice announced that, with the exception of the concert hall, all pier amusements had now been closed down for the duration of the war. She had long since felt her nervousness subside into dull resignation. He would not come. How could she have had the arrogance even to expect him to remember. Both of their previous meetings had been accidents, the first fortuitous, the second perhaps fateful. And if she had been Maud waiting here, alone? But she was not Maud and, as on so many previous occasions, must act only for herself. Casting one last resentful look towards the ridge where Whitehawk Camp crouched under belts of sweeping rain, she set off to wander blankly among the shuttered shops and arcades.

She was soon at the end of the pier, having long since passed Maud's old fortune-telling booth. Now, above the waves, she found she could shed her disappointment, if only because its melancholy landscape of hill and combe, manor house and quarry, seemed impossibly remote. She had come to where a funfair had operated even as late as this summer. Now everything was padlocked and sheeted over, giving the place the atmosphere of a small town suddenly abandoned by its inhabitants. Here, like a temple to some overturned and exiled idol, stood the carousel, its animal demons no longer screamed at by excited children. Opposite rose the helter skelter, a blind watchtower, its spiralling slide greasy with rain, its mounds of mats like pelts discarded from some looted storehouse. Nearby a garish Rosetta stone read *Ghost Train. Most Horrific in the County.* But the coloured gas lamps that would have flared here during the years of peace, were now permanently quenched, their ribald evocation of a contrived terror grown bleakly inappropriate. Over the old entrance to this chamber of comfortable horrors, a tarpaulin sheet whipped miserably, revealing the painted hat of a witch, a cauldron and four skeleton legs chained together. How hard it was to imagine the shivery joys of those who had once thronged here. And how easy to imagine it all passing, without a sound, into oblivion. Sadly, Beatrice sat down for a moment in the front carriage of the little wooden train that now waited forever to take its vanished passengers into the heart of the mystery. Ahead the rails ran down a slope towards a tunnel surrounded by ghouls wearing sheets as shapeless as the capes issued to convalescents at the hospital. Suddenly the whole train gave a little lurch. Then the front carriage detached itself and began to move forward down the slope. The acceleration was too rapid for Beatrice to be able to jump off safely so she clung on, reasoning that, at some point, the force of gravity would slow the carriage down. But passing through the tunnel entrance, the carriage actually seemed to pick up speed despite the absence of its engine. This and the way some invisible tripped mechanism shut a door behind her, threw Beatrice into a panic, so that she screamed like any holidaymaker. Meanwhile the journey continued and there was nothing for it but to hold on. Once or twice a clammy softness brushed past. On a corner a skeleton rose up clutching an axe. The carriage came close, slowed down then sped away. Now it was lurching through a series of flapping doors each of which revealed ghostly suspended shapes. And through all of these gimcrack visions, Beatrice kept up a childish squealing and alarm, her heart thudding at each new revelation. It was too ridiculous. She who had dealt with the wounds of the living dead, she who had washed and scoured and bandaged the suffering victims of war, could not bear to face a few papier-mâché fright-masks on a pier.

Then the carriage stopped. How long she waited in the darkness and whether this ordeal was perhaps the preparation for what was to come, she could not say. Certainly, she seemed to go out of herself for a while, as if her body but not her mind were asleep. Then she seemed to be in a ravine of some kind. There was a reek in the air, which she remembered having smelt before, in the aftermath of explosions in the quarry. Now shapes were jostling past. *It's gone up. Like a bloody fountain. A fountain as high as the fucking sky.* Then darkness. Followed by a long silence in which men seemed to be shouting for things, *Water, Mother, Shit, Christ,* but mainly *Water.* Now she too was scrabbling up out of the ravine. *Charles! Where are you Charles?* Then another long silence during which she experienced unendurable heat and thirst.

– Here's a new one.

Her eyes snapped open. She was back in her body in the dank tunnel of the ghost train smelling of urine and excrement. She was not alone. Ahead in an alcove a woman knelt on hands and knees while a man, naked below the waist squatted behind her thrusting. She could hear the wet slap and suction.

– Haven't seen her in here before.

She turned to see another couple gouging at each other's bellies against a wall.

– You have her first.

The hand was on her shoulder. She screamed but out of a terror that no longer had any time for ghosts.

– I'll take her. C'mon this way. Miss Lumley, isn't it. I thought so. Here's the way out.

It was him, the real ghost, the real guardian of this place. The other apparitions were sliding away, abashed. Gratefully, she allowed Eric Wren to lead her into the salty gull-filled light.

She had not seen him since the night of the second tug o'war. Like Charles, his face bore the traces of the intervening months in many lines and furrows. But whereas, in Charles, this ageing process had eroded without shaping, so that the features seemed those of a man who, in his experience, was still a boy; the limeburner's face suggested a longing for innocence even as it registered the shocks and hardships of a new, more restricted life. If this sometimes gave him a furtive look, an impression compounded by the way he nervously dragged his lower teeth across a newly shaved upper lip; it also made for a certain authority. Privileged by the military hierarchy, Charles Tremain still seemed dangerously passive. But Eric Wren had assumed a new purposefulness. To what this might lead, Beatrice could not guess. But she felt obliged to attend to the signals generated by this unexpected source of power. He was helping her now through the gate in the arch. She smiled.

– We always seem to be meeting in caves.

– You oughtn't to be here by yourself. Not at this time, Miss.

His hand was cold and bore some newish scars. From inside the ghost train there came a chanting chorus.

– Wren's a wanker.

He nodded towards the sound.

– We're on leave tonight.

– You mean that's some of the battalion in there. What on earth . . . ?

– Tell us about God, Wren. Tell us about the devil between your legs.

The former limeburner grinned apologetically. Beatrice suddenly understood his extreme isolation. And pitied him.

– Kids, that's all. Clerks. They don't know any better. But it's no place for a lady. I mean a lady and a nurse.

– I came to meet someone.

She had not meant to say this. But felt driven by a compulsion that was not altogether unwelcome.

– I know, Miss Lumley. I'm sorry he can't come.

He knew already. She had not expected to be pre-empted in this way. The memory of the Salisbury Plain letter rose up like bile. *Mr Wren thinks . . .*

– You? You're sorry? Let go of my hand. I'm not an invalid. What business is it of yours?

There were figures now at the ghost train entrance, faces peering round an arch.

You going to give her one? What's her name. C'mon Wrenny. Let's see how she spreads.

Eric made a sudden darting movement and the faces scattered in an alarm that was not altogether playful. Isolated but feared. From within the ghost train a woman's voice screamed.

You've shortchanged me, you fucker.

Beatrice made as if to walk off down the pier. But felt his hand on her shoulder a second time.

– Miss Lumley. Beatrice.

She turned in her outrage.

– It's the old story isn't it? You and him together. And me on the outside. But I'm older now. I have my own life. I have . . . friends.

They were standing by the carousel. A giant cockerel stared down, famished for attention. Or worship. Eric Wren reached up and stroked a wooden wattle.

– Miss Maud . . .

She started. So he knew of her too.

– I didn't come because he told me to. He wouldn't, nowadays. I came because I wanted to tell you about . . . – He stopped and dragged his teeth across his raw lip again. – You know, Miss Egerton and he were very close once. Well, – here he glanced up at the cockerel as if it might speak for him – they're close again. Or might be. There. I've said it. And Charlie will kill me for it one day. Or try to.

Her voice was small when it came, the voice of her old self, timid, troubled by period pains.

– Why are you telling me all this. Now. So late in the day. I'm older. I'm . . .

– Because there's still a chance to save him. You have that chance. But if she does what I think she's going to do. Look, Miss Lumley. It's like we're all tied on a wheel. Like that wheel over there with the animals on it. But you. You can climb on and off when you like. Climb on again. Just this once. Before the wheel goes round so fast we're all broken by it, thrown off in pieces. Hey! Not up there! Come down you blokes!

233

Eric had run over to the helter skelter. Down its spiralling slide came a succession of soldiers, shouting. He waited until they were all at the bottom, sprawled on their mats, then drew them all to attention. They were surprisingly docile. He walked back to Beatrice.

– I'm supposed to be in charge. Poor lads. They'll be over it soon. When we go out.

She saw that his eyes were full of tears. But whether for the poor lads or Charles Tremain or Maud or herself she could not say. Certainly, in the end he would weep only for himself, out of the face he had stolen from the moonlight under the rhododendrons at Ecclesden Manor.

The sky fast and white and broken. Like flocks of sheep, Maudie says. Wouldn't you like to be up there? Driving them. Faraway. Oh ever so far.

Dragon Pit dusted yellow with pussy willow.

It's like powder when you brush against it. Does it have a scent?

Careful you don't put a touch to it. It'll explode sure as . . .

Eric, don't be an ass. It won't, Maudie honest.

Eric laughing now in that way he's copied from his dad. Hoarse and high.

She doesn't know anything she doesn't. She's just from a town.

London's a very elegant place. Not like this old hole in the ground.

She doesn't know anything.

I do. What do you know, anyway? Bet you don't know the name of the highest mountain in the world.

I do.

Tell us then.

His dark flush. Horrible. Oh Maud, you shouldn't have. From Greenlands icy . . .

Thundersbarrow of course. Even though some say the Beacon's a foot or two higher.

There see. See, Charlie. That's what comes of living in a filthy smelly old hovel. That's what comes of being a quarryman. It's Everest, you ape. Didn't you even know that?

Oh Maud. Don't. Please don't.

Don't you even know the name of the highest mountain in the world?

Oh high and white and fast. To be up there. Among the flocks of the clouds. Looking down.

And where's this cave you're always blathering on about? I don't believe there is one.

Her hair straggling the braided coat collar. Yellow. Fawn. 'Like yours, Charlie,' Eric said. That first time they met. 'Like yours.'

There is but I'm not showing you.

Eric, I did promise her. We can't break a promise.

It's ours, Charlie. What's she got to do with it. The stone and the blood and everything. A girl.

Please, Eric.

Oh, don't mind me. I'm just visiting. And if you must know I can't wait to get back to London.

High and white and fast. Eric moving slowly through their shadows towards the cave entrance.

Go on then.

Not out here. Oh look at all these snowdrops. Can I pick some?

You said you would. Up in the cave. You said you'd show me.

Not with that friend of yours. Wren. What a weensy name for such a stupid hulking brute.

You shouldn't have teased him, Maudie. He can't help being unlettered.

I don't see why I shouldn't tease him if I want to. And what's so interesting about your cave? Another hole in the ground. That's all.

Yes I suppose it isn't interesting. To you. But you shouldn't have teased him. Mater says he's a bit simple. He has fits. He'll never be brainy.

That's what you think.

I . . . I don't understand.

He's already brainy. Too brainy. That's why I did it. To stop him.

To stop him what?

To stop him getting power over me. Like he has over you.

Oh don't be an ass, Maud.

That's what you said to him. What's this place?

The boathouse. It's not used now.

235

Old voices. Honeysuckle. 'It should have been nipped in the bud.'

Oh it's so dark. And musty. Look at this old settee. The stuffing's started to come out.

You could show me now.

All right then. There.

But I didn't see anything. It was too quick. You're just scared.

I'm not. Not one jot.

You are. Like you were in the cave when you saw the bloodstain.

I'm not scared of anything, Charles Tremain. I'm not scared to show you. There.

The raised pinafore. A white foam of undergarments. Then the place where tummy and legs meet. A hairless pink seam. She does not move. Her lips parted. What do you do now? In this cave whose air pounds and pounds.

Now you, Charlie-dinkums.

Moving nearer.

Let's do what you told me you did with him.

What did I do? When?

You told me he rubbed it till stuff came out. You said he said he was making milk.

I can't, Maudie I can't.

She holds it between finger and thumb. It hangs limply. Nothing comes out.

There I knew it wasn't true. It was all a big lie. Like the lie about the ghosts in the cave. Silly fat floppy worm. Ugh. Put it away.

I wasn't lying. Eric wasn't. It's just that.

What. What's just that?

Oh go away. Just go away, won't you.

I am going away. Back to London. And I shan't be sorry. So there.

Gone. But not the pink seam. Nor the glint of moisture threaded across its rift.

I can now, Maudie. I can now.

Gone. Crows arguing in the elms.

Maud Maud Maud Maud.

— I do hope you're eating sensibly dear, you look so pale.

It was Sunday afternoon and Beatrice was sitting with her aunt in the back parlour at Orion Parade where she had first met Maud and then, not many weeks later, come across Maud and Charles together. Her aunt glanced critically at the peacock arm-covers on her chair.

– It seems dirtier than on my last visit. – She rubbed a thumb along a greasy antimacassar. – And more vulgar. Would you look at that. – Here she turned to a velvet screen framed with gold leaf. Maud had hidden behind it once, to give Mr Birkett a fright.

– It comes from Italy, aunt. An heirloom made in Naples. Mrs Birkett has Italian blood, I believe.

– That explains it then – her aunt sniffed, having disposed of an entire culture. Beatrice glanced out of the window. Mrs Birkett was standing in the unkempt bottle-littered garden staring up into the bare cage of the plum-tree. Her voluminous flowered housecoat billowed like a dirty sail. Meanwhile Ulysses went prowling with savage intent along the top of the cracked wall that had begun to give up its fight to keep the garden from plunging down into the kitchen. Aunt Millicent sighed for her attention.

– I could wish you had continued teaching. That nice Mrs Eddles. And so close to the manor. What an entrée that would have been. – Her aunt sighed again, evidently having bathed her previous suspicions of the Tremains in a blueblooded glow. – But I suppose the war has changed everything. Even the trains don't run on time anymore. Would you believe I was delayed for half an hour this morning because of some troop movement.

– That would be the First Battalion.

Her aunt looked up quizzically. She had not expected this headstrong niece of hers to be conversant with military matters as well. Beatrice continued, warmed by the thought that, in speaking of these things she was silently inviting Charles back into her life – They've finished training up north and come down to join the Second Battalion. The regiment's due to leave for Egypt soon.

– Where half will die of dysentery no doubt and the other half get wounded and come home to be nursed by you. Well, well, I suppose it had to be. And I can't say I'm not proud of you dear, working down in that dreadful fort. It's just that I'd hoped you might have found better lodgings by now. Somewhere, shall we say, more refined.

Her aunt raised a little phial of sal volatile to her nostrils as if reminding herself of a more salubrious world. Beatrice walked over to the window and leant her forehead against the grimy glass. It was true. Orion Parade was a desolate, constrained and indigent place. With a little shiver of disgust she remembered how, going down into the kitchen that morning to fetch milk, she had come across broken egg shells half full of some nameless jellied substance floating in an empty potted meat can on the draining board. When you walked across the communal bathroom the floor-tiles shifted on a bed of slime. Smears of excrement lodged under the rim of the lavatory bowl on the first floor and there were dark urinous stains behind the sink. Yet for a while she had been happy here, with Maud, two friends against the world. Dislodged from a crevice by Ulysses's progress along the brickwall, a snail was crawling slowly up the pane, leaving a wake of frothy bubbles. The delicate horns wavered in the wintry air. She turned back into the room.

– It's a place to stay. And one shouldn't make too much of one's own comforts in times like these. Look at what our soldiers have to suffer.

Once, not so many weeks ago, such words would have carried a certain conviction. No longer. For she was not happy any more. How could she be? Maud had grown distant since the incident in the cloisters, as if sensing her dismay and confusion. After writing to apologise for not meeting her on the pier, Charles had made no further contact. Sometimes Beatrice felt she would have preferred her original loneliness, when she had first come to Chalkhampton as a VAD. Then at least she had been troubled by nothing but the past. No. She was not happy. Yet could see no way of escaping this leaning tenement where a woman in a flowered housecoat stared for hours at a tree trunk and a snail dragged its frilled body up a filthy window. Suddenly sickened by her life, she went and knelt with her back to her aunt's knees, in a gesture that recalled long ago afternoons of childhood. Her aunt touched whispery lips to Beatrice's coil of hair.

— What if you came and lived with me?

Beatrice, who had grown used to the idea of fighting an endless rearguard action alone in Chalkhampton, was shocked and not a little displeased at the rush of excitement which this question induced in her. But reined herself back.

— I couldn't leave Chalkhampton, Aunt. I couldn't stop nursing.

Her aunt gave a little laugh.

— No one was suggesting you should. But what if I left home to come and live here. What do you say to that?

Again Beatrice attempted to restrain and control her turbulence. But felt herself falling inexorably back into the circle of a long-missed family protection. Aunt Millicent was sniffing the phial again.

— You recall Dr Blake's plans. That I should come down to live by the sea. It seems now my health makes a move imperative. In fact I already have a property in mind. Number one, Artillery Row. Do you know the street? Appropriate name don't you think in these militaristic times.

Beatrice draggled after her aunt though the empty rooms of the house in Artillery Row as though she herself were a ghost, doomed to haunt the site not of her past undoing but of some future escape into soul-destroying security. Although the house had been cleared after the death of the previous owner, little signs of his occupancy lay littered here and there: a broom in the larder, a pair of gumboots in the scullery, a broken-spined copy of *The Cloister and the Hearth* on a window-ledge in an upstairs bedroom. Out in the front garden some conifers swayed dimly in the wintry gloom. At the back a long strip of garden sloped between more conifers mixed with shrubs towards the embankment of the very railway she had travelled along that Good Friday before the war. Letting her gaze cross unkempt vegetable beds, some ruinous cold frames and the brick plinth of a cess-pit, Beatrice finally came to concentrate on the distant ridge of Thundersbarrow. With melancholy relish she sat down by the window and imagined herself already living here whilst the war still raged, endlessly, on the far side of the Channel. She would grow old, a spinster. And still Charles and Maud and Eric would come to haunt her dreams, as if searching for some appeasement which only she could provide. Then it was that a most extraordinary happiness seemed to flood into her, from Thundersbarrow or the embankment or the frowsy tummocked back garden. It was, she knew, a happiness quite independent of any personal fate, a happiness without source or end. In this upstairs room with its peeling flowered paper and its solitary damaged book, she had been shown how the stream of happiness might come to her if she were to let it. So that she stood up and went running downstairs in an access of excitement and joy. This was where she wanted to live, now that she had been allowed her vision, here in Artillery Row. So that her aunt who had been inspecting cupboards and running a critical forefinger along the tops of pelmets was quite taken aback and had to sit down under the burden of Beatrice's vehemence.

– Goodness gracious dear – she gasped fumbling for her scented phial – I was right after all. There's colour in your cheeks already. And on such a cold day! I shall tell the agent to go ahead at once. Though the sale back home may take some little time.

And Beatrice, who had realised in the sudden uplifting of her soul that the stream of this happiness was threaded with pain and remorse, nodded furiously, her eyes brimming tears.

It was late when Beatrice arrived back at Orion Parade after a three course meal with her aunt in the restaurant of the Grand Hotel. If the mood of elated melancholy which had descended on her in the empty house lasted throughout the consommé, it was beginning to fragment into a more restless gloom by the time she was halfway through her plate of devilled kidneys. Beyond the great curtained restaurant windows the waves were slapping against the iron girders of the pier. Forking at her now regretted choice of urinous organs, how could Beatrice not be reminded of the ghost train or before that, of a certain locum fortune-teller in her booth. After the main course had been cleared away and she had started, under the unctuous gaze of her aunt, on a dish of chocolate-coated profiteroles, it was Frith's words that came back into her mind: *I saw you going up together in the lift at the Grand.* Then, biting into the sweet mush ('horse turds' Maud had called them, once), she was assailed by Charles's *I couldn't keep away* overheard from the parlour in Orion Parade. So she who, looking out that afternoon across the back garden of the empty house in Artillery Row, had found herself willing to embrace a radiant loneliness, plunged now into the old chaos of feeling, a chaos made the more intense by thoughts of what lay awaiting Charles's Regiment, on the other side of the Channel. By the time she had finished a second cup of coffee, Beatrice's agitation had coagulated round a persistent and fierce dyspepsia.

Orion Parade was quiet, so quiet that, creeping up the stairs she was obliged, with much embarrassment, to endure the yelps and squeals of her own stomach as it attempted to digest an unaccustomed opulence. She passed Maud's door which was closed as usual, her friend having taken to going out almost every night over the last week, although Beatrice dared not guess where or with whom. So to her own room and the mechanical rite of pacing which had emerged almost as a mirror of Maud's absence, driving Beatrice back and forth ten paces each way between the window and the door, as if the sheer monotony of the action would somehow erode anxiety to something softer and more malleable. But the rite never succeeded, however Beatrice blanked out her mind by counting her steps or reciting *The Lady of Shallot*. Always they would creep back in, then arrange themselves slowly, lasciviously, in various entangled and alarming postures on the back of her flickering eyelids. Tonight there were sounds as well, low and irregular which she made a feeble attempt to attribute to Mr Birkett who, she knew, must be up still, planning a new running order for the concert, now it was definitely known the Regiment would contribute entertainment as well as audience. But always the sounds flowed back to circle the nightmare of Maud and Charles's coupling. So she tramped on, moaning and hugging herself, while in the dark region below her stomach, several cramps

241

announced a monthly that she knew would test to the limit her new-found acceptance of all bodily functions.

Suddenly she stopped, her heart pounding. There had been a new noise, a noise that could have nothing whatsoever to do with her landlord. At first she thought it might be rain blowing hard against the window. But she had been outside an hour earlier and the November night was quite windless then, as well as clear. She waited. And would have gone back to her rite of pacing, if the noise hadn't recurred, more forcefully this time and accompanied by the murmurs which earlier she had wanted to attribute to Mr Birkett. Quickly, with a feeling of hot guilt as if she were somehow herself an intruder, she went across to the window and twitched back the curtain. At first the back garden seemed crammed wth shadow. Gradually, as her eyes grew accustomed to the darkness, there came into focus the plum-tree which Mrs Birkett had stared at so forlornly that afternoon. Against its trunk leant a figure in a trenchcoat. His hands were cupped to his face, funnelling a voice that combined urgency and an almost drowsy insouciance.

– Drop the key down, darling. Do stir yourself and open up.

Beatrice flinched as a third shower of small pebbles spattered against the glass. She saw now that the salvo had originated from a second figure who was closer to the house, on the gravelled area in front of the kitchen. The face of this figure, though raised in her direction, had no distinguishing features at all and with a little shiver she remembered the rhododendron alley at Ecclesden, the mask eaten by moonlight. Tonight, if anything, the effect was more extreme and she would have cried out if, at that very moment, the window next to hers hadn't rattled open. She had already recognised Charles's voice despite its slur. Now she was certain his summons had not been directed at her. Swaying back into the darkness of her own room, she wanted nothing but oblivion and curled up with her knees against her chin on the cold bed.

They had been summoned by the number of paces. Six hundred and sixty-six steps she had taken, between window and door. A magic number that could not be ignored, being the number of times a peacock will display to its mate. They had flown all the way from Ecclesden, in the darkness. Now they would dance for her. Here in the room. And sing. The dance of love and loss. The song of him and her.

Her watch was over on the sideboard so she had no idea of how much time had passed since she had lain down. But the softening drag in her loins was urgent. She must get up and go to the bathroom at once. It was then that she realised the dream had not dispersed. The song of the peacocks was all around her in the room. Only it wasn't peacocks any more but human sounds. She sat up shivering on the side of the bed. In place of the voices she had heard coming from the garden, there were cries now, the cries which voices die into when all words are exhausted. Groping for her dressing-gown Beatrice heard and did not want to hear. The air was vibrating like a membrane, swelling and shrinking and swelling wth an urgency she could neither flee from nor repel, a repeated, monotonous, rhythmic cry that strangely parodied Maud's sup- pressed stammer. For it was Maud, crying in her locked room, crying out of the mirror of another's desire. Terrified, her arms across her face as if she were running toward a sheet of flame, Beatrice plunged into the corridor. Passing Maud's room she paused for a moment, despite herself, straining like a thief and heard the tide of cries resolve itself at last into the simplest of all speeches.

Oh yes yes yes yes.

So Maud's chanted affirmation dragged Beatrice down into the pit of herself. Yet at this darkest moment when, independent of any volition, her eyesight pierced the door, illuminating a rumpled bed on which Charles's thrusting buttocks lay cradled between Maud's rather bony thighs, Beatrice felt again, briefly yet intensely, the elated resignation which had come to her at Artillery Row. And feeling it, she knew too that the time for such things was not yet. It was as if the echoes of the empty house had sent a message to her here, on the cold landing, saying: *Do not come to me yet. You have still to struggle with these friends who turn to demons; these ghosts transformed into lovers.* And in the clammy bathroom where diarrhoea and blood had to be dealt with in swift and scalding succession, she found herself gritting her teeth to expel not only the waste matter of jealousy but a more sweetly subtle essence, absorbed in part from her aunt, which would have had her hide away, numbed and afraid. But she would not be afraid; and she would not grow numb. Or not yet. When she returned to her room it was empty of noises. They would begin again of course, if not tonight then tomorrow night and on every other night of her life. But for now, lying alone in Orion Parade, Beatrice felt a cold certainty. Charles would never love her as he loved Maud. But she would love him despite his betrayals. And that love would bind him more tightly to her than he could ever imagine. So that in the end, perhaps, he would die for her.

The next morning she felt too unwell to go to the hospital and was obliged to send word by one of the other tenants. She lay in bed with cramps that were partly gastric and partly menstrual but folded together and swaddled in the sweetly dark knowledge of the night. Maud's room was deadly quiet. For a time she could have imagined that her two betrayers lay there still, like a couple trapped in the lava flow from Vesuvius, frozen in their interlocked writhings, faces racked with satisfaction, mockery and rage. But, stumbling to the bathroom, she noticed that the door had been left on the latch. She peeped inside. The bed was made once more and Maud's hairbrushes lay as they always did, in a semi-circle on the little glasstopped dressing table. Nothing seemed out of place. Standing there in her anguish, Beatrice was assailed with the thought that Maud had, in fact, been out all night. What she had seen and heard must have been illusion brought on by pain and suspicion. But then she noticed the muddy bootmark near the fireplace. Her relief was unspeakable. So that she actually thanked Charles aloud for having left this unmistakable clue. To have been betrayed was one thing. To have been deprived of all evidence was quite another.

So she went back to bed, her relief issuing in tears which induced a headache, the headache in its turn producing the familiar slowly turning blood-sphere somewhere at the centre of her skull. Deep within this revolving disc of pain she seemed to come to a narrow place where many people jostled this way and that, cursing and shouting. Then the crowd vanished and she was alone, running down a slope, in terrible fear. Even as she ran she knew that the dream, or a variation of it, had occurred before. And knew too that its obscure meaning seemed to prefigure as much as it remembered. Then the slope too fell away. The red sphere dissolved.

– Yes yes yes.

Had they come back to torment her a second time? Were they doing it in her room now, beside her own bed, on the floor?

– Yes. He's right for once.

– Maud? Is it you. What time is it? Where are you?

Either her eyes wouldn't open or the room had filled with some of the darkness of dream. Then the shadow materialised, standing beside her bed. Beatrice felt a coolness brush her forehead.

– Walt told me. You've slept all day. The old trouble is it?

Maud's voice was soft and cool like her fingers. Beatrice struggled to rise. To escape the soft pressure of Maud's being.

– No. It's not. Or not just that. – A wave of revulsion swept through her and she dragged Maud's fingers away as if they were parasites, sucking her strength. There was a pause. Then Maud rattled something on the sideboard.

– I've brought you some broth. On a tray. Do you want to sit up? Or shall I leave it for later?

Another pause. While Beatrice wrestled with the desire to scream at her former friend, *Go away. Leave me alone.* Knowing all the time that she wanted her to stay. If only to confirm the mystery of things. Maud sighed.

– It's only a period dear. And perhaps a stomach upset. You're not dying.

Yes yes yes.

Involuntarily, out of a humiliation which was also dependence, Beatrice moaned a long low moan. She had loved this woman, in her new-found sense of freedom after the suffocating summer at Ecclesden, loved and respected her. For Maud had been the beacon of that freedom. But now, with horrible rapidity, she was guttering back into the same darkness and suffocation that had engulfed Charles. Maud had sat down on the bed. Beatrice could feel the warm weight of her. So close. Yet remote as a star. Unknowable. She sighed again.

– If you think I'm going to apologise.

– Perhaps I should. For living.

Beatrice hoped her bitterness had a suitably ice-hard ring. Yet suspected it would always be damp. At the core.

– Oh don't be so soppy, Beatrice. Self-pity doesn't become you. – Then with a sigh that wasn't altogether disingenuous, – If you must know, we thought you were staying with your aunt. At the Grand. Walt got it wrong as usual. It was just an unfortunate mix-up. A coincidence.

So the terror and excitement of the world could, in another's eyes, become one more weary link in an endless chain of causes and effects. Beatrice gulped to swallow her tears. But said nothing. There was another pause. Maud leant over to the sideboard.

– Won't you have some of this? Mrs B made it specially. A sort of Dickensian gruel. But then she's a bit of a Mrs Crupp herself, don't you think? Do you remember that character? In *David Copperfield*?

The tray was floating towards her. Beatrice lurched at it, shouting,

– Why me! Oh God, why me!

The soup rose in a ragged sheet and spattered the lino. The bowl had shattered into many shards. Beatrice slumped back, into her misery. Maud had stood up.

– Shall I go then? You want me to go? – Then *sotto voce* – Sheer bloody hysteria that's what it is. Womb-fever. I'd better go.

Beatrice could not reply. For she did not know the answer. A voice on the stairs quavered up.

– Is everything all right?

– Quite all right, thank you Mrs B. Just a small accident. Miss Lumley says the soup is delicious.

Then Maud was busying herself gathering up the fragments of the bowl and piling them on the tray.

– I'll tell her you'd finished it before the plate fell accidentally. Have you a towel for the floor?

Still Beatrice lay dumb. *Yes yes yes.* Maud drew nearer again. But did not sit.

– Look, Beatty. He's just a man. A fuck. If I like a man and he likes me. Well. And this was for old time's sake. The Regiment's leaving soon.

Still Beatrice lay, hearing but unable somehow to connect what she heard with anything in her own memory or experience. Maud ran her hand back over her head. And sighed again.

– He wanted you, of course. I always knew that. But you frightened him off. You were too, how can I put it, pure. That was why he didn't meet you on the pier. He'd come to the conclusion that it was better that way. He told me something of what happened that summer you see. So I do understand.

And Beatrice, lying in her Vesuvian coffin, all fish below the waist, lying and not wanting to lie, there on her bed of shame, knew for the first and last time that nothing can be shared, that each howls in the cave of the heart alone forever. And in this knowledge found a tiny part of her voice again, dry and withered and old.

– You disgust me.

Just a man, a fuck.

She had gone. But later that evening, when Beatrice was obliged to change her protection in the bathroom, Maud came back briefly across the threshold from which she had been so utterly and despairingly dismissed. Beatrice had failed to lock the door properly and looked up in alarm from where she must squat on the bowl in a chaos of towels and paper. Maud smiled out of the great distance into which, so she implied, she had completely, if temporarily, withdrawn.

– If it's any consolation he's no good. Between the sheets I mean. Limp in fact. And you should see his skin. Like a dragon he is, all scaly. Why he hasn't consulted a specialist I don't know.

Beatrice's feebly flapping hand might have raised a wind to blow her former friend off the surface of the earth. Or underneath it. When she glanced down into the flushed bowl, an egg of blood remained, its crimson yoke dissolving round the central ruby seed.

She flushed again and cried to see the egg turn to a bronze and green eye at the centre of a peacock feather.

I don't think she likes me any more. Your mater I mean.

Why do you say that?

(Not that I don't know. Your hair. Your small bust. Your gift of blazing, unaccountable insight. Mirror mirror.)

You like me though, still, don't you, Charles?

Whatever makes you say such a daft thing? Of course I do, Maudie.

Call me Maud now. I prefer it. I'm not a child any more.

Maud, yes.

Is Eric still your friend?

Eric? You're pulling my leg.

I'm not. I want to know.

After the landslide in Dragon Pit? After the way his old man went for pater. In the quarry. With a pick. Only pater's too strong for him of course.

(That's not the version I heard.)

Eric still my friend? After all that? Enemy more like. Not that I'd deign to give him the satisfaction of thinking us at war.

I think your pater likes me. I caught him looking at me in the hothouse the other day.

Yes. I'm sure he likes you.

Aren't you jealous?

What? That he likes you?

Because he looked at me I mean. Aren't you just a teeny bit jealous.

Of my own father. Maud Egerton. Don't be preposterous.

(But he was looking. Looking and undressing. So that you should have felt exposed. Under the Brown Turkey Fig. Hung all over with hard green flasks. But didn't. As though it were natural to be looked at in that way. By him.)

He wants me to go abroad with him this summer. A sort of Grand Tour. Says it'll broaden my education. But I don't want to go. I don't want to leave you.

Why not? I'm only a cousin several times removed. A poor relation.

Maud don't say things like that. It makes you sound so. Well. Bitter.

Why not? Why shouldn't I be? Down here? Amongst all this? You don't know what it's like not to have a father and mother. To be an orphan.

You've got Aunt Constance.

That cow!

She brought you up.

To be inferior. To be told I was worthless. To be reminded of my ill-starred birth. Constantly. By Constance. Don't talk to me about my Aunt Constance.

But you can't help the fact that your mother died when you were young.

Having me, Charles. She died having me. Eclampsia. I killed her.

No you didn't.

I did I did. I killed my mother. Oh why don't you go? Go on your Grand Tour with your cheating vindictive all-powerful father.

If I go you'll go. That's what I meant. You'll go away from Ecclesden and never come back.

Of course I'll go, Charles. I have my work to do.

You mean the pamphlets. The what do you call it, women's union or guild or whatever.

The WSPU. Women's Social and Political Union. Which is another reason why your mother hates me.

I think it's all rot. The votes for women talk.

Of course you do. You're a man. Men don't have to give birth.

You don't like me any more do you, Maudie?

I told you, don't call me that.

But you don't.

It can't work, Charles. We've grown up. I knew this would be the last holiday.

(Yes. The last. And then you'll go. And never come back. Or not until it's too late.)

Charles stop crying. Please.

It's just that. . .it's just that. Oh bloody hell, Nimrod. Stop panting. I'll take you in a minute.

It had to be like this, Charles. Like they say in the quarry chapel. It was ordained. Long before our births. A sort of destiny.

Lully lullay. Lully Lullay.

The falcon hath borne my mate away.

What's that girl screeching now? Doesn't she know I have a headache?
It's for Robert, mother. He'll only settle for her.
Where's the governess, for God's sake. Where's Jupp?
Robert won't have her mother. Only Maud.
She will have to go. It's come at last. Though God knows I tried.
No Mother. Please no.
Don't paw me like that, Charles. You're not a girl. Are you?
(It was ordained. Long before our births. A sort of destiny. Oh Maud Maud Maud Maud they were crying and calling.)

It was a measure of Beatrice's painfully won independence that, after the scarifying encounter with Maud, she did not, as she might have been tempted to do a year previously, take refuge in any long-drawn-out and debilitating illness. However self-pitying she might be inclined to feel, she knew that her responsibility still lay at the hospital where she was back the day after, dealing with three new cases just in from France, all of them wounded by the same sniper on the same stretch of Front. She knew too, that many of her initial reactions after the shock of her return to Orion Parade had been, if not downright false, then coloured at least by a certain grandiosity of self-regard. Walking through the bleak November light of the ward, with her period still in full spate, attending now to a novice's uncertain bed-making (how this reminded her of her own tentative beginnings), now to a cry for water that summoned up a ghostly no man's land to hover round its haunted victim, she was inclined to cast a more sober eye on the things she had thought and said. However painful it had been, that night of sounds and imaginings, it could not by any stretch of the imagination be accounted a betrayal. Hadn't she long ago given up any claim on Charles's heart, as long ago at least as the letter from the camp on Salisbury Plain. Absurd then to behave like the wronged virgin in some melodrama of unrequited passion. The two meetings which she had subsequently had with Charles had done nothing, if she looked hard enough, to mend this absolute break. Indeed, if she took time to relive the second encounter in the parlour at Orion Parade, it became obvious that both Charles and Maud had, in their different ways, been trying delicately to hint that they had a prior claim on each other. Then had come the aborted meeting on the pier. After which she had done nothing. Not because she was too frightened or confused. But because she had already accepted unconsciously the fact of Charles's distance and unattainability. And not only accepted but welcomed it. If Maud meanwhile for whatever motive (*He's just a fuck, Beatty*; although even now such would-be cynicisms seemed more smoke-screen than revelation), had stepped in where she, Beatrice, had had no real desire to venture a second time, could she complain? Such behaviour was not only absurd but hypocritical too. She had had her chance. Now leave the stage for others. Having arrived at this cool peak of self-analysis, Beatrice could be seen to grimace in a thin-lipped way that had a few of the younger, fitter patients referring to her somewhat unflatteringly as The Hag.

Yet underneath her frozen exterior, Beatrice still burned with a desire to understand and to love. Indeed, her swift resignation to the fact that she could not count herself a victim, actually seemed to deepen and clarify this desire. Often, whilst travelling to and from the hospital (Maud had discreetly taken to journeying at different times), she would be reminded of that strange emptiness of exhilaration which she had experienced in Artillery Row. Although she had already adjured herself with a talismanic *Not yet* (there was in any case the complicated business of buying and selling in which her aunt was now embroiled), Beatrice came to see that this shock of estrangement must be a sort of prelude to the coming change in her life. And if this meant that she would somehow lose all those who had been dear to her she could not, she realised, allow the loss to occur without taking steps to understand, to ferret for explanations, in short to confront those she loved with the fact of this imminent loss. She must talk to Maud again. And Charles. And Eric. She could no longer be passive. She must see through this love, such as it was, to the end.

But however much she attempted to put this new-found belief

into action Beatrice was continually rebuffed. She had hoped at first that Charles might repeat his clandestine visit, so that she could confront him in some quiet, unassuming but ungainsayable way. He didn't. Meanwhile, Maud would come back late or not at all and leave before anyone was up. Beatrice thought of writing to Charles. But decided that this would compromise her dignity. Then she thought of going to see Eric; until the memory of the ghost train put all such designs to the torch. At last when she was beginning to sink back into a despondency that could only presage the return of self-pity and inaction, two things happened which simultaneously galvanised her and introduced a new inhibiting force into her life. It was like climbing to a ledge in the quarry and finding the ground drop away from you. Or so she remembered afterwards. When it was too late.

The two things happened on the same Saturday morning, after a rehearsal the evening before in which Maud had not only studiously avoided her former friend, but sung in an offhand and slapdash way that had had Mr Birkett beside himself with rage.

– Up. Up. Think of your mouth as a hole in which the divine afflatus vibrates . . .

– Walt. You've got your holes mixed up again.

The usual sniggers from the chorus. While Beatrice, beyond both shock and amusement, simply stared.

Then in the morning Maud was gone. *For the weekend*, according to her impresario, who evidently associated this disappearance with the unfortunate rehearsal. *To London. About some business.* His words trembling with the fear that she might not return. Beatrice too, felt apprehensive, peeping in at the room from which Charles's boot print had long been erased. There was some sort of tailor's dummy in the corner. And a profusion of sewing materials which she had not seen before. If this was indeed the end, the end of their friendship as well as their estrangement, how could Beatrice cross to the next phase of her life, when she would live with her aunt, then become a ward sister and finally leave England altogether to nurse in France? There was too much unfinished business. Too many frayed threads like the ones in that green canvasy-looking cloth swaddled round the feet of the dummy.

– Oh and there's a letter for you. – Mr Birkett called up, from the hall.

It was not a letter. But a ticket: *Admit one. Whitehawk Camp. Open Afternoon. 3 to 6 PM. Sunday the —th November.* Wrapped round the ticket was a newspaper cutting: *Omnibuses leave the Clocktower at 2.30 precisely. Do not miss this golden opportunity to be with friends and loved ones. Remember! The regiment goes overseas in less than a month's time.*

Who had sent this information. Charles? Eric? A ghost? Its arrival not only seemed to comment obscurely on Maud's sudden departure, but also pre-empted Beatrice's desire for action. If she went to the camp now and confronted Charles it would be because she had been summoned. Yet if she didn't go it would seem that she had achieved none of the difficult resignations and acceptances of the last few days. Charles, who by now had undoubtedly learnt about Beatrice's presence on the night of his tryst, would suspect that beneath her womanly exterior lurked the same raw and timidly forward girl he had known at Ecclesden. She could bear to be alone; she could not bear to be underestimated. The ticket and the newspaper cutting, so nearly screwed up and thrown into the fire, were carefully slipped back inside the envelope and put in a place of safe-keeping.

The omnibus route ran east along the promenade then followed the cliff road out to Whitehawk Camp. The mood on board was festive. Some sang. Many had brought drinks and sandwiches. All looked forward to seeing husbands, brothers, fiancés. Only the nurse, huddled in her trenchcoat near the front, seemed not to want to take part, ignoring one man's slightly slurred imperatives to *Join in the chorus*, refusing with a firm politeness all offers of fruitcake wedges, hardboiled eggs, swigs of cider. She preferred, it seemed, to watch the road, which had turned away from the cliff to make its increasingly rough way through allotments, over the blurred ramparts of a camp where the charred skulls of primitive men had once been unearthed, suggesting to the horrified diggers a race of cannibals, sucking their enemies' brains in the windy lee of a chalk rampart. Beyond this ancient place of murder or worship, the wire and nissan huts of a more modern encampment lay, no less desolate, though reeking more of drudgery and petty discipline than pagan savagery. The singing in the omnibus stopped. People were seen to draw their coat collars up and hunch down as if the wind had grown suddenly stronger. Only the nurse, from her fastness of trenchcoat, seemed positively to welcome the sight, leaning forward and squinting as if she could see through solid matter. Now, from inside the camp, a faint crepitation and wheeze of brass floated out to greet them. *They're going to play us in*, someone muttered, his croaked words sounding more like a premonition of emprisonment than a delighted anticipation of festival. So the bus entered the gates to the accompaniment of 'Men of Harlech'. When the band had finished, the civilians applauded decorously and began filing down the spiral staircase. Their mood had grown sombre. Although soldiers hugged and kissed and were hugged and kissed in return, there were few smiles. All knew how many meetings like this remained. Some turned a brief wary gaze on the Channel where the Regiment would soon be sailing. A few glanced in admiration or resentment at the nurse. She, they now realised, had known all along. Somehow she seemed already to have suffered what they could only guess at, then shy away from. The thought made them angry yet resigned. They turned back to their loved ones.

Beatrice for her part felt numb and alone. Lingering by the bus she deeply regretted the decision to come. There was no one here to meet her. The letter had never been meant for her in the first place. Maud should have been the recipient. And now she must endure her loneliness afresh, in this crowd where everyone seemed to have a partner or a companion. On the roof of the camp HQ a Union Jack slapped hollowly in the wind.

– Hello, Miss Lumley. It's grand here isn't it. Have you got a brother in the Chums?

She turned to find a rather lanky boy in blazer and short trousers standing between two nissan huts. Almost simultaneously a warm muzzle pushed against her hand.

– Robert! And Nimrod? No. Of course not. It's the other one. The bitch he named after that Tennyson poem. I forget . . .

– Oenone. Though I always call her Oene for short. Come here Oene, don't jump up like that.

– Oh I don't mind, – Beatrice lied.

– You won't be able to do that in Egypt you know. Jump up and paw the fuzzie-wuzzies. You're going to be Charlie's secret weapon. Did you know that?

Snuffling happily, Oenone slid her paws down Beatrice's coat, leaving two muddy trails.

– To Egypt, you say. He's taking her with him?

– Oh yes. And to France afterwards. Because that's where they'll be going eventually. Charlie's had it from high up. Some friend of mother's. A brigadier. They'll be in France by the spring. Though I'm not supposed to tell you.

Looking down at the dog, who had decided to roll on a patch of grass, Beatrice felt a curious sadness, as if its unquestioning involvement in what it could not understand somehow reflected on the emotional storms she had endured over the last few days. When she looked up it was through a film of tears.

– But not Nimrod, – she said, if only for something to say.

– Oh no. Nim's too old. He just sleeps all day now. But I say, have you got a brother then?

Beatrice hesitated, hoping to be rescued by the sight of the man she had come to see, out of a desire which was still not wholly clear to her. All around them soldiers and their families were moving off in the direction of the rifle range where there was to be a short speech given by the Colonel followed by a football match between First and Second Battalions.

– No. I . . . I've come to see Eric.

At this the schoolboy burst into an alarming peal of laughter.

– What, the limeburner? Haven't you heard? He's been banged

255

up. In the glasshouse. For desertion. If it hadn't been for Charlie, they'd have shot him. You can't see the limeburner. – Then, with a little catch in his voice. – I used to like him. I used to think he was brave. But he's not. He's just a bloody coward. Fancy running away from the best regiment in the world. – Robert paused to scratch a violet scarred knee. His look brightened. – Charlie wouldn't run away. D'y know he can hit a target at fifty paces. With his Webley. He's going to bring me a Picklehosen. And a stick grenade. Defused of course. Charlie's the best brother in the world. – Robert paused again and looked down. – She's coming back you know. Back to Ecclesden. And I don't want her to. Not any more.

Aghast, Beatrice looked on as her former charge began to sob uncontrollably. She did not know whether to comfort him or tell him to pull himself together. It was too embarrassing. And confusing. Coming after such a torrent of obscure announcements. But she must do something. She glanced over to where Oenone was chewing absentmindedly on a piece of four-by-two.

– Robert. Would she like a stick thrown? I think she would. Show me how you do it.

Wiping his face on his sleeve Robert obliged. But even as the stick arced away he was snivelling again. Beatrice put her arm around him. He flinched.

– Who's coming back? Your old governess? But you're at Tongdean now. Didn't I see you once in the quad? After a rehearsal?

He nodded.

– I didn't mean the governess. I meant Maud. Maud's coming back. Because she and Charlie are going to be married. And I don't like it. It's not fair.

Oenone was bounding back with the stick. Still wrestling with the weight of Robert's unburdening, Beatrice tried to compose her thoughts. What should she say? How should she phrase her questions? About Eric. And Maud. And Charles. But suddenly a car horn sounded in the distance. Robert started.

– Crikey. Mother wants me back. She won't stay for the footer. Says it's vulgar. – Then, shifting into formal gear. – Goodbye, Miss

Lumley. It was a pleasure to talk. I like history now, you know. Especially the battles.

And he was gone. With Oenone in hot pursuit. Beatrice felt suddenly tired and cold. It seemed peculiarly pointless now to try and find Charles. Even if he had sent the invitation, which she very much doubted, he would be busy saying goodbye to his family. Her presence would only be resented, especially by his mother. Almost without realising it she had wandered in among the nissan huts and sat down on a bench by a door. The events which Robert had so hastily described tumbled back and forth in her mind without rest. How much of it was true? And if it was true what did it mean? Eric a coward? He who had shepherded his men away from the pier with such an easy authority. Maud about to return to a place she had always said she hated to the bottom of her heart? And she and Charles to be married? So Beatrice peered down into herself, searching for answers to questions that a cynical experience should have told her to dismiss, if a lingering innocence did not oblige her to ignore.

She must have dozed off in that windy duckboarded ravine, for when she opened her eyes he was standing right in front of her. She struggled to get up but he put out a restraining hand and pointed behind her.

– You're not waiting for him, are you? You'll have to sit there a long time.

Craning round she saw a blackboard leaning against the wall of the hut. Its chalk notice read: *Sweeney Todd, Your friendly Demon Barber*. Charles smiled. Then his face darkened.

– I didn't believe him when he told me. My little brother I mean. How did you get hold of the ticket?

Bridling under an interrogation whose peremptoriness seemed to imply she was beholden to military authority, Beatrice blurted,

– Because you sent it. I don't know why. Guilt maybe. Or because you wanted to say goodbye. And now you regret it and want to pretend you didn't.

257

– Me! I can assure you, Beatrice. Wait a minute. Eric. He's behind this. Even though I got him out of a tight spot. He still wants to humiliate me. But I've got the measure of him now.

Again Beatrice felt the tears start to her eyes. Yet determined to pretend they were caused by the whipping wind.

– You mean to say my presence humiliates you? You still know how to pay a girl a compliment and that's a fact.

The rash on Charles's neck deepened, despite the cold.

– I . . . I thought you were going to harangue me, Beatty. For what I did. Yes. She told me everything. We didn't want to cause you pain. It was all a damn silly coincidence.

– Pain? Pain? Why should I care what you do. Now. After all this time. Because we spent half an hour together in the aquarium? You're an acquaintance, Charles. That is all. At least do me the honour not to assume anything deeper.

She paused, depressed at the anger in her words, at the knowledge that such anger could still be summoned up.

– Then why did you come? Why did you expect me to ask you?

Charles folded his arms and waited. She could not answer. It was true. Her attempts to distance herself always ended like this. She looked up.

– Because of Maud. Because she was, I mean, is, my friend. And I need to know.

Charles did not meet her gaze. Over on the HQ roof the ropes on the flagpole were gibbering as if tormented.

– All that's over now. It was just a game. Something we never finished when we were young. With you it was never a game. And I thought. After the aquarium. That we might. Oh hell, Beatty. I always get things muddled, don't I?

Beatrice determined not to be drawn into the morass of Charles's motivation.

– Is that why she's gone to London? Because the game, as you call it, is over?

They're going to be married. Robert's words vibrated in her mind. But she would keep them sealed in. For the moment. Charles looked round as if he expected an eavesdropper. Then leant forward.

– Can you keep a secret?

It was the old trick. The promise of some fascinating intrigue in a clandestine world which she was expected to acknowledge and pay court to, even as she accepted her perpetual exclusion. Once she might have been drawn. But not any more. Beatrice sighed with cold resentment.

– If it's a secret worth keeping you wouldn't be telling me.

Charles ignored this and hurried on.

– She's gone to see about a marriage licence.

He had pre-empted her, cheerfully confessing what she had supposed she must prise out of him. Her chest pounded. The moment had come.

– I'm not quite sure of the details. But she had a letter from her guardian saying that some information had turned up about her natural mother. At Somerset House I suppose. You can imagine she was feeling pretty sensitive about it.

The moment withdrew. This had nothing to do with Robert's revelation. Which she decided to bring forth now, in desperation. But Charles, to her consternation, merely laughed.

– The little rat. That must have been, let me see, at half term. I was on leave. I argued with mater about her. I can't deny it. And Robert must have overheard. And got the wrong end of the stick. He's not happy at the moment. Tongdean's a hard place at first. But still I'll have to reprimand him.

Beatrice suspected guile but felt too weary to pursue the matter. She turned instead to the final puzzle.

– Why did Eric go missing?

– No one knows. It's something to do with those fits he used to have. When he joined up they seemed to disappear. Which was as well since he might have been pronounced unfit for active service. He was happy about it at the time, if only because he didn't have to endure what he used to call his tongues. But recently he's been hearing the tongues again though without the fits. And he's been disturbed by it all.

– So he wandered off. Charles he shouldn't be in the army at all.

– You might be right. But it would destroy him if he had to leave now. No. I've done what I can to protect him. I only hope that when we get near any action he won't funk it. That's what his voices have been telling him you see. That he's a coward underneath. And, if you must know, I suspect he is.

– So in the end, after the dig and everything, you have the upper hand.

Charles sighed.

– It gives me no pleasure I can tell you, Beatty. But gosh, look at the time. Your bus will be leaving soon. Look I can't say I was glad to see you at first. But now I am.

– Thank you for the compliment I'm sure.

Charles glanced quickly at her, abashed.

– You've changed, Beatty.

– We all have.

– I suppose it's the war. Your work.

Once again she felt his fascinated fear of sights and sounds that were daily occurrences for her but must, for the time being, remain locked in his darker dreams. It was almost as if he had grown younger since joining up.

– But we're friends still, aren't we? Despite everything that's happened.

It sounded like the pleading of someone younger even than the boy she had known at Ecclesden. So that Beatrice, who had meant to leave this place only after having said something final, went up on tiptoe to peck him on the cheek, a gesture which was nothing if not provisional. Nearby in a barred window a face stared out and blinked.

I suspect you know why I called you in here.

Yes, madam.

You may call me Aunt. Because that's what I've tried to be to you. Like Constance. A guide and a protector.

(A bully and a hypocrite.)

And all for what? This . . . this . . . filth.

'The Suffragette'? Filth? What . . .?

Don't interrupt. Look at this one on the cover. With her vulgar stole. And her hussy's smile. 'Irrepressible' indeed. I suppose you want to be like her. Eh? Do you?

I want to be like myself.

Oh clever. Clever. I suppose you thought it was clever to hand these round in the quarry too. Amongst people who can barely sign their names.

(That's part of the problem we're trying to address.)

And that card game I caught you playing with Charles. Panko. Another product of these demented women's imaginations.

(Charles thought it was dull.)

And don't think I don't know about the other matters. With Charles I mean.

(That maidservant who spied on us in the boathouse. What a baby Charles is. I shall be glad to escape this place. These people.)

I have written to Constance and await her reply. Your place now is in London. I wash my hands of you.

(Out, out damned spot.)

(I'll destroy you all in the end. One day. Somehow. I'll be here. Sowing salt in the ruins. One day.)

Hello, Maudie. I mean Maud. Want to come rabbiting? Wren's got a new terrier. Lob. Look. Oh he's off again.

Your mother had the magazines I distributed in the quarry. How did she obtain them I wonder?

How should I know?

I've no doubt your friend Wren knows. Don't you Wren? Did the voices tell you to do it? Did they say I was one of the damned?

I'll thank you not to be blasphemous. There's some round here that don't take kindly to it.

I'll be as blasphemous as I bleeding well like.

Maud.

Shut up Charles. Well, Wren. I always knew you were a sanctimonious bastard. But I didn't think you were a coward as well.

Who are you calling coward?

261

You.

If you weren't a woman I'd . . .

Well I am. I suppose you could always rape me. But then you've probably cut off your balls already as a sacrifice to Jesus Christ or whatever male idol it is you worship.

Now that's enough. Both of you. Maud, after you've gone . . .

And good riddance I say.

Eric. I don't want to fall out again. After you've gone I want to remember happy things. Please, no more hatred.

Why, because you'll cry? Is that it, Charles? Because you'll turn into a great big slobbering baby. You see I don't believe in your tears any more. You only cry for yourself.

I don't. And I don't want you to go. But mother. Oh I just thought this last day we could all try to be happy.

You'd better catch your religious lunatic up. He's almost on top of Thundersbarrow.

Won't you come too. He doesn't mean to be rude.

No. He can't help it. Go on, Charles. I'm not coming with you. I'm staying here.

Pity. I'd grown rather fond of her.

It would be tantamount to incest.

It was your idea, Katherine.

Only because I thought she might be moulded. But there's bad blood there. Her mother . . .

Or her father. Very well. I can bear the imputation. Bad blood and money. How old is she now?

Sixteen.

A pity she's so wild. But you would choose Constance. That dodo. Is it true the girl's been taken up by those Pankhursts?

In a manner of speaking, yes. And that's where the money will go. To the cause.

Eleven twelve thirteen fourteen . . . Nineteen-fifteen. She'll be twenty-one in nineteen-fifteen.

In the November.

She'll know it all then. She'll be told everything. That lawyer Annabel brought in hated me from the start. He'll rub it in hard. How much she's inherited from her mother. Who her father was. You think she's our enemy now. You wait until nineteen-fifteen.

We have no choice, Colin.

We may regret it.

Regret not having her in the house you mean.

No. Regret her money.

Don't be preposterous, Colin.

The quarry won't last forever. You know that was why old Wren wanted to open up Dragon Pit.

Are you suggesting we're dependent on the quarry. With your investments?

No of course not. It's just that there might come a time. Well. Anyway. Perhaps it's just that I'd grown fond of the girl.

Which is hardly surprising. When do you travel?

In two weeks' time. Glad to see the back of me, eh?

Are you taking Charles?

Of course. That is if I'm permitted. If you think I can be trusted not to corrupt the poor innocent.

Not so innocent. But yes. Take him. He needs distraction. He needs to forget.

Beatrice came away from Whitehawk Camp convinced neither of Charles's ability to tell the truth nor of Robert's unreliability as a witness. She realised with bitter hindsight that she should have pressed Charles harder; Robert too had been allowed simply to leave his remarks hanging in the air. But in the end it was she herself who must bear the brunt of the blame. Beginning to long now for the time when she could leave Orion Parade behind, she cursed herself for being so tenacious of the past. At the same time she found herself growing obsessed with the idea of Charles and Maud's imminent marriage, so much so that the words *She's coming back to live at Ecclesden* echoed lucidly through her dreams however murky these were, with their tangles of faceless figures and grey twilit landscapes.

Maud did not return after the weekend as expected. Mr Birkett, nervously aware of the coming dress rehearsal for the concert, grew increasingly distracted, a mood which seemed to infect Beatrice with a whole new series of anxieties. What if she never came back? The munitions works had already sent a letter to the lodging-house which the landlord took it upon himself to open, announcing in dire tones that Miss Maud was risking the sack. What if she and Charles eloped? Or died in a suicide pact? So Beatrice dragged herself to and fro between her room and the hospital, nursing the first seeds of that guilt which whispered, *It's all your fault. Telling her to get out. Prudishly lavishing on her a disgust which you felt only for yourself.*

Then, on a drizzly Wednesday morning, Maud's letter arrived. It was addressed to Mr Birkett but this increasingly gaunt and harried man had gradually taken Beatrice into his confidence over the last few days, so that she was hardly surprised when he came running up to her room and barely waited for her to make herself decent.

— Ah, Miss Lumley. News at last. They are both up there. In London. Maud and the Captain.

Beatrice's hand went instinctively to the secret pouch in her bodice. Her suspicions had been correct. She would at least allow herself a little sarcasm.

— Really. Next stop Gretna Green, I suppose. They're probably already on their way.

Mr Birkett started to laugh then stopped, not understanding. She felt an unaccustomed power flowing from her long anticipation of what would happen.

— Well, his family never approved. So it must be an elopement. The letter was probably sent after they left London.

Still her fingers stroked and stroked the invisible talisman. Strange to think that, now it had happened, she felt no emotion. An elopement before the Regiment left England. It seemed right somehow. Almost a part of some natural order of things. She found she could almost begin to approve. Until Mr Birkett whooped.

— It's . . . yes, oh I must take off my glasses, yes . . . it's a good joke. Very dry. But no they are in London still and coming back in time for the concert. The will has proved more difficult to unravel than she had expected. The Captain has gone up to assist. It is a blessing really. She never was good at keeping deadlines. But a military man. An officer. He will not allow her to shirk her duties. Married you say? Hardly. Unless some clause in the will demanded that . . .

Again he laughed, clutching the fluttering notepaper. Beatrice's mood passed rapidly from bitterness to outright rage. She fairly lurched at her landlord.

– Give me that. I must see it. Give me the bloody thing.

But Mr Birkett proved unexpectedly strong in warding off her attack. Soon she had subsided on to the bed in numb misery. The irony that this misery was caused by the absence of the very event which she had most feared, did not dawn on her until much later. For the moment she could only feel that Charles had been playing with her in some way, even though he had denied that there was anything between him and Maud. Above all she felt terribly inadequate for not having anticipated events correctly.

– What will? – she muttered at last. – He never said anything about a will.

– It's to do with her twenty-first birthday. I never gathered she *was* twenty-one, did you Miss Lumley?

Beatrice shook her head. A Scorpio.

– Yes she plays her cards close to her breast as they say. Well she has reached her majority now. It was the Friday she left apparently. How modest she can be.

Friday. A Scorpio born on All Hallows Eve.

– And that is when her natural mother's will can be read to her. She has known about it for some time it says here. There have been meetings with Lady Tremain who, of course was always something of a protector to her. It is all really rather exciting. And the Captain is such a friend to her.

Oh Charles, yes yes yes. If you must know he's no good. Between the sheets I mean. You disgust me.

Her landlord's mystifying and inconclusive précis of Maud's letter ignited in Beatrice an intense longing to confront her friend. Yet this longing was accompanied by, indeed almost seemed to arouse, an equally strong desire to avoid Maud altogether. So that each morning Beatrice prepared for work with the same hopeful fear that today would be the day her friend returned. And each evening she returned from work to find the room next to hers still empty and the fear and the hope inside her stronger than ever. For Maud did not return in good time as Mr Birkett had predicted, shepherded by the reliable Captain Tremain. Indeed by the afternoon of the Saturday of the dress rehearsal, Mr Birkett was beginning to curse all army captains as shirkers and malingerers. He even went up to Beatrice's room to ask if she had had any further thoughts about the possibility of an elopement. Hearing her own nightmare trembling on another's lips, Beatrice found herself touched by an unexpected realism. Soon enough her conviction that such an event was in fact unlikely, seemed to be confirmed by a telegram from Charles. 'Delayed By Indisposition. Apologies. M goes direct to Tongdean 1900 hours.' Mr Birkett was now beside himself with relief and would have kissed his lodger if she hadn't jinked aside telling him she must change.

That evening, when Mr Birkett burst into the hall at Tongdean with Beatrice in timid tow, Maud was already sitting by the radiator, having arrived early, as Charles had promised. Seeing her again, Beatrice was shocked by the violence of her reaction. It was like a physical version of her emotional state, for she experienced a simultaneous attraction and repulsion. But even if she had managed to reconcile these opposites, walking up to Maud to take her by the hand and thereby begin the long slow process of healing which both of them would surely require, Beatrice found herself wrongfooted, somehow, by the occasion. It was not for her to greet Maud; Mr Birkett had that honour, in tails and patent boots, at once unctuous and reproachful, conciliatory and barbed. Meanwhile the swirl of activity which the conductor's arrival in the hall generated, simply swallowed Beatrice up, so that before she knew it she was standing in the third rank of the female chorus, as distant from Maud as if she had still been in London. It was at that point, studying her friend as

266

one would a statue in a gallery, that Beatrice understood how, even if they had met, there would have been scant communication. Maud seemed to have aged during her week away, aged and hardened. There was a resolute apartness about her now, as if she had learnt personal truths that had no need of others' recognition. Then, with a little shiver of concern and puzzlement, Beatrice saw that her friend was unwell, with a high colour and a staccato way of breathing that made her clench her shoulders together, forcing them upward to expel some unwanted presence from her lungs. She smoked incessantly, dragging and puffing on a succession of Army Clubs as if the unwanted presence could be exorcised through the medium of smouldering tobacco. Surely she should not be here at all. If this was the 'indisposition' to which Charles's telegram had referred then it must have worsened since her arrival back in Chalkhampton. But if Beatrice's first instinct was protective, this soon melted into ambivalence. For the more she looked the more she became convinced that Maud's state of health was intimately linked with her new sense of herself, which had no need now of mockery or foul language, but could rest on its own security and certainty. And this in turn she felt had something to do with what Maud had endured or undertaken in London. Maud might be unwell but it was with the kind of illness that derives from revelation and a sudden access of unfamiliar power. Maud was strong in her 'indisposition'. She had no need of her friend's instinctive pity.

The first part of the dress rehearsal was a ragged, desultory affair. Both the raggedness and the desultoriness seemed to stem from the star soprano, rising up through the cloud of cigarette smoke to distract, disorder and disturb. During the Handel, Mr Birkett kept losing his place in the score; the choruses sang persistently out of tune; the violins came in too early; the horns too late. Worst of all Maud herself sang her solos with a kind of reckless abandon; it wasn't that she didn't hit the notes, more that she didn't care. At first Beatrice attributed this strange insouciance to her friend's evident ill-health. Slowly however she began to see that Maud wanted to sing like this. For this was not the voice she had inherited, to be nurtured thereafter over many years under the watchful eyes of others. This was a voice that had descended on her and her alone, suddenly, like the rage that descended on the Queen of the Night. She had caught the voice and guarded it now, jealously, in the oubliette of her racked throat and lungs. In fact the more she sang in this way, the more it became obvious that this was how she would always sing from now on. The effect was close to ugliness yet charged with a strength and authority that transcended mere aesthetics. It seemed to Beatrice that Maud's coming of age had released many unforeseen forces.

During the interval there might have been an opportunity to approach her old friend at last. Certainly, she was left well alone, the rest of the society being at once too disturbed and too impressed by this new incarnation to want to risk being near her. Even Mr Birkett kept a respectful distance, as if he recognised that a talent had tonight been transformed into something greater yet more difficult to handle. But just as Beatrice was plucking up courage, Charles, along with several other officers, came striding into the hall and, catching sight of Maud, walked straight up to her. The next moment they were both deep in conversation with Mr Birkett. Beatrice hung back. It would have been difficult enough dealing with Maud by herself. But to have Charles inserting his comments into the proceedings would have been intolerable. She was not ready, not yet. Meanwhile she could see how Maud at once grew more animated yet more guarded in front of Charles, coughing now and again into a handkerchief pulled from her sleeve. Charles was talking about the Regiment's contribution to the coming concert. There would be a brass band he said, a mime, some parlour songs. Beatrice heard his voice in that echoing place and turned away. Even when she caught sight of him trying to wave her back from the curtained entrance she pretended she had not seen and walked on into the cold night air.

– Miss Lumley, isn't it? Could you come? He needs someone like you. A nurse I mean. Quickly.

White as if powdered, set with two dark-rimmed puffy eyes, and fringed by hair that had turned from carrot to rust, Timmy Frith's head floated out of the door, the dreadful door that led to the library at the end of the cloisters. She was not going there again, not for anyone, especially this demented childman, who no doubt associated her with the exciting humiliations he had experienced at the hands of Maud. She turned to walk swiftly away, back to the real world, not realising it was ahead of her too.

– Don't go. I . . . I think he might be dying. Look. You're not allowed just to go.

Something in his shaking, unbalanced voice made Beatrice pause.

– Who is. Who is dying?

– Him. The limeburner. But he's not a limeburner now, he's a soldier. Oh why here? Why to me? I can't . . .

Frith's stifled sob dragged her forward. Into the cloister.

He had led her to a small cell of a room that lay at the bottom of some steps running down under the first of the Stone Age portraits. The walls of the cell were lined with mahogany stands on which rifles stood in rows. Frith glanced furtively out into the cloister then shut the door with a click. They were locked in. Beatrice's fingers tightened round a hatpin in her handbag.

– It's out of bounds you see, the armoury. If I'm caught down here I'm done for. No one knows I come. No one knows why. And now him. Barging in. Shouting and waving his hands about. You've got to calm him down, Miss Lumley. And get him to go away. I want to be left in peace.

These last words were spat out as if Frith's lungs were filling fast with some noxious fluid. He was drowning in himself, Beatrice realised, with a little shudder that quite excluded pity. Her hand relaxed on the hatpin. Meanwhile she had noticed an inner room which held a table on which a map lay spread. Frith pushed past and swiftly scrambled the map up into a crackling heap.

– It's the Front. I wanted to join. I know where all the battles have been. And where they will be. Oh yes. It isn't a crime, is it?

Beatrice shook her head, wondering now whether she would ever escape this demented creature.

– Of course it isn't. But they won't have me. I'm too young. But I'll get there. I'll show them.

– You said Eric Wren was here. Where please? I haven't much time.

– Not in there. In here.

Frith drew back a tarpaulin curtain that might have been the very one which used to hang over the entrance to the cave in Dragon Pit. Beatrice had a familiar sense of darkness coagulating into lumps then sliding greasily aside. Frith had retreated.

– You won't get me in there. Not again. Not after what happened on the hill. And then that bitch in the library. I can't stand it. I can't stand any of it. I'd rather be buggered all night by Jessy. That's why I'm going out. Going. Out.

Eric Wren was spreadeagled among a heap of cut-out figures that had once been used for target practice. All around lay a scatter of cartridge cases. A rifle range disappeared into the darkness behind him like a low-roofed gallery in a flint mine. So this man would always call up the ghosts of Thundersbarrow wherever he chanced to be. Frith was gibbering incoherently in the background. Eric looked up and wiped spittle from his mouth.

– I'm better now. They're gone. But it's always worse when they come these days. Much worse. Not so you'd see, mind. I just sat down here for a rest. It's the feeling they give me is bad. Still, they got you here.

– Me? You mean you planned this?

Eric Wren laughed and sat up.

– Don't plan anything, Miss. Least of all the voices, now they've turned.

– Turned? Charles said they went away for a while. Is that what you mean?

She was kneeling down to loosen his collar and take his pulse. Grand mal? Or petit mal? He really shouldn't be in the army at all.

– Went. Then came back. But from somewhere different. Not

270

from the ground any more. I can't really remember what that felt like when they came, up on the hill. Except that I used to forget myself like. No. Now they come from inside me. And stay inside. I don't forget myself now. Now I can go on drilling or what have you without anybody knowing any better. But what they say is. Different. And makes me cry longer afterwards, inside myself.

– Yes, now I come to think of it Charles did mention.

– Did he now? That's because I told him. Which was a mistake. And I bet he mentioned other things too. About how I knew I'd funk it. Did he tell you I tried to desert too? I saw you, you know, up at Whitehawk. But you were too far away for me to hear. From inside the glasshouse.

The knowledge that she had been watched while she talked to Charles so wearily that cold afternoon made Beatrice blush despite herself. She grew angry.

– Well you're all right now so I can go. I don't know how you got away with joining up in the first place. But if what you say's correct then I should think most of it's fantasy anyway. You'll be different once you're at the front. You'll forget your voices then. Or they'll forget you.

She had not meant to say so much so bitterly. And lingered, feeling guilty. Eric stood up.

– You're right to be angry. Do you remember when I asked you to climb back on the wheel? When we were on the pier?

She nodded.

– Well don't. Whatever you do, Miss Lumley, don't.

Then he told her how it had been Charles who had tried to desert, after a bayonet practice in which he had been found trembling and weeping beside a dummy spilling sawdust from a gaping hole in its side. He, Eric had gone after him, catching up with his drunken superior in the back garden at Orion Parade. The tryst with Maud that night had apparently been intended as a prelude to some more elaborate flight. But Eric and Maud had managed to persuade Charles of his folly. Later however, when they were back inside the camp, Charles had turned on Eric and accused him of desertion, seemingly out of resentment or sheer malice or shame. Got him banged up for a week too. He paused. Beatrice had squatted down on some mats used by the boys at rifle practice. She believed yet did not want to believe.

– Do you remember, Eric? At Ecclesden. When you brought me the moorhen chick. We were all on the side of life then. What happened?

He did not answer for a long time. Was this the period when he must, as he put it, cry inside?

– It's him that's the coward, miss. Not me. The new inside voices told me as soon as they started. He'll betray us all in the end.

– And Maud? Don't think I don't know about him and Maud. I was there that night you know. I heard the gravel.

– That's different too. It's not like I said it was on the pier.

– But they've . . . been together.

– But they're not going to be married or anything like that. She's going back to Ecclesden to take it over. Charles and his mother think they can rule her but they can't. She wants to destroy it all. Ever since she was told to get out all those years ago. That's what she's wanted. And now she can.

– How Eric, how?

– With money. The money they want but can't have. Unless she gives it them. Which she will. For a price. Oh yes.

– You mean because of the will. Who was her mother, Eric?

– That I don't know. But what I do know is you've got to climb off our wheel. I should've known it long ago when we rode down Thundersbarrow together in the dobbin cart. But then I was all hymn-singing and prophecy. Them's were the wrong voices. But the new ones they tell me truth. Get out, Miss Lumley. Get out now.

It was an uncanny echo of the words she had hissed at Maud. She knew he was right, this man who had never been wholly her friend, yet had shadowed her through the crises of her young womanhood. Yet where was she to go? Back to Orion Parade? Where Maud awaited her. Forward to Artillery Row where, she suspected, this platoon of ghosts would follow her, making the old intimation of a solitary and voidlike joy wither before birth. It could make no difference where she went. So she shook her head, gazing despairingly into the darkness.

– It's too late, Eric. I can't leave any of you.

Then they were hugging each other, a bereft brother and sister there in that gallery smelling of cordite and pull-through. They would never, perhaps, be as close as this again. Timmy Frith came writhing towards them.

– I know what you're talking about. You're talking about that bitch and Tremain. Paint my tummy, darling! Oh I know everything. I'm Lazarus see. Ever since you – here he writhed up and jabbed Eric with a trembling forefinger – ever since you brought me back to life up on that hill. And now I've got to die again. But they won't let me. They won't let me die.

The tears were caking the powder on his cheeks. He had slurred rouge across his lips making it look as though he had two mouths, the one superimposed badly on its failed predecessor. Now both mouths were screaming.

– I want to die. Get out. I want to die. Get out. No not that way. Back there. Down the secret tunnel. Into the hill. That's where they are. All of them. All the dead. Waiting.

Eric and Beatrice parted at the cloister entrance, their formal handshake accompanied by the subterranean wailing of Frith.

Eric was clutching two Boer War Lee Enfields from the armoury which he had been detailed by Charles to pick up for use in the mime scene at the concert. He had not been able to work out a way of seeing Beatrice in private until his voices came to tell him to fake a fit and send Frith to fetch the nurse. Now he would wait for his superior by the gate. Beatrice hurried back to the rehearsal but found that both Charles and Maud had gone, the former because of duties, the latter because of a temperature. She could not pretend she wasn't relieved. She would need time to digest Eric Wren's account of the last few weeks. Once or twice Mr Birkett caught her with eyes closed when she should have been singing. But said nothing.

Pater, I thought I'd just look in . . . Oh.

The young Count from England would like to see the pictures.

I'm not a Count and I was waiting for my father. He's just coming.

No. I see him with the Signore. There. By the trough. Talking.

Oh. Yes. Very well take me to them, these pictures.

City of ghosts. Or no. A city without ghosts. Emptied of everything but itself. Haunted by its own emptiness. There was a city in the hill you thought. Beyond the cave. Where people went when they died. This is a cave. This gloomy red barrel-vaulted place he is leading you through, his teeth clicking as he walks. That seat. Its legs have the claws of a beast. A dragon.

You like them?

A room within a room. In the heart of the hill. Figures frozen on the flaking walls in postures of love or death. Entering each other. Destroying each other. Here is the emptiness. It flows out of them. It will become a flood flowing out of the hill. His hands on her buttocks. From behind.

There are more. Many more.

I cannot look. I must look. I. Maud?

No Charlie. Not Maud. But what I could have been. If you hadn't driven me out. If you hadn't tried to destroy me.

Me. Destroy? It was them. I'm just a child. I loved you.

You stood by. And did nothing. Now I'll never come back.

Come with me now. Walk with me through these tunnels. I'm so scared.

I can't, Charlie, not any more. One day you will find someone else to walk with. Together you will visit the city under the hill you dreamed about as a child. Then the flood will come and wash your mind of its pain.

The English Lord is not well? Too much sun?

I need . . . I . . . need . . . air.

Out out down peristyle's flashing gauntlet out out through the halls of sin and thick wet flame.

Maud come back come back.

Padrone, I want money, lira, money.

Who were you talking to just now, father?

Eh? Oh no one. A ghost. You meet them all the time in these places. An American archaeologist I used to know.

Her nose. I saw her nose in his. But not her eyes, sea-green shameless eyes.

Just imagine the chaos and destruction. Lava. Mud. The sea itself withdrawing. Gases that choked and suffocated. It's all so quiet now, so peaceful.

There is no past only a present waiting to be born.

Just thank the Lord, Charles, we live in a northern latitude. No volcanoes. No earthquakes.

Thundersbarrow is a volcano. And there are earthquakes waiting in all the chalk places. Eric knows. He knows it all.

Yes a nice man that archaeologist. But broken. His beloved only daughter died young.

Her nose. I saw it. Maud. In the past that is no past.

It was late when Beatrice arrived back at Orion Parade, ahead of Mr Birkett, who had had to stay behind at Tongdean to discuss arrangements with the leader of the orchestra. No light came from Maud's room and, to Beatrice's enquiry, Mrs Birkett replied vaguely that she seemed to remember the lodger coming in about nine and going straight upstairs. Once or twice during the night Beatrice fancied she heard a cough and then a moan through walls whose thinness had once channelled sounds more exalted or demonic. But she herself was finding sleep difficult tonight, so that the coughs and moans, if that was what they were, soon blended into a fitful waking dream in which Eric and Charles went running ahead of her along the pier, laughingly refusing to slow down and listen to her gasped and endlessly repeated entreaty: *Tell me where it's hidden oh tell me where it's hidden.* By dawn Beatrice had had enough of these ghostly doings, plunging into a deep dreamless sleep from which she woke unrefreshed to hear a tap-tapping at her door.

Mr Birkett was jigging from foot to foot outside.

– Such a time to answer. I thought you must have already gone. But quickly. She seems quite delirious. And as you are a nurse.

This entreaty reminded Beatrice too forcefully of the unsavoury encounter on the previous evening. She had had enough of being appealed to as some sort of ministering angel. Besides which she was tired and, she noticed, glancing at her watch, late for work. She turned back coldly into her room.

– I should fetch the doctor. I'm only qualified to deal with war victims.

The barb was quite lost on her landlord but Beatrice did not care. She was still too raw to put aside her defences. Trapped in the landing skylight a rapidly dwindling flock of stars glittered on the dawn sky's orange field.

That evening, when Beatrice climbed up the steps and unlocked the front door, the stars had returned in a dense metallic host. All day the thought of Maud lying on her sick bed had risen up to block out the real beds in front of her, as though her parting taunt had somehow turned back on itself. Tending a wounded soldier she would find he had her friend's eyes or hands and be obliged to withdraw for a moment, trembling. It was Charles's fault she decided, for having brought Maud back from London in such a condition. Yet hadn't she too passed by on the other side? Back at Orion Parade, Beatrice was inclined to be more forgiving.

Her first encounter reinforced this new mood. Dr Blake was coming down the stairs, having completed his second visit of the day. She had often seen him at the hospital but always at a distance. Tonight he seemed to recognise her instantly, which only served to soften her feeling still further. After some small talk regarding Aunt Millicent's imminent move south, he began describing Maud's case as if Beatrice weren't a trainee nurse at all but his professional equal. She glowed, despite herself, when he told her that an old tendency to pneumonia had reasserted itself after a bad soaking in London; that her condition wasn't too serious but that she would need constant watching; that he had administered quinine and a sleeping draught in such and such a measure; that the crisis would come most probably tonight or tomorrow night. Finally, when he appealed to Beatrice to take responsibility for a patient whom 'your landlord has told me is a special friend', she could hardly resist. Her weak protestations about the hospital were brushed aside; he personally would square it with the authorities. She could take two days off to tend the patient on his instructions. In the end Beatrice had to assent.

So began the vigil that Beatrice had sworn never to keep, watching over and tending to the needs of the one person in the world who had promised so much at the beginning yet latterly caused her so much pain. Despite the sleeping draught, Maud was delirious that first night, periodically raising herself up out of the wrack of tangled bedclothes and sweat-stained pillows now to demand that her nurse, whom she insisted on calling Annabel, save her from them, over there, in the corner; now to threaten a dire revenge on the whole damned crew; now to sob that she hadn't meant to do it, not to Beatrice whose soul she promised she would pray for throughout the rest of her natural life. So that, trying to calm or cajole or reassure, Beatrice had the distinct impression that the two of them existed in different times, Maud looking back on a friend whom she had pitilessly murdered, Beatrice watching over someone who had changed so much, she lived in a future with which the present would never catch up.

All night the Wright's vapouriser flickered in its moat of water, the chemical-soaked cone evacuating a pungent penetrating odour which Beatrice would forever afterwards associate with the writhings of a woman in fever and her own gigantic shadow, warped on the grimy plaster ceiling, as she bent down to administer or comfort. Maud's temperature rose so high that Beatrice was obliged on several occasions to call for tepid water and towels. Then, stripping her charge, she bathed the long yellowy white legs and arms with gentle strokes, admiring in spite of herself, the symmetry and declivities of a body that Charles Tremain had desired but never truly possessed and that she had both feared and envied. Gradually, she came to know every feature of that body from the birthmark in the shape of a fish on the back of the left knee, to the jagged white childhood scar above the navel; from the wispy reddish swirl of the mons Veneris to the flaky mole on the neck below the right ear. Like a lover she pored over these unique signs, these unrepeatable features that made this woman Maud and no one else; like an archaeologist she squinted to decipher the underlying pattern which these features made, piecing together the shards of some scattered lyre; like a master criminal, poring over a safe, she strained to crack this body's combination whose countless digits lay concealed in every cell of every structure, from the bruised half-moon of a big toenail to an oxter's shadowy mauve crater, from the white-gold burr of a forearms's hair to the wrinkled coral flaps of stuck-together labia. Only then, Beatrice felt, would she be able to touch for herself the mysterious treasure of the life this woman had lived. Afterwards, with the code still unbroken, the unique signs still not wholly penetrable, the special alphabet still undeciphered, Beatrice would slump back in her chair exhausted. Meanwhile, purified by the ritual of such attentions, her matted hair swept back from her tortured forehead, her nightdress rearranged and demure, Maud would lie like a draped archaic statue, recently dredged from some offshore wreck, then cleaned and polished in readiness for the day when it would again be viewed and marvelled at by unthinking multitudes. Then dragging herself up out of her fatigue, Beatrice felt an almost maternal protectiveness. It was she who had created this beautiful idol of fever, she who was responsible for the delicate equilibriums of its extraordinary transfiguring condition, she who must keep the world away. When Mr Birkett knocked before bedtime to see how things were progressing, Beatrice dismissed him with an angry abruptness. How could he understand what they had been through together, the two of them there in that muggy, muffled cell?

After the landlord's puzzled and apologetic withdrawal it was given to Beatrice to see that Maud's fever was something that belonged to them and them alone, an almost palpable emanation which they shared, as twins will share the same amniotic fluid. They were united by this bodily conflagration which glittered in the patient's aquamarine eyes, oozed from her pores in coagulating beadlets of briny moisture and sang and crackled in her chest as if the lungs were two braziers packed with a fuel of tissues and tubes which could neither be replenished nor consumed. The fever was their secret, their love, an embodiment of an absolute interdependence that had flared miraculously out of the ash-heap of disappointment and betrayal. Then Beatrice would lie down beside her chattering hot-cold double, thinking, since she had failed in her attempt to unlock the treasure-house of her life, to absorb the fever itself, entering into a condition of fervent mutual possession, her arms entwining Maud's shuddering chest, her pelvis pressing against Maud's heat-heavy hips, her legs entangling Maud's goosepimpled thighs. Slowly they would drift like that, together through the shallow shoals of exhaustion, their voyage accompanied by the high-pitched wheezing of Maud's chest, as if a flock of distant gulls were following the wake of a boat. Then, when they were beyond the straits and roads of the small hours and lay becalmed in that deep sea whose darkness swells to an absolute black an hour before dawn, it seemed to Beatrice that the boundaries between their bodies had indeed broken down and they were sharing the same bloodstream, the same memories, the same heart.

The expected crisis did not come that night, but by dawn Maud was a little cooler, her flock of demented seagulls a little quieter, so that Beatrice was able to separate herself from this creature who had demanded so absolute a union (as she supposed), creeping away to her own bed to try and find herself again in the solitary, unencumbered dreamless sleep of those who must act as well as suffer. But by noon she was back once more by Maud's bedside, bathing limbs in which the fire of the night seemed to have condensed and grown heavy, so that she seemed no longer to hover like a scrap of paper in the updraught of her own conflagration, but to have sunk down into a fleshy molten crater from which Beatrice must try to raise her as best she could. Now was no longer the time for mutual merging or the delicate would-be-lover's study of skin, hair and cuticle. Submerged with her patient in this new liquid heaviness of fever, struggling with her at the heart of the body's lava wilderness, it was all that Beatrice could do to drag towel across limb or raise a cloudy glass to bluish parched lips. The fever now seemed to slow everything up and penetrate all areas of thought and feeling with its numbing fiery ichor. Maud was for the most part wordless; groaning now and then after a fit of coughing that seemed to bubble up like marsh gas through thick blankets of weed and mud. Beatrice too could find nothing to say, falling back from the angelic heights of the night to a more sober evaluation which reminded her both of her estrangement and her determination not to be wholly defeated. So she became a nurse again and welcomed Mr Birkett's occasional hushed entry with Bovril (*I'm dying to get into this*) *For the one who's doing all the work*; even as she resented his implicit assumption that, compared with the fever-racked woman on the bed, all of them were mere adjuncts. Dr Blake came too, around lunchtime and sat listening to Maud's chest with a stethoscope whose cold metal disc made her shudder from the depths of her feverish trance. Then he lifted the nightdress to tap her shivering back, cupping an ear to the torso like someone lying on the ground listening for a subterranean disturbance. Pronouncing the patient stable but not out of the wood he glanced at Beatrice confidingly, as if to say, you know how to look after the sick. At which Beatrice found herself strangely tearful, wanting not professional congratulation but some deeper more personal recognition of her sacrifice which could only come, she knew, from the very person least likely to vouchsafe it since, despite their continuing enmeshment, Maud must remain forever distanced from her old friend. So that she had to turn away and busy herself with fluid for the vapouriser, in preparation for the long night to come.

But first there was the even longer afternoon. Years afterwards, Beatrice remembered those hours as having been more unendurable than anything she had hitherto experienced, either in the hospital or at Ecclesden or there in Orion Parade, listening to the whispered endearments of her betrayers. The fever grew heavier and more solid if that were possible, seeming to fill the whole room with its ugly base metal bulk, its taste of brass and ashes, its smell of salt and greenish thick-threaded urine. Bowed under the weight of this squatting odiferous presence, Beatrice felt as if her marrow were being sucked out morsel by morsel to feed the slow remorseless blaze in Maud's vitals. Then it was that she came to hate the illness as a living embodiment of her misery and disappointment. Firstly, she had been betrayed; now she must minister to the poisonous gnawing force that had erupted in Maud as a consequence of that betrayal. Would she never escape this room, this woman, these thoughts? Through the dense enshroudings and smoky veils that seemed to choke the sickroom, she caught herself moving towards the bed with arm upraised, intending to smash it down on the supine earthbound monster that Maud had become. The terrible suspended moment passed. Staggering back to her chair (whose wingless straightbacked structure she realised, in a glare of ironic lucidity, had once been intended for a nursing mother), Beatrice fell into a fitful doze, trying to control her body if not her mind.

Meanwhile, as if her skull was slowly being filled by a grey cement of fever, Maud's heavy tongue and cracked lips spat out one curse after another. At first she could manage only single words, all of them obscene. But gradually the vile and endless rope of profanity looped itself into a more coherent enunciation, wherein Charles and Eric and Lady Tremain must wrestle together at the bottom of some final slimed oubliette of her revenge and triumph. Beatrice tried to ignore these heavy outflowings of the fever's venom, eructated from a mind that had been and still was its own worst enemy. She shut her eyes more tightly. Then hummed. Then put her hands over her ears. But always they got through, this troop of ghosts she wanted so desperately to be rid of until she could stand it no more and went over to Maud and shook her violently, screaming at her to shut her foul mouth *now now now*. Which of course Maud did, the shaking having dislodged or stirred some deep-seated silting at the bottom of one of her lungs, so that all she could do for several minutes was cough and retch, retch and cough, then lie back limp as a scarecrow on her pillow, while Beatrice knelt at her side, her head buried in the damp sheets whispering, *I'm sorry dear, so sorry*.

But worse was to come. At four o'clock in the afternoon, when

Maud's ponderous and scatological tirade had subsided into a fitful muttering and Beatrice was just wondering whether she would have the time to leave her patient and indulge in a quick all-over wash, when there was a familiar knocking at the door. She had grown to accept Mr Birkett's hovering attendance since the morning, making use of him to sit in for her and genuinely feeling grateful for the cups of tea and other refreshments which he insisted on bringing her himself. If this solicitude had more to do with his anxiety for his star singer than his concerns for her nurse, Beatrice could for the time being overlook the humiliation. But on this occasion, when she opened the door she was confronted not by one but two men.

– I've brought the Captain as you see. May he look in? Just for a minute? It might do her some good.

Remembering the curdled and livid stream of curses that had just recently oozed from her patient's lips, Beatrice could not help an explosive, if sardonic laugh. Charles looked discomfited. And glowered a little.

– I suppose you blame me. For letting her catch that chill. But really I couldn't stop her. She wanted to do it, alone, in the rain, along the embankment. It was such a shock you see. The will.

– She has inherited much?

Mr Birkett simmered with the prospect of his protégée's wealth. Charles sighed,

– Of course. But there were other private things to do with her parentage. I expect Beatty, I mean Miss Lumley here, will tell you. – Beatrice smiled non-committally. She did not want to reveal to Charles that she had no idea of what those private things might consist. Charles continued. – And then the night we came back she seemed so much better, if a little weak. Well. Are you going to let me in?

Buried somewhere in this quilt of half-hearted apologies was the ghost of his old guilt over what had happened. But it lay very deep. While nearer the surface stirred a more assertive truculence. Maud was his now and he was going to see her whether Beatrice liked it or not. Beatrice suddenly didn't like it and blocked the door.

– It would do her no good at all, – she said in a voice that she hoped sounded as brusque as the ward sister's. – You can rest assured she is receiving all due care and attention.

Beneath Beatrice's words were many similarly hidden messages which she hoped Charles would read. That she knew he and Maud were no longer lovers. That she would like to be told about the business of the will. That she half forgave him for his actions. But Charles was peering round her as if trying to catch a glimpse of some forbidden performance.

– Really Beatty, you must you know. You must let me in.

And all might have been lost if at that moment Dr Blake hadn't reappeared and dismissed the very possibility of Maud's having visitors. Charles shot Beatrice a parting glance that contained more than a shade of anger. When the doctor had gone for a second time, having said that the infected left lung sounded a little less congested (*It's almost as if something has been dislodged, dispersed*), Beatrice sat down at her familiar post, depressed and weary. It was obvious that Charles regarded her nowadays as little more than a nuisance who intruded awkwardly on matters of interest and excitement. When Maud had recovered from this illness she too would turn away from her nurse, back to the world which had begun to absorb her again, the world of Ecclesden and Thundersbarrow from which she, Beatrice, had always been excluded, staring in through the glass at exotic fragile creatures whose lives would forever remain a scented mystery. So she sat on, waiting for evening, dulled into a sense of inescapable futility.

Then at last the afternoon stagnated utterly. In the pool of the little room, from which weak dregs of winter light were slowly evacuating themselves, the two women lay as heavy and incommunicative as stones under the sludge of fever. Neither spoke nor moved. Neither slept nor woke. They had descended, it seemed, to the very bottom of things, the sump where light hardly penetrated and nothing could be thought or done or remembered, beyond the fact of illness. How long this clammy inertia lasted Beatrice dared not guess but, when the change finally came, she could see the Plough quite plainly in the window from which Thundersbarrow was sometimes visible, while downstairs two lodgers argued vociferously over a last game of cards. The change was sudden and irrevocable and frightening. But it dissolved the muck and effluent of the fever's low point, so that fresh molten streams began to flow into the room's crater, merging and dividing and merging again in a riot of glowing cross-currents which, if they threatened to carry the two women away, promised in any event not to fossilise them.

It was Maud who inevitably signalled the change. Into Beatrice's fitful sleep her cry whined along its trajectory like a high velocity shell.

– I'm one of them!

Beatrice opened her eyes to find her patient standing up, her hair flying, her eyes glittering and, most disturbing of all, as if she had reverted to the little girl who had been so enamoured of Ecclesden all those years before, her nightdress lifted to the neck in a gesture that mixed vulnerability and defiance. In response to Beatrice's sharply embarrassed adjuration, Maud simply laughed.

– I am you know. She didn't think I'd find out. But I did. Mother told me. From the grave.

Then, dropping the nightdress, Maud half-ran half-pirouetted across to the starry window. Swiftly she began wrestling with the catch.

– It's over there. I'll go now. I want to go at once. But they keep tring to stop me.

As if the last mineral deposits of the afternoon were still silting her limbs, Beatrice struggled in a dream slowness to reach Maud before her wrestle with the catch proved successful. Luckily it was stiff (she remembered the difficulty her friend had had when opening it to throw down the keys to Charles), so that eventually after many millennia, Beatrice did reach her charge, wrestling her away from the window in a gruelling contest. Maud was burning again but with a different kind of heat from the previous night, a heat that seemed at once more unstable and closer to explosion. She was light, too, where she had been heavy and strong where she had been limp. So that before Beatrice knew it, she had wrenched out of her sleepy grasp and was moving around the room making for the door. It struck Beatrice as she watched, that Maud had acquired an almost serpent-like agility, as if the fire which raged inside had taken on animate form through the sheer intensity of its combustion. Again she made a grab and again Maud jinked away.

Then began the most terrible game of all, in which Beatrice, increasingly exhausted and Maud, growing uncannily stronger by the minute, stalked each other round a room which was also the landscape of their lives, containing ghostly images of Ecclesden and Orion Parade, the hospital and Whitehawk, Thundersbarrow and that most phantom place of all, the ever-present Front across the Channel. During the playing out of this game, which was also a war to see who would devour whom, many came to watch as they had once watched Charles and Eric in the pit of the quarry. Every item of furniture was an onlooker, every mark in the faded rose-petalled wallpaper an eye or a mouth. Here was Mrs Eddles and here Old Joseph; here Molly Dadger and here Katherine Tremain. Sensing this wraithlike audience, Beatrice felt possessed by an angry defiance. Was she expected to lose now, at this critical moment, in front of all these accusatory watchers? So that, trapping Maud at last between the wardrobe and the washstand, she flung herself upon her patient, as if the game must, indeed, be fought to the death. Then the two women were rolling over and over together, across the grimy threadbare carpet, until both came to rest beside the nursing chair, in a tangle of limbs that recalled the previous night, except that now their bodies were in desperate heaving scrabbling conflict. While the heel of Maud's palm was jacking her chin back, Beatrice pressed both knees down on her opponent's bony shoulders. Then Maud's pressure relaxed so that Beatrice could clamp the offending hand with her teeth. After a flurry of shouts and imprecations, Beatrice found herself on her back with Maud bearing down from above, both hands trying to grip her windpipe. It was terrifying to feel how strong the sick woman had become and awful to smell the sweat of desperation wafting from the neck of her nightdress.

– You won't get me again, – she whispered through clenched teeth and for a moment Beatrice really believed Maud was addressing her personally. Until she looked into her blank unseeing eyes.

So it might have gone on, this cross between a game, an assault and a coupling, if the thunder of their bodies and the lightning of ravaged furniture hadn't alerted Mr Birkett below. Bursting in without knocking, he was at first too shocked and fascinated to move, for Maud's nightdress was ripped almost in two at the front and Beatrice, having discarded her housecoat for ease of movement was herself in little more than a shift and fluffy slippers. Then, in response to the nurse's hoarse entreaties, he groped back from the realm of masculine reverie and began slowly but firmly to disentangle them. Although the fever had not abated, Maud was quieter now, if only because she seemed to feel she had attained her goal of not letting 'them' get her. Put back to bed with a hot water bottle she lay wide-eyed while Beatrice recovered her equilibrium and her housecoat and Mr Birkett went to fetch coals for the fire.

That terrible struggle, during which Beatrice had felt she was fighting not so much to rescue Maud as to prevent herself from being sucked back into the old ways and false habits of feeling, ushered in a period of calm. Still wide-eyed Maud talked in a rambling way about Ecclesden which seemed, in her mind, to have become a ruin.

– They blew it up you see. The soldiers. But that was on my orders.

Wincing at the smart of Maud's fingernails across her collarbone, Beatrice remembered Eric Wren's account of her friend's thirst for revenge. Now Maud had begun to merge Ecclesden and the quarry, announcing that they were both being attacked by forces under her command. The newly kindled coal fire roared as if to confirm the sick woman's story. And Beatrice, slumped in her nursing chair staring into the flames, began to feel unutterably tired.

Someone was trying to force something hard and thin down her throat. She gagged and gagged but still they forced. *Quick Nurse I.*

She awoke to find the fire a heap of cooling embers and Maud's bed empty.

Maud's disappearance inaugurated the final progress of her delirium towards its grand climacteric. At first, rushing out on to the chilly landing, Beatrice was inclined to shout out the alarm. Then, glancing at the window where once, long ago, waiting for her friend, she had finger-rubbed a stick man out of the streaming condensation, she realised how late it was. Over Whitehawk, where even now Eric Wren and Charles Tremain were stirring in their nissan huts, in preparation for a day that would inevitably bring them closer to the real war, there was the faintest flush of dawn. It must be five o'clock at the latest. Orion Parade was still deep in slumber. To disturb the lodgers now would only complicate matters and introduce the possibility of frightening Maud into running further away, assuming she was still on the premises. Realising that even this assumption must be doubtful, Beatrice tried to collect her scattered thoughts. She must first check if Maud's keys were gone. Then, whether any of her clothes were missing. Both searches proved negative but this only fuelled Beatrice's anxiety, inducing a waking dream in which the patient ran across Five Lords Burgh in her ripped nightdress pursued by Nimrod and Oenone. *Oh Maud, Maud, don't blame me*, Beatrice blurted, less to assuage a sense of guilt for having dropped off to sleep, than to exonerate herself from the sadness of the past. By now she was in her own room, gathering dress, trenchcoat and outdoor boots so that she could begin a wider search. It was then that she heard it, a distinct giggling from inside her own wardrobe. The giggling formed itself into words accompanied by the jingle of metal coathangers.

– Really mother, I knew you were hiding in here. Why didn't you tell me? Come on. I want to introduce you to someone.

Beatrice stood transfixed. Then her transient frisson of terror gave way to relief. For all at once Maud emerged from the wardrobe wearing one of her wimples askew and the old muslin dress which had seen duty during the Thundersbarrow excavations. Suppressing the bizarre notion that, by this ruse, her friend had attempted to usurp her role as betrayed victim, Beatrice stepped forward with a would-be matter of factness. Maud raised her hand.

– Beatty, this is mother. Mother, you may be dead but that doesn't mean you can't meet the only woman I ever, I ever . . .

Whether her mother had disappeared or refused to emerge from the wardrobe or simply melted back into Maud's fever, she could not go on and allowed herself to sink gently into Beatrice's waiting arms. All the clogged heaviness of the afternoon had vanished; while the evening's frantic violence seemed no more than a bad dream. Maud had now attained to a new clarity of fever which made her at once transparent and infinitely soft. So she burned there in Beatrice's arms, a bird of pure fire and when her voice came again it too was clear, a hot, utterly clear jewel, without flaw or seam.

– Beatty. Do you know what I found out in London. Well. It's this. I'm a Tremain, too. I'm one of them.

The pure flame-feathered bird must rest in Maud's mind and body for its allotted time before once again taking flight. Although she had spoken with complete lucidity she could manage no more communication that night or for the two days that followed. The inexperienced observer would have said that her fever was now worse than ever but Beatrice, having been among many deliriums since becoming a VAD, knew that the crisis had passed and was pleased when her diagnosis was confirmed by Dr Blake. The body might still burn but the fire was running out of fuel. And by the same token the mind which had been startled into more and more outrageous leaps of logic and sense, must withdraw now and curl up in a recuperative silence. Maud's dumbstruck condition did not signal some worse agony but, rather, the beginning of her long slow descent back towards the vale of health. The next night her temperature was lower, her lungs less congested. The next day Dr Blake only needed to call once. Then for twelve hours of the following night she slept almost perfectly, with hardly a wheeze or a moan. Coming in at dawn after the first real night's sleep which she herself had been able to enjoy since the beginning of the vigil, Beatrice found Maud sitting up against pillows she herself had plumped and looking critically into a hand mirror, her head on one side.

– Don't I look a sight. Those bags under my eyes. I've lost weight too. What have I been doing all this time, running up a hill?

And Beatrice who, even in her joy at her friend's recovery, knew that things between them would never be the same again, could not resist a mild barb.

– That and talking. You never stopped talking. Such things. But I won't embarrass you. Yet.

Maud sensed the barb and winced, laying down the hand mirror.

– Have I been very ill?

The question might have been asked by the most guileless of little girls. Yet Maud managed to give it an edge of pride. And a darker tone. As if being very ill was akin to being very bad and both must be accounted highly desirable achievements. Beatrice took a non-committal line and asked her if she was hungry.

– I think, Beatty – Maud said – I think I should very much like a glass of milk.

To which Beatrice responded by promptly rushing out to the kitchen, her eyes filling with tears of frustration and remorse.

Have I been very ill?

Maud's simple question echoed down the days that followed, becoming by turns, a taunt, a promise and an agonisingly long farewell. That she had been very ill but was very ill no longer, did not at first make much difference to the pattern of things. The patient still needed nursing and Dr Blake promised that he would arrange an extension to Beatrice's leave of absence from the hospital. Maud herself was very weak and even relapsed into fever for half a day, regurgitating all the old obscene threats and opaque recriminations. Now, for the first time, Beatrice became aware that Maud's tendency to chest trouble could be traced back to one specific incident in her recent suffragist past. While confined in Holloway she had been force-fed. Dr Blake confirmed both the fact and the diagnostic connection with pneumonia. But any drift back into compassion was quickly checked by a renewed sense of exclusion. Otherwise Beatrice 'soldiered on' as she put it, grimly yet with pride, one afternoon when Mr Birkett paused in the doorway with a tray. She felt more tired than she had done a few days ago; also more relaxed, given her patient's slow progress.

But otherwise her mental landscape had not much changed. She was still unable to communicate with her former friend, still unable to address the mysterious business of her London journey. She was still, in essence, alone.

But not quite. For hadn't Maud herself gone some way towards answering some of Beatrice's more pressing questions when, emerging from the wardrobe, she announced that she was in fact related to the Tremains? The shock of this revelation had not properly sunk into Beatrice's consciousness yet, primarily because she was not entirely convinced that she shouldn't attribute the words to illness, giving them no more value than the endless sewage wash of profanities. But gradually she began to feel that the words, uttered out of the transparent crystal heart of her fever were, in essence, true. Wouldn't this explain the curious way in which Charles and she had moved from being lovers to something less unravellable but more involved? Painfully coming to terms with this knowledge, Beatrice was soon confronted by the more prosaic business of work and nursing. After two more days Maud was sufficiently recovered not to need her friend's night-time attendance. Then all at once the days too became less onerous, as Maud found she could sit up for longer and read or sew, concentrating on the costume for the soldiers' mime at the concert, a costume that for some reason had to remain secret, being stuffed under the chair when anybody came in. Finally, one damp December morning, with a sense of regret that had her looking back on the terrible fever as a time of heightened experience, even (if she was honest with herself) happiness, Beatrice found herself on the tram travelling down to the fort. The old round had resumed. She must lose herself in her duties once again.

But the expected plunge into selflessness proved hard to achieve. Beatrice could not simply expunge the experience of the last few days. Indeed she often felt as though she were back at Orion Parade, the woman attending the Fort hospital being a mere mechanical substitute, a fetch almost, without substance or feeling. This fetch was frequently reprimanded for carelessness and, on one occasion, even put on washroom duty, the hospital equivalent of military defaulters, a link with Eric Wren's punishment that had her feeling distinctly uncomfortable. There was, too, the more painful because less easily quantifiable business of her alienation from the wounded and the dying. It was as if Maud's deranged fever had come between her and the men in the ward. What they were suffering no longer seemed important. She knew that objectively this was absurd, even culpable, especially since the Chalkhampton Chums would soon be leaving for the very places where such suffering was inflicted. Yet she could not help being distant now and, having to endure the anger and resentment which this distance provoked, began to realise that Maud's illness had eaten into and tarnished the image of the very man for whom, in a sense, she performed her duties. She had lost her faith in Charles Tremain a second time and was not inclined to ingratiate herself with these simulacra of him, these mirror images that orbited round his crumbling idol like satellites round a dying sun. That her distance also had much to do with continuing love, a love that feared to find Charles in one of these very beds before too long, only intensified her cold aloofness, causing even the ward sister to advise her to unbend a little if only for the sake of a good atmosphere.

During all this time Maud grew considerably better, though remaining weak. Beatrice was at first puzzled then irritated to find that her former patient appeared to feel no sense of gratitude for what she had done. It was as if, indeed, she expected it as her birthright, a product no doubt, Beatrice brooded bitterly, of her discovery of an imminent wealth. This in turn made her resent her charges at the hospital even more, as if their continuing gratitude were a deliberate reminder of its absence elsewhere. Seething and impotent, she would come back to her lodging and refuse even to look in on Maud, who only made matters worse by seeming not to notice anything was amiss. Then one day, after a particularly gruelling afternoon (a corporal with an amputated arm had tried to escape the hospital by jumping naked from a ward window thus necessitating the amputation of the other arm), she walked up the stairs at Orion Parade to hear Maud weakly humming the Queen of the Night aria. The humming stopped.

– Is that you, Beatty? Will you come in for a moment?

She would not and made resolutely for her own door.

– Beatty. I want to talk. I never see you nowadays. Please.

It was the first or last offer of the olive branch and Beatrice was too much in turmoil to refuse. Still she would not sit down. Maud looked up from the nursing chair.

– How is work? – Then, not waiting for a reply – I'll never go back to that factory now, thank Christ.

Beatrice snorted.

– You don't need to. With your money.

– You know about that? How?

Maud seemed genuinely surprised. Beatrice laughed, shortly.

– I should have thought everyone knows. And just as soon as you're well enough we won't see you for dust. But then that's what money does. Changes people. We won't be fit to lick your boots then will we, here at Orion Parade.

Maud was pale. But smiling.

– I seem to remember someone who rather looked up to money when she thought it might be connected with a certain manor under the Downs.

Beatrice could not ward off that blow. The fact that Maud was now potentially rich had made her more envious than she had expected. But the fact that she had been received back into the world of the Tremains was infinitely worse. Still, she must recover somehow.

– I'm not the girl I was, Maud. It's Charles who hasn't grown up. Or should I say your brother. Which he is in a spiritual sense since you're all apparently related. Or how did you put it? Oh yes: I'm one of them. What's the relationship then, Maud? On what branch of the Tremain family tree do you have the good fortune to perch and sing?

Beatrice had the uncomfortable feeling that, in spite of all her resolutions, she was still fatally liable to offer herself as a one-woman audience for the self-absorbed melodrama of these people's lives. It didn't cost them anything; but for her it was a perpetual haemorrhage of emotion. Maud was still smiling, evidently unable or unwilling to register Beatrice's ponderous sarcasm.

– I remember now I told you something of that. What a state I was in. You must have thought I was mad. But, yes, it's true. – and here she drew her shawl (a new silk one Beatrice noticed, where had that come from?) round her shoulders. – Sir Colin and my mother. It was a whirlwind romance apparently. Of which I was the product. So yes, he is my brother, my half-brother.

Beatrice felt a nausea bordering on faintness. This was worse than anything she had heard from the depths of fever. Worse than all the imprecations, the curses, the threats. Yet the words brother and half-brother had been let fall so casually, Maud might have been alluding to some defunct lineage. Would she never know as much as those around her? So envy and regret rose up to fight with her plummeting self-esteem. Greyly, at last, she managed to mutter.

– It must have been quite a moment.

Maud laughed.

– You could say! – Then, growing more intense and, Beatrice fancied, less sincere. – Oh Beatty, you've no idea the affect the reading of my mother's will had on me. I who had always thought she died a pauper. To find out that not only did she come from one of the most respected families in Virginia; but also that she married (and divorced) Joshua Cohen, the financier. I who had been treated by the Tremains as a cross between a menial and an inconvenient relative. To find out that I was their equal. No, their superior. Thank God, Charles was there. Not that he could stop me running out, later, along the embankment. But you're right. I am changed. Not by the money. But by what lies behind the money. I'm someone now. I don't have to work, making munitions for a man's war. I don't have to sing for an old lecher if I don't want. I don't have to . . .

293

A fit of coughing truncated her speech. Beatrice realised with a chill that Maud's speech impediment had quite vanished. She determined to shock it back into existence.

— So when's the happy day?

Maud removed the handkerchief from her mouth and took a couple of gulping breaths. She looked unexpectedly solemn, pious almost.

— Beatty, Charles and I are blood-related. It wouldn't be right.

— It was right when you thought I was down at the hotel with my aunt.

Maud was red despite her pallor.

— Isn't that just bloody typical? When somebody has some good fortune everybody forgets what they were before. You forget that I didn't know then. You forget that I was nobody. We were, well, friends from way back. Oh I've explained it all to you before. Please, you can be quite obsessive sometimes, Beatty. And distasteful. Would you like a blow by blow account? It wouldn't last long.

— Please don't call me that any more.

— What?

— That patronising diminutive. I'm Beatrice. Nothing else.

— Well, really. You are on your high horse tonight. All blame and sanctimonious lectures and don't call me this don't call me that. Am I not to receive even one word of congratulation?

Maud might have been a pouting child, eager for adult approbation.

— No more than I receive one word of thanks. What is there to congratulate anyway? You haven't done anything. You're just on good terms with fate. While I . . .

Beatrice choked back a sob. The self-pity had come unbidden. She had not intended so craven an appeal. But to find out that Maud and Charles were half-siblings, after everything else. Maud seemed genuinely moved.

— I don't want to be in conflict with you, Beatty, sorry Beatrice. It was my old self, the one I like to think my fever burned up, which was likely to cause you grief. If I hadn't been like I was, all fire and selfishness and resentment, I wouldn't have done what I did with Charlie. It was a meaningless thing, Beatrice, because my life had no meaning. All that smashing of windows and sticking hatpins in horses (which in any case ended with the war) was just a veil really, covering a hole in my life. Because in a sense I didn't know who I was. Do you see? And now I do know. Oh I can't describe the joy I felt when that fat dandruffy old solicitor handed me the envelope with the photographs of my mother. She was beautiful, Beatrice. Not like me. And now I must honour her memory. The convalescent wing for officers will be built at Ecclesden with her money. The money that her husband settled on her and that she left to me. Perhaps after the war I may even go out to America and make contact with her family. That's how I've changed, Beatrice. For good.

Throughout this speech Beatrice had been studying the shawl which Maud was wearing. Its border was embroidered with silvery horses. She had seen it somewhere before. Where? Meanwhile Maud's voice wheezed on. It was as if she were talking from a great distance, or in a dream. The voice sounded assumed, a concatenation of sounds that had somehow found refuge in her body by chance. This was not the Maud Beatrice had known. It was not even the Maud the old Maud might have become. The fever had washed her away on its receding tide and left in her place this transparent and inadequate substitute, talking about change and good and honour. The old Maud would never even have countenanced accepting an inheritance tainted by the outmoded laws of marriage and property. And as for revelling in what it could do for her! Beatrice knew then that the friendship between them was over. And moved instinctively towards the door. The olive branch had withered. Maud looked puzzled.

— I thought you'd be glad, Beatrice. I thought you of all people would understand.

But Beatrice could only shake her head. She had remembered where she last saw the shawl. On the narrow shoulders of Lady Tremain when she had hired her to coach Robert one summer morning in the hothouse at Ecclesden. She turned at the door.

– He's a coward you know, your brother or half-brother. And a liar.

Maud's face went unexpectedly hard, as if the transparent softness had suddenly ossified. She brushed her hand back across her hair, in the old way.

– Poor Beatty. As if I didn't know.

Failing to win Beatrice over to a belief in her new self, Maud had dropped her guard for a moment, revealing the old self still intact, though buried in the silt washed up by illness. And Beatrice would have felt almost relieved, if she hadn't suddenly sensed that Maud was now doubly powerful in her ability to call on two quite distinct personalities.

If the shrivelling friendship between the two women had been finally amputated that night, it still continued to sprout phantom vibrations of feeling and pain. Beatrice was convinced that Maud was now seeing Charles regularly, not only from the evidence of the shawl but because of the way Mr Birkett grew nervous when she mentioned The Captain, as if he had been sworn to keep a secret. This would have been hard enough to bear in the old days, when Beatrice had fancied a possible renewal of affection; but now she knew not only that the renewal had been aborted but also that Maud and Charles were connected by blood as well as other attractions, the knowledge was a profound burden. Inwardly, she cried out to be relieved of it; outwardly, she stiffened her mask of impersonality so that the soldiers in the hospital took to calling her by a new nickname, The Nun, presumably because of her silent unapproachability.

Then her own collapse struck. Dr Blake had warned her of this, on his last visit to Maud the week previously. It took the form, as he had predicted, of an intense dragging fatigue. When she came on as well, Beatrice knew that she would have to ask for yet more time off, but for herself now, not another.

She arrived home early that day determined to go straight to bed but, on opening the front door, immediately heard voices in the back parlour. At first she thought she must be hallucinating, mixing the present with that time when she had chanced on Charles and Maud, alone for the first time. But today, apart from those two voices, she could hear at least one other. Desperate to go upstairs and lie down, she found that her exhaustion was determined to conspire against her. Despite herself she struggled forward along the hallway.

– Why, look who it is. Mother. Bobby's old teacher. Bobby get up off the floor.

– I want to play with the cat.

– Kill it, morelike. Look at the poor thing, it's run behind the bookcase.

– Stupid moggy. I'd like to pull its ears off.

– I thought you already had. Beatty, are you going to stand there all night?

– She probably has other business. And we really must be going. Maud, it has been so good to see you looking so well. And we have had such an interesting chat about the wing.

– You don't need to try too hard, Katherine.

– Well no, I didn't mean . . . But we are looking forward to having you, aren't we, Bobby.

– Um.

– Bobby.

– Yes, if you say so.

– Especially once the trust income starts coming through.

– Now Maud, that really is below the belt.

– Fuck off, Charles.

– Maud! The boy.

– He's heard worse.

So, after the long vigil of Maud's nursing, Beatrice saw and heard how little had changed; and understood that, whether she were a witness or not, things must always happen, relentlessly and without reference to those who merely hover on the threshold. Later, she would remember how Lady Tremain's hauteur had been besmirched by a craven self-abasement in front of Maud, her new daughter; how Charles had put his arm round Maud and kissed her like a half-brother on the cheek; how Maud had looked sharply, gloatingly from her to them and back again, sensing her power, revelling in it. The cat Ulysses had made a dash for the doorway where she stood, only to have his tail pulled by the scowling Robert. Ulysses squealed and Beatrice uttered a faint, *Please don't do that*, as the doorway collapsed into her bed and the faces in the parlour dwindled to motes sliding up the walls of aching eyelids. But they had left their voices behind, as some venomous swarm might leave a slick of poison:

Beatty. That's what I used to call her. Eh, Beatty. But you don't like that name do you. Beatty. Beatty. Beatty.

Beatty, red as a beetroot.

Bobby!

She is though, isn't she.

Well I must admit.

Yes. And common.

A common little bit of snatch. Who can't get spread to save her life.

Beatty. Beatty. Beetroot Beatty.

So the sulphurous voices danced round her and clambered over her and thrust inside her all the time telling her she was nothing and nowhere until she had indeed found where her body and mind vanished in a dry sump at the bottom of a shaft up which nevertheless she must gradually climb toward the crusted grey of morning. Where Mr Birkett was standing, as on so many other occasions.

– Now it is your turn, eh?

– I need rest, the doctor says, after what I've been through. – She smiled. Now at least Maud would have to tend her.

– Well be thankful you're not ill. If you want anything ask my wife. I have to go down to the pier. The concert is tomorrow.

She called him back from the landing, hoping for some glimmer of sympathy.

– I'm afraid I shan't be able to take part.

– Of course not. Maud though is better. We are all so glad. It is just such a pity she has seen fit to stay with Lady Tremain at the Grand. I should have liked one last night, to run over one or two things. Now I must see about renting out the room.

298

Beatrice lay back on her pillow. She had not even the strength to weep. The day stretched ahead of her. A barren waste.

So now you know. Poor thing. Poor poor thing.

The dragon was leaning over her. Why did he not breathe fire? Why did he not simply burn her up? The dragon shivered. His body was strangely cloth-like.

It had to be. Like the voices said. She'll live there now. She'll see us all destroyed.

I nursed her. I brought her back to health. And now she's left me. It's so, so . . . humiliating.

You'll be healthy again too. You'll forget us.

The dragon's paw touched her forehead. But it was a hand. A man's hand.

I'd rather forget myself. I'd rather not be myself. Do you understand that. Can you?

The hand stopped. Withdrew.

I can. Surely I can.

– Did the soldier come for the costume? The Captain's servant?

It was Mr Birkett. In the cool light.

– I think so. I told him to look under her bed.

– So silly for her to forget. But she is very busy.

A dragon. Eric Wren was a dragon.

Under the hill waiting for the thunder so that he can wake and unleash the second flood.

Cool light. A tremor of returning strength. You are a woman again. Alone. In a town beside the sea.

. . . and they wanted the carpets, even that old rug on the backstairs which was so stained. Naturally, I said yes, all included in the price. So now I leave on Sunday. It's strange to walk round the rooms and think of the past. Well dear, I expect you're keeping busy at the hospital. This dreadful war. I am not happy though about your plan to go abroad. We will talk more about this. Have you remembered to give in your notice, dear? We don't want to

have to pay that man more rent than he's due. Well I look forward to seeing you Monday week at the new house. Dr Blake writes to say it will do me a world of good, though I must admit I've been getting the pains again lately. You will have to help me with the furniture when it arrives. I'm getting a local firm to do the removal. But they always break something. Or leave something behind. Is it true your local regiment goes abroad soon? I read it in the Advertiser. Such heroes. Or fools. That Tremain boy too. What his mother must be suffering now. I'm so glad I don't have any children of my own . . .

CONCERT IN AID OF CHUMS. A GOOD TIME HAD BY ALL. HIGH ART AND LOW HUMOUR. A TRAGIC ACCIDENT. OUR BRAVE BOYS. LOOK OUT FRITZ WE ARE ON OUR WAY. GOD SAVE THE KING.

Last night at eight o'clock sharp in the old theatre at the end of the pier, occurred the long-awaited concert for the First and Second Battalions, 4th —shire Regiment, better known by all and sundry as our very own Chalkhampton Chums. Designed as a bon-voyage and God Speed for the two Battalions, it was also, in the more than capable organisational hands of Lady Katherine Tremain, a very successful fundraiser for the Regiment, ensuring that the Comforts Fund will now be more than able to supply much needed and outstanding items of equipment and kit.

The hall was packed, so that those who had not managed to acquire a seat were forced to make use of whatever standing room could be found, some even perching precariously on a ledge overlooking the seaward side, of which more later. After a rousing performance of 'Jerusalem', in which the entire audience joined in with full throats and fuller hearts, the first half of the concert got off to a fine start with three choruses from Handel's Messiah *performed by the choirs and orchestra of the Tongdean Choral Society under the baton of Dr W. Birkett. Dr Birkett himself cut an imposing figure, spruce in his immaculate frock coat and with a dramatic way of conducting that was never merely ostentatious. The choirs too sang well, despite absentees owing to illness, while the small chamber ensemble was never less than sparkling. The choruses finished, there now followed the high spot of the first half and the spectacle of what can only be described as High Art in the making. To tumultuous applause, looking pale but determined (she too having recently endured a bad illness), Miss Maud Egerton came on stage to sing two arias from Mozart's most popular operas:* Don Giovanni *and* The Magic

Flute, *the latter presented in an estimable translation by Dr Birkett himself, obliging your correspondent to reflect that, even in the land of our enemies, darkness and militarism have not always triumphed. Dressed in a long mauve and white tulle gown with bare shoulders and a single Christmas rose at her bosom, Miss Egerton was the picture of elegance and refinement. Her voice, however, transported the audience to other realms, fairy lands forlorn of Mystery and Romance where the grim business of war could mayhap be forgotten. Her voice was as free as a bird's and as seductive as a siren's. Many of the hardened soldiers in the audience were seen openly to weep.*

After such heights, everyone in the hall required rest and refreshment which was amply supplied in a half hour interval. Only one event marred the happy atmosphere. Among the aforementioned spectators clinging precariously to the ledge in the gods nearest the seaward side, was one young man who fatally lost his footing, plunging down into the savage briny below. A rescue operation conducted promptly and efficiently by a platoon under the capable command of Captain Charles Tremain, son of the late Sir Colin, the noted philanthropist of Ecclesden Manor and much mourned husband of the aforementioned Lady Tremain, was to no avail. The poor unfortunate had sustained a blow to his head during the fall and could not be revived. He was named later as Timothy Frith, a pupil of Tongdean. Next of kin have been informed.

But in a time of war such accidents have to be taken in our stride. Sobered but not downcast, the audience returned to their seats and prepared to enjoy the second half. Now the Regiment came into their own. The first item on the agenda was a very amusing comic band followed by a mime in which George and the Dragon fought for possession of a maiden. The symbolism of this by turns exciting and humorous conflict was not lost on the audience. It was whispered, too, that the bold St George was none other than Captain Tremain himself, a rumour confirmed when he removed his helmet at the end to take a bow. The fortunate maiden whom the doughty warrior had sworn to rescue (Belgium, Let Thy Cries Not Be Forgotten) was none other than Miss Egerton while the dragon (clad in a superb costume made anonymously from green canvas and balsa wood), turned out to be occupied by one Lance-corporal Wren who, despite his evil leer, received the biggest cheer of all. Then came a selection of parlour songs sung to the accompaniment of Dr Birkett's scintillating piano. Among many performances, one stands out, that of a setting of A.E. Housman's famous poem 'Bredon Hill', by a young contemporary composer who has himself recently gone over to France, Mr George Butterworth. This was sung in a sweet if slightly thin baritone by Captain Tremain. It can safely be said that the tolling of the one bell left not a dry eye in the house. Then came more songs, led by Miss Egerton, of a somewhat indelicate nature which your correspondent proposes to pass over as not fit for discussion in a family newspaper. Suffice to say they were just what the troops ordered and who can blame them? Even the majestic figure of Lady Tremain herself, ensconced in the old Royal Box, was seen to smile at some of the more risqué lines. So, finally, to God Save the King and three cheers from the Regiment in honour of the town that has done so much to succour them. Then all filed out into what had become a windy night, each clutching to himself thoughts of the future and fond memories of the past.

Aunt Constance, who was my mother? Why do you never speak of her?
    There's nothing to say. She died when you were born. Now your father . . .
    He's dead too. A diplomat. Born in Washington DC. But my mother. What was she? She didn't just die.
    Are you going out this afternoon dear? On that march.
    Of course.
    Do wrap up well. And do keep away from the police.
    Why are you trying to change the subject? It was the same at Ecclesden.
    It was for the best, your leaving. As Katherine said.
    (You thought you loved him. Absurd. Only yourself. Love only yourself from now on. And mother.)
    She hates me.
    No. Not hates. But really dear, do you have to go out. Again. It's so. So, well, unpleasant.

The window I break will release her face. From the past to which it has been consigned.

How do you do.

Charles.

Dull party.

They always are when Constance does the organising.

I was up in town and thought. Mother doesn't know.

Of course not.

I heard about the court case.

Did you?

I did. I was worried. I . . .

Look. I have to go. Finish my wine for me. If you like.

Maud. I saw the ruins. I saw the place of bodies. 'And the force of the blast was such that the sea withdrew for many leagues and under the sea were revealed many monsters and shipwrecks and crawling slimy things.' Maud. Your grandfather. Your nose. But your eyes. Your eyes are like mine. Maud. And I think . . .

Cigarette smoke aswirl in the draught of her going. Army Club. Gone.

Hold the head still, Miss Seymour, the head.

Shake it keep shaking it like a terrier with a rat Wren's terrier what was his name Nimrod no Lob that's it shake it like Lob so that they can't oh but they can and she's got your head now in the vice of her cold hands Miss Costello the fatarsed old warder

Watch that kicking, Mrs Abbott. The right leg. Are the straps in place? Good. That's right.

Can't move pain in my leg digging in the buckle

Very well. The tube now. Pass me the tube. Thank you. Now.

Might be a demonstration a student's seminar so relaxed they are and everything so slow but I can't and the tube oh fatarse armpit ghastly shaven crater pissing sweat no I won't I won't open not to you not to anyone

I love your mouth, Maudie. It's like a flower, a flower opening.

Balls, Charlie.

So now the mouth is redundant. The tube inserted thus. Hold her steady, Miss Costello, can't you. Yes that's it. Into the nostril. To avoid choking.

I can't I can't who are you leaning over me now your waistcoat smelling of eau de cologne sucked up into my forehead and down the back of my throat a whole man in there I am being fed a whole man

The funnel now Mrs Abbott. The patient, I mean prisoner, seems calmer.
Yes. Right. Thank you. And the mixture. And down we go.

Darkness darkness is a light wheeling pain which is food which is breath
My lungs are swallowing me
Oh

Struggling again. Remove the tube.

Some of him still down there where the tunnel divides Oh why I can't
Prisoner choking, remove tube. Straps. Head between knees, Miss
Costello. The back. The back.

Gelid white mash like fly's eggs on the stone floor now bile and blood to
make it moist

Shall we look at the butterflies, Maudie? Daddy collected them. Such
colours yellow and blue and red.

Red red I have vomited my death and am still alive

You get uppity with me again and we'll pour that lot back down you as
well, so help me Christ.

Frankly, Miss Costello, I deplore this business but the authorities insist.
Perhaps this will discourage her from her ill-advised protest. You can remove
her gown now and take her back to the cells. And provide plenty of water,
mind.

Eaten by breath swallowing myself I will never again not
Darkness
Swallow

I see she's been released.
Already?
Ill apparently. Pneumonia.
(Oh Maud.)
She's only got herself to blame.
(Oh no not herself. Never herself.)
The vicar will be coming at five.
Do I have to, mother? Do I have to read the Lesson?
Your father would have wanted you to.
(Eric by the kiln the day after Daddy died. Shouting, 'He brings down
the fire from the skies.' As though he had caused Daddy's death.)

But my voice. I may not be able.

The passage he loved. That's all. From the Psalms. Tell the vicar and that will be that.

(That will be that. But nothing finishes. Ever. Mother earlier today at his desk. Shuffling papers. Looking up. Face pale. – I'm afraid, Charles, your father has left us with many problems. Debts. A second mortgage. Well. We shall just have to manage. –)

Maud Maud Maud Maud they were crying and calling.

On a December morning of wind and rain, just a week before the first evacuations from Gallipoli, the Regiment left Chalkhampton to begin its long-awaited overseas service in Egypt. A grand parade had been planned to take place on the square in front of the town hall. After an address from the mayor the troops, led by their regimental band, would march away to the terminus from where they were to travel to Southampton by way of Waterloo. Half an hour before the regiment was due to arrive in the square, a crowd of people had already assembled on either side of the cobbled space which still bore the traces, so some averred, of a terrible martyrdom in Queen Mary's reign. But no heretic's bonfire would have burst into life there today; the cobbles were shining wet and rainy billows, torn it seemed from the crumbling masonry of waves, hurled themselves in swift succession against any available roof or wall. Hung over upper storey windowsills and across the entire frontage of the town hall (a nineteenth-century structure built on the foundations of a villa sacked by marauding Saxons), Union Jacks of every size and state of preservation flapped disconsolately; while bunting, looped in a huge cross over the centre of the square, writhed and snapped without rest. At the top of the town hall steps, under a canvas awning which was already beginning to sag with the weight of accumulated water, the mayor and several local dignitaries waited stiffly. Lady Tremain was among them, her white Ulster glowing like a lily in the murky air. Beside her, in a green-belted gaberdine, her pale hair scraped up and hidden inside a low-crowned Spanish hat festooned with glass grapes, stood a younger woman whom some in the crowd recognised as the Diva of the pier concert, while others talked about her fabled wealth which was apparently being put to good use in the conversion of a wing at Ecclesden into a home for convalescent officers. Meanwhile the wind grew stronger, if that were possible, so that many had to furl up their black flowers of umbrellas, for fear they would turn inside out. Two gulls swept past on the rain, commenting shrilly on the proceedings. The minutes passed slowly.

To Beatrice Lumley, looking on from the back of the crowd, it seemed that the parade had already occurred, that everyone in the square had somehow been bewitched, so that the salt rain could go unhindered about its business of expunging the memory of the regiment forever. The sight of her former friend up there under the distant awning only deepened this feeling. Had they been through so much together simply to arrive at this absolute emptiness? Having left Orion Parade at the beginning of Beatrice's short but savage collapse, Maud had had no further communication with her, obliging Beatrice to rely on second-hand accounts of her perform- ance at the concert and the subsequent removal to Ecclesden. At first the bitterness had been intense. But as exhaustion withdrew she began again to look about her and prepare for her own move to Artillery Row with her aunt. Indeed she had told herself that her presence in the square today was as much a matter of civic duty as a nod to the painful past. Perhaps it was. Yet her stomach still griped. And she could still, if she was honest with herself, come close to tears. This was, after all, the first time she had seen Maud since the evening of the voices in the back parlour. She had been prepared to feel a certain sadness; but not this intensity of mourning.

Making another partially successful effort to control her tears, Beatrice looked away from the town hall back towards the rain- lashed square and concentrated again on the reason for the crowd's patient assembly. Was the parade in fact the figment of some communal fantasy? Perhaps indeed the soldiers had come down from Whitehawk after all, but as ghosts to caper invisibly under the bunting, mocking the solemnity of church and state. She closed her wet eyes for a moment then opened them on Mr Birkett who stood a little to one side of her, struggling with an umbrella that appeared to have become possessed, its stem jerking in his fists like a dowser's rod, its metal ribs already warped by the force of the wind. Did he too have the strange sensation that, though the soldiers had come and gone, nothing had changed? Her soon to be ex-landlord had taken Maud's departure hard. After the excitement and the plaudits of the concert, he had come down to earth to find himself alone with his wife in the lodging-house. At first Beatrice had sought the sympathy of a fellow sufferer. But Mr Birkett was exclusive and egotistical in his loss. Coming out of the bathroom last night, she had passed Maud's old door and, peeping in, seen the landlord spreadeagled on the bed. Taken aback she had allowed her housecoat to drift apart revealing a complex lattice-work of tapes and towelling. Turning his head, Mr Birkett stared without seeing. Then she knew that her own misery could not be shared.

— I think I can hear them. Listen.

And indeed it was as if Beatrice's voice, drifting up on a particularly strong gust, not only broke the spell that had descended on the square, but actually helped in the slow process of bringing the soldiers into being. Now everybody who, until that moment, had heard only the dull tattoo of flags, the shrill lament of stretched wire, could suddenly make out the tramping of many boots. From this distance the sound had a fiery edge as if a conflagration had been ignited somewhere near Whitehawk and was gaining in intensity and proximity by the second. People actually huddled closer together as if expecting this miraculous and terrible fire to burst into the square and envelop them all, plunging the windy wet morning into a furnace of light. Glancing at the imperturbable Lady Tremain, the mayor fingered his chain of office nervously. It was he who would be obliged to address and, in some sense, control this dark fire smouldering before him in a thousand pairs of eyes. By his side the bishop remained more sanguine. His prayer of blessing would have about it an air of elegiac finality which, he comforted himself, would be chilly enough to quench the harshest blaze.

— They're in East Street I should say. Under the clocktower.

Again, Beatrice's words had the effect simultaneously of drawing the troops nearer and making the people who had come to watch and say farewell, flinch reluctantly out of their waking dream. The entire collective consciousness of the square seemed convinced it was about to be invaded and overrun. The soldiers did not belong to Chalkhampton any more; they belonged to war, that vast smoky conflict being conducted, for all the crowd knew, in some noisome cave at the centre of the earth. The soldiers were not coming here to be encouraged and wept over; but to threaten and expose. Everyone in the square was suddenly a naked thing, cowering at the imminent arrival of a force which, though few were prepared to acknowledge it, they themselves had helped to create. Only Beatrice was different or felt herself to be different, glancing this way and that and encountering the crowd's apprehension. How strange they all looked, how remote. Did they not see that this was necessary, this alchemy which had transformed the Regiment into a monster with fiery feet and a furnace for a heart? But no. Her virgin soul, so bitterly resented in months gone past, had today set her apart from and above the rest. Only she could quell the beast which even now was winding its slow way through the town. Only she could stare unblinking into its bitter hungry eyes. So Beatrice, once more mistaking humdrum disappointment for a fabulous election, relinquished the bucking zone of her landlord's umbrella and went to stand at the very front of the spectators. Here, so close yet far away from her former friend and rival, she would make Maud acknowledge her power even if she did not admit it. *Look, I am still here*, she wanted to say, *You have not defeated me*, and, glancing across to the canvas awning, fancied she detected just a flicker of a smile under that soaked hat. She felt a surge of self-vindication. So that even if her next words were heard by no more than a handful of people, it seemed to Beatrice that they rose spontaneously out of the whole body of the crowd. And stood like Mary in the wall-painting at Ecclesden waiting for the transfiguring shaft. Or blow.

– It's here now. The Regiment's here. It's turning the corner. Now.

And so for the first and last time this Being materialised in the middle of Chalkhampton, in distant sight of Thundersbarrow and a few hundred yards from the shore. No longer a motley and disparate assemblage of those who had volunteered a year ago last August, the two battalions had become the single creature of the crowd's generalised fears and Beatrice's specific longing. Through its many limbs only one idea surged; and only one bloodstream circulated round its many hearts. Yet the beast had barely been brushed by the conflict it sought to embody. In time, great scars would appear on that rippling khaki hide. Holes would be punched. Rents torn. Pieces ripped off. In time, the beast would go down on its knees like Eric Wren in the dumb show on the pier. Then, through its tattered costume, many strange things would be glimpsed. From behind the lines or above them, observers with binoculars would see how the beast had been constructed, what bones had been used, the weight and colour of its musculature, the texture of its bloody tissues. Meanwhile, floating back towards the ravines from which it had risen at dawn, the cries would come, as Beatrice had once heard them: single words like *Water, Shit* or *Mother*, or longer unintelligible statements. By this time the beast would be on its stomach, stretched out among a thousand craters it had briefly hoped were caves. The cries from its now collapsed structure would grow fainter as night came on, then cease altogether. The particles which had seemed so full of life and colour when initially exposed, would have begun to turn a neutral shade halfway between mud and chalk, as they sank into a profound stillness. So the beast would die out there among the belts of coiled and picketed wire, leaving a few of its many parts to turn back into men who must crawl with painful slowness back towards the land where they had been born. Some would die on the way in advance dressing posts near White City or under the bell-tents of the casualty clearing station outside Doullens or back at the base hospital in Dieppe; others would manage to take ship and sail back across the Channel where yet more hospitals awaited them, such as the Fort in which Beatrice worked or the officers' convalescent wing at Ecclesden. Some would die there; while others, having recovered, returning to what they were before the war, would find that they could never quite bury the memory of those caves at the bottom of the world.

For the first and last time. The Regiment in its glory; the beast in its glittering dream of war. Everybody in the square was vanquished by the sight; everybody would have knelt to do homage if they hadn't already utterly abased themselves in more complex and obscure acts. For in recognising the power of what stood in front of them, the crowd had also to accept its defeat. In cheering imminent embarkation, a cheer orchestrated by the mayor and involving the hurling upwards of many dark hats to hang suspended for a moment in the opaque air like a flock of birds glimpsed through mist, the cheerers had to say farewell. Many ties were broken that morning, silently, between one billow of wind and the next, or between the mayor's pompous recitation and the sharp cry of a gull sheltering in the town hall's pillared portico. Blood bonds and bonds of affection fell away as if rotted by the wet atmosphere. Mother said goodbye to son, sweetheart to sweetheart, sister to brother. But there was one bond which proved even harder to break than all the others. And when it did fray apart, strand by reluctant strand, the whole square, the whole of Chalkhampton perhaps, as far north as Ecclesden and the brooding bulk of Thundersbarrow, was left numbed and adrift, a vessel whose moorings had been slipped. It happened just as the bishop was finishing his Prayer To Be Said In A Time Of War And Tumults.

– '. . . that we being armed . . .' – he intoned, his cassock whipping about him like sea foam – 'with Thy defence may be preserved evermore from all perils, to glorify Thee that art the only giver of all victory; through the merits of Thy only son, Jesus Christ Our Lord. Amen.'

Amen and all knew it had happened. The bond with the past was broken. No one could go back. What had happened before this moment was now utterly unreachable. Amen. The soldiers stood each in his section, his platoon, his company, his battalion. Each waited to go. Each longed to go. But stood still. Watching as the past receded. Amen. And the crowds of civilians watched them watching. Beatrice watched. Handkerchief tightly screwed up in her gloved fist, her satin hat quite sodden now and limp. On the right of the square, in the middle of the Second Battalion, she could see Charles standing at ease at the head of his company, his greatcoat plastered to his back. Nearby, leading his section, stood Lance-corporal Wren. They were facing away from her. Maud was watching them; but watching her also. While Beatrice in her turn included the two soldiers and the canvas awning in her gaze. So it was as if they were all still linked, the four of them, in that turbulent place, but linked negatively. For no one of them could tell exactly what the other three were thinking. Then Beatrice felt a timid plucking at her sleeve. She turned to find Molly Dadger, her black hair hanging in dripping ropes to her shoulders.

– Don't they look fine, Miss. So 'andsome.

Beatrice, who had been gripped by the terrible charge of the negative circuit, could only nod. Molly pointed to the dripping back of Eric Wren.

– Funny to think what I used to feel for that one. And all he did was use me for running errands. You know, – and here Beatrice's old pupil drew confidingly close – I reckon he never had what you'd call a real man's as you might say *urges*. – She paused interrogatively then hurried on. – Still, all that's in the past. I'm walking out with a proper down-to-earth bloke now. He's an under-cook at the Grand. Earns almost forty quid a year. We're engaged. But my Jack don't have to join up. He's got bad eyes.

Again Beatrice nodded, seared by the energy of the circuit.

– And you're a VAD now. Doing your bit. To think I might have married that one. Lor what a thought. – Molly giggled. – Like lying next to a bit o' cod! – Then more timidly, absentmindedly sucking at one of her caked ropes of hair. – Have you met anyone, Miss. Anyone to walk out with?

Then with a supreme effort Beatrice did drag herself free and stood laughing into the rain, scorched but free.

– Oh yes, Molly. I've found someone. Someone to walk out with. Forever.

And laughed again, so that a few of the nearest spectators turned and tutted for the impropriety of it, during the bishop's closing peroration if you please and Molly, whispering a doubtful *I'm so glad for you, Miss* moved away from this woman who had once been kind to her but must be touched in some way now because of the terrible things she'd seen and was really not the sort of person you wanted to be acquainted with for all that she was a VAD.

So the ceremony in the little square ended. A bellowed 'shun' from the RSM sent a thousand detonations echoing into the rain. Then as the band struck up with 'Tipperary', the Regiment wheeled away, company by company, past the cairn of kit bags which had been piled up at its arrival, as if to mark the start of some great conflict here in the heart of Chalkhampton. As each man passed, another stone in the cairn was removed, so that in the end nothing remained except a space. This particular battle, unbloody and without a result, had left no survivors. Then, in a damp huddled mass the civilians followed, a few children capering despite the rain to the tunes of the now distant band, or running on ahead to march in step with an older brother. Meanwhile the mayor, the bishop, Lady Tremain, her new protégée and all the other dignitaries, were swallowed up by the town hall like statuettes disappearing into a clock-face. The awning was dismantled in a deluge of rainwater. The flags and the bunting came down. Soon the square was almost empty under its shifting shrouds of rain. A couple of gulls landed to root among a mess of half-trampled currant buns. Their savage beaks glistened as they hopped from tidbit to tidbit. Glancing back from amongst the crowd Beatrice saw these things, how they existed in a frame of light, an echo of words, a roughness of stone. Then turned to tramp uphill to the terminus.

Beatrice was standing in a chaos of noise and movement under the great hangar of Chalkhampton terminus. On every side farewells were being exchanged, kisses imparted, reassurances given, promises renewed. It should have been an intense scene, naked even, yet everyone seemed dominated by a diffidence bordering on constraint.

For the real goodbyes had been said elsewhere, in darkened rooms and corridors, under the wet skeletons of leafless trees. Only in the way fingers stroked and lips touched could there be detected the diminishing after-shock of other more intimate moments. Beyond, the train waited to begin its journey. Steam rose in thick grey clots to the roof of the terminus where pigeons roosted on girders, their heads tucked under their wings. A small soldier wearing a paper rose in his lapel brushed roughly past, knocking against Beatrice's right breast, the painful one.

– Mind who you're knocking into, you great fucking clumsy oaf.

And indeed the little man remained a great fucking clumsy oaf despite his gasped apologies. Beatrice turned away, her breath coming in short angry bursts.

It was an anger fuelled by searing self-doubt. Why had she come here? What good could it do? In the town hall square, when Molly Dadger had spoken to her, she had been gripped by a wild elation. She would go to the terminus and say goodbye to Charles whatever the consequences for her peace of mind. Why shouldn't she? There were many in that crowd who had only the smallest claim to be involved with the proceedings. Many had come out of idle curiosity or because they felt it their duty or because they took a morbid interest. She at least knew two of the soldiers personally. And was herself a nurse. Besides she wanted to see Maud.

But on the uphill walk to the station she had begun to question her motives. Perhaps she was as morbid as the worst of them. Perhaps she merely wanted to gloat. Then she had seen Maud and Lady Tremain in the back of a new Rolls convertible threading slowly along the street through the crowd. Maud, she was sure, had noticed her. But refused to register the fact, her face blurring to sepia behind the smoked glass. It had been all she could do to carry on and not go scuttling back to her miserable comfortless room in Orion Parade. How would she face these two when the moment came, on the platform with the man she had thought she loved? By the time she reached the station she was teetering on the verge of desperation.

– Hello, Miss Lumley, I thought you'd gone abroad. Mother said . . .

It seemed she was fated to be confronted with this childish doorkeeper.

– Robert. And with Oenone again. Is she still going out?

– Oh yes. Doesn't look too happy about it though, does she?

And indeed the young bitch did seem discomfited by the noise or the crowds or simply by some undefined terror of what might happen next. She panted wetly into Beatrice's lap.

– I'm looking after her till he comes back from the bar. Charlie says he's got to have a skinful. But Wren's with him.

Beatrice was again assailed by a desire to run away or hide. But stayed on, squatting down mechanically to rub the nervous retriever's ears. Suddenly Oenone jerked away and gave one short high bark. Of recognition or warning.

– Here you are, Robert. Lemonade. I . . . Oh it's you. I thought I recognised you in the crowd back there. Seeing someone off?

Maud seemed taller than Beatrice remembered. She had relinquished her green gaberdine for a fur-trimmed coat and stole. Yet she retained something of that transparent and treacherous composure visited upon her by fever. There flashed before Beatrice's eyes the vision of a woman clutching her nightdress to her neck as she danced girlishly toward a window. A long back. Pear-shaped drooping buttocks.

– Of course. Both of them.

Maud laughed shortly.

– What Charles and Eric? Really, Beatrice. Will you never learn? The icy manner could not conceal a certain quiver of apprehension, even perhaps a lingering spark of their old intense friendship. Maud rearranged her stole and took Oenone's lead from Robert.

– Come. Your mother's sitting on that bench near the platform. We will wait there.

– I don't want to go with you. I want to stay with Miss Lumley.

– Honestly, Robert. Don't make a scene. Not here. Not when the Regiment's about to leave. Remember what Mother said. Any more scenes and we'll have to think about a special school. And we don't want that do we?

Robert was snivelling and looking around wildly.

– Mother doesn't say anything. You do. You're not my mother. You're not the Maud who sang the song about the falcon. You're an imposter.

The noise of the slap was instantly lost in the cacophony of that place. But it had penetrated Beatrice's soul. Once she had pulled this child's hair in a fit of self-pity. She watched Maud dragging him away and felt a sudden access of calm. She had come to see someone off. And would do so.

He was leaning unsteadily against the newspaper kiosk outside the bar. Eric Wren had just disappeared into a tiled convenience.

– Charles. I came to say goodbye.

She had not meant to sound so matter of fact. Or so yearning. His face was flushed.

– Is it? It can't be. I thought you'd gone abroad. Mother had it from . . . Oh I can't remember. But you haven't. You're here. I say, Beatty I . . . – Then as if a veil had descended. – They're waiting for me. Over there. Maud and mother and little Bob. I must go.

She was desperate now. Desperate to keep this man standing or rather swaying a little longer in front of her alone. And suddenly remembered what she always carried. Turning away to fumble in her clothes she was at last successful. He stared at the amber cylinder she placed on his palm.

– You find them in the quarry, don't you?

His voice betrayed a tremble of old feelings. She looked up at him, as if they were alone again, in a place of wind and light.

– I wanted to give you it. As a charm. – Then with a supreme effort that almost tore the words from her lips. – A Devil's Thunderbolt. It's for luck. It brought me luck.

– Luck? – He was echoing incredulously. – You? After all that I . . . that she . . . Beatty, you're incredible. Or mad.

She was muttering with tears in her eyes.

– Oh but it did. In a way. It did. And I'm not mad at all.

Then his mouth was on hers, stopping all further movement. His breath oozed whisky. She struggled then relaxed. She had glimpsed Maud in the corner of her eye.

– At your service, Miss Lumley.

It was Eric. With the grey closed face of those who frequent bars to drink soda water.

– Charlie. I mean Sir. We must go.

Charles came sleepwalking out of the tunnel of their farewell kiss.

– Of course. Just saying goo'bye to my other sister. Yes. And now brother lead on. For you are you know. A brother to a dragon.

Eric Wren turned to Beatrice and winked. As if to say he would take good care of this slightly squiffy officer.

– Its dragons sir. Not dragon.

Charles burped.

– Poetic licence. Anyway if you want to know it's not dragons at all. It's jackals. You've got an old deflec . . . defective translation. Brother to jackals. Doesn't quite have the ring though, does it?

He turned to Beatrice. Who shook her head. She could not speak now she had seen him take the belemnite and place it like some living fragile thing gently in his tunic pocket.

Charles had been reclaimed by his family, while Beatrice watched from a distance, knowing that Maud watched her. The kiss between the two half-siblings was perfunctory, almost truncated. Lady Tremain looked on vaguely from her bench, as if she no longer saw much of what went on around her. Robert shouted out a mechanical list of keepsakes he would like brought back from the front – *A lüger and a pickelhosen and a mortar and a* – until Eric Wren lifted him up and spun him round his head, making the others laugh nervously, while Oenone barked her high-pitched warning. Beatrice remained excluded yet, retaining the taste of Charles's breath on her lips, was prepared to accept her isolation. A whistle blew and suddenly everybody was moving toward the waiting train. Once on the platform there was a slow-motion separation of soldiers and civilians. The Regiment was being reformed and brought to life again, under the pressure of so many kisses. Now soldiers were easing themselves into the waiting carriages. Beatrice saw Charles pushed up into the train by Eric and both turn to wave. She caught his eye. And blew a kiss. Which simultaneously made her feel ridiculous and special. Then, as the civilians themselves thronged forward, the carriages began sprouting hands and faces while the civilians, running alongside, superstitiously tried to touch them for cure or a charm. Beatrice herself ran for a while then gave up as the train gathered speed, leaving the civilians standing or sitting on the platform like so many drab fragments of shed skin. She turned and realised she was almost at the end of the platform. Below her on the rails lay torn newspapers, a dead pigeon, two yellowish brown coils of excrement. The train was a door receding on to the horizon. She turned to walk back and came up with the Tremains who studiously ignored her. She didn't care, not now Charles had kissed her. Then suddenly from nowhere Mr Birkett came puffing up too late to wave and wrapped his unwanted arms round Maud and Beatrice at once. Both flinched away, from him and from each other, yet were joined, strangely, by the absolute intensity of their longing to remain apart.

— *Ars longa vita brevis*, dear ladies remember that. – Mr Birkett squeaked and was a little taken aback not to say abashed at the way both young women simultaneously burst out crying.

3. Horizon of Storms

June – July 1916

It had been sultry and still for days. The air lay heavy in the streets and squares of Chalkhampton, a thick dry but invisible wadding in which all aromas and malignancies, all gases and foetors seemed to hang and intermix. Down on the tar-caked pebble beach, the sea heaved slowly like a sheet of mercury. The pillars of the pier took on the black opacity of basalt columns, where they rose from the water's impenetrable silver, seeming to support not timber and iron but an infinitely heavy heat haze, whose surface rippled now and again as if something had plunged down into it from an unimaginable height. Sealing the town within its dense gauze, this heat haze turned the surrounding landscape into a mirage, opening out on to ever more remote and impossible vistas, in which the bulk of Thundersbarrow or the long low ridge of Whitehawk floated, apart from the earth yet attached by countless unseen burning sinews. All day the sun hovered overhead, its circumference blurred like the rim of a kiln stokehole, its mouth seeming to ooze heat without light; while at night, eroded of its separate hard gemstones of stars, the sky glowed feebly, with the ashen dimness of a bed of smouldering chalk.

This weather, at once sterile and pregnant, would normally have been dispersed by one if not several thunderstorms, but this year for the first time anyone could remember, the storms did not materialise or rather, would build up as low contusions above Thundersbarrow during the evening then melt away overnight without a single flash of lightning or one refreshing fat drop of rain. Chalkhampton, it seemed, had finally sunk into a stagnant crater, whose smooth surrounding walls of hills had just enough height and bulk to hold off all change or disturbance. As if this suffocating inertia wasn't oppressive enough, the dry heat and the stillness which no storm arrived to disperse, had been announced and then regularly punctuated by another kind of storm whose muffled almost impacted echoes brought anxiety rather than relief.

This storm had begun on the last Saturday in June, during the morning when the heat was just beginning to intensify. At first its noise seemed so distant and the sky so lacking in clouds that the townspeople, struggling about their business through the sticky ravines of streets hardly noticed it. Indeed after an hour and twenty minutes, the reverberations lessened to the point where they could be ignored. But only for a while. For, gradually, as the day progressed, it became apparent that the dry muffled thunder had not vanished but was continuing to echo somewhere below the invisible horizon. Now people began to listen in earnest, looking not at the sky but down at the ground, as if instinctively associating the sound with something subterranean and earthbound. Then there would be murmurs under the breath, strange nods of the head, or brief and cryptic exchanges of glances. After three days and nights of this persistent but strangely soft almost ethereal thunder, people no longer had to guess or speculate about its origins. They knew now that the great bombardment of the German lines had started, the prelude to the Big One, the Breakthrough, the Push into Open Ground, Cavalry Country. They knew that the greatest battle of all was about to begin.

The knowledge brought no relief. Even when, after seven days and nights, the great man-made storm died down a little, becoming less continuous and more subject to periods of calm, even silence, people still went about their business with the hooded, slightly furtive look of those who know too much yet not enough. For if they understood the battle had now begun, they knew also that many of their own loved ones and relatives were directly involved. It had been three months since the Chalkhampton Chums had left Egypt. Postcards and letters soon established without a shadow of doubt that, after entraining at Marseilles, they had travelled north to disembark somewhere behind the British lines near Albert. All knew, or if they didn't know soon found out, that this area of the Front, an L-shaped sector running south from Gommecourt to Fricourt and then east from Fricourt to Montauban, would be the theatre for Haig's Big Push. Yet now that the bombardment had given way to the battle itself, the inhabitants of Chalkhampton discovered that their knowledge was at bottom a terrible haunting void. No one could imagine the nature of the battle, let alone the role their menfolk might be playing in it. The names on the maps remained names; the landscape (like Downland, some said, only more rolling) a distant abstraction. Gradually, as the days went by, the local *Herald* began to carry longer and longer lists of casualties, accompanied by tessellated pages of grainy photographs. Yet even this knowledge was not enough. It did not take them into the heart of that storm still echoing on and off below the horizon. Even when a handful of casualties turned up at the Fort hospital, their own accounts of what had happened or not happened only aggravated the raw wound at the heart of the town. It was as if people had begun to connect their unutterable ignorance with the continuing sound of guns until this terrible link was in its turn enclosed by the rainless sweltering heat. So that someone only had to mention the lack of rain and his listeners would immediately comprehend an underlying vision of bloodshed, carnage and grief.

It was a Tuesday afternoon, towards the middle of July and the little cul-de-sac of Artillery Row lay quiet as usual. So far the day had been little different from any other during the previous three weeks. The closeness of the atmosphere had not diminished. Clouds were gathering once again along the horizon. An occasional low rumble rose from across the Channel where, unknown to the citizens of Chalkhampton, three German regiments of the Eighth, Fortieth and Fifty-Eighth Divisions had just launched a savage counter-assault on Delville Wood. The Row itself was quite deserted. At the bottom, near the tram shelter, the yellow roses under Mrs Christie's parlour window had the papery, slightly tarnished look of flowers obliged to bloom in the middle of a long drought. Further up the short steep road, a child's wooden horse lay undisturbed in the gutter. Nearby a crumpled three-day-old *Herald*, bore the bold headline, 'Gains All along The Somme: Substantial and Steady Progress in the Vicinity of Longueval and Pozières'. The front page fluttered slightly, as if trying to turn over, abashed at a too easily won optimism. Directly opposite in an overgrown front garden, bees entered and emerged from a stand of self-sown foxgloves. The owner was indefinitely away, having lost her husband on the first day of the battle, though the circumstances of his death bore little relation to the account given in the standard letter which she had received a week later signed on behalf of the colonel of the regiment. Attempting, as part of his company's second wave, to climb out of a support trench, he had not acted 'bravely' but mechanically, his mind having already vacated a body anaesthetised by Navy issue rum; nor, being hit by a piece of shell casing that tore the face away from the skull could he be said to have died 'gallantly'. Knowing nothing of such things the bees went on murmuring inside the funnels of the foxgloves. Far below, on the promenade, a tin sign advertising sticks of rock flashed milkily in the dim sunlight.

But there was one figure in this, the most stultified corner of a stunned and stagnant town, who was behaving with a combination of physical vigour and extreme mental caution which, assuming there had been anybody in the neighbourhood to watch, might have been impressive if it hadn't looked so uneasy, the product not of decisiveness but paralysing fear. At first you might have thought it was the very likelihood of his being observed and his consequent determination that this shouldn't happen, which made this man so furtive and so quick. But it soon became apparent that his mental and physical world was dominated by the thought of what was not there. He had appeared initially some five minutes before, clambering up the nearside embankment of the branch line which ran alongside this last outcrop of the town before forking off in search of the Rother, the weald and Thundersbarrow. Now he was already halfway down the twitten, a narrow path overhung with an unkempt mix of dusty overgrown hawthorn, hazel and conifer, which passed along the southern or downhill side of the last house in the row. Coming to a gate which evidently led into the back garden of this house, the man paused, muttering, and ran his hands along its wooden surface as if he were reading some hidden braille message. Having long-since lost its latch the gate creaked open. The man jumped back and glanced with terror over his shoulder. Then muttering again, he moved forward through the gate which he was careful to close behind him.

The man was in his early twenties, of medium height and build. His hair might have been fair but had become so dirty and matted, so stuck with seeds of dandelion and dead thorns, that its fairness had to be inferred rather than observed. The colour of the moustache too was indistinct, being speckled with the white dust that had lodged in every zone of his weeks' unkempt growth of beard. Despite the heat, he wore a greatcoat of the kind issued to the army, but this he had buttoned and belted up so thoroughly, it was impossible to tell what rank he held or if he were in uniform underneath or not. The coat was ripped under one arm and bore the mark of many grass stains, as if its wearer had recently been rolling down a bank. He appeared to carry no hat and his boots were so caked with chalk and dried slime they looked like natural excrescences. The man moved forward, through a belt of shrubs, pausing once to scratch the purplish rash round his Adam's apple and continually checking behind him with sudden darting swerves of his head.

The path led him to a deserted backyard. Here, in front of the scullery, a small paved area lay bordered by a shed and a coal bunker. There was a white jasmine too, flowering against the shed and, as the man moved blinking into this arena of intense heat, a tabby cat came yawning from its shade, his dusty fur lying in flat glistening wedges. Then all at once, sensing something about this visitor and electing to be cautious, the cat withdrew and sat watching. The man moved swiftly up to the scullery door and tried the handle. It was locked. Turning away, he made a quick survey of the scene then darted to the coal bunker. Sliding up the coal door he thrust his hand inside to the elbow and groped briefly amongst the scraping nuggets. Then hand and arm returned, dusted black with coal but bearing a large brass key on a string. The key fitted the lock and with one last rapid glance behind him, the man passed inside and shut the door. Soon afterwards there was a rattle of bolts being slid with some force. Under the jasmine the tabby lay down with his front paws folded and closed his eyes.

Beatrice Lumley leant back in her chair, dragging both palms across her eyes and down on to her cheeks. Briefly, in negative, the image of a single window floated across her darkened vision. Then, palping her neck with her fingers she yawned, allowing her surroundings to come back into focus. The basement room where she had been working was large and cluttered. There were filing cabinets along one wall and ranks of box files obscured another. The window which had apppeared in negative lay high up in the whitewashed brick wall opposite her desk, a single pane that provided the room's only natural light. In front of her on the desk lay papers covered in columns and figures. She glanced at them again and sighed.

Although she still wore the apron of a VAD, its red cross turned a pale pink by many bleachings, Beatrice was no longer nursing in the ward ruled over by Sister Macready. A combination of events and coincidences had come about to ensure that, soon after the New Year, she had been transferred to the hospital's VAD administration wing. At first she had wanted to believe the implication that this was a genuine step up. Her qualifications as a teacher had been the prime movers apparently, convincing the authorities that she would be better employed using her brain than wielding endless bottles of lysol and iodine-soaked wads of gauze. Flattered by the attention and painfully conscious that her nursing skills had not developed much since the day she had hesitatingly swabbed out and hot-dressed the groin of the boy soldier, Beatrice had come to feel that the appointment represented a sort of banishment. Her work in administration had largely to do with capitation claims for those soldiers with amputations or other disabilities. It was, in effect, a branch of accounting, for which she was by no means qualified. Still, reasoning that all work in a time of war must contribute something, she had knuckled down to the business of registers and card indexes, at first under the lazy tutelage of a flatfooted male orderly who had been a solicitor's clerk in peacetime, latterly alone. In those early days she took a certain pride in the work, the business of compiling lists of those with one leg or one arm or no arms and no legs demanding a vigilant responsibility. She was glad, too, to be away from the rather oppressive ward sister. But most of all, though she found this difficult to admit, she was relieved to be spared the sufferings in the wards. Indelibly associated for her with the dark days of the previous winter, the ranks of wounded evoked a pain that mixed pity and horror with something more self-absorbed, unsatisfied and vengeful. Her early phase of enthusiastic nursing had soon become hopelessly entangled with the false dawn of Maud's friendship and Charles's return. And now that both were gone again, Maud back to Ecclesden and Charles overseas with his regiment, these feelings would not disperse but hovered round her as she emptied bedpans or made up beds. Registers and sums seemed preferable at that time, making even Macready's evident delight at her 'promotion' easier to bear.

After the departure of the Regiment, Beatrice had spent only a further week at Orion Parade, before moving to Artillery Row to live with her aunt. The change at first had seemed a desirable necessity. If the expected calm and freedom from all base desires had not descended as she had hoped it might, on that distant afternoon when she had first entered the empty house, she could at least comfort herself with the feeling that she had escaped what had become a mean and restricted life. Artillery Row was not only situated in a more salubrious area than her landlord's lodging-house, it was closer to the Fort hospital. The house itself was comfortable and despite Aunt Millicent's sometimes petulant domination of kitchen and scullery, Beatrice returned to it every night with the feeling that she belonged there. During the first few weeks, while the furniture settled into its new surroundings and Beatrice set about redecorating her own bedroom (the one which looked out on to the back garden) with some discounted green flock wallpaper whose leafy pattern reminded her of Ecclesden, it seemed as if the years of exile, of not belonging, were over. Even at night when, more from duty than love, she was obliged to sit and read *Emma* to her shawled and sallow-fleshed guardian, Beatrice would catch herself glancing round the little parlour and whispering *home*.

But things had soon begun to change. Firstly, there had come the alarming and rapid decline in her aunt's health. It seemed that the move to Chalkhampton had exacerbated rather than improved her condition. At the beginning of the third week Beatrice had come home to find her aunt sprawled on a settee, her breath short, her face grey. Dr Blake diagnosed a minor heart attack and admitted her to the civilian wing of the Fort hospital for observation. Returning a week later, Aunt Millicent seemed better for a while, but then two more strokes followed hard upon each other, the latter a violent seizure beside the pit from which an obsolete filter bed had recently been removed. Beatrice was just in time to stop her plunging in. Then had followed bedridden weeks, for which a nurse had had to be engaged at, in the patient's words, *outrageous expense*, the implication being that her niece would have been better employed tending her, rather than the unknown wounded soldiers at the fort. As a consequence Beatrice suffered a guilt which became acute when, one day after work, she returned home to find Dr Blake already in solemn and, he hinted, final attendance. Drugged by morphine, Aunt Millicent slept into the small hours then woke, gasping for words. Holding her birdlike frame up against the pillows, Beatrice saw how the heart hopped and fluttered weakly under the breastbone as if seeking escape. She had been witness to many such moments down at the fort yet could not help being moved, now, in a different and perhaps more selfish way. So that laying her cheek briefly against Aunt Millicent's forehead, she cried for herself or for the part of herself that must lie there too, inside a failing body. Then it was that the spirit of the feverish Maud visited her again, reminding her of a past that seemed now to be bathed in a heroic light, despite the undershading of despair. For Maud had been strong, a strong girl whom Beatrice had loved, whereas this woman whom she could at most respect, had passed beyond human frailty. Then too, Maud had filtered many truths through her fever, truths about them both as well as others; but Aunt Millicent could only ask for a glass of water or mutter something inconsequential about spring-cleaning the attic. At one point she did beckon Beatrice to lean forward so that she could warn her not to enter into any hasty liaisons *after I'm gone*. But if this admonishment drew on some hidden fund of knowledge about her niece's life, it did not succeed in appearing to be anything less than an afterthought, a last almost indifferent glance back across waters that were already beginning to close over her head. Even at the end, Beatrice was marginal to this woman's life. And must sob for that too when, finally, her aunt lurched forward as if seeking to touch something, then lay back for a last time, her blue-lipped mouth frozen half-open in its cracked and perspiration-streaked powder mask.

The funeral was sparsely attended by a few London relatives whom Beatrice had met once or twice in her forgotten childhood, along with a couple of local tradesmen who had appreciated Aunt Millicent's prompt payments by return and hinted heavily that a continuation of that tradition would be much appreciated. After-wards the relatives came back for tea at Artillery Row, arranging themselves stiffly for the ritual recital of war and weather news. None wanted to stay long, knowing that the house had been bequeathed to Beatrice, along with what little money and bonds her aunt had managed to salt away. Then had come the first night spent alone, when Beatrice became a ghost in her own house, gliding from room to room, seeking yet not seeking her image in pierglass and silverware, her hands raised before her in supplication or farewell.

It was that first night alone which brought home to her how tenuous her ties with Artillery Row really were. At the bottom of the little hinged drawer behind the frilled skirt on her dressing table, inside a spring-loaded jewellery box wrapped round with a wad of cotton wool, lay a creased and smudged card which Beatrice had often taken out and kissed since receiving it back in February before her aunt's illness had entered its last phase. On one side there was a photograph of the Sphinx; on the other a short message in Charles's sloped elegant hand. *Eric says this creature is a speaking likeness of Behemoth. When we visited it he launched into a veritable sermon. I think he's just a big cat with a badly mauled nose. How far away Blighty seems. We are longing for action. Hoping this finds you as it leaves us. In the pink.* Reading it that first time, Beatrice had been unable to restrain her tears, running upstairs to conceal not only the sadness of separation but the deeper pain of renewed isolation. Aunt Millicent knew nothing of these people. It was as if, outside the aching confines of Beatrice's own skull, they might not even exist. The thought filled her with fear and self-disgust. Why had she never been able to express her emotions? Why must they always remain hidden and unaddressed? If she had managed to be more open, confessing to her aunt at least some of the trouble of last winter, instead of sitting night after night ploughing through Jane Austen, then she herself might have gained in confidence and stature. As it was she remained alone and disregarded. This was why the card was so flippantly terse, more brusque even than the letter from Salisbury Plain. Little Beatty won't mind, what with her aunt and her work. She's so mouselike anyway. Meanwhile back at Ecclesden, perhaps in the butterfly room itself (though the shattered cabinet had long since been consigned to the attic), Maud would be scanning some profuse and detailed missive from her half-brother, full of passion and shared jokes, and mentioning Beatrice, if at all, as one would a slightly exasperating maiden relative. So she had reasoned, hearing her aunt moving painfully in the scullery, already draped with the miasmic shroud of a last illness. Yet the postcard had not gone unanswered. And for the next month Beatrice had waited for a reply, longing yet dreading a Charles both more expansive and less familiar. Hadn't he kissed her goodbye on the station? In front of Maud? Hadn't she given him the lucky Devil's Thunderbolt like a sweetheart? Buoyed up by these memories she even sent off (Oh heights or depths of folly and longing!) one shilling for a cheap 'Pendant of Service and Sacrifice' to be worn *by all those with husbands or sweethearts overseas*. The pendant came and was duly pinned inside her bodice where the charm had once been concealed. But Charles did not reply. Gradually, her dressing-gowned morning vigils at the top of the stairs before breakfast became more irregular. She grew to treat the postman's gravel crunch as a sign of continuing desolation rather than imminent promise.

And now her aunt was dead. Taking out the card once more she saw it as a sum total of all her failures. So small and faded and soiled a thing. It whispered to her, in its soiled prosaic voice: *Go away. Escape. Now that there is no one. Now that you are truly alone.* Yet the very next day, as if Aunt Millicent's death had unscrambled a blockage in the gearwork of days, a reply did finally arrive. It was a card again, this time postmarked Marseilles and at first Beatrice thought it had been sent by mistake, since it contained no message, only a series of printed alternatives meant to be used by a wounded soldier who had been sent back down the line. Her heart shuddered. Then she saw that whoever had sent this card was having an amusing time with the rigid military language, crossing out words to make a stumbling, staccato sentence: *I am quite sick have received no letter from you for a long time.* The signature was indistinct and might have been either an E or a C. This would-be playfulness only confirmed what Beatrice had felt the night before. Although she wrote again, sending socks she had knitted during the spring, she again experienced an overwhelming desire to act in some decisive, incontrovertible way. That this desire conveniently linked a new phase in her life with the likelihood of moving nearer to Charles's regiment, Beatrice was not inclined to question. There was excitement in the idea, not least because in moving nearer, she might actually discover a new apartness (France after all was a big place), in which she and Charles might meet on some more nebulous spiritual plain. Perhaps that had been the meaning of the vision she had had in the empty bedroom all those months ago. So the card was placed with its brother in the wadded jewellery box, as an earnest of things to come.

By this time it was June and the press was buzzing with rumours of a new campaign in northern France. At first Beatrice did not pay too much attention to these reports. Then one day, the solicitor's clerk with the fallen arches put his head round her basement door to announce that the Chums were definitely on the Somme. He himself had a brother in the First Battalion whom he looked up to inordinately. *Harry's written saying they'll be in the thick of it,* he shouted shrilly then disappeared, leaving Beatrice to wonder why he had chosen her for this announcement, then to brood on her own circumstances. The thought of Charles and Eric being involved in a great new battle at once alarmed and excited her. To these emotions was added a certain tincture of bitterness at their continuing silence, which she tried to sweeten by reasoning that they probably had no time. The upshot was that she experienced a great longing to nurse again. It was almost as if the very association with her friends made it her only means of self-expression. Gradually as June passed into July, some of the first casualties from the great offensive appeared at the fort. Watching the stretchers being unloaded from the ambulances, Beatrice tried to imagine their journey home. Denied knowledge of their complex and gruelling progress from aid post to advanced dressing station to casualty clearing station and thence to base hospital and the Channel ships, Beatrice found that her imagination would not function. With the result that her longing to nurse became merged with an equally insistent urge to know. Since she was now certain that Charles and Eric were themselves involved in the Big Push, it seemed suddenly imperative that she return to being a VAD pure and simple. Only thus could her mounting anxiety over their fate be assuaged. Every day she scoured the local *Herald*, possessed by a mood in which hope and dread were equally balanced. If there should be a photograph of Charles, or if Eric's name should appear in the casualty lists, then dread would predominate; but if Charles's name should be mentioned in the honours list, or Eric should be quoted from where he lay lightly wounded in a base hospital, then hope would triumph. Since none of these eventualities occurred, the anxious equilibrium was maintained. Once or twice Beatrice thought of writing to Maud (she could not bring herself to approach Lady Tremain directly) to ask for news. But resisted, if only because, from the day of the Regiment's departure to the present, there had been no communication with her old friend whatsoever and to start now was more than her pride could bear. So she waited, listening for the postman's tread in the morning and buying the late edition of the *Herald* in the afternoon. Meanwhile she had put out feelers regarding a transfer to a theatre of operations. At the beginning of the year it had been announced that VADs could now serve abroad, given three months' training and a minimum age of twenty-three. It had been this last requirement which, at the time, had caused Beatrice to pass over the newspaper reports without comment. Now however that stipulation seemed laughably irrelevant. Who during such a crisis would question her that closely? She would be no more rejected on account of her age than any male volunteer, some of whom were as young as sixteen. A weekend trip to the Red Cross headquarters at Pall Mall confirmed her hunch. Today, two weeks later, she had only to receive her transfer instructions which she had recently been promised were in the post. Then she would be on her way to France, a move nearer the conflict which she could not help but feel was propitious.

Missing her usual tram Beatrice had to walk a good quarter of a mile to reach the bottom of Artillery Row and felt quite faint with exhaustion by the time she came to the twitten below her own house. It was the muggy heat she told herself, pausing in the shade of a conifer to get her breath. That and the tedium of her work. But even as she wiped the sweat from the wings of her nose Beatrice was troubled by a thought that would often come nowadays, unbidden yet insistent. Her fatigue had to do with something more than simple physical exertion. Since Christmas her cycle had become irregular, to the point where she could no longer anticipate from month to month whether her period would be even heavier than usual or simply non-existent. With this disruption, there had developed attacks of dizziness accompanied by disabling hot flushes. For all her diffidence, Beatrice would have consulted her aunt on the subject;

but by that time Millicent was already sequestered in her illness and could not be approached. So she turned to the dog-eared *Enquire Within* but could find little under Change of Life that seemed relevant to a woman as young as herself. Dimly she seemed to remember her aunt mentioning just such a case, long ago in the old house when one of the neighbours called round. *Hardly of childbearing age and yet her womb was already giving up. Extraordinary. Like a Judgment from Heaven.* Could this be happening to her? Dr Blake might have been helpful but somehow, what with her aunt's death and then the plan for going overseas (she had put the house in the hands of a letting agent), Beatrice had allowed the matter to slip. And indeed for most of the month hardly thought of the business. Until the symptoms returned. As now.

Dizzy, and increasingly nauseous, Beatrice chose not to take her usual route down the alley to the back door, but went straight round to the front in order to pass inside and lie down as quickly as possible. As she groped in her handbag for the key, rustling the newspaper which she bought religiously every afternoon but often did not dare scour until evening, the tabby cat who had been asleep under the jasmine at the back, came sidling round the corner of the house. Rubbing with tail erect against her skirts, he followed her into the darkness of the hallway, where a letter glimmered on the mat. Still sweating, Beatrice sat down on the settle to read it. Here at last were her orders abroad. In two weeks' time she must report to Red Cross HQ then take the afternoon train from Victoria to Folkestone and thence across the Channel to the base hospital at Boulogne. Despite her condition, Beatrice could not help a little shout of triumph. Almost simultaneously the cat, who had been engaged in purringly pushing his chin against the edge of the letter, suddenly jumped down and, with ears back, ran low-bellied towards the parlour. Beatrice scolded, laughingly.

– Ulysses. Whatever is it? Have you seen a ghost?

The cat had sat down in the parlour doorway and was staring fixedly towards the scullery. Beatrice followed his gaze. Nothing.

– Really puss, you're so . . .

334

But her words died in her mouth. There had been a movement. And a choked sound like someone suppressing a cough. Her pulse began to pound. The gas meter above her head ticked with unnatural loudness.

– Who . . . who's there?

How thin her voice sounded in this suddenly alien house that she had dared call her own. Shakingly, she stood up and groped with infinitely heavy steps forward or downward into the darkness. And would have fallen if he had not caught her, proving thereby that he was no ghost, returning like so many before him to announce his own death at the Front. Yet for years afterward Beatrice would remember this moment as the beginning of a kind of haunting, in which human fear and excitement took on an almost supernatural intensity. Perhaps in the end the terrified reaction of the cat had not been so very wide of the mark.

– Charles. How did you find me? How did you get in? Oh I was so frightened. Why are you here and not in France?

So the questions poured sweatily from her, as she attempted to steady herself, detaching her body from his grasp, until everything was swaying again and he came back, leaning over her as if from the top of a steep, barely scalable slope to steady her ascent, his hot hand closing on hers which had grown chill and dry. The ascent was difficult, since it involved leaving so much of the past behind, but together they achieved it and then she was at the top of the slope of days looking deep into the ravine or cave from which he had emerged. Again, the voice was asking, begging to be answered, but now the spasmy sick feeling had begun in the very pit of her stomach, smothering all sound so that he had to guide her now through the sick feeling into the depths of a house which had briefly seemed so strange and other. The sick feeling did not evaporate, but she felt calmer for his having shown her that it was her house after all and not a cellar under some ruin in the middle of a devastated plain. Yet still he had not said anything nor even appeared to hear.

In the cool darkness of the scullery she leant against the enamel chill of the butler sink and retched with long dry coughing spasms.

His hot palm cupped her forehead. His other hand stroked her back. Now a thin thread of greenish bile was dangling from her lips. The thread was braided with nasal blood. She looked at it quizzically, wondering how it had formed there, deep in the empty cave that had suddenly yawned inside her body, then risen without her prompting to connect her to this moment of unlooked-for tension. Then the shame began and wiping the thread away she cried into the sink for the humiliation of his seeing her like this, throwing up the air of which her life had so dreadfully come to be composed.

– That cat. Didn't I see him once at old Birkett's? The drooping jaw. Its unmistakable. He had a classical name, didn't he? Ajax or . . . No. I forget.

The incongruity of these words, the first she had heard from his lips since the troop train had chugged out of Chalkhampton terminus, filled some of the emptiness in Beatrice's body so that a little part of her could laugh despite the tears of shame. Struggling to stand upright she glanced to where the cat was sitting with one back leg over his shoulder licking gently at the sprout of a pinkly exposed penis. Evidently, he no longer regarded the newcomer as an apparition.

– Ulysses. He was at Orion Parade, yes. But then he came here. It was quite strange. Walked I suppose. He was always a bit of a wanderer. I offered him back but Mrs Birkett's developed an allergy. So now he's mine would you believe. And I never even liked cats. Much. – She paused, remembering yet not wanting to remember the woman who *had* liked cats. Then in an access of misery, turning away to dab her mouth with a soiled dishcloth – Oh Charles. I'm so embarrassed you should see me like this. But it's that time. You know.

Which was true, except that Beatrice was obliged to omit the fact that nowadays the sickness would often come instead of a bloody discharge. So the old coyness settled back into place after the nudity of antiperistalsis.

– Don't worry, old thing. I'm sorry I gave you such a fright. And the heat can't help.

He paused, as if forgetting what he had intended to say and Beatrice, despite her condition, was seized by an intense joy which had to find words, any words.

– Oh, but Charles you're back. And not hurt. Or not badly. You don't know the anxiety I've had. And the papers. And the casualty lists. And . . .

So joy relaxed into tears and he was leaning forward again, drawing her head briefly to his shoulder.

– That's all over now. – Then, pointing at her faded armbands – I say, you're still a VAD then? In that hospital?

He had stepped back and stood looking at her from the treacly shadows. A wasp which had been buzzing angrily against the grille in the larder came stuttering out to be swatted by Ulysses. The cat sniffed at the striped body fastidiously. Then ate it, shaking his head.

– But I told you all about it, didn't I? My transfer to administration. In my letter.

The one you never answered, she wanted to add. But resisted. Her joy had been shortlived. The rim of the butler sink dug into the small of her back. She would have liked to retch again but alone, in some concealed place. She dabbed her mouth with the tea towel.

– Of course you did. How silly of me. And they work you hard, I bet. How's that old battleaxe Macready? Still making you empty bedpans?

It was as if he had heard what she said but not registered the sense. And where had that tremor in his voice come from? Perhaps it had been there before, unnoticed like a slight flaw in a jewel. She could not remember. But now the very syllables of his words seemed rifted, so that sense was forced to jump across, blindly.

– It's you soldiers. – She was speaking through the mufflement of the towel, glad of its protective shield. – You keep getting wounded. And so we have to make you well again.

She would be a nurse once more in Macready's ward if that was what he wanted. Perhaps the ghost of a joke might simultaneously quell her humiliation and draw this phantom firmly into the land of the living. But Charles barely smiled. Then seemed suddenly anxious, staring up at the ceiling.

– Where are the rabbits? He might want them. He might come for them. I shouldn't want . . . Oh Christ . . .

So the rifts between his syllables opened up again letting out an acrid smoke. Then as quickly closed over. So that even as she was throwing the towel into the sink and stepping forward, he was laughing, making her wonder whether she had heard his intervening words correctly, if indeed they had ever been pronounced.

– Yes, you're so right. But you see they will keep shooting at us, those damned Boche. And sometimes we forget to duck. Look Beatty, I'm most awfully sorry for coming inside without permission but I arrived here before you and . . .

She was close to him now and could smell both his rank breath and the sickly odour wafting from his clothes. She would have to wash them she told herself, then wondered at how easily she had accepted the outlandish idea of his staying here in Artillery Row. His eyelids were flickering as he went on.

– I guessed where the key would be. I might be seen outside. And I wouldn't want . . . Oh no . . .

Again that other voice, the one shrouded in some sort of smoke. She was swaying once more or he was or the air in which they stood together, responding to some unheard, unimaginable detonation. Then through the grainy aftermath of the blast he moved towards her, enfolding her at last in a tight embrace which, she found out later, branded the red shadows of three brass greatcoat buttons on left breast, sternum and navel.

– Oh Beatty, you've no idea how I've longed for this moment. But poor dear. You must lie down. You look whacked if I may make so bold. Come on, lean on me. That's it. This way.

So, like a cross between a phantom and an escaped slightly delirious convict, Charles Tremain re-entered Beatrice Lumley's life for the last time. Stunned by his sudden unexpected presence, she did not think to question the proprietorial way he invited her back into her own domain.

The light was fading in the back parlour when Beatrice and her

338

unexpected guest sat facing each other across a table over whose green chenille cloth linen had been spread to accomodate a meagre meat tea. Charles had already drawn the curtains and would not allow Beatrice to light a lamp. Occasionally, there was a distant rumble in the direction of Thundersbarrow and once, a blue light seemed to rise up over the sea like a sheet shaken out by some giant hand. The jubilee mug in Charles's hand shook, spilling a thin brown stream. But he did not seem to notice. He was busy talking. Not to Beatrice. Or rather not only to Beatrice. For behind the mask of words this man seemed always to be communing with other unseen presences he had summoned to be with him there, among the cutlery and piled shortbread, the dish of tinned Scotch salmon and the soft clustered brains of dumplings.

After her initial surprise and consternation, Beatrice had experienced a calm blankness of spirit, lying upstairs on her bed fully clothed, sucking a tablet of crystallised ginger, while below her Charles moved about restlessly in a twilight he himself had created, by pulling across curtains and dragging down blinds. She had even dozed for a minute or two, then woken with the distinct impression of having been back on Thundersbarrow but at night, among the shallow depressions that marked the shafts of the ancient flint mines. Charles's white tapes had still been in place but in a different pattern of straight parallel lines which for some reason she had to walk between, slowly, like a blind person, while far below in the darkness a lone peacock called. Waking to her room and the memory of all that had just happened, Beatrice found that her calm had quite vanished. In its place she was possessed by a nagging anxiety in which anger, disillusion and fear jostled for pre-eminence. Before venturing toward the kitchen to see who or what was making the noise, she had had the foresight to tuck her letter from the Red Cross into her sleeve. Drawing it out now, she realised that it was this innocent piece of paper which had become the focus for her new mood. Why had Charles come back now, at the moment when she was about to go abroad? It was as if he had deliberately pre-empted her resolution to act and act decisively. Worse still he had,

339

by his sudden reappearance, quite destroyed the dream on which her transfer had been founded. Hadn't she hoped, shyly and with only the vaguest notion of any actual meeting, for some communion of souls, out there in France? How could such a communion ever take place now that he had confronted her in her own house with the reality of his new self: rank, haggard, shaking, self-obsessed? Gloomily, she lay and listened for signs of his presence. Not a sound. Had he perhaps gone the way he had come, back down the twitten and out, over the hills. For a moment she was filled with an unspeakable relief which made her realise just how much she had feared not only his presence, but also the strain on herself which it must exert. Why had he come there? What for? How long had he intended to stay? What had he expected her to do? But the questions, rising up out of her brief vision of his departure actually seemed to summon him back, so that down in the kitchen he reasserted his presence with a cough and a scraped chair-leg. Then to her amazement Beatrice found that she was glad after all. Glad that he had come to her. Glad that he had chosen her, now, today, whatever else might have happened before on other days and in other places. And rose up off her bed with a renewed determination to prove herself worthy of his choice, whatever it implied. The ginger pastille had done its work. Her dizziness and nausea were quite gone.

An hour later, sitting opposite him in the little parlour, with Ulysses purring proprietorially in her lap, Beatrice found nevertheless that she could summon no appetite whatsoever. Her sense of glad pride had long since evaporated, to be replaced by all the old questions, thrown into relief now by many new ones. What had happened at the Front? Had he indeed been involved with the Chums in the Big Push, as she had assumed in her daily scouring of the newspaper? If so, had he been wounded? And was this why he had come back? Or was he on leave? Had he already been to Ecclesden? Had he seen Maud? Where was Eric? Oenone? When was he going back? Or was he not going back at all? So far, from this vast armada of questions she had been unable to launch a single ship.

It was as if Charles had bolted the back door on the whole world. Outside there was a familiar distant rumble. Charles dropped his fork, still caked with dumpling and half rose in his seat.

– That noise. What . . . what was it?

Frightened by his fear Beatrice had consciously to control herself, glancing across at the briefly luminous curtain.

– Thunder, I expect. Do have some salmon, Charles.

– Thunder? But it sounded so fucking loud. Are you sure?

His face was sweating.

– Of course I'm sure. What else could it be? The guns don't sound like that.

– Guns?

He was standing now, gripping the chair. She regretted the remark. But pushed on.

– I thought you'd know. How we hear them, sometimes. But that's thunder. Thunder with no rain. And how we need the rain. The garden's quite dessicated. Oh Charles, you're so edgy. Please.

Then, as would often happen over the next few days, Charles's face suddenly cleared. And he was sitting again, talking with happy disregard through wolfed mouthfuls of food.

– Did I tell you about my blighty one? A piece of shrapnel in the leg. God, how it hurt. It was hot too. But it got me back here. Yes. Look I'll show you.

Then all at once Charles was standing again, this time to turn and drop his trousers for all the world as though he were attending some military examination. Long inured to the sights of hospital, Beatrice still found herself girl enough to be startled into a blush. Moreover, she could not at first decide where the wound had been made. In the crook of either knee, welts of eczema lay, their crusts bloody with recent scratching. Then, on the left calf, indistinct and seemingly long-healed, she did at last pick out a thin scar. And would have subjected it to professional examination if Charles hadn't suddenly swung away, busily rebuckling his Sam Browne belt. He still had not removed his greatcoat.

– Bad enough to send me home. To send me here.

Beatrice sat back and, despite her still queasy stomach, munched ecstatically on a chunk of salmon stuck with small crunchy vertebrae. A faint uneasiness that so well-healed and shallow a scar could somehow constitute a 'Blighty wound' rose up to trouble her mind. But who in the end was she to question the vagaries of the military machine? Charles might not be telling the whole truth; he might be strangely ill-at-ease; but he was, as he himself had just acknowledged, indubitably here. Not at Ecclesden. Not with his mother. Not with Maud. But here. Only a few hours ago such a set of circumstances would have seemed beyond imagining. The salty clot of fish slid down her throat with the piquant luxuriance of a long ago picking of raspberries. Even the worrying manner of his arrival, finding the key and to all intents and purposes forcing an entry, could be explained. He was a soldier after all and soldiers did such things. Or were reputed to. This soldier was sitting down again cupping his still full mug. Suddenly Beatrice felt she could begin to broach the many questions that had accumulated, like a silt.

– And you came back from France alone?

She was launched. Although it was not yet the moment to mention other names.

– On a troopship yes. With plenty of others. No doubt you noticed.

– The influx? Yes.

– I ended up in Southampton, in one of those big clearing hospitals for a few days. And then when I got my invalidity papers made straight for here . . .

– Invalidity? You mean you're invalided out?

– Not indefinitely. But it tore the ligament you see. I can't walk well.

Again a slight doubt rose in her mind and seemed to be mirrored in his ever-shifting eyes. She had seen him walk without difficulty not a few minutes ago. Once more she must suppress the feeling.

– And Ecclesden? Have you been there?

– Well, first of all I . . .

She waited, luxuriously anticipating the admission that he had

342

come to see her first. But Charles's mind seemed to have frozen in mid-sentence. The mug shook. There was another flash like an emerald slit in the very fabric of the curtain. The air in the little parlour sagged, still and heavy. Perhaps at last there would be rain. Charles had begun counting.

– One. Two. Three.

A low growl truncated his litany at four. He took a noisily desperate slurp of tea.

– Not that close. Not yet. Oh Beatty, what shall I do?

And then he was on his knees, arms hooped round her waist, his face buried in a lap still warm from Ulysses, who had jumped off in alarm at this stranger's latest violence of gesture. Flinching at so absolute a contact, Beatrice nevertheless found the courage to stroke Charles's hair, feeling how thin and brittle it had become, as if scorched in an exposure to some source of flame. Electrified by the atmosphere, a few dry follicles stuck to her fingers. She must resolve to be calm. Here was a soldier who, having fought and suffered, had surrendered himself into her care. Nor could she deny a certain sense of triumph. The prey who had eluded her net for so long was now firmly in her grasp. She would not let go again lightly. He had entered her kingdom and must take the consequences wherever they might lead. So she patted the shaking head with a grimly possessive gesture, deliberately forgetting the many anomalies she had already encountered.

– Well, you can't go anywhere tonight. Not in this weather. You must stay here. I'll make up the bed in the spare room. Are they expecting you at home?

He shook his head but did not raise it. Then she allowed herself to grow brisk.

– All the better then. All the better that you chose me. Come on Charles, pull yourself together. It's only a storm. Only thunder.

But she knew that it wasn't, despite her mask of practicality. And knew too that her deepest desire involved his not pulling himself together at all, but staying with her to be nursed this side of breakdown but on the far side of health. What this would mean for herself and her imminent move she hardly dared contemplate. Shocked at her own duplicity she could not help surrendering to another stomach spasm. Charles raised his head, seeming to guess her discomfort, both physical and moral. Although his cheeks were still wet he seemed to have mastered himself again, looking up at her with the old slightly impertinent air of condescension. A boy in a man's body.

– You're a brick, old girl. A really good sort.

Disliking this false bonhommie more thoroughly than his irrational fearfulness, Beatrice threw caution aside.

– And Mr Wren. Did he – she was going to say *survive* but winced still from too great a flow of reality into that sacred place her house had become – did he come through?

The merest glimmer in those cloudy blue eyes. The merest twinge of muscles under skin that she suddenly realised was strangely grey and wrinkled where the jaw bone articulated. As if it had somehow been stripped off then stuck back on.

– Oh yes. I saw him at the aid post not long after I got mine. The merest scratch. He's quite indestructible. And taught me such a lot. You know, out in the desert he showed me how to throw grenades as if I were chucking coconuts at the fair.

Charles had torn away from her and, all disability forgotten, was walking quickly between mantelpiece and doorway, too quickly, trying to outpace something. Or someone. Beatrice must somehow change the subject.

– Did you know Birkett's trying to organise another charity concert? He's just the same. It's a wonder how his wife puts up with him.

Marching. Marching. Hardly hearing.

– Yes, it's supposed to be at Ecclesden this time. In the new wing your mother's converted. I've had to opt out of course. Things are just too hectic now down at the hospital. But Maud will be singing so I've heard. I shan't be missed I'm sure.

She would not tell him yet about her transfer to France. Indeed his arrival had made all such practicalities recede beyond reach.

344

Meanwhile, as if he were trying without success to recall something, his march eased for a moment. Then speeded up again, the memory quite forgotten.

– Charles, I think you should go to bed, rest.

She had not intended her voice to sound so tremulous, as if she were suggesting something indecent. Which in a way she was. The storm had entered the room now.

– Charles?

He had stopped opposite her, the room seeming to march on, desperately, with its sealed canisters of storm. He was raking his fingers through his brittle old man's hair. Trying to rub something out or in.

– If I stay, all the doors must be locked. Do you understand? And the windows, I shall have to check the windows. He can only – he gasped, his chest heaving with the exertion of his march – he can only pass through an opening. Do you promise, Beatty. Do you promise me that?

Again this obsession with pursuit, with someone seemingly trying to track him down. For one terrible moment Beatrice entertained the thought that Charles was unhinged. Then with an effort controlled herself. Not mad, no. Just tired. A tired soldier who has endured. But he doesn't remember her. He doesn't remember Maud.

– Come help me with the bed. The storm is coming closer. It sounds as though it might be over Thundersbarrow by now. And I must have those clothes. To put in the dolly tub.

The face of a little old boy looking down on her through the banisters.

– Up the wooden hill to Bedfordshire.

– Why did you die? Oh why did you die? Why did you?

The voice rose and fell in the interstices of thunder. She had stopped on the landing on her way to the bathroom after having seen him settled an hour back. A glass of water and a handkerchief on the bureau beside the single bed with its single sheet under which he had climbed, trembling and a little hot, to assume the foetal position, one arm over his face. The pillow plumped up, the window checked. Quite fast. *Goodnight, then. I'll leave the light on in the bathroom. And the door a little open. So. Too much? Yes? Like this then. Good. Goodnight.* Her child. Her invalid. Her charge. And now this. Forcing her to listen at the open door. Forcing her to realise that once again she knew nothing of this person or how he had lived.

– Why did you why did you you bastard you fucking impossible marvellous bastard because because the shrapnel i didnt mean to white city rum scoop too much too much i didnt mean troops of midian the quarry's gone up just like your shaft i was frightened then and im frightened now up and over thats it oenone cmon girl no faster the tapes oh yes its here the shellhole keep low i dont want i cant i dont want to meet him like pater maxim no weve got to turn it on them no it only needs two sir youre in command with the toffee apples creep forward through the wire you bastard oh no shes hit cmon sir just feed the belt in water pour the water in the jacket so it doesnt overheat no she needs the water i bastard you bastard im off come back stop running youll be no why why did you how can i where will we o die

The litany ended. But the storm continued, shuddering back and forth through the little house. Beatrice staggered away from the door as from the entrance to a furnace, stunned by the heat and turmoil of Charles's mind. Shivering in her own bed she grew frightened and confused. What were these events that seemed to rise up out of his mind like smoke from an explosion? Who was he talking about with such bittersweet regretful venom? Was she host to an incurable, someone who had travelled beyond not only physical help but the sort of tenderness which, she flattered herself, only she could provide? If so, what kind of help should she seek and where? Outside a dry wind was driving against the house, rattling panes and knocking over a spade in the back yard. He seemed quieter now yet she dared not venture back down the landing to linger outside that cave of pagan curses. She crouched under the eiderdown and waited. Why had he come back out of the storm to mutter and blaspheme?

Why should he be allowed to destroy the hardwon calm of these last few months? For a moment, as the lightning blurted again across the window, so that the walls of the room seemed to warp and expand, she hated this uninvited guest and would have gone screaming at him to be off, back to Maud and his mother or back to the Front where no doubt Eric and the others awaited him with an impatient love. But the desire to exorcise was short-lived. With the ebbing of the wind, a calmer love returned. She must help, not condemn.

– Charles, are you there?

She dared not switch on the bedroom light for fear of shocking him. Her voice sounded frail and old. Then the thunder returned, a series of percussions like something huge and heavy being pushed down a giant staircase. She waited for the next flare of lightning. When it came she saw without looking that the bed was empty. He had gone. Sensing her unspoken but furious imprecations he had returned to his own world. And she, who for the first and only time in her life, had been vouchsafed the chance to understand another's soul was alone again with her shrivelled nut of nauseous virginity. It was she who had put a curse on things not him. If she had only bothered to listen instead of retreating into self-pity he might still be here. It was not that this second entrance didn't have an ulterior motive. She was ready to admit that she had intended coaxing him into her bed if only (her period might or might not be waiting in the wings) to lie back to back and head to toe for the sake of animal warmth. How feeble that plan now seemed, how childishly duplicitous. So she wept, sitting down on the still warm bed. Until the singing began.

If you want the old battalion,
We know where they are
– Hanging on the old barbed wire.

A rhythmic punching of sounds, the words rose in the gaps between lightning and thunder to the accompaniment of a lower more metallic noise. Beatrice pulled back the curtain and squinted down into the darkness. He was out there somewhere, in the back garden, digging.

347

Hanging on the old barbed wire . . .

Another burst of lightning lit him up at the bottom of the sloping lawn where the previous owner had cultivated a cucumber frame. The glass was long gone but the brick wall survived. He was inside the wall excavating with the spade that had fallen down in the wind. All at once the rainless darkness closed in again and he was invisible. Beatrice groped blindly forward. Then a fresh flare showed him naked, his frail body glistening with sweat. She saw too, in that brilliant instant, how the rashes behind the knees had been mere outliers of a more general eruption. Upstairs in the spare bedroom, she had averted her eyes from his undressing. Now as the lightning pulsed once more, she stared shamelessly, glimpsing in the hollow cave of his loins a remembered shrivelment. *Quite limp in fact. And as for that skin trouble . . .*

– Charles, come in. You'll catch your death.

She was determined still to treat him like a slightly errant youth. He carried on digging, swivelling round slightly to address her.

– Fetch a lantern will you, Lumley. The dugout's OK. It wasn't a direct hit. There's some corrugated sheets over there. *We know where they are . . .*

She did as she was told since this too could be part of the game. Or nightmare. But fetched his clothes as well, like any solicitous mother.

– Put these on again, Charles. I can wash them tomorrow.

Then scared as she was she found herself laughing in a sudden soaring exhilaration. He looked up from his struggle with the deeply unfamilar garments. A caveman.

– War is no laughing matter, Lumley. Quickly help me with these.

Then he was leaping out of his shallow trench and dragging the corrugated sheets across, balancing either end on the brick courses. Beatrice moved to assist but found she was only really required to hold up the lantern. A few loose bricks kept the sheets from slipping. She found herself wondering briefly about the neighbours but managed to dismiss the thought from her mind. At least Charles was here and had not deserted her for a second time. And if she humoured him in his fantasy of digging and trenching, she might in time be able to lead him back inside and run a hot bath in the scullery. Who was to say that this physical activity might even help to clear the darkness that had come oozing up from his mind back in the house. So she stood there watching Charles Tremain build a dugout.

– There. Now wake me when the wiring party goes out. 0200 hours precisely. Goodnight.

He had hacked a hole in the side of the brick wall with a crow bar. He slithered through and disappeared.

– Put out the lantern, there's a good lad and tell Wren I want to see him at stand-to about the rations.

Mournfully, hopelessly under the disturbed midnight sky, Beatrice did as she was asked. Or commanded. He would not come indoors tonight. The darkness was thicker than she had supposed. So she trudged back to the house alone. Behind her from under the ground came a deep hoarse circular chant:

We're here because we're here because we're here because

She shut the door and locked it. No one else would enter uninvited until morning.

The next morning Beatrice woke early and lay for one timeless moment in a state of perfect forgetfulness, her mind filled with the voice of her dream, a voice that had seemed angelically intimate, speaking to her and her alone as she walked through a wood that might have been the hanger beneath Thundersbarrow except that its trees had been carved from chalk. There were blossoms under the trees and it was when she knelt to pick one that the voice came, out of the cathedral of the trees, whispering solely to her: *That is the Venus and Adonis flower; in the autumn it withers away*. Such happiness in the words, despite their tincture of melancholy. Such vistas of delight. And then, within or around the voice the echoing of many streams and waterfalls until the white columns of the trees were drowned in the noise, becoming the foundations of a city at the

349

bottom of the sea. She was floating now, among the pillars and crenellated battlements, deep into the white city under the waves. The flower in her hand glowed green as she floated and she had an overwhelming sense that ahead of her in some aquamarine square she would meet the ruler of the city and all would be, all would be . . .

A grey light had oozed through her drab curtains, hardening on the green wallpaper into a flocculent crust. It was all there again, the day and the evening and the night, the shame and the anxiety and the fear. Dragging herself from her bed (her stomach still aching from the exertion of vomiting), she tore back the curtains. The clouds of the previous night had drawn off a little, allowing a pale sun through. There had been no rain, despite the thunder and the wind. Out among the parched yellows of the garden the new corrugated roof of the cold frame flashed dully. He was there still, she was sure. But today there could be no repetition of last night's simple drama. Most of the questions had been asked, if not answered. She had done the right thing and taken him in. Now in the grey pitiless light she must decide what would happen next. She must act on both their behalves.

If her decision-making centred on the preparation of porridge and toast; and if her will to act was exhausted by the mere effort of carrying out breakfast on a tray to her guest, then Beatrice could perhaps be forgiven. The man who had once been her social superior, moving through worlds which she could barely comprehend, was now wholly in her power. He had fallen from the heights of Thundersbarrow to throw himself helplessly at her feet, here in the backgarden of a suburban house. An heir without his estate, a captain without his company, a man without a home. Yet if she were to offer to be these things she must never forget that he had also, in however incomplete a way, been her faithless lover. Her desire to nurse and protect was tainted by the bitterness of the past. Had he in fact chosen her because of that past, because he sensed that, unlike Maud or his mother, she was weak and biddable? This was bad enough to contemplate. But when she started to speculate as to the possible background to this extraordinary singling out, her thoughts jumbled to panic. Why should she believe his account of wounding and hospitalisation? His erratic behaviour over the last few hours would have caused even the most indulgent of witnesses to doubt Charles's reliability, if not his sanity. Had he in fact escaped from some secure institution whither he had been taken after breaking down at the Front? The thought of this and the possible consequences both for herself and the man she already looked on as her patient should she fail to do the right thing, made her stop halfway down the garden and stare into a framework of poles which she had erected for her runner beans a month previously. The beans themselves had begun to flower but, because of the dryness, had already dropped many blosssoms. Beatrice saw yet did not see the scarlet petals on the parched ground. Then, out of the darkness of her mind, the strange chalk forest of the night before rose up. What should she do? What should she not do? Again the old resentment at being chosen or used rose up like bile. To be swallowed when his voice broke through the white trunks.

– Ah! At last. I'm starving. Quickly, Beatty. In here.

The fact that he had reverted to her old diminutive, combined with the steadiness of his voice, gave her hope. So that she tore herself away and went stooping through the tarpaulin (he must have found it in the shed), down two wooden steps into the dugout. Here, under the corrugated sheets all was dampness and twilight. On one side of the space was a shelf of earth covered in his greatcoat. On the other a table and rickety backless chair, both likewise uncovered and commandeered from the shed. Beatrice placed the tray on the table and sat down opposite Charles, who took her proffered bowl of still steaming porridge. He looked up at her, his mouth working.

– I expect you think I'm up the loop, eh, Beatty? Coming out here. And so forth.

She returned his gaze until, inevitably their eyes sheered away from each other. She felt a sudden overwhelming pity.

– No, Charles. It's not for me to pass judgment. All that you've been through. I don't understand but I can try to accept.

He smiled and stirred the whirl of salt into his porridge.

– I must, you see. Can't sleep in a room any more. It's like, like rooms are caves while this hole in the ground is a room. It's crazy. A paradox. But that's the only way I can describe it. Can you put up with that? I'll try not to be a nuisance. It's just that I need, need . . .

The old tremor had returned, to Beatrice's renewed dismay. But it made her bolder.

– Charles, I don't mean to be rude. But how long – her throat was unexpectedly dry and she had to stop to swallow for saliva – how long do you intend, I mean do you want to stay, here, with me?

So much for the brisk authority of a nurse. She was a girl at Ecclesden again. Hopelessly out of her depth. Charles frowned.

– I can go now, if you like. Yes. Leave now. He'll get me in the end anyway. Yes, why don't I? It was patently wrong of me to assume you'd help me. After all no one else has. The whole fucking crowd of them. Not one. And now you. I can't . . .

The tears rolled slowly down his cheeks and plopped one by one into his porridge, like clear pebbles. She stood up aghast, not only at his volatility but also at the burning desire to keep him here, indefinitely, which suddenly flamed up inside her.

– Oh, Charles, of course you can stay. I didn't mean to imply. But what about your family? And the army? I might even add, my neighbours.

He too had stood up in that low garret, bending, his wispy hair brushing the earth-caked roof. He was shaking now, uncontrollably.

– Here I'm safe. In White City. Doing what I can. I thought it was houses that were safe. If you bolted all the doors. But he was in the house last night, so I had to come out. I had to, Beatrice.

She had noted this reversion to her full Christian name. It made her feel more powerful somehow.

– Charles. Who is this person you seem so frightened of? There's no one in the house apart from me. And Ulysses. Is it Eric? But you said Eric's at the Front still. So he can't be here. Can he?

The munitions factory siren was wailing down in the town, signalling the end of the night shift. Maud had worked there. In the old days. Charles ran the back of his hand across his mouth then suddenly lurched forward. His fingers at her throat burned and tightened.

– Don't ever ask. Don't ever. All right?

His voice rose in a crescendo. For a terrible moment she thought he was indeed going to strangle her. Then the fingers relaxed. The pulsing vein on his forehead sank back beneath the skin. He was shaking again.

– Don't. All right. It isn't . . . him. Not exactly. It's . . . Beatty, you think I'm mad but I'm not. Not yet. If I go, I'm finished. If I stay I might, just might survive, escape, I can't explain. But you've got to help. Do you understand? Without you, I can't do it. But if you keep on asking questions before I'm ready to answer, well . . .

He sat down again heavily and Beatrice half-fell, half-sank at his knees. There she rested her head and sobbed in a mirror image of last night's tableau when he had needed her lap. His hand came to rest eventually on her head.

– You must give me time, Beatty. And be patient. I have to go back you see. Not across the Channel, but here – she looked up and saw him tap his temple, then resumed her posture of reproachful obeisance – I have to go back inside myself. I could feel it starting last night. Then this morning when I woke it went off a little. Now it's starting again. And I must give in to it. I have to work out what happened, Beatty, back there. What and why. Then perhaps he'll go away. Yes it's starting again and I have to give in to it until it's finished. Oh yes. I have to.

His words had seeded the rank air in the makeshift dugout with a compressed fury. She felt unable to lift her aching head under so much impending weight. Her neck where his hands had gripped throbbed and stung. Yet she must lift her head. And accede to his abject power.

– Well, if that's the case and you're determined to go through with it, you must have clean clothes. Really, Charles Tremain or should I say Captain Sir, these smell absolutely foul.

Ten minutes later she was walking back toward the house with an armful of soiled clothing. The handover had taken place through the tarpaulin sheet (or gas curtain as he insisted on calling it), and represented a significant pact. The sun had now risen above the house roof and, deep amongst the white sprays of jasmine, a robin was singing his summer song, a song in which Beatrice had always detected a melancholy autumn note. *This is the Venus and Adonis flower*, she whispered to herself and passed into the scullery. After she had handed Charles an old raglan of her aunt's along with a pair of men's dungarees which she sometimes wore for gardening, she set off for work, secure in the knowledge that her haunted guest would indeed be there on her return. His filthy kit lay soaking in the dolly tub.

All through the long day at the hospital Beatrice was gripped by a new sense of unreality. The lists of names and dates, the cards in the card indexes, the box files, the paper clips, all the paraphernalia of her job danced before her eyes as if they were fragments of some other universe, separated from her by an invisible film. So that she sat back and stared until the little basement room itself floated away on a gentle tide and she was sitting in a void, hearing only Charles's strangely cracked voice, seeing only his bent, prematurely aged, yet curiously tensile body. He had come back and he was living in her garden. She could neither laugh nor cry, question nor complain. She was simply existing in the knowledge of his presence, a feather plucked out of time, drifting hither and thither without volition. By the end of the afternoon she realised she had neither worked nor eaten. She was dizzy from her long dazed vigil. Yet must go back to the source of this strange new existence, to the derelict soldier, singing in his dugout under the moon.

It was the clothes that brought her back to earth, before she had even taken off her coat, let alone tickled Ulysses or looked out shyly to see if her guest was indeed still in residence. They lay where she had left them in the morning, a tangle of brown seaweed soaking in lye at the bottom of the dolly tub. Possessed by an almost maternal protectiveness, Beatrice suddenly wanted to see her captive soldier looking as smart as he had done on parade that cold December morning and, throwing off her coat, filled the copper and set it on the range, then turned to what, until this transfigured moment, would have been the indescribably tiresome business of rubbing each garment on the scrubbing-board attached to the tub. How her back used to ache after a few minutes of this labour. Not this evening. It was as if she had been visited with a new strength. That this strength had as much to do with a desperate desire to stave off disaster as with any straightforward intimation of happiness, did not enter her mind. Charles was here and she must care for him. That was all.

It was just as she preparing to rinse the scrubbed clothes through that she noticed Ulysses tap-tapping something shiny over by the larder door. It was a Wills Gold Flake tobacco tin, much rusted and with a dent in its lid, which must have fallen out of the shirt pocket when she had carried the clothes into the scullery earlier that morning. She would have put it aside on the draining board if Ulysses, jumping up to retrieve his catch, hadn't dashed it to the ground, so that the lid came off. Inside there was no tobacco. Instead a tiny booklet fell out, its pages shedding two small creased pieces of paper. Gathering up these items in her already chapped hands, Beatrice glanced first at the pieces of paper. One was a handwritten pass which stated that *Captain Charles Colin Tremain has permission to be absent from his regiment for the purpose of proceeding to England on leave from July 11 to July 17 1916 returning by train from London (Victoria) at 4 pm on July 17 signed Major G. Bristow VC on behalf of Colonel Foster.* The second piece of paper was a railway ticket stamped *Boulogne Route Only*, allowing for a *Return First Class Journey from Chalkhampton to France on July 17*. Beatrice carefully slipped the papers back into the booklet and went out into the hall. There was a Red Cross calendar hanging by the mirror. Today was a Wednesday. Her red trembling finger stopped in the third column: Wednesday, the nineteenth of July. The man in her garden had gone absent without leave. He was, in effect, on the run.

Beatrice had not been prepared for the shock this simple deduction caused. Sitting down on the settle in a vain attempt to control a sudden attack of breathlessness, she reached back and tore the calendar off the wall. Again her finger ran up and down the columns of dates. Again it stopped on the nineteenth then jumped back and forth between the eleventh and the seventeenth, as if trying to find some anomaly in their sequence. But none presented itself, even after she had checked the year at the top of the calendar, then counted off the days on her lye-wrinkled fingers. Finally she took out the pocket book from where she had tucked it in her bosom and began once more to read the stark handwritten note, only this time silently enunciating every word as if to test whether what it seemed to say to the eyes could indeed be corroborated by the lips. Again she was confronted by the stark unwillingness of things to be other than they were. The words and the dates all agreed. The timeless trance in which she had been immersed all day dissolved. With the shudder of displaced air after some distant explosion, time and the war rushed back into her life and almost overwhelmed it. It was then that she turned to the pocket book.

Each page had been divided into three portions by two roughly inked horizontal lines. Above these lines were dates, while between them, in a rushed and nervous hand that Beatrice could nevertheless recognise as the same that had once written her letters from Tongdean and a postcard from Egypt, lay a record of Charles's recent experiences. Holding the diary, Beatrice could barely manage to stop her hand shaking. She was possessed by a delicious sense of guilty pleasure that, she realised, was not so very far removed from the excitement of giving sanctuary to a runaway. Instinctively, she flicked forward to where the last few days would be. Disappointed to find nothing about herself she turned back to the last entry dated *July 10. Maud Maud Maud they were crying and calling.* Hot misery welled up, yet she forced herself to go on, backwards into the mystery of the trenches. Again nothing for several days then: *July 7. Have reached Boulogne. Thank Xist I met that Brigadier friend of mater's at that clearing station. – Where's the wound, Tremain? – Calf, sir. Only a scratch, sir. – Damned unlucky show that. Still you all showed pluck. I see there's at least one recommendation for a DSO. In your company too. Fellow by the name* of Wren. Not that he'd know anything about it. – Dead then! He's dead! Oh thank . . . But no. Just badly wounded. – And how would you like some rest? After you've recovered, of course. Go and see your mother. Give her my regards. I'll square it with Colonel Foster. – Yes. Yes. To get away. Back. He is under my bed still you see and . . . Still going forward into the past. Two more blank pages. Then 3 July. I couldn't help it. He made me do it. It's part of his revenge. He made me do a bunk. He made me make him follow. So that. When the shell. His face. 2 July. Why didn't he tell me this place was Thundersbarrow. That crater. The chalk caves. The tunnel. Why didn't he warn me we were going back to where it all began. Then I might have been braver. And when the maxim jammed. I might not have run. Beatrice stopped, her heart racing. She ought not to be looking at this, she ought not to be tearing off the scab in this secretive, ruthless way. But her eyes would not allow her to shut the book and she would have gone on, jumping three more blank days that had wrapped their silences round the thunderous core of the battle, if there hadn't been a sudden detonation out in the back garden. Going to the scullery door, she saw Charles crouching beside his dugout, her old dungarees gripping him at the waist so that his belly hung in folds over the belt. He was waving his arms wildly. She slipped the pocket book in a drawer and went out to him.

– Charles. That noise. The neighbours.

– Not Charles, Lumley. Captain. Now listen. I want to take you to see our jumping off point. Then you can bring up rations. Come. Quickly.

With horror, Beatrice noticed the holster with its recently replaced service revolver, barely concealed by the ill-fitting raglan. Last night he had begun to strangle her. Tonight he had revealed his weapon. Yet the dream somehow drew her on, if only because the words of his diary still echoed mysteriously in her ear. To understand fully she must participate in whatever re-enactment Charles's fever had dredged up.

They were lying now in a shallow depression which had once been a bed for the previous owner's prize leeks. Charles was peering through his binoculars, another piece of equipment which he had magically produced.

– This, Private Lumley, is Jacob's Ladder. Over there, in No Man's Land is Sunken Lane, sometimes known as Hunter's Lane.

She followed his pointing hand to where the old field ditch ran across the garden, dividing its cultivated areas from the overgrown part. The ditch was perhaps three feet deep and full of nettles.

– We must be deployed in Sunken Lane before Zero Hour. Then when the mine goes up, – here he pointed to the right, indicating the circular depression which had once contained the filter bed – we can rush to occupy the crater before Jerry does. But how to get from here to Sunken Lane without being seen?

So absorbed had Beatrice become in Charles's nightmarish transmogrification of her suburban plot that she quite overlooked the questioning note in her captain's voice. A punch on the shoulder drew her back from reverie.

– Well?

– Ouch, Charles. I mean, Sir. How? I . . . couldn't you just crawl?

– Crawl! Don't be a sodding arsehole. They'd spot us in no time and have their maxims trained on us, especially that one, you can't see it clearly but we think it's under that little rise in their second line. The Bergwerk.

Beatrice squinted as if she were indeed surveying the enemy front.

– Second line? Oh you mean the railway. Yes I see.

Charles appeared not to have heard the mention of the railway.

– Of course, our guns should have knocked it out before Zero Hour. But you can't be too careful. So, how to achieve our ends. Why, dig is the answer. Dig a tunnel or two tunnels. It's only fifty yards. And with men like . . . men like . . .

Suddenly Charles was shaking again. His head fell against Beatrice's shoulder.

– Beatty, I'm so tired. I don't know whether I can go on. I want to just lie down and go to sleep. Forever.

I couldn't help it. He made me do it.

Suddenly Beatrice felt a great pity for this man. She discovered too that she nursed a fierce desire to vindicate him, to show the world that he was not the coward he believed himself to be. So that it was she who insisted on perpetuating the nightmare, ordering him back to the dugout where he must wait while she brought up the rations. For which he seemed pathetically grateful. Only later, back in her house, did she brood on the strangely exciting thought that, while she was pretending to be a soldier at the Front, her supposed captain had been dressed in clothes she herself had worn.

Thursday June 29. In billets. Today should have been the day. But no. Another forty-eight hours to go. Oh God, the waiting. Last night I tried to tell him what I was going through, outside the estaminet. Our guns were flashing all along the horizon. You'll be all right, Sir. Just you wait and see. Oh Eric I won't. I can't.

Tonight it was difficult to tell if the distant rumbling was another approaching thunderstorm or just the familiar undercurrent of the artillery in France. It was hotter than last night so that, alone in her bedroom overlooking the garden, Beatrice had thrown off all the blankets then, not without checking that the curtains were drawn, taken off her shift and lain down naked on top of the sweaty sheets. She had brought the makeshift diary up with her to bed, determined to suck out whatever secret it contained before the morning obliged her to slip it back into his dried and ironed shirt. As before she worked backwards.

Wednesday June 28. 1100 hours. Attack postponed until Sat. Because of the weather. Rehearsal with the white tapes again. All very jumpy.

Tuesday June 27. I dreamed of her last night. On the hill. In a white dress. Which she let me unhook. But there was another dress underneath. And then another.

Beatrice let her eyes wander from the diary down the bed to where her free right hand lay among her pubic hair, tugging at it gently. How remote the hand looked, as if it did not belong to her. Now its forefinger was sliding down to the labia. Who had Charles dreamed of? What did the dream mean?

Monday June 26. Eric's remark to me after I'd supervised the delousing in the barn. – You had your chance, Sir. When you met her again in Chalkhampton. – He could see I was looking pretty choked. He always did see. Which is why I hate him. And can't do without him. – You had your chance. – You mean I should have fucked her instead of my half-sister? – His ghost of a smile. Or smile of a ghost. But I should have. Oh yes. Before it was too late.

Her detached, wilful forefinger lay still now in the cleft that was always dry nowadays, as if all her youthful juices had drained away in one emptying flood. She watched the finger which suddenly jerked into life and began to make slow circular rubbing movements. How strange she felt. Sad, yet excited. While the disembodied voice of the man she had loved echoed in her head and the real Charles lay outside under a sheet of corrugated iron.

But I should have. Oh yes.

Oh Charlie yes yes yes.

Her finger moving faster now scraping at a hard kernel of scab whose itch was also emptiness, the emptiness of living.

Oh yes.

The juices seeping back a little, out of some final reserve, so that the soreness diminished, allowing her finger to attempt a more vigorous assault.

Oh Charlie you should be here. Yes. Not there. Yes. You should be. Oh yes yes. Oh!

The diary slipped to the floor.

Years later, when memory required her to adopt a more conventional view of the past, she would tell herself that he had been wearing full battle kit and that the polished brass of belt and button had glinted in the moon. But there was no moon and the figure who appeared suddenly and fleetingly in the corner of her half-closed eye, wore what looked like an army issue hospital gown. She froze where she lay, both hands moving instinctively to cover her breasts then absurdly abandoning these to protect loins that even now shuddered a little with the first frustrated spasms of release.

– Why? Why have you come?

She whispered to the figure who already wasn't there, then leapt up and without a thought for probity, flung back the curtains to peer at where she knew the dugout to be. Silence. Heat. No movement, unless in the undergrowth where Ulysses was hunting. His face had not been visible. Or rather it had been a face made up of isolated features her memory dredged up from different times and meetings: the thick moustache, the old white scar across the forehead, the full lips arced in the ghost of a smile. *Which is why I hate him.* So Charles had been right. Eric Wren was here. Feeling suddenly cold Beatrice crawled back under the sheet and lay shivering.

So the strange new order which Charles Tremain had brought with him from across the Channel was established in Beatrice's life. By day she lived in the world of VAD administration, by evening within a hundred yards of the German front line and by night in a restless turmoil of dreams and waking visions through which the figures of the recent past walked or crawled or ran in smoky silhouette. All day the clouds built up on the horizon, all night the rumble of thunder vied with the more distant shudder of artillery fire. And still no rain came. And still, moving between the house and the garden, in response to Charles's regular signallings with the old paraffin lantern, Beatrice could see neither a resolution nor an escape. It was as if, having entered her world with such confident stealth, Charles had proceeded to extinguish it utterly. There was no time any more, only a succession of lights and darknesses punctuated by the routines of the front line, routines that were at once darkly necessary and ludicrously out of place, so that Beatrice caught herself crying between smiles, or laughing after a sudden urge to cry. Charles's mood was still liable to swing between grim determination and irrational violence at a moment's notice and he still occasionally admitted to the folly of his behaviour. But for Beatrice this was as nothing compared with the blessed fact of having him there. She suspected, after a further study of the diary prior to slipping it back into its tin, that Charles might well be using her property as a conveniently obscure bolthole; yet at the same time, given his refusal ever to come indoors, she was not convinced that he was simply putting on a cynical act to throw her off the scent. After all, a real fugitive wouldn't dare sing as he did, or flash in morse when darkness fell, or even on occasion fire his revolver. And it was this continuing intimation that, as Charles himself had told her, the war at the bottom of her garden was in some sense real, which finally forced Beatrice to accept that time couldn't stand still forever. She would have to seek help or advice from somewhere. Surely an honourable retreat to hospital or asylum (from which perhaps he had escaped in the first place), would be better than some neighbourhood witchhunt. She would have to act and act quickly. For her own sake as well as his.

Beatrice had not gone to Dr Blake for advice over her cycle; now she was determined to see him about the fate of the one man who had betrayed her. At first he proved difficult to track down until she discovered that his office had been moved closer to the new wing, which had been converted from an old stable block. Beatrice, long out of touch in her basement full of filing boxes, assumed the wing would contain more beds for the wounded, who were still pouring in at the number of about twenty a week. Dr Blake glanced out of the windows at a bed of petunias. He wiped his forehead. It was still muggy.

– No, Miss Lumley. Nervous cases. We take our first consignment tomorrow as a matter of fact.

Beatrice started and blushed. This was too extraordinary a coincidence to be missed. She must act on it.

– Nervous cases? I thought the army didn't recognise nerves.

Dr Blake drummed his fingers. He was a busy man.

– They haven't any choice now. Not since the Big Push.

– And you are going to treat them? Here.

She hoped her voice didn't sound too tremulous.

– Of course. It's hardly an arcane science. They need quiet mainly. And rest. Is this why you asked to see me? You'd like a transfer perhaps?

Again Dr Blake drummed his fingers on the desk. Beatrice remembered Mr Birkett remarking somewhat bitterly that the doctor had only agreed to treat Maud because of her connections with Ecclesden. *A fine snob he is.* 'It takes one to know one,' she had thought to reply at the time. But kept silent. Now the memory seemed vaguely troubling. There were enemies everywhere. Hadn't Charles taught her as much during their evening vigils? She had better hug the coast a little.

– Oh no, Doctor. I'm being posted abroad soon. It's just that, well I wonder if you could give me some advice before I go to France. It's my cycle. I seem . . .

She had not meant to use this ploy. It had simply risen to the surface, driven by her sudden fearful need to shield Charles from a sharp-witted series of deductions. Dr Blake stood up. He did not suspect anything. His impatience was purely practical.

– Not now, Miss Lumley. As I said our first consignment's in tomorrow. I only give consultations by appointment. See my secretary on the way out. I expect she'll be able to fit you in early next week.

Beatrice too had risen and nodded gratefully as if this brusque dismissal were the most generous of welcomes. She had what she needed. A strategy and a hope.

– Charles. Where are you? Cooee. I want to talk. Please come up. It's important.

She was standing at the entrance to the dugout. It was almost dark, the time when Charles had told her it was safe to bring up the rations. *They're eating too. The snipers included.* A blackbird was singing in an elder overhanging the twitten. She felt a sudden irritation with this charade. Hadn't the doctor said that nervous cases needed quiet and rest. Not this endless rehearsal of what couldn't be changed. She put down the plate of beef and potatoes then called again, only less cautiously. And was immediately pinned to the ground in a flurry of dust and hoarse breathing.

– What do you mean man, shouting like that? We'll have every maxim between Gommecourt and La Boisselle trained on us. And there's a patrol out in a minute. Checking the tunnel into Sunken Lane. It's finished you see. He worked like the quarryman he is. At heart. I . . .

Beatrice was sobbing, her hair tousled, her housecoat soiled with dirt. She could not look in his eyes. Charles placed a hand on her shoulder. She flinched.

– I'm sorry, Beatty. It's just that . . . – Then with a wail of anguish. What am I going to do?

His head was in her lap again even though she still felt aggrieved at his treatment of her. She must speak now.

– Charles. They've opened a new wing at the hospital. For nervous cases. Shellshock. Don't you think. I mean – here she coughed with embarrassment and felt the muscles in his neck stiffen, so that she must stroke them in silence for a while, feeling the wispy hair where it curled under his collar and then, further round, the fine sandpapery feel of recently shaved skin. Not a soldier at all. What should he do? What should she do? The silence grew unendurable. – Look I don't know anything about what happened or how you got here. – She stopped again. She had read the diary from cover to cover. And seen the overdue tickets. They were looking for him even now. – But surely, if you went down there and gave yourself up. They'd see how ill, I mean how unhappy. Charles you must. For my sake. For his.

Silence again. The blackbird fluttering away, calling in alarm at some movement in the twitten. Then Charles was standing over her, his silhouette against the cloudy sky.

– We take prisoners. But we don't surrender. You're coming out with me tonight. Through the tunnel. Chop chop. Look sharp. They'll be sending up Verey lights soon.

Charles had been busy while she was working down at the hospital. Between the old hot bed and the field ditch, there now ran at right angles a shallow three-foot-wide trench covered over with all kinds of vegetation culled from the rougher areas of the garden: elder and ash branches, cow parsley, dock, seeding grasses. Charles had woven this mass so skilfully together that it did indeed seem like the roof of a tunnel, especially in the twilight. Now, adjured to a strict silence, Beatrice was crawling along the tunnel, in the wake of Charles's earth-caked boots. To think that only a few days ago she had gone to the trouble of washing all his kit. Now he was as filthy as ever. It was like having a big child to look after. A thought which, coming out into the field ditch, she decided not to pursue. Charles was squatting by a contraption which appeared to consist of a pole and two small mirrors, long since left to gather dust in the shed. Another raid. Another lurch back into fantasy.

– What is this, Charles, I mean, Sir? – she whispered, pulling an elderflower's creamy disc from her hair. She too was muddy now and would have to devote herself to even more washing.

– It's a trench periscope, of course. And don't call me that name. Captain to you. Actually I can't get it to work at all.

Beatrice felt under pressure to compliment, as one would the indifferent effort of a small child, out of love and the duty to reassure that is love's obligation.

– It looks all right to me. And the trench. I mean tunnel. It must have taken you hours.

The periscope rose up into the air and landed with a thud in the twitten. There was another scuffling of foliage.

– It's useless. I can't. And how am I to be expected? And as for the tunnel. It was him. I told you. That bloody madman. Who doesn't give a fuck about life and death. Who just goes and does it. And we're all supposed to do it too. Or at least I am. Being his superior. But I can't. I tell you. I mean I couldn't. When. Oh the Gatling's jammed and the Colonel's dead play up play up and play the game play up play up play up play up oh play play play play play . . .

How could she not shrink away, as the howling storm inside Charles attempted to suck her into its vortex of panic and stasis? Compared with this, Eric Wren's fits had been almost benign, with their fragments of received Biblical law and reassuring prophecies. Charles was simply writhing in his own entrails and could not be reached. Yet she must try.

– Oenone. Charles, where's Oenone? You took her with you. I remember her on the station. Did she come back?

If, by the mention of a simpler bond of affection between man and animal, Beatrice had hoped to drag Charles away from the many invisible hands that seemed to be pulling him under, she was disappointed. In fact, she realised with a little start of apprehension, everything now seemed to be driving Charles deeper and deeper into his nightmare.

– She's back there, of course, – he replied absently, gesturing vaguely in the direction of the house.

– What, indoors? But I haven't seen. You haven't fed . . .

– In billets. She's being looked after by the quartermaster. We'll be there soon. Out of the line. Before . . . before . . .

Again Charles seemed to lose himself in some inadequately focused perspective. Then, with renewed vigour, plunged back into the details of the moment, a moment which Beatrice ruefully reminded herself, was already weeks in the past.

– Have you got the grenades?

She nodded, touching the paper bag filled with stones which he'd given her earlier.

– And your face is blacked?

Reluctantly, she had daubed some wet earth on her cheeks, reasoning that it might act as a mud pack.

– Right. Pass me the wire-clippers. – She handed him a pair of rusty secateurs. – Over we go and quietly does it.

The raid had been successful according to Charles, although from Beatrice's point of view, the business of scrambling down the railway embankment then indulging in a spot of stone throwing at a brick coal bunker, was hardly her idea of a romantic evening out. Yet still she felt driven to go alongside him, if only to play for time until she could think of a way of getting him to the hospital. She would see Dr Blake on the Monday and be more forthcoming. For the moment she felt cold and tired and supremely bored with this endless game of soldiers.

– What's he doing, Miss?

– Who is he?

Beatrice had left Charles to his meal in White City and was trying to walk like a normal civilian back towards the house. The voices of the children came from the twitten where they had evidently been spying. Her first instinct was to pretend she did not know what they were talking about; then she intended shooing them away, these troublesome sprites, from a path that was half hers. But the days of solitude told against her. After all, hadn't she just been indulging in a kind of childish, albeit deadly game. And these were children. In the end she might find she had made some allies.

– That man you mean. Over there. – She gestured vaguely as if to include an entire unseen army.

The children nodded, giggling. Miss Lumley was hoity-toity like her aunt who'd snuffed it.

– Well, – her mouth felt dry. She glanced desperately at the cold frame and the leek trench, at the concealed tunnel and the field ditch. Several cairns of earth and chalk rose glimmering in the twilight. There were two spades leaning against an upturned wheelbarrow. And, she realised for the first time, a faint sweet smell of human excrement. She gulped and turned back to her moon-faced inquisitors among the elders.

– Well, he's my gardener actually. He's digging hot beds. You have to remove the soil you see. And replace it with manure. Then I can grow all sorts of things. Melons, gherkins, aubergines. –

Briefly the conservatory at Ecclesden floated past, a silver ship crewed by ghosts.

– Auber what? Do you mean the battle of Aubers? – The boy wiped his hand across his nose. His sister gave him a punitive shove. Her mouth hardened into a sly grin.

– Hasn't grown anything yet then, has he? Been at it for days too.

The ghost ship of Ecclesden conservatory had foundered on the grimy reality of this ransacked suburban garden. Purple glossy aubergines came tumbling out alongside red peppers, bunches of purple grapes, orange melons. They melted in front of her on the darkening grass, a devil's feast. The girl was picking at a scab on her neck.

– Does he sleep in the garden, too?

Realising she would have to appear to be more nonchalant, Beatrice tried smiling the confident, lazily condescending smile of the adult she had never quite believed herself to be.

– Actually, I was joking. Actually, he's a builder. He's putting in some new pipes for our earth closet. The old ones cracked in the winter . . .

– Is that why there's a pong? – The boy pinched his nose and gasped. – Dad uses the, you know, from our earth closet to put on the garden. Night soil he calls it. Is that what you're going to do?

Beatrice breathed a little more calmly. Now at least the boy seemed prepared to chat. But suddenly the thought of excrement had this putative ally giggling uncontrollably, so that his sister eased him aside and stood there, arms crossed.

– You're lying you are. He's mad, your bloke. He's mad because he's a coward who ran away from the war. I'm going to tell our dad all about him. Our dad fought and lost two fingers.

– And shrap . . . shrapnel, Cissy, in the chest.

– And shrapnel. Your man didn't fight. He just ran.

All the agony of a child's efforts to make her companions believe in her version of events flooded back over Beatrice in a choking wave. Gnats were spiralling in high coils over Charles's dugout. It was still stiflingly hot. There might even be another storm tonight. How she wished she had not allowed him to invade her life so thoroughly, making everything so difficult and dark.

– He's got a wound too. – So, wielding a child's desperate logic, falling back on truth to support a falsehood, Beatrice saw the entire mirage of her adult fiction dissolve.

– Where? – The inquisitors sensed blood. They were keen.

– On his leg as a matter of fact. Quite a bad one.

– Back or front? – The relentless chorus continued.

– Well, I don't see that it. Well, back, actually. Yes, on the back of the leg. – Beatrice looked shyly at her judges as if seeking clemency. And knew she would receive no such thing.

– Told you so. I told you so. In the back when he ran away. A cowardy cowardy custard who's got less spunk than mustard!

Now the demonic sister was dancing from foot to foot on her witching ground of dry pine needles. Years later Beatrice would still associate the scent of resin with a final descent into a hell of her lover's making. The midges coiled their incomprehensible oscillating dance. *Dancing the Second Coming*, so Eric Wren had said to her once, in a different world. *If we could only understand the signs.* Another madman. But loved too, in a way. Dead probably now, swallowed by war then regurgitated to haunt poor Charles for some imagined wrong or omission. Oh would no one protect her from this world, its gross battening of flesh on flesh? She turned away in tears. The terrible children were chanting their dark triumph. They screamed.

And all at once he was beside her. Black with earth, white with chalk, grinning hugely. The one she loved but who could not love her. He grinned again at the blanching children.

– Well now, here's two brave new recruits I'll be bound. Would you like to come and see my den. I'm sowing it with dragon's teeth. And using dead men for manure. I collect them with this shovel. And dig them in nice and deep. Upside down so their souls can go straight down to Beelzebub.

But the children had already run away, whimpering, through the stagnant air of the twitten. Beatrice didn't know whether to laugh or cry, resting on Charles's bare shoulder. He, meanwhile, had managed a few smiles before the paper-thin grey look returned and he began muttering to his ever-present invisible companion, *You bastard why did you make me say that why did you?* Back in the security of their own house the children were already spilling the details of the whole terrifying mystery to a shocked and outraged mother.

At the end of this longest of weeks, Beatrice was forced to confront two changes which, so she told herself later, led to the final disaster. Or victory.

The first change was a consequence of the encounter with the children and had, in a sense, been prepared for. No child would be able not to confess to such a dreadful meeting as the one that had been engineered by Charles that evening. So that when, on the following Saturday, the front doorbell rang, Beatrice was already more than prepared. That Charles had been a fool to reveal himself in such a way she had long since accepted. But latterly she had begun to wonder if he hadn't seen it as an escape route, obliging the neighbours to sever his links to the past with an impersonal suddenness which neither he nor his protectress could somehow manage.

The neighbours were certainly determined. Blinking in the dazzle of early sunlight which reigned at this hour, burning off the Channel and the lead dome of the pier theatre before the heavy clouds rolled in, Beatrice found herself confonted by two figures, a woman and a man. The man she recognised as her next door neighbour, Mr Gorrod, heroic father of the two children who had fled her ghost the previous evening; the woman was the elderly Mrs Christie who cultivated roses at the bottom of the Row. The man looked both determined and vaguely harassed, as though undecided as to whether he should behave with amicability or aggression. Mrs Christie accrued a complex chill. And released it in dense waves. She was the leader.

– Miss Lumley. I fancy I may address you, having known your aunt quite well before she was called over, poor soul. And she, I'm sure, would approve of my actions. To think of such goings on under her own roof. Such immorality.

Beatrice studied the mole on the woman's left cheek. The hair growing there was strangely withered. Another of war's witches. Gorrod coughed, a neighbourly confiding sort of cough. If hollow.

– We have no right to interfere I know. – Here he looked almost apologetically at his ally then bit his lower lip and turned back to Beatrice. – But frankly, Miss Lumley. It's not right. We have children after all. And there's a war on. In fact speaking as a former combatant . . .

Beatrice, who had been clutching the doorpost for steadiness, let go and felt a vertiginous rush of righteous anger. That the anger might have its roots in self-pity was at this juncture neither here nor there.

– There is a war on, yes. I've nursed some of the victims. I've seen the wounds, Mr Gorrod. The cavities oozing pus. The gangrenous limbs . . . She stopped, knowing her neighbour had been injured in a training accident which left him unfit for active service.

– It's a just war. A war to end barbarism. – Mrs Christie was winding and winding the noose of her jet necklace. Mr Gorrod put up his good hand.

– We all know the noble work you perform. This had nothing to do . . .

– Noble. Hah! It's nothing of the kind. Disgusting, yes. Demeaning of course. This is the agony of a dying god. A god who can't be resurrected. Except as some evil, some force that will cause even greater destruction in the future. I know. I've looked into the eyes of that god. He's in my back garden. He has a hole in his mind so large all the gauze in Europe wouldn't begin to fill it.

She finished, aghast at herself, at the way the absent Eric Wren had somehow spoken through her. As if he were indeed as close as Charles said he was. Terribly close.

– That settles it. We go to the police. This is some criminal or other. Some renegade. A deserter even. – Mrs Christie had created a row of red indentations on her liver-spotted hand. She turned to go where justice could be found. Gorrod put his hand on her arm.

– Mary. Wait. Miss Lumley has never given us any cause until now. She is a sister of mercy after all. And off to the Front soon so I hear.

Beatrice nodded. Then realised she was expected to speak. To tell them about her letting arrangements. To reassure them that she would not be leaving Charles in charge. So she would say nothing. Obliging the trembling Gorrod to continue.

– Whatever has caused this . . . – here he seemed to gag at the very thought. – Whatever irregularity in her own past has obliged her to act in this way, we must give her a second chance. A few days. Yes a few days and then we go to the authorities. – He looked at Beatrice for the first time. – That gives you time to find this, this person a new berth.

– We must have a limit, George. How many days? Three?

Gorrod licked his dry lips. He would have preferred not to be here. But his wife and this neighbour made a powerful team.

– We must be fair. Let's say ten, yes, ten days.

Gorrod closed his eyes, as if experiencing a satisfactory bowel movement.

– Seven, George. Seven at the most. And even this I am most reluctant to allow. My niece is coming to stay next weekend. She is exceedingly delicate. Some of the things I've seen these last few days. Some of the songs. You'd think there was a whole regiment in there, bellowing that filthy drivel.

So the supporter of Just Wars deprecated their engines of prosecution.

– I must admit I've often wondered if there was more than one. Some of the choruses . . .

– Oh I've no doubt she'd allow others in.

Beatrice had had enough. She came forward, out of the house. Murderous, if afraid.

– You mentioned the songs. The songs men sing about their own deaths. What would you sing if you were about to die? Tell me. I'm longing to know.

Mrs Christie raised her eyes which were bloodshot at the rims. She knew where her dead god resided.

– A hymn I should hope. Something uplifting. 'From Greenland's Icy Mountains' perhaps. The estimable Bishop Heber.

Eric had sang that. He sang it now, raised by the spell of words.

– Fuck hymns. Dying men don't sing hymns. They sing about home or food or . . . or . . . fucking.

The old woman had staggered backward in a fluster of crêpe and jet. She was inclined to levitate.

– Come away, George. She is plainly corrupted. And probably half-mad as well. I've got a good mind to speak to the hospital board. I know Lady Tremain quite well. Apparently she's been quite poorly. – Then turning to Beatrice who stood blind and trembling in the pitiless sunlight, horrified at how close her neighbours had come

372

to identifying her guest. – Seven days, seven days. I know your sort. I've seen the Whore of Babylon. Oh yes.

Once she had used the same expression on the summit of Thundersbarrow. The thought made her laugh.

– Right. Seven it is. As long as it takes to create the world. Or begin a battle.

They departed leaving the gate ajar, a curious lapse in refinement. Beatrice went to close it and saw on the pavement against the garden wall a dog's turd gloved with flies.

– Good show, old girl. That saw them off. These peasants. Creeping back into the war zone. Loot. That's what they're after. Anything left lying around. It's a wonder they weren't carrying shovels to dig up their neighbours' savings. Bloody tomb-robbers.

The shock which Charles had given Beatrice was, if anything, stronger than the one she had received on the day of his arrival. It was as if she had lived so intensely under the strange regime of the last few days that any breach of its strict laws threatened to overturn her whole life. Hadn't it been an absolute decree that Charles would never come inside the house but live permanently at White City? Yet here he was standing in the hallway, with a rucksack (more raids on the shed) dangling from his arm. She fell back on to the settle, gasping for words.

– Charles . . . I . . . you quite startled me. Inside. Did you hear? They're just busybodies. They don't matter. We can . . .

She stopped and attempted to grasp the enormity of the situation. Charles put his knapsack down and squatted in front of her.

– Take your time, old girl. You've no idea how jolly it is to come back here. They seem like they belong to another world, the trenches and all that. To be honest I'm simply glad to be alive.

Beatrice looked up sharply. He was smiling at her, with friendly concern. Could he mean what he had just said? Had he really returned? Or, having lived through the hell of the last few days, had he finally realised that he was home? If this was indeed his real homecoming then she herself, by playing along with his dangerous

373

games in the garden, must have helped to make that homecoming possible. She looked at him again. He was smiling still. This wasn't an act. She could have shouted for joy. And pride. He was home. Her Charles. Sound in mind and body.

– Five days we've got. Five days of heaven. Then back to that. – He swivelled round on his haunches and pointed towards the kitchen. – Can you hear? Of course you can. It's the preliminary bombardment. One hour and twenty minutes of sheer unimaginable fury. Every bloody gun along a fifteen-mile front. 18 Pounders and 4.5 inch howitzers. 6 inchers, 9 inchers, 9.2s. And after that day and night until Thursday morning at Zero Hour. Think of it. I wouldn't like to be Fritz now. Nor one of our front-line fellows come to think of it. Wren wanted to stay behind. To make sure the tunnels into Sunken Lane don't cave in. I told him not to be such a bloody fool. And ordered him back. Now he says he's going to go up every night with the rations. Typical. Just because he dug the main one himself. Lying on his back with his feet against a sort of cross between a shovel and a screw. The type the sappers use. Says Pedgell Wright gave it him. When they met at Gordon Dump. Lying on his back and singing. Christ, I hate that hymn. Screwing out the chalk in lumps. How the troops of Midian. Thinks he owns the chalk. Like he thought . . . he thought . . . Thundersbarrow . . . I . . .

Gently, in slow motion, Charles was dropping down on his knees, then sliding sideways to the floor. He lay there motionless and for a horrible moment Beatrice imagined he had had some massive seizure. Then the snoring began. It was obvious. He had probably been missing sleep. He was dead-beat.

The next two hours seemed to pass more slowly than the previous three days. Although Charles had not returned sound and whole as Beatrice had so wildly thought, it was plain there had been some kind of change. The problem was to discover its nature. Clearly, the Captain no longer occupied a forward trench; yet just as clearly he had not sailed back across the Channel. Where then could he be? Logical deduction suggested some sort of rest area behind the lines. Hadn't he alluded to the closeness of the barrage and Eric's pigheaded determination to 'go up with the rations'? The house then must be situated in a village of the kind the army called a billet, hence his belief that the neighbours were peasants who had ventured illegally into the war zone. Beatrice's despair at this point was bottomless. Sitting on the settle staring down at Charles's shrouded form (she had wrapped him in a blanket and put a cushion under his head), she saw time opening out ahead of her in a potentially endless series of oscillations between the Front in the garden and the billet in the house. It was as if the nightmare in Charles's head had got stuck like a gramophone needle, teasing out from the wax cylinder of his memory an endlessly repeated double refrain: trench billet trench billet trench billet. The anxious knowledge that she would have to report to the Red Cross in ten days' time or forever lose her chance of serving abroad combined with her neighbours' ominous threats to make her want to shake Charles and order him to get well. Then came the miserable thought that her whole intention of going to France had been bound up with her longing for Charles. In any case she couldn't just abandon him. Once again hospital seemed the only answer. But how? And when? Her guest was beginning to stir. A kettle on the hob was whistling. Ulysses wanted feeding. She decided to go about her business as usual, hoping thereby to ground this new fantasy in a continuing commonplace. The trouble was that her guest had commonplaces of his own.

He was leaning with his back against the range, his arms behind him, the flats of the hands lightly touching the hot surface. He seemed rested. But Beatrice, bent over the dolly tub in which she had left some sheets to soak, sensed a deepening of the dream, in the shadowed eyelids and twitching drawn face.

– And wine. *Du vin*. I'd like some *vin du pays, s'il vous plaît. Comprenez? Avec les oeufs. Oui.*

He was talking yet not talking to her. During his sleep, the topography of the 'billet' appeared to have sharpened, metamorphosing her house into an estaminet. The garden shed was now a 'stables', in which Charles and a couple of other invisible officers slept, along with Oenone who he insisted was looking fitter than ever, despite the quartermaster's indulgences. She struggled desperately in the grip of this new scenario.

– You said five days. What happens after that?

– I say. Not bad English. But call me Captain if you please, Mademoiselle.

– Captain. You mentioned Zero Hour. And a bombardment?

– Goodness! Don't you know? Don't you listen to the men talking. It's like all top secrets: common knowledge. The Big One, Mademoiselle. What we Anglais came over here to do for you. Break through Fritz's line. Roll him up.

Beatrice stood transfixed, the baton which she used to stir the lye, standing upright like a groyne in a silted pool. How could she have been so stupid? So lacking in foresight? All at once, the vision of a wasting alternation between house and garden faded. It was true that Charles's enactment of a continuing war had, at the beginning, been disconnected and timeless. But now time had appeared to frame and give it shape. He had entered on a journey towards the very moment that had precipitated him into her arms that first afternoon in Artillery Row. He was beginning to work forward in meticulous detail to the moment (still mysterious, still haunted by what Eric Wren had or had not done), when he had been wounded and so begun the long journey home. Even the initially puzzling mention of a five days' bombardment corroborated this interpretation. Hadn't the diary (which recorded Charles return to billets on a Saturday), made it clear that the original attack had been scheduled for the following Thursday but had had to be postponed because of bad weather? Charles was now deep inside the events which led up to the first of July. To Beatrice's amazement, what at any other time would have provoked shock and sadness, was today a source of deep reassurance. The very accuracy of Charles's vision would mean that she could predict every turn. And if she could predict she could also plan. Charles's movements and motivation were no longer a mystery. With the help of the diary (which she could remove tonight from his shirt), she would be able to come up with a strategy for admitting him into hospital within the time set her by her neighbours. With a light heart she went out to the offsales at the pub on the corner to see if they had anything that could pass for wine. Her soldier had gone down the line to rest and prepare. And his salvation seemed assured.

– Yes. It seems there has been some trouble there apparently. To do with the son. You knew him, I believe. Colin was it? Or Robert?
  – The eldest? Charles?
  – Yes, Charles. The one who joined up. Came home and went missing apparently. The mother's beside herself. In fact she's had another stroke so they tell me. Her specialist is an old friend of mine.
  The weather was still warm and still the earth cried out for rain. Dr Blake sat in his shirt sleeves relishing both his vicarious excitement in retelling someone else's drama and a deep-seated snobbery of connection and inside knowledge. Beatrice was fumbling sweatily with her dress behind a screen. Between her legs she could still feel the slide and cold weight of the jellied speculum then, sheathed and soft, the entry of his probing fingers. But when she shuddered it was for other less explicable reasons.
  – Yes. And they can't find him. You'd think an army that can move hundreds of thousands of men around France could track down one miserable deserter.
  – How can you be certain he deserted?
  She had emerged from behind the screen and stood adjusting her belt with what she hoped looked like unconcern. When he had been inside her, Dr Blake had sighed once or twice as if her vaginal tightness were a deliberate insult to his professional skills. She had felt hotly ashamed even of that.
  – Well he can't have forgotten his leave dates can he, my dear?
  The dear had only appeared in this man's speech after she had removed the clothing from the lower half of her body.
  – He might be ill. Sick. Or shellshocked. Like one of your patients. And in need of help.
  Dr Blake put his head in his hands as if to exclude the gnat whine of female logic.

– He was given a thorough all-clear before he was discharged from the base hospital. And the Brigadier who arranged his leave has apparently vouched for his mental state. It's suspicious in my opinion. They ought to visit everybody he was known to be connected with. For his mother's sake.

She was suddenly aware of his scrutiny. Had he sensed something in her bearing? Had he picked up a certain longing to tell all, inadequately masked by the desire to run back to the sulphurous shared dream that had folded its dark wings beneath her roof? Beatrice bent down as if to adjust a shoe tongue. She heard the doctor sigh and scratch his head.

– Anyway, I daresay they'll catch the poor fellow in the end. Now my dear, about your condition.

Charles had spent three days in billets and everything was going to plan. He still slept in the shed opposite the coal bunker, insisting on calling it the stables. Eric Wren and the other men of A Company were lodged in the flint barn which, long disused and roofless after a fire, lay beyond Beatrice's boundary at the top of the Row. Coming into the kitchen for meals (Beatrice's estaminet, one of two in the village, was apparently out of bounds to other ranks), Charles affected a swaggering ease which quite took his landlady's breath away. Confident, conventionally flirtatious, even to the extent of slapping her rump on one occasion when she bent to fetch a dish out of the oven, he became an officer at rest. On the Sunday, as the diary (carefully extracted from his shirt pocket) corroborated, there was a rehearsal of the attack, staged solely by Charles (but accompanied by many importunate ghosts) in the rose garden at the side of the house. For a time Beatrice had been worried he might seek out his old trench system for this mock-up and so be drawn back prematurely to the Front. But now it was as if the back garden didn't exist; or rather as if it had magically reverted to what, for her, it could never be again. Charles meanwhile busied himself with reels of wool (taken without permission from her knitting basket) and looked momentarily nonplussed when she furiously questioned why the roses had been thus draped and festooned. Then patiently, condescendingly, seeming to think she was a new recruit who had only just come out to France in time to join the battalion for the Big Show, he demonstrated how the vertical blue strands represented a five-yard spacing between each man in an attacking wave, while the horizontal red strands were spaced so as to suggest the hundred-yard gap between each wave. Beatrice squinted at the ghostly woollen checkerboard, fascinated despite herself by the absolute precision of this plan. Charles swivelled away and began addressing a climbing rose on the wall of the house as if it were an audience of squatting and sprawled men. *Each Company will attack in two waves of two platoons each; there will be ten waves in all, the seventh wave consisting of Battalion HQ and the tenth of stretcher bearers. No, we won't be needing them; Fritz will. The first eight platoons will be fighting units, the next eight mopping up, support and carrying. You'd like to be carried, eh, Wilkins, all the way to Berlin I bet. Well, since you mention it I can tell you now that A Company will be off first. Yes Wren. From Sunken Lane. And remember, no running. Two minutes for every hundred yards covered. Yes like a one-legged race. Do I think it will work? Why of course not. The attack will be a complete failure. All right Wilkins, don't look so glum. Even officers joke sometimes. Just remember all this when you're sat guzzling schnapps in a captured Boche dugout. All right. Company dismissed. Go and get some grub.* Bees were humming in the pink depths of the climbing rose. Charles turned back to Beatrice. There were tears in his eyes. *Wren doubts their wire will be broken. I do too. But how can I tell them that? How can I even begin to tell them what I know and feel and fear?* Then he too was gone, leaving Beatrice to gather up the snagged wool in sorrowful wonder.

– From what you tell me and on a preliminary examination I would say no, it is not the beginning, as you feared, my dear, of a premature climacteric or, as you ladies call it, the change. But we should need to carry out more tests to make certain. There may be a case for curettage. But as to the irregularity of bleeding, I would suggest your emotional state has a part to play.

The doctor, having delivered himself, peered at her over the top of his glasses. Beatrice nodded understanding with miserable fervour. Everything was drifting awry. News that, at any other time, might have filled her with exhilaration, seemed now to lack all meaning. She wasn't concerned for herself. The whole visit had been a pretext anyway, masking her plan first to announce Charles's presence in her house, then to ask Dr Blake to take him in next Saturday afternoon. But before she had had time to compose her thoughts behind the screen, he had leapt in with the bombshell about desertion. Worse still he claimed that Charles had already been to Ecclesden, thus giving the lie to Charles's own assertion that he had come to her and her only. Disappointment fuelled a simmering rage. She was absolutely not going to be betrayed and humiliated again. She stood up.

– I can't say I'm not relieved, Doctor. And perhaps, as you say, my emotional state . . . But I'm afraid that when you mention tests, well, the war can't wait can it, but I suppose my body can. Now if you'll excuse me.

She had not believed she could be so brusque with a figure of male authority, refusing even to have the door opened for her, so that the doctor was forced to abandon his gynaecological condescension.

– As you wish, Miss Lumley. Good luck in any case. There's plenty of work out there so they tell me.

– And plenty of mutilated bodies afterwards.

Then she was gone.

– Well?

– There certainly is evidence. As our sources suggested. And as you, madam, were so good as to, ahem, corroborate. A proper little camp.

– So what are you going to do about it?

– Report back of course.

– Report back!

– That's our orders. And that's what we have to do. Now if you'd be so kind . . .

– But aren't you going to arrest him?

– Fact is, madam, he was there but he isn't no longer.

– Isn't no, I mean, isn't any longer? He's there all the time. Singing and shouting obscenities. What about the house? Have you tried the house? Have you been inside?

– Fact is, madam, we don't have a warrant. We're just the scouts if you like. Just ordinary bobbies. And the owner isn't in.

– Of course she isn't. She's a VAD. But she'll be back this evening. You can come back this evening.

– Fact is, madam, we're conducting this investigation. Isn't that right? 'Course it is. So please allow those who know best . . .

– Best! Best! It's a travesty. If only Mr Gorrod were here. If only he hadn't gone to London.

– Rum place that.

– It's my opinion he's got wind and done a bunk.

– You would with that old hag breathing down your neck.

– There's a lot of them about nowadays. Mad old women.

– We'd better get back to the station.

– There's been something going on, that's for sure.

– It's one for the military, I reckon.

– Huh. Wouldn't like to be that poor bastard when they catch up with him.

– Exactly what the super' said this morning.

Coming home that evening Beatrice went straight to the shed where he slept. She had been nagged all day by the knowledge, culled from the diary, of an exchange about her between the Captain and his batman. Would the memory of this jolt Charles back into the present, something which she had longed for last week but now dreaded since, apart from the excitement of the business, she had begun to feel a growing interest in the mystery of the two blank days which Charles's actions would soon, she supposed, fill in.

There was a mattress in the shed now, evidently dragged down without her permission from her aunt's old bedroom. Also a primus which he must have found up in the attic. Was nowhere safe from his prying? It was like being constantly burgled. Charles was not there. On the mattress lay a crumpled, torn and grubby sheet of paper. It was typewritten and marked *Secret* in the top lefthand corner. Idly she let her eyes pass over the already fading text. 'On a date which will be communicated later . . . A Company will leave its forward position in the Sunken Road and move in a north-easterly direction . . . the German salient . . . followed ten minutes later by C Company already assembled at Jacob's Ladder . . . Nettoyeurs to wear a yellow badge on their shoulders . . . Companies to be distinguished by coloured arm bands as follows . . .' She looked up. Two pigeons were calling to one another in the conifer alley: *It's awful, Henry. It's awful.* What strange rift in things had allowed this invasion of nightmare? She had had enough. It had been a mistake to go along with what she now knew was a ruse and a lie. Even this piece of military jargon had probably been left there for her to find. He had run away. And he was a coward. Not only because of his desertion but also, and more importantly, because he had been too craven to tell her the truth: that she was a convenient and temporary bolthole, nothing more.

– And I thought I might help you to get well again. I'm a poor deluded bitch. That's all. And ought to go to France tomorrow. If I . . .

His hand was on her shoulder. She smelt spirits.

– 'selle, old thing. Only two days to . . . two days to . . . Oh why didn't I screw her? When I had the chance? She was there for the screwing. That's what Wren says. But you don't know what I'm talking about do you, so I'll shut up.

Charles had staggered past her to slump on the mattress where he lay breathing heavily. She was filled with renewed rage, if only at this further coarsening of what must once have been a romantically tender regret.

– I want you out, Charles Tremain. Out and off my property. I've had enough of this charade. If you want charades you should go back to Mummy and Maud Egerton who, so I'm told, you've already visited. I won't be used any more. Do you hear?

But he did not hear. Or could not. The pigeons were still lodging their fastidious complaints. About the light or the trees or the earth. Beatrice went out to the standpipe in the yard, filled a bucket and returned to fling water on Charles's sweating head. He started up then, seeing her, shook himself and smiled.

– Still here? That brandy you keep in your cellar isn't half bad. Wren says there were two gendarmes here earlier. Beats me how they got so near the Front. Snooping around. After some criminal, apparently. Lucky they didn't come into the barn. I was in the middle of supervising the delousing and in none too good a mood. – Beatrice was about to interrupt but he swept on. – Oh and did you hear about the dance tomorrow night? A sort of farewell party. In the square, here. Hope you'll come. Have a dance with me. Say yes, won't you.

That night, listening to the darkness, Beatrice saw how far she had drifted out from the shore. Hour by hour the ghostly world of the Front had crept up a little closer, a little closer, until now she was quite surrounded by its noises, sounds and smells. England was far away. Her house, which should have enclosed her with an absolute solidity, had grown thin and transparent, allowing the darkness of the Front to pour in like smoke. Her garden, where all day the birds used to sing, where light trembled in the veined green tissues of runner bean leaves, her little plot of English earth, had been furrowed and gouged and blasted and undercut until hardly anything remained. And in the midst of it all stood this man, orchestrating the invasion of her life with a mixture of cynicism, frivolity and insane conviction. All at once she sat bolt upright and raised a clenched fist. She had decided. She would go to the Agent tomorrow and see if the tenants couldn't be moved in earlier. Charles would have to go then. She had abandoned all hope of hospitalisation. Later, in the depths of sleep, Eric Wren appeared once more at the foot of the bed, holding his terrier in his arms.

In the morning the night's clearcut route to freedom seemed to have tangled over and grown hopelessly narrow. What difference would a few days make? And how did she propose to evict Charles, short of calling the police, the very route which she had so desperately wanted to avoid? Her mind grew cloudy, brooding on these difficulties, while outside in the sunlight, Charles cleaned his Webley, peering into its barrel as if it were a tunnel leading to some source of light. With the result that she went to work in a daze compounded of mental exertion, sleeplessness and continuing anxiety over her health. All morning she sat in her gloomy basement, then rose at one and went out, unseeing, into the town. The faces that she passed seemed to contain a hidden knowledge of her dilemma and mocked her with long contemptuous looks. She could hear sharp whispering behind her back and once, at a crossroads near the aquarium, thought she saw Eric himself, in the distance, leading a dog that seemed much larger than the terrier she remembered. So she walked on, pursuing and pursued through a world that appeared to know everything about her yet had no use for the knowledge, since it involved lies, deceits and vanity. Until the tenement rose up, as it always had, in the old days, like a crumbling cliff, stuck with the dirty grey lichen of curtained windows.

Mr Birkett stood looking down on Beatrice with a consoling almost piteous smile. He had grown more gaunt since last winter and had shaved off his rather wispy beard. This new nakedness gave him a blue simian look, revealing a wide shovel-blade of a chin and beneath it the creased stalk of the neck. He ran a finger along the mantelpiece and hummed the opening of the champagne aria from Don Giovanni.

– But yes, this is an unexpected visit. I heard about your aunt. So sad.

Beatrice felt confused and uncertain. Why had she come here, of all places? It was as if she had been led, or driven. And what now did she intend to do? Plead for help? Confess all? Passing along the hall she had encountered a knot of tenants in the dining room hunched over some card game. They had looked up with savage resentfulness.

Other faces had appeared at the banisters to leer and whisper. Was this the house where she had met Maud for the first time; where they had shared their evenings together, where for a brief period she had been happy, happier even than at Ecclesden in the early weeks? Of course it was. For here Charles had come; here he had met his half-sister again; here Maud and she had become estranged. Like Ecclesden, Orion Parade had opened up to reveal many dark, cold rooms behind the seeming warmth of its thresholds. Would Artillery Row behave likewise, now that poor Charles had come there, to live out his sickness in her presence? With a conscious effort she tried to concentrate on this present trouble. This man, she realised with a shiver, was her last hope. She coughed.

– Mr Birkett, I must be honest with you. This isn't exactly a social visit. I came – she swallowed nervously – I came for advice.

Then, as Mr Birkett turned from a nonchalant and expansive host into someone at once more suspicious and less accommodating, his rather bony fingers stretching and contracting on the dusty mantelpiece as if he were trying to palp some invisible substance into a shape, Beatrice told as much as she dared of the last few days, omitting names and transferring the whole drama on to an imaginary friend who lived next door in the Row. Her voice sounded strange to her. It was as if she sat slightly to one side of herself, listening. She knew that what the voice was saying could provoke at worst a disgusted incomprehension, at best a meddling fascination which might end in disaster. And she didn't care. Let the voice go on. She had fought alone for too long. Sun struck the mirror behind her old landlord's head so that a stream of watery light went flickering along the ceiling. That mirror had held Maud once. Mr Birkett coughed.

– Thank you, Miss Lumley, Beatrice if I might be so bold.

He might not. But she no longer had the self-possession to withhold the liberty.

– You have come to me for advice and I must say I am honoured. But I still have a difficulty understanding. You have a friend you say who lives alone and she has been visited by a soldier who is not well. This soldier, he is the Wren person who came here once, is he not?

Beatrice nodded, blushing at yet another deceit.

– This soldier is not well in the head you say. And the neighbours are complaining. Has he no family?

Beatrice glanced out at a line of washing strung between the plum-tree and a hazel sapling. Pegged handkerchiefs and smalls flapped like skins on a vermin post. She turned and nodded again. Mr Birkett's eyes looked as if they were about to begin unhooking her bodice.

– Very well. But you are a nurse. If a man has a wound it can be treated at your hospital. If this man has, as it were, a wound in his mind then he must go to where they treat such things. This war.

Mr Birkett waved his hand as though to brush away the blowfly of a conflict that had settled so obscenely on his life, laying its eggs on the encrusted empty casket of his aestheticism. But his eyes were busy about her underthings and had perhaps successfully penetrated her petticoat.

– This is my advice to your . . . ahem . . . friend. Beauty is the only truth, Miss Lumley. The beauty of art. All this ugliness – again the flapping hand as if threatened by maggots – it must be put away, out of sight. But a thing of beauty is a joy forever, as Wordsworth once said.

– Charles quoted that once. But he said it was by . . .

– Ah the Tremain boy. I heard he has come back on leave. Let us hope this war will spare him for higher things. You have seen him I expect?

Beatrice shook her head vigorously, blushing again for the deceit and for the memory of Charles's health which she suddenly felt she herself had helped to undermine. But also for something else, a tone in her old landlord's voice which rang slightly thin, like an overtuned piano key.

– I . . . I see very few people.

Mr Birkett smiled. His teeth were no longer brown. Had all the money raised at the concert gone to the Regiment?

– Of course. Of course. But you are a comfort to a great traveller.

Her heart shook. He had guessed after all. It wasn't that she hadn't wanted him to. Her eyes filled with tears.

386

– But what must I do then, Mr Birkett. Go to the police? To the Military? I should hate him to be hurt in any way. And I just can't see how to persuade him to go to the hospital. Oh it's too awful.

– What all this has to do with Ulysses I can't quite . . .

– Ulysses?

– The great traveller I mentioned. And now it seems you don't have a friend in trouble after all. Well.

So she had let him discover her secret. And felt an insane rush of lightness. And was standing up now, lurching across to the landlord, forcing him to fold her in his consoling embrace and so endure a closeness which had been unthinkable when they had lived under the same roof. Mr Birkett seemed curiously tentative, almost timorous. But if Beatrice had seen his eyes she would have pulled away from the scented waistcoat and sought refuge. He had seen what he must do. The seeing was hard and pitiless. But could be concealed in a lilting voice.

– There, there, Miss Lumley, Beatrice, no situation is irreversible. Shall I come out tonight and see what can be done? You are a woman on your own and cannot be expected to fight every battle singlehanded.

And Beatrice who had realised how desperately she had wanted not to surrender her secret up to the world, nodded meekly.

Come Tonight Stop 1800 hours Stop News Stop Jackals Stop WB.

Mr Birkett listened to the clerk and nodded his head.

– And that's Miss M. Egerton. Yes. Ecclesden Manor. Near Thundersbarrow. Yes. Good.

A tram passed by in the sunlight, its side blazoned with a poster for the Military Service Act.

Their two shadows moved back and forth across the scullery wall, warped and vast. The wind-up gramophone on the draining board vibrated to the sound of Caruso singing an aria from *La Bohème*. Next would come Vesta Tilley's version of 'Burlington Bertie'. Then Caruso again. They were the only two cylinders he had been

387

able to find, in the attic where Beatrice had deposited the gramophone not long after her aunt's death. Beatrice shifted her gaze to the man who was dancing with her now, moving slowly from foot to foot, his eyes closed. Flushed with the remainder of the French Spirit (the empty bottle was lying on its side under the table), Charles seemed oblivious both of her and his surroundings. Earlier that evening when she had arrived home it had been a different matter. All animation and excitement, he had showed her the X of bunting he had strung across the yard with two pieces of rope and some crayoned paper. *For the festivities tonight. We've got to have a good send off.* Then he had followed her indoors, at one moment whistling, 'If you were the only girl in the world', at the next chattering about the battle to come like a child anticipating some long-looked-for treat. It had been hard to persuade him to sit down, let alone eat. Then had come the preparations for the dance. The pushing back of table and chairs; the fetching of the half bottle of eau-de-vie and finally, triumph of triumphs, the unveiling of the gramophone. *You never told me you had one, Mademoiselle. And it works.*

Beatrice felt near the end of her tether. Not only was there the constant strain of having to play up to Charles's obsessive re-enactments; she had also begun to develop a slight fever which she traced back to her brief contact with the solicitor's clerk a week ago at the hospital. He had been off work ever since and she realised with a dull foreboding that he must have passed on his infection. Since her nervous collapse the previous winter, Beatrice had found herself to be generally more vulnerable to chills and infections. On top of all this sat the ambivalent knowledge that Mr Birkett would be arriving soon, the first person from outside to penetrate their shared world. What would happen then? Would Charles collapse at last and beg to be taken to see Dr Blake? Or laugh and reveal that it had all been a play contrived so as to help him keep his mental equilibrium while he wrestled with the terrible secret at the heart of the battle itself? Beatrice could not help feeling guilty about what she had done, especially since she had long-since guessed that the re-enactment had four more days to run. What would Charles say to her now when he found that, instead of helping him as she had promised, she had gone outside for assistance, willing in the end to sacrifice his delicate, strangely tender re-creation of the front-line world to her own needs and scruples. Would he blame her? Reject her? Surrender to her? Breaking out in cold sweats, hearing Charles talking to his ghostly companions in the yard, clearing away the tea things, then going upstairs to change into her best gown, Beatrice could not deny that she was about to betray her guest. Yet, felt convinced that it must be done. She could hardly stand another night of it. Yet alone four more. Bent in front of her dressing-table mirror and trying to concentrate on powdering a face whose contours would keep blurring, she remembered Maud's sickness and its aftermath. How long ago that seemed. And how innocent she had been then. Her body flared again as if to remind her of what it harboured, some slow-burning spiritual corruption. Yet, she must play the part to the end. And go gliding down to dance with a deranged deserter in the scullery, while outside the yard echoed to the distant shudder of another imagined bombardment.

But Mr Birkett did not arrive. When, at eight sharp, there was a knock on the front door, Beatrice almost jumped back from Charles's encircling yet curiously impersonal embrace. Another hot sweat found her briefly unable to focus as she went out into the hall, so that she banged her shin on the settle. The boy at the door handed her a sealed envelope which she tore open with trembling fingers. Mr Birkett begged her to accept his apologies but unavoidable business had detained him. Would tomorrow evening be acceptable? He would assume so unless he heard otherwise. With her shin still throbbing, Beatrice could not help a certain elation and went back into the kitchen to embrace the next phase of Charles's delirium. But Charles was not there. For a panicked moment she wondered if he had misinterpreted the knock as a danger signal. Then she saw him, out in the yard, taking down the bunting and looking up at the clear sky. She went to him, suddenly afraid. He looked pale and old.

– Doesn't look good. This rain. I wonder if they'll call it off.

Charles hunched up his collar and rolled up the two ropes. Beatrice stared at the perfectly clear sky. The evening star glimmered high above Thundersbarrow.

– Rain, Charles?

– You know my first name. What's this if it isn't rain? God's tears? Either way it'll do for our attack on Thursday. The observation planes will be grounded. No show.

He yawned and stretched.

– Anyway I'm turning in for an early night. Thanks for the dance. Can you hear that singing? That'll be Wren and the others up in the barn. Won't they be jiggered if it's postponed?

So Beatrice, who had not wholly discounted the possibility that as the estaminet owner she might be called upon to spend the night with the English Captain, rearranged the scullery and crept up to bed, shivering. In the night it did rain, if only in her head. And she heard the sound of ammunition carts going up the line.

In her dream the knocking was that of many soldiers' boots marching past the schoolhouse at Ecclesden. Charles waved as he went past, at the head of his company, riding his mother's gelding. Eric Wren did not wave and kept his face turned away from her. Then the shaft on Thundersbarrow opened up again and all the soldiers began filing down its sides in a long black spiral. She wanted to warn them not to go into the caves but had lost her voice. Then someone else began calling and she was suddenly wide awake, hearing the knocking on the front door and other less distinct noises round the back. Frightened and hot, she flung on her housecoat and went to look out of the window. There were two men below, in blue uniforms and red caps. For a mad moment she thought they must have come to collect the rubbish; then, that they were from the letting agent. But her fear and foreboding told her otherwise. By the time she had reached the hall she knew they were military police. She had been betrayed.

– Miss Beatrice Lumley?

She nodded, her mouth too dry to speak. The card in the man's hand wriggled like a fish. She could not read the writing on it.

– Did you know the officer in your house has been absent without leave from his battalion for over a week?

She nodded again, then shook her head violently. Betrayed. She had been betrayed. But not by Birkett. Not by the army. By herself. Betrayed by that person inside her who always said no, who always ran away, who always refused. It had happened at Ecclesden and again last year at Orion Parade. And now today for a third time. She had succumbed to the treachery of her own timid soul. And would have wept in front of these eidolons of men. If a choleric rage hadn't suddenly spurted up inside her, drowning all circumspection, all logic. She had found her voice again. And would speak.

– Absent you say? Without leave? Bollocks. He's been at the Front. In fact he'll never leave it now. He'll always be there. Don't you understand. Always.

The taller of the two men, the one who had shown her his identity card, stroked his chin and smiled contemptuously.

– The Front's in your bedroom, is it?

The slap sounded loud in the dawn quiet of the Row. The man staggered a little and flushed a dull ruby.

– Bitch. You're lucky we ain't got orders to take you too. Though I can't see why not. Harbouring a deserter and all.

The man's companion coughed. He was nervously fingering an unlighted cigarette.

– Extenuating circumstances, Mick. That's what they are. It's his family. They know the Brigadier. And they told him . . .

– I know what they told him, Bill. You can have the son but this here bitch is to be let off the hook. So just thank your lucky stars you've got friends in high places, Missus. Now as for your fancy man if he isn't at the Front now he soon will be. As a private going over the top. What do you think of that?

Beatrice was swaying with fever. The tall man and his companion would keep merging then splitting apart like reflections in the hall of mirrors on the pier. Their words too were loud one minute, then soft the next, echoing now in her head, and now from far off in the middle of the town. Their meaning was largely beyond her. Except that, increasingly, as the tall man's mouth moved to the ventriloquism of her fever, she heard again and again the same desperate command, *You must get to him. Before they do. You must. Must.*

– 'Ere, where do you think you're going. If you think you can save him you're . . .

The tall man's voice died away as, obedient to the command in her head, Beatrice ran back through the hall and across the kitchen into the scullery. Opening the back door, she blinked in the glare of the rising sun and saw what she had dreaded. She was too late. On top of the dugout where he had evidently run for shelter, Charles was struggling violently with three more military policemen. His Webley flashed in the sun then went arcing away across Jacob's Ladder. Charles cried out something inarticulate and was suddenly felled by a blow to the stomach. When she came up he was still writhing in pain on the dented corrugated roof. She knelt down and stroked his damp forehead.

– Had quite a hideout here didn't he, Miss? I've heard of ex-soldiers living rough but this was a complete little redoubt, all to himself. A real Leipzig Salient. Lucky that gun didn't go off.

He was looking at her now in a way that she remembered from long ago when they had talked by the peacock run. A different world. She could not speak for tears.

– It's all right, Beatty. I couldn't have made it. But you can. For me. Change it, Beatty. Try to change what happened. I'll be with you.

– Move aside there, Miss. Prisoner's got to go now. You've said your goodbyes.

His finger on her cheek. His dry, unkissed lips. Gone. Hauled along like a limp carcase between two military police. The sun warm on her back. More terrible than the darkest arctic chill. Gone.

And in the sad, empty air of the dugout, fallen, unremarked on the tamped earth floor: the belemnite she had given him at the station. Picking it up she held it to her parched lips for a long time. And felt the cold strike like a splinter into her heart.

– I suppose I owe a thank you. For being let off the hook I mean.

– Not me. No. Thank the old witch at the manor. She had just about enough strength to get on the phone to the Brigadier. And seemed to think you shouldn't be implicated.

– Whereas if it had been left to you . . .

– Really, Beatty. What have you been playing at? We were driven half-frantic looking for him. He might have done himself an injury.

– Whereas now the army will simply arrange to have him injured. Free of charge.

– Beatty, he went absent without leave. The army, perhaps I should say the Brigadier, has been really most understanding. They even agreed not to begin a search until we had made our own private enquiries. Then when nothing came up (I must say that we never dreamed he'd land on you), we even went to the trouble of putting them off the scent with a cock and bull story about a fiancée in Yorkshire. If it hadn't been for my, our, intervention, he would have ended up on a charge before a courtmartial. You would have been responsible for that. Hiding him like a common fugitive. And a coward.

– He chose to come here. To me. He hated you. And he wasn't well. How can he go back to France?

– I can assure you he was quite well when I saw him off at the station this morning.

The doorway was swaying in the thick evening light. It would collapse soon and leave her suspended in a quivering void of fever. Maud went small then came back again, looming. She seemed about to demand to be allowed indoors and Beatrice could not bear that. She attempted a last ditch collection of thoughts.

– So why have you come? Now? I was just preparing dinner. I can't . . .

She had dreaded the humiliation of crying in front of her old friend. But the image of the empty house and ravaged garden was too much to bear. He had been here and he was gone. That was all.

– Poor dear, you're quite whacked aren't you? Why did you do it, Beatty?

– Don't dear and Beatty me.

Maud smiled. She was cold and Beatrice was hot. She wore cold, opulent clothes, a pale linen jacket and a string of chilly glistening pearls. Beatrice stood simmering in her ragged housecoat and hastily pinned up hair. She could feel the shock of contact between the hot and the cold. On her threshold. There was a movement behind Maud and Ulysses appeared, wrapping his tail round her booted calf.

– Oh a cat. No. Not on my dress thank you very much. We don't like cat hairs. Be off with you. Shoo.

Amazed yet contemptuous Ulysses sidled round to Beatrice and miaowed soundlessly.

– I thought you liked cats. That one anyway. Don't you remember him? From Birkett's?

Maud was brushing her dress fastidiously with a gloved hand.

– No I don't, I'm afraid.

Cold. The old Maud had been shed like a skin. Revealing this ivory replica. Beatrice felt her face flushing once more. She licked her dry cracked lips in vain.

– If Charles wasn't ill why did he come to me? Why did he desert?

Cold and infinitely knowledgeable. Yet still she would not let her in, to defile the hot cave of the house with her slippery unfeeling coils. Coils of blonde hair, under a ribboned boater.

– A funk that's all. He got windy that last day at Ecclesden. We were up on Thundersbarrow and he started remembering the battle. You know about the battle, I take it?

Know about it! She who had lived through its prelude. Who was still there, behind the lines, a day before the regiment was due to move up. Watching them going to and fro in the village square, or swimming in the pond by the mill, or lounging under the sweet chestnut tree, playing an endless game of Crown and Anchor. She laughed now to think of where she was. And where Maud wasn't.

– It was something that happened between him and Eric.

She knew. And was even now watching the two of them in conversation outside the stables.

– You're nodding, so I suppose you know that much. Well we haven't found Eric, though he hasn't been reported dead. Molly Dadger's gone over to France to see if she can locate him in one of the base hospitals. But it was something that happened . . .

– Yes. And when it does happen I'll understand. He'll be there too. With the captured maxim. But Oenone . . .

– Beatrice, do you need to lie down? You seem, well, confused if you must know.

– Confused! I can't afford to be confused. I've got to check all the kit. And then go over those plans for bombing along Stuff trench into the Bergwerk. Confused! I've never felt clearer-headed in my life. It's just that unfortunate delay because of bad weather which threw us all. But now we're on course again. Two days to go. Yes. Two days. Oh Charles now I know what you meant. I'll be with you.

Dear Walter,

Well it's all over now. And the family honour has not been besmirched. All thanks to your quick wit. She's a rather pathetic case now, don't you think. Quite old-looking. And if you ask me a little gone in the head. Charles admitted he'd had an attack of the blue funks as he called them. And more or less hinted that she'd taken advantage of his weakened state, keeping him in that pokey house like a virtual prisoner. Would you credit the nerve of the woman! Sheer desperation, I suppose. The sort of malice only a frustrated spinster could harbour. Well he's back in uniform now and has already written from somewhere near Etaples. He's been demoted of course but says he'd rather be in the ranks. Being a captain involved too many responsibilities. Still no news of Wren. Except a report that he was wounded about the same time as Charles. Once again, many thanks for your swift action. All might have ended in disaster otherwise. Looking forward to the concert in the autumn. Regards M.

My poor boy my poor poor boy taken at the very last moment taken from me forever yet you want me to understand don't you you want me to go on as you would have gone on through those last two days those last forty-eight hours of your real life before that other posthumous life began you want me to go forward and understand how the posthumous life took over and when it took over and where in the shrieking void of the battle with Eric Wren beside you you want me to be there don't you to heal what you were prevented from healing either then in the chaos and carnage or now in my garden of phantoms which you brought into existence my poor poor boy building and digging and tunnelling until the necropolis was finished and you could summon them the dead like a necromancer summon them into your city of ghosts which I must guard alone now now that you have gone because that's what you would have wanted yes and I will I will because then at last I might come to understand not just this final mystery but all the others as well on the hill and in the quarry and under the shaft and in Maud's bedroom and that's what you want isn't it because then I'll be free at last like you made me feel I would be once long ago outside the peacock run Oh tell me tell me Charles that that is what you want that you want your Beatty to do this for you who looked after you when you were frightened and fed you and protected you but couldn't in the end save you Oh say it now just say it.

Yes, Beatrice, I want you to do this thing for me.

Shall I begin then? Shall I begin now?

Yes. Begin now. Where are we?

In the backyard. The washing. I was too tired, too sad to unpeg it.

The village square. What time is it?

Four o'clock in the afternoon. The clouds are boiling up again. There'll be another storm. With rain at last.

1600 hours on June 30. Weather fine. We have just paraded. The men are falling out. Soon we shall be marching up to the assembly trenches. Listen. Listen to what they are saying. He is among them.

Rifle. Bayonet. Pull Through. Ammunition Pouches. SAA. Small Arms Ammunition. A Bandolier of same. Knapsack. Holdall. Gas Helmet. Ground Sheet. Water Bottle. Housewife. Mess Tins. Cutlery. Iron Rations. Four repeat four empty sandbags. Pick. Entrenching Tools. Sixty-six Pounds in all. That little lot should last us till we reach Berlin.

We've got to cross No Man's Land first. Sixty-six bleeding bloody pounds.

You should be so fucking lucky. Look at this bleeding barbed wire. A whole roll of it just for little me. And as for those poor fucking sods the Bomb Carriers.

And you'd better not forget them nail scissors. Most particular Haig is, about the nail scissors. Wouldn't do us capturing a Boche dugout and him noticing we'd got long fingernails.

Over in the corner near the ostlers. They were sorting through their equipment and one of the detonators must have been faulty. Two dead and three wounded. But we couldn't wait. We had to be in the lines by six. I was so windy. So bloody windy. And he knew. And kept close. He was always so close. Where are we now?

On the path leading past the runner beans. I haven't watered them today. Some of the flowers are dropping. And oh, flying

Ants. On the track near the bombed-out sucrerie. I remember. Jet-black swarms of workers and amongst them the males and females all big and clumsy with their floppy wings they were climbing something and Oenone kept barking as they climbed

The bean poles. Launching out from the top into a gathering darkness. The worker ants scribbling their manic zigzags. They know there'll be a storm. Ulysses is curled up under the runners. Asleep in the shadow of the

Rifle pickets. A regular battalion going down the line. Lucky blighters. Missing the Big Push. Singing at the tops of their voices. Hullo! Hullo! Here we are again. But the ants. Hundreds of them. Crawling up the stocks and on to the barrels. Then launching out against the flash of our

Thunder. In the quarry. The cave

Where we. Oh Eric, do you

Remember

When we were so high and the ants were flying and we went into the cave and heard

Our guns sir on the horizon and

Where are we? Where are we now?

A heap of grass cuttings. In a wire frame. At the base a rat hole. Like the entrance of a tunnel into

A tomb. Mass graves. Some of the men crossed themselves, spat, muttering

For Fritz, Tremain says. Don't you believe it. Don't you bloody believe it. Haig's got everything planned. But

Eric, I don't want to lie there. When she. When I

You won't, Sir. Just try to be calm. We're all in the same boat

Up shit creek without a paddle. Where are we now?

In the pergola alley. Roses. Oh so tired. So tired I am and lonely and

Many of the men had blisters. It was the wet. After the rain two days
before. Made the trenches like flooded

Ditches. The crawl. That's what we'll be doing soon. The bleeding
sodding crawl. Where's this mate? The Nile Delta? The

Old Beaumont Road. Esau's Way. Tenderloin Street. I had memorised
the entire terrible topography of our journey. When we had to fork left and
when right. Where there would be a munitions dump and where a sector
exposed to enemy sniper fire. And always down, down, oh always down into
the darkness, the dark underkingdom that leads

All the way back to

Where? Oh where does it lead, Eric? Why won't you

Speak of the devil

And Oenone

Had to be carried of course

Like a bleeding baby. This ain't no place to bring a lady. She might see
something unpleasant and

Get down now, Oenone. That's a good girl. And

Remember

The thousands trying to move both ways at once. In trenches clogged with
mud and rivulets of thick chalky water. Trenches that had caved in. Trenches
too shallow to afford protection. They carried their Enfields above their heads.
Swaddled in canvas. To keep them dry. And

Remember

The hundreds squatting or leaning on either side. The stretcher bearers
already beginning to return, splashing stumbling back along the dog-toothed
communication trenches, their burdens joggled uncertainly aloft, swagged dirty
canvas pallets on which the first wounded groaned or cursed, forbidden or
unable to die. An hour it took us. Just to reach the assembly trenches. And
once

Remember

Through a chink in a gas curtain men playing poker their ringed stubbly

faces stained from beneath by a lantern's amber and the noise up ahead louder
now than I'd ever heard it before. And the light, darker yet more brazen than
a thousand mingled sunsets, pulsing

Here in my head as I struggle to remember
The flint mines Oh Eric, I can't
You can, Sir, you must. For
Her sake. Yes. Where are we now?
The cold frame. You loved her not me. You said
White City. We've come to White City where
It has begun. The thunder. Her not me. Maud Maud Maud they were
crying and

Wailing so loud it was like silence, a silence of utter implosion as if your
body had swallowed the air and could not regurgitate it so that men moved in
that sunken world of grey-white chalk ravines between parados and firestep
traverse and firebay dugout and forward sap like heavy divers only able to
communicate by signs slow waves of the hand or infinitely burdened and
heavy shakes and nods of the head. Have you brought

The tapes. Hems and ribbons ripped from my pure and incorruptible
underthings. Oh forever untouchable. Cottons, silks, elastics. And the
Gas
Mask Aunt wore as a young girl at the Venetian Carnival in Tooting
Bec. Oh I'm well prepared. Unlike you, Captain. And then
We were filing down into the
Cold frame
Forward HQ
Under the corrugated iron which you
Found empty. The previous lot had been only too glad to scarper and it
was
Cushy enough, a table, bunk beds, look sir they've even left us
An India paper Palgrave, Titbits. Do you remember Eric in the cave, her
bodice, the darkening stain, oh if
I turn there's a clump of pearl-grey eggs secreted in the earth just above my
head. Woodlice. The metallic ping of fat rain drops. Shall I
Brew up, Captain? With the pull through soaked in whale oil and the
cigarette tin

Primus stove slopping paraffin

In a time which was no time. A single extended minute lasting forever and
What should I do now, Eric? Should I lie down, or check the men or
Pack up your troubles

Lad. He'd never called me that before as though I were his son. As though
our fathers had never

Existed in your old kit bag because we're here because we're here because
we're

Here, Oh Eric, thank you thank you for being here and for not saying
How long? How long must I tolerate all this? The cold and the dampness.
You peed in here didn't you? I can smell the reechy tang of it. Like a little
boy in a cave. And now it's started to bucket down. Between blue flashes of
lightning over Thundersbarrow. And will you hark at that thunder. Like an
actual bombardment. But I'm so cold. Can't you see. So cold I'm shivery
hot. How long, Captain before they stop

Moving the furniture in heaven. That's what Miss Jupp used to say when
there was a storm. Do you

Remember
Eric
If you say so
Lad call me that again it's cushy here isn't it under the ground curled up
in this bunk call me

No, Sir. I can't. It ain't right. Sir. It ain't fucking
Stupid governess. How Maud hated her and made faces behind her back.
What time is it?

Midnight
2400 hours and time to lay out the tapes sir. In
The bath once remember she
In No Man's Land and
Once she
Time to lay out
In the bath
In No Man's Land. The tapes
Buttocks so young she yet even then I even then touched
Tapes. In No Man's Land

But splayed and Oh melting suds the crack I

Sir you don't appear to have heard a bleeding fucking word I've been saying if you'll pardon the

Fact is it isn't like furniture at all. Nor books falling down a staircase. The fact is it's like

Nothing no one's ever heard in the whole fucking history of the entire fucking

Remember

Bombs not a storm. Metal not air. A seven days storm of metal to end the world. What do you say Eric? Will there be a flood too? Will we be

Going Sir. I've got the tapes

The hems and the ribbons

All rolled up in

My canvas Sewing

Ammunition

Basket

Box

Where are we? Where are we now?

Crawling out of

Jacob's

The leek

Ladder

Trench down Eric's tunnel

Of pure pent up screaming

I heard once in the ghost train when you didn't

Remember

To come and I heard

The sound as though it had been imprisoned underground for centuries and was escaping now in a single extended wail of pain and despair and endless

Oh endless suffocation of myself in myself and flesh too hot too hot to breathe Oh

Eric. Why did you hate me? I couldn't help what I

That's enough of that now. Here's the

Christmas

Verey

401

Candles
Lights
And the Toy
Pistol
Derringer (three ha'pence from Woolworths) which the boy next door
dropped over the wall and I confiscated like the teacher I always will be saying
Where are we? Where are we now?
In the field
Sunken
Boundary ditch
Lane. You go first Eric up and over I
Can. And must. Now that the dragon. Go on
Oh out into darkness under the cracking chalk
Roof
Dome
Of the cave
Sky
Remember
Dodging between the sudden upwellings of flame that would pick us out,
blue-white against black
As the lightning stretches my shadow across (oh soft and incorruptible
virgin vestments) white torn hems and ribbons and elastics laid out in rippling
lines, as far as
Their first belt of
Brambles
Picketed and coiled wire
On the bank near the railway line. I tripped once and cut my arm on
something sharp and
Two of the men were hit by shells that fell short. I can't remember
Seeing the wire cut
Crawling back to our own lines, then the dugout again
Under the cold frame
In White City. Where I slept the sleep of the dead. But always oh always
stark wide awake and upright. Seeing yet not seeing that shaking earth and
chalk

Cell where I am shaking too. Don't forget that. Don't you ever

Remember

The cave, Eric, I dreamed I was back in our cave under the hill eating sponge cake I'd stolen from the kitchen and listening to the rain. Oh how I longed to be back there in my childhood Eric while you

Never

Nor I. Whose childhood is a forgotten vagueness. Who must lie now listening to the storm. And the hot flutter of my own heart. A frightened rabbit, quaking at

Explosions you see I never told anyone it's funny but I was always frightened of explosions yes in the quarry called them airbangs it's funny when I was a nipper would you believe yes and it's funny you see because later you see I

Went running down a path

Still windy

I saw you running down

Thundersbarrow away from

Me

The past. Don't you see. That's why I joined up. With him. With Eric. Don't you

Remember

A boathouse on a wet afternoon. A settee spewing my white incorruptible

Remember

What time is it?

Four o'clock on the morning

Of the last day

0400 hours. Oh time drowned underwater in that green sunken world. I must go up now into the light and the wind on the hill out of this fug of fear and shame my bowels cramping quick I'll have to be

Careful, Sir! We've got wounded here and

Stumbling over a legless torso blurting screams. Then down a communication trench and into the foetid latrine. How much longer Lord. How much

Longer, crouching in the wet darkness outside the cold frame among the lupins. The scalding rush. Then a sharp stabbing pain. Haemorrhoids. But out here in the garden I've no

Field Dressings big enough Captain and as for TCP

Poor fellow. He looks so

White and you'd be too if you had a belly full of

Shh. Not so loud. The Captain might

Hear. Of course you could hear a pin drop in this trench. You could hear a hedgehog fart at forty yards. Why it's so quiet you'd have to shake a bleeding baby to wake it. Fuck off will you. Just fuck off into

The darkness before dawn. Candle flame on the trestle quivering in the percussion

Of the final bombardment. A hurricane of every calibre of shell we have from now until

The end of time

Zero Hour

Rum ration sir

The cooking sherry

In a petrol can (Soon Runs Dry)

Milk Bottle

With a ladle

Medicine spoon that I

Dashed from your lips

Tucked back into my nightdress, always the nurse because

I would have gone on drinking oh yes gone on and on but he was beside me as always his eyes on me blank somehow but seeing and then it was as if

You were the only girl in the world and

We were the only two left in that wilderness of noise and violence and endless endless

Waiting for one who never comes who will never now oh why her why her why not

Both of us looking away his voice whispering

And I were the only boy

We won't reach the mine crater

What's that Eric, what's that you say old Mole from

Greenland's Icy Mountains from India's Coral

Parapet. It's only a hundred yards we'll

Not get there first. The Boche will. To their side of the crater. We'll have to swing left

Back down
The other way
Into the flint mine
The other way
Together where
Only man is vile

How much longer? How much longer do I have to sit here waiting for the end of things? I'm so cold and hot at once. And empty but

Don't eat before. That's what Eric says. If you cop one in the belly it all spills out. Time to

Check the arm bands
Coloured wool swatches
And the metal triangles

Which I cut from a tin of Huntley and Palmer's Digestives (one and thrupence, reduced, at the grocer's on the corner)

Fixed to every haversack to flash in the sunlight so that our observers in the rear can plot our magnificent

Massacre and
Where are we? Where are we now?
The field ditch
Sunken Lane
Again. It's nearly
Five o'clock
0500 hours and
The rain is slackening
There's still some low cloud and a light drizzle. But
Clearing by dawn and

Keep your heads well down you men. Especially at that far end, Wilkins. My feet like lead and my heart full of air. What would I do? How would I move? Let alone command. Oenone lay at my feet and looked up lugubriously now and then as if deploring my state. Meanwhile Eric was singing about the troops of Midian while others lay and smoked or squinted over letters from home or checked their paybooks or tightened the covers on their Enfields or just stared with that look no one has seen who hasn't been there, a look at once blank and bottomless, a look that mixes stone and water.

Our bombardment was so loud now it seemed to be inside and outside at once, a part of the very structure of our bones and a thing more remote than the farthest galaxy. I shifted my knobkerry from left hand to right and saw that I had been gripping it so hard my palm was serrated with its grain. Time to synchronise watches. Then just as I

Lifted the whistle Aunt Millicent inherited from her policeman father

The mine went up

Like a dirty great bleeding

Eruption of pure darkness, a single dark blossom unsheathed only once in a millennium rising vertically on its black stalk to bury the light then slowly with infinite slow collapsing of unfolding falling petals of chalk and mud and concrete crumbling and falling away, the pillar of a

Sodding great bloody black fountain

Crumbling back into vaporous spray. One man screaming my back my back slithering down from the parados where grinning a moment before he had braced himself against the shock waves while the debris hit Sunken Lane, lumps the size of footballs

From their redoubt. Under the

Hill

Remember where the dragon

Where I saw

Stop shaking man

Then their bombardment renewed its intensity so that we all lay hunched, praying for the moment

Which came

And brought with it the second silence. A silence buried deep down at the black core of all noise. The sun had risen now and there was a low mist. The larks were singing too and when at last I put my whistle to my lips a small butterfly with spotted red and brown wings landed on a burst sandbag. And folded its

Wings. A comma. Among the lupins. A sort of

Good omen that, Sir, don't you

Remember our oh so long and lost lonely summer day when we stood side by side the only girl and

The only boy in the darkness

Of the butterfly room
Poor pater's cabinet that shattered when
You left me. Don't you
Remember
Nothing as, blowing my whistle and raising my knobkerry I rose up. Both bombardments had begun again, ours lifting to the second line, theirs concentrating on our forward positions, the balls of shrapnel turning from white and white-yellow to pink in the sun-drenched, dissolving
Mist at the bottom of the garden. It's going to be a
Fine day for a football
Massacre
Walking forward, as had been decreed, with exactly five yards' spacing between each man and at a speed not exceeding two miles per hour, two platoons to each wave of each battalion, we officers striding out at the front, through the seas of purply pollinating grasses, from which rabbits would dart every now and then, Oenone shaking and barking soundlessly at my side, wanting to chase the rabbits but knowing there was a more serious task ahead, the grass rapidly melting away as the ground became pitted and rucked and churned and we headed for the
Brambles
Coiled and picketed barbed wire
Shrouding
The railway line
Their forward trenches
Which was when I saw them, beyond the barbed wire, the figures, rising up out of the mist and the smoke and the shuddering, the men whom we had supposed were ghosts, whom our seven-day bombardment had reportedly dispatched to another world, arranging themselves now with an infinite slow patience in dark formation on the parapet etched against the sky kneeling or standing in the clear hot morning light each ghost raising a barrel to his shoulder and
If I didn't know better I'd hazard a guess that they were
Aiming to
Christ they've come up from underground without a scratch between them they're not dead at all Eric they're

Feeling jolly chipper and looking forward most awfully to mowing us all flat you were about to say, Sir? I couldn't have put it fucking better myself. So

We must find shelter. But not
The old filter bed

The mine crater as some had hoped. Fritz was already occupying its further side. As Eric had prophesied. Who was next to me now, shouting

Down Sir, down here
And suddenly I was with him and a shaking Oenone spreadeagled in
A dip in the ground
A shell hole
Where the old earth closet stood perhaps
Ground still warm from the explosion
Of morning sunlight and
A slight lip to flinch under. But where are the
Others? Isn't it obvious where
Oh look Eric, look behind us there
Sir, I've already had the pleasure
They're all behind us still but

Not totally upright as you might say I know Sir it's that maxim in the Bergwerk now the way I see it is we've got to

Stretched out horizontal like a wind had knocked them down like when *you flick one end of a row of lead soldiers and the whole lot topple over in sequence still keeping the wave formation they were walking in when*

Go forward you and I
Like they're asleep

Well you can't say they didn't have a disturbed night. Sir keep your head down, the Bergwerk Sir, can't you

Hear the patter patter of bullets as the maxim traverses from right to left *pausing to pick out those who shift slightly in their final dream then travelling on then pausing again to drill a few more rounds into a man who is already a corpse hanging on the old barbed wire his brain spattering away in blood-flecked mustardy gouts so that*

We've got to before the next wave we

Can't leave Oenone. She's shaking scared shitless. And they're all asleep anyway aren't they all gone to beddybyes

Up the wooden hills

Sir, pull yourself to-fucking-gether if you'll excuse my French. It's you and me who've got to do it and look here's some

Windfall Bramleys from the tree Aunt wanted cut down

Toffee apples.

What a spot of luck. We'll get into that trench and bomb our way along the firebays until we reach

But the wire. Oenone. I can't

Sir! Charles! Charlie lad. We must. Don't you see, we

Must now I see. I see why you brought me here. It's the shaft again isn't it? And he's down there. The one daddy said was waiting. He's waiting for me now, isn't he, Eric? The naughty man waiting to kiss me night night and don't let the little fleas bitey Oh

Pull yourself together Charlie for Jesus Christ Almighty's frigging sake. You're not a kid any more. Before the next wave comes up out of Sunken Lane we've got to

Oh but that's where you're wrong you see. That's where you're so dreadfully and utterly and luminously and spiffingly

Fucking bleeding hell. We're going. Look the dog's wagging her tail. She wants to come don't you dearie so why can't you just

Where are we? Where are we now?

Amongst the brambles. Crawling. Snagging my hair. Wet dankness. A fox's corpse. Flayed skull and eyeless sockets. Stripped backbone. Forepaws and

She's hit Eric. Oh she's bleeding. I can't, Eric. Come back. It's Oenone. She's

C'mon there's a gap. That bloke found it. The one with the head the bastards used for target practice. Don't worry mate, we'll take 'em out for you. They won't even have

Time to stop let alone weep. How I bawled at Eric up ahead for the unfeeling bastard that he

Quick, crawl through here. One sodding tiny gap. So much for our fucking artillery. So much for the devastating effects of shrapnel on enemy barbed wire. Devastating my arse. Now

Where are we? Where are we now?

By the railway line

The Bergwerk. It was Eric who cleared Stuff trench, bombing his way from firebay to traverse to firebay. I just followed, hardly seeing, stumbling over their dead and wounded, through a thick stagnancy of cordite. A ghost who must

Keep up. Keep up with me, Charlie lad. Soon be there, when I've just said cheerio to this little lot and

Pulling the pin wiped out the entire fire crew. Then it was Eric who turned the maxim on their lines, enfilading them. I just lay there feeding the belt through and keeping an eye on the water jacket while he cursed and fired fired and cursed not a man at all with his

More water Charlie from that dixie look lively we're overheating

And his

That's for Dad and that's for Dad and that's for

Until suddenly I couldn't stand it any longer I tell you

And started blubbing like a girl

The only girl

I couldn't help it I tell you I couldn't help it when I

Legged it

Made a strategic withdrawal

After crawling through the brambles again because

I had to, don't you see. He had come up out of the shaft and was after me. I had to run away, back down the slope, to where Daddy was, he'll protect me and I won't have to die, not ever, I

Sir, Charlie lad, come back, don't be a sodding fool. You'll be

Hit. And I was. And fell down with a sharp pain in my

Calf. I saw the wound. That first night. It was

Where they kicked me when I was

A traitor

Ambushed in the quarry by Eric and

Remember

But not this time. This time he came back. The stupid great fearless insane bastard came back and half-dragged half-carried me to Sunken Lane. After everything that had happened. And then

What

410

It happened

What

Because of me. I was the reason why it happened. Because I ran. From the one who was chasing me, back into my childhood, looking for a place to hide

In the field ditch

Sunken Lane. It was chock-full of our lads, the ones who had managed to crawl back or hadn't even climbed out in the first place. One chap he just stood there grinning from ear to ear shouting over and over again Play up play up and play the game. Then Wilkins was beside me with a field dressing and

Stop whimpering. You're like

The only girl in the world. Crawling back through the brambles, my leg

Scratched, that's all it is. A pin prick. You're not going to bleed to death is he George and did you

Play up play up and

See the way Wren took out the maxim? Then carried back Tremain here slung over his shoulders like

The only girl sitting on the rain-damp grass in the field ditch dabbing at my bramble-scratched leg while

Bugger me if he hasn't started off back for that Boche trench like he's going to try to

Play up play up and

Retake the maxim. Do you see, George. He's dodging and weaving like a wing-half. He's reached the wire. He's

What, what's happening. Won't someone tell me what's happening to him. I need to

Play up and

Shut your mouth can't you Christ I don't mind telling you you're a windy ponce even if you are an officer. He's. Oh

What? I want to see. I must see if he's

Down. The poor bastard. Stretcher bearers. Where are the buggers when you want them. It's no good. George, you with me? We'll

Bring him back in yes

No. Not you. You stay where you are, Captain Sir. George and me'll bring him back in. What you want to come legging it back for in the first place if you can't wait to get out there again. And if you don't mind me *saying, Captain Sir, if you'd stayed out with him in the first place he'd still be*

Alive not dead. Dead not alive. So I waited for Wilkins and the other soldier to bring Eric in while the wounded groaned around me and the shells whined overhead and the man with the grin endlessly screamed his Newbolt refrain as if the forward flow of time had been forever blocked by the piling up of bodies until at last they did come back half-falling down into Sunken Lane and I looked on him for what was to be the last occasion before a belated stretcher party appeared to drag him away and in the face that was no face in the depths of that bloody disc from the scorched hole of his once mobile mouth I heard

Remember

And that was when I knew. And that was what I came back to help you to know. That I loved him. And betrayed him. And condemned him to the darkness I myself deserved. All because I broke and ran. Because I hadn't the decency to let myself be

A brother to
Dragons, and a companion
To owls. My skin is
Black upon me, and my bones
Are burned with heat.

– I think it was for the best.

– You are entitled to your opinion, Mr Gorrod. But I believe we should have acted sooner. Why she's half out of her wits. And barely decent. If that man had been taken away sooner, as I advised the police on Monday.

– There was something she had to do. Something that we can't grasp. I feel it in my bones.

– What are you talking about, man. Ah! Now the doctor's persuaded her to go indoors. All that writhing about on the ground. Most unseemly. Well I hope that's an end of it.

– I doubt it.

– Pardon.

– I said I doubt anything has an end. Or a beginning for that matter.

– Really, Mr Gorrod, you're talking in riddles today and no mistake. But hasn't this rain done the gardens a power of good?

4. Return

October 1924

It was an icy-blue late October afternoon. There had been a frost the night before and, as the train drew into Ecclesden Halt, the breeze dislodged scores of withered chestnut leaves from the holt beside the platform, sending them fluttering and scurrying across the rails. The wheels of the carriages ran over some of the leaves, crushing out the few remaining juices so that they oozed together into a brown pulp. The engine squealed its arrival and gouts of steam puffed up into the clear hard air.

The woman in the first class carriage looked out for a moment longer, then shivered and turned back to pat a wicker basket on the seat beside her. The basket was rectangular with a wire grille at one end. The woman lowered her face close to the grille and clicked her tongue.

– Won't be long now, puss.

For answer the cat, a large tabby with a drooping lower jaw, rubbed his chin repeatedly against the grille so that the whole basket shook and threatened to topple over. The woman tutted.

– Don't be such an impatient puss.

The woman was in her late twenties but looked older. This was partly because she wore a rather outdated black dress that had taken little account of the rise in hem lines since the end of the war. But the impression of a premature and not altogether unwelcomed middle age had more to do with her neck which, emerging from the high-collared black blouse, looked wrinkled and leathery, an effect compounded by the face with its splays of crow's feet and a thin-lipped, downturned mouth. Her forehead too was lined, not to say grooved, a feature she had made no attempt to conceal, having scraped up her grey-streaked and rather sparse black hair into a severely constrained bun. She wore no ornament of any kind except an oblong silver locket on a chain which she swung now in front of the basket in a gesture that combined playfulness and a certain obscurely articulated threat.

– Soon be there.

If this high, rather girlish voice, containing as it did the merest hint of a buried petulance, gave the lie to what was in essence a pretence of age, the eyes, glancing away from swinging locket and patting paw, revealed a brief, dulled weariness that had nothing to do with the endurances of time. But the weariness passed and the eyes grew bright again. There had been a movement in the far corner of the compartment. A sighing stir that must be attended to in a condescending sort of way.

– There'll be a car of course. To collect us.

The woman could have almost laughed. But snorted instead.

– A car. At Ecclesden. You don't know Ecclesden, Walter, and that's a fact.

Again the laboured stirring and rustling as of someone attempting to insert himself into a suit of ill-fitting clothes. Which was an act Walter Birkett had often been obliged to perform, if only in his mind.

– But the ceremony. You are a VIP, are you not?

– The attendance of a deputy headmistress is hardly world-shattering, Walter.

– Our memorial service then. When Robert and the vicar came to their agreement and approached me I was assured I would be given all due consideration.

– Robert doesn't live there now, Walter, you know that. The house is shut up. He probably doesn't even remember he gave you any assurances.

– Very well. Lady Tremain. She too knows about the memorial.

– Lady Tremain! Her involvement's almost posthumous.

– Nevertheless, – Mr Birkett was standing now and reaching up to

418

take a strapped case from the netted luggage rack – they have agreed and you would think . . . – here the too hastily pulled case fell down on to the seat and gaped open, spilling a sheaf of sheet music. – Botheration.

– Here, let me help you with these. The train won't stop for long. No, I'm afraid there won't be a car. – The woman squinted at a sheet – What are these?

– Eh? Oh some Bach and a setting of something medieval which he was supposed to like. *She* left a note about it. Before . . . before the end.

The barely concealed barb of remorseful bitterness which the tone of this last remark let loose was quite blunted however, for the woman had already turned away to busy herself with her cat and other luggage. Another shoal of chestnut leaves poured down past the window, scattering across the deserted platform and coming to rest along a row of rotten moss-caked palings. Against the brittle blue of the sky Thundersbarrow lay darkly etched and silent. The grey arc of a transparent moon hung tilted above its summit.

When Beatrice Lumley received news of Mrs Eddles's sudden death back in September '24 she had thought little of it. Then, a month later, had come the official letter, inviting her as a former colleague of the deceased and a distinguished educator in her own right, to attend a commemorative ceremony at Ecclesden schoolhouse, during which a teak bench of remembrance would be dedicated to the former headmistress's memory. Studying the letter over breakfast, one autumn morning in Artillery Row, Beatrice had been surprised at her inability simply to put it to one side. Surprised then saddened. After what her aunt had once correctly prophesied would be the 'hiatus' of the war years, she had returned to teaching in 1919, rising by the spring of '24 to the position of deputy headmistress at Chalkhampton Grammar school. Established upon this august pedestal, Beatrice Lumley no longer supposed herself to be a woman whom chance emotions could disturb. Indeed the very words which people used to evoke such emotions had long-since absented themselves from her perspective, shrinking behind a life of deliberate solitude and drab almost wilful probity. Yet now, because of a thin official communiqué, this life itself seemed to have withdrawn, leaving her horribly exposed to the chance breath of any passing desire. Without knowing how she came there, she found herself standing outside by the recently refurbished cold frame, reading the letter aloud to a sleepy Ulysses. Her voice changed with her changing emotions. Amusement first, shading into an ironic acerbity, then a certain tender nostalgia followed by importunate longing, into which guilt and resentment poured with equal measure. Finishing the letter she felt quite unable to move. Ecclesden. Where it had all begun. To go back. It was simply too ridiculous. In the cold frame the leaves of winter lettuce were beaded with dew. *He* had lain down there, night after night. And once, she too, in a fever that was also a going beyond nature, a nightmare that transported her body and soul to a world she had never imagined existed. And now they wanted her to go back. To begin what couldn't be begun ever again. *Oh Charles*, she moaned and knelt down beside the hot brick of the frame, *Oh Charles, what should I do?*

To see her like that you might have assumed that she was often in the habit of communicating with the soldier who had re-entered and then so precipitately left her life eight years earlier. This was not the case. After Charles Tremain had returned to his battalion and the vigilant, if patronising regime of Dr Blake had restored her to health, Beatrice had found it surprisingly easy to regain her old focus and determination. It was as if the terrible re-enactment in her garden, conducted at first in Charles's wake, then latterly alone and among many importunate ghosts, had emptied her out of any further desire to know or discover or forgive. A great gap had opened up, at the moment when she found herself lying in the depression which Charles had called Jacob's Ladder, surrounded by the faces of her neighbours, that morning of the Big Push and Eric Wren's mutilation. She would never recross it; never return; never understand. But to go forward. That was different. Indeed for all its ferocity, her illness had seemed to prefigure just such a development.

Looking back, she saw it as, among other things, a prelude to her complete gynaecological recovery. As she remarked to Dr Blake, whose face immediately expressed both smug omniscience and a certain disappointment at the loss of an interesting case study, it was as if the sluicings of fever had performed their own, natural curettage. Her cycle reasserted itself with all its former intensity and, by the autumn of '16, Beatrice was once again making preparations to go out to France.

There was no dream of spiritual communion now to fuel a feverish desire to serve. Charles had left her, not only physically when the military police dragged him vomiting air through her front gate, but spiritually, when his disembodied form had confessed the abiding unrequitable love of his life at the bottom of an invisible trench among the ghosts of the dead and the dying. Eric Wren, too, could no longer command her uncomfortable allegiance. Having finally returned to England, he was being treated in one of the big London teaching hospitals where, it was rumoured, they could even construct a vanished face, out of electroplate and other magical substances. A short letter had come from him, written in somebody else's hand, telling her these bare facts and alluding briefly to the disaster in France. It made no reference to Charles and, after a laconic mention of the DSO, ended by asking her not to visit. Beatrice respected this wish. What had been done had been done, once at the Front and a second time behind her house. He too had no further need of her. And so, freed of these presences, in better health than at any time during the previous three years, she had only to rearrange the letting of the house (ensuring that Ulysses approved of the tenants) and reapply for overseas service. With the result that she was on her way to Boulogne by the middle of September and serving in a casualty clearing station set up in a château near Doullens when the news came of Charles's death.

Molly Dadger was the messenger. She too had crossed the Channel but not to nurse. Despite his myopia, her husband Jack had been drafted into the army as one of the first batch of conscripts. Sent out to Charles's old regiment, which was regrouping behind the lines after its terrible mauling on the first of July, he had seen action in High Wood during the battle's last autumnal days and been badly wounded. Now he was at Dieppe base hospital, too ill to be moved. But not to speak, apparently. For again and again he reverted to the fate of one poor sod who was found wandering behind the lines, having ineptly attempted to inflict a Blighty wound on his left foot. Courtmartialled, this bloke was sentenced to be executed at dawn, a sentence which was carried out, Jack knew, because his mate got roped into the business. They did it in a quarry. Just like the ones up on the Downs. Prisoner so pissed he could hardly stand.

Molly Dadger had breathlessly poured this story out as if expecting her former teacher to rave or attack her. When Beatrice did nothing she became more breathless than ever. And a little frightened. But Beatrice experienced an immense calm. Long afterwards she remembered how one of the green slatted shutters on the window in her little office (she was an assistant matron now) had come loose and begun creaking in the wind. There were poplars beyond the gravel terrace, dimly swaying. It was right. He was at peace now. He had paid his debt.

During the weeks that followed, Beatrice wondered whether she ought to write to Maud but found that here at least, the old wrongs would not be assuaged. She did write to Eric but received no reply. So the war dragged on, while her nursing became an end in itself, existing in a sealed space, apart from all emotion, all fear. During Passchendaele she was near Ypres for a time; then the following year she became caught up in the great retreat. When withdrawal turned into advance she realised she had been living on a rapidly dwindling reserve of nervous energy. A partial collapse that autumn found her back in Chalkhampton, where the ministrations of Dr Blake brought her round once again, in time to watch the armistice celebrations from the hospital window.

Then peace and a deeper callousing over of what had once been a raw wound. She could not deny that teaching came more naturally to her than nursing and, after a couple of years at the grammar school, could look back across the divide that separated her from her younger self with something like impunity. She began to entertain the idea that what had happened to her since the war might be just as important as her experiences during and just before it. Now at least she was answerable to no one and had no need to rely on others for a vicarious intensity. In fact, a certain complacency set in, so that she shifted from thinking *I no longer want to remember* to the harsher, more dogmatic *I do not remember*. More recently the attentions of a certain middle-aged works manager, whom she had met at an end-of-term sherry party, had only served to increase the seeming distance between now and then. Although she did not for the moment wish her solitude to be disturbed, least of all by a balding and slightly corpulent fifty-year-old, Beatrice allowed herself to be courted, if only to confirm her complacent self-reliance.

If she were honest with herself she would admit that this complacency had been tested on several occasions. Firstly and most intensely in early '22, when news came of Maud's death from double pneumonia. For days she struggled to regain the equilibrium which this event threatened to destroy. She knew that, in a sense, the old Maud, the Maud whom she had loved, nursed and lost at Orion Parade was already quite dead. But still at night she would be visited by her ghost, pleading, mocking, accusing. Eventually, though, she won the struggle. Even the account of her funeral which a distraught Mr Birkett brought back from Ecclesden, failed to stir a now thoroughly numbed memory. Eighteen months later and she heard that a third disabling stroke had necessitated Lady Tremain's removal from Ecclesden to a London clinic. Robert, who was now eighteen and training to be a pilot, had closed down the house preparatory to putting it on the market. Meanwhile Eric Wren had been moved out of London to a home for disabled ex-servicemen somewhere on the Kent coast. He refused visitors. To all these developments, Beatrice responded with the same dully indifferent *So be it*, then, settling Ulysses on her knee (none the worse for the years of separation), returned to her stack of marking.

The letter from the school governors had changed all that, bringing to life through its stiff official prose a world which no amount of intimate contact could have resuscitated. It was as if Charles had spoken through that collective bureaucratic voice, possessing it like a messenger from the dead until Beatrice, exposed and alone, must submit with all the credulous intensity of a novice attending her first seance. *Go back*, he was saying. *Go back once more for my sake. And for yours. And for Eric's. And for hers. There is still something to be done. You must do it, you who were always outside and apart. You are the chosen one. The priestess. The keeper of the flame.*

And if this voice, rising up out of the jade opacities of lettuce leaves, merged something of Eric Wren's old prophesying with the more matter-of-fact tones of an infantry officer, then wrapped them both up in the sweetly low tones of a woman who, in the end, had abandoned them all, Beatrice could not be blamed. A flame had passed through her and left her scorched and trembling. She was alive once more in a way that she had thought gone forever, with youth and desire and trust. So Beatrice decided to attend the ceremony (which coincided with her own half term) as a guest of the St George's school governors. The works manager and would-be suitor had already suggested a trip up to London and Beatrice could not deny experiencing a certain pleasurable power when putting him politely but firmly off. She would be staying in the old schoolhouse itself where, since the new headmistress could not take up her post until the spring, the new assistant was standing in, helped out by a succession of supply teachers. This ghost of Beatrice's own youthful self was none other than Molly Dadger who, after her husband's death from wounds, had herself undergone the same teacher training course as Beatrice. A brief correspondence with Molly revealed that the half term ceremony was going to coincide with another event that, six months before, Beatrice might have read about in the *Herald* with the merest tremor of recognition. Now she took it as an omen and a confirmation. The vicar and Robert Tremain had finally come to an agreement (originally mooted by Robert's mother), that Charles should be commemorated by a service and dedication of a plaque inside the church. There was to be no reference to his less than honourable fate, the rank of captain being silently restored.

With Lady Tremain's Brigadier acting as go-between, the permission of the Regiment's current Colonel had been sought and granted. Mr Birkett had been asked to provide a small choir from the reformed Choral Society and some music, befitting the occasion. Back in '16, after the military police had taken Charles away, Beatrice had been briefly inclined to cast her ex-landlord in the role of betrayer. But she had soon accepted her own mixed motives in going to Orion Parade in the first place. Mr Birkett too had shown himself supportive during her illness, finding new tenants to move in when she had gone abroad. Over the following years a wary rapprochement had grown up between them, based less on real friendship than on their mutual awareness of a shared obsession. Both had been fascinated then disappointed by the starry centrifuge of Ecclesden. Both had had to come to terms with an exile that, after the news of Maud's death, had come to seem permanent. When Beatrice boarded the train at the terminus with her old landlord in tow, all the signs seemed right. She was going back because she must. Even the presence of Ulysses, from whom she could no longer bear to be parted, seemed part of the pattern.

– Ah the provinces. No sooner do we leave town and they return, the dark ages. When will culture take root in such a place? Never, I tell you, never.

Mr Birkett's peevish lament encompassed the entire platform of Ecclesden Halt. As Beatrice had predicted, there had been no one waiting to take either their tickets or their cases, from which even now a stray sheet fluttered appealingly.

– You should have gone with the choir, Walter. Didn't they hire a charabanc?

– And miss the pleasure of your company?

Beatrice knew that her ex-landlord had taken the train because he regarded himself as socially superior to his amateur singers, many of whom worked in a bakery housed on the premises of Maud's old munitions factory. They were little more than a glee club in fact and had severely limited his musical ambitions, raised to such dazzling yet evanescent heights by the vanished Maud.

– Never mind. There'll be a van or something.

– A cart. We'll end up jogging along in a cart.

Reminded of a long ago journey in just such a vehicle, Beatrice could not resist a certain wafting of low spirits. All around was desolation. In his once carefully tended tubs, a fur of self-sown forget-me-not pierced here and there by sow thistles usurped the stationmaster's vanished reign of wallflowers. Swirls of lime were forming and reforming along the platform, joined now by the scratchy shoals of chestnut leaves. No one. Not even Molly, who had promised she would walk over to meet them. Beatrice sighed.

– I heard the stationmaster's ill. Ever since his only son was reported missing at Arras.

Mr Birkett did not hear. He was peering through the ticket office window. Dust of lime had been allowed to encrust the sill, drifting against the panes like snow. Mr Birkett sneezed.

– I do believe . . . yes . . . some sort of primitive human being does inhabit this place after all. I say. You. Can you understand me?

The figure floated slowly through the little room and came to rest, rubbing its hands in front of a meagre coal fire. On the far side of the glass Mr Birkett began gesticulating, as if to signal across great distances. At last the figure by the fire looked up. His wizened red-eyed visage had something naked about it as though it ought by rights to have been covered by fur or fleece. A dewdrop hung from the tip of the nose. Smearing it away with the back of his hand, he let his gaze travel from Beatrice to Mr Birkett and back again. The man he did not recognise, done up like a Christmas pudding, in a three-piece suit with a fob and a Homburg, some stranger come to make trouble as usual. But the lady. His eyes flickered recognition. Beatrice too came forward, pushing open the flimsy door.

– Joe.

– Miss Lumley. I never thought I'd live to see the day. And you just a slip of a thing.

Beatrice blushed. Mr Birkett coughed through the ticket opening, a prize exhibit. The shepherd continued to look her up and down with the shamelessness of extreme age.

426

– And is it true, are you coming back to the schoolhouse? – Beatrice nodded.

– But only for the weekend, Joe. Only for a visit. There's to be a bench . . .

– That old hag Eddles hung on too long. But by crikey you're a woman now and no mistake. Well what would the old quarry lads say now. Supposing any of them were left to speak.

Joseph wiped a rheumy eye and drew out a huge spotted handkerchief from his smock. Mr Birkett leant forward like a man staring through the headhole of a pier amusement, its screen painted with a body whose incongruity only served to make the head more startlingly real. In this case, a torn old recruiting poster from the first months of the war supplied the body of a child looking up from his toys to ask his father what he did in the Great War. Mr Birkett's head nodded there on juvenile shoulders.

– Here. Take our tickets. We have valuable luggage. And there should be a brougham. Look lively man. I've come for the memorial service and Miss Lumley here . . .

Joseph, continuing to gaze fondly on the transmogrified school-mistress, spat into the grate, an oyster of phlegm that sizzled while he spoke.

– The memorial service, eh? Any brougham went long ago. It's at the bottom of a shellhole in France now I shouldn't wonder. Along with our boys. It's a wonder more didn't take heed of that there recruiting poster. – And here he gazed contemptuously at his questioner. – We might have got the business over a damn sight quicker.

Mr Birkett's face grew larger above the borrowed body of the child. He stuttered.

– Some of us were held back for essential war work. Charity concerts you know and . . . and . . . other things.

But Joseph had glimpsed something in this man's face which made him remember a long ago night spent in a lodging-house at Orion Parade. There had been a dream. And a voice. He turned to Beatrice who was beginning to sweat this close to the fire.

– Many changes since you were here last. The Tremain boy and poor Wren. And the manor shut up. And Lady T swallowed up forever inside some fancy London clinic. A sorry business. And that flibbertigibbet Miss Egerton. Who they did call Tremain though I can't for the life of me see why. Anyone could guess she wouldn't make old bones.

He had remembered them, the words in the dream. *All this because of her.* It was terrible to have to remember. He had lived long enough. This winter would be his last. Beatrice fingered her locket.

– I was expecting Molly Dadger. She's not ill I hope.

– Ah, that was what was mithering me. She sent word. She's delayed and could you come direct to the schoolhouse.

Beatrice was possessed by a sudden exhilaration.

– I think I know the shortest route.

Joseph laughed. Or cackled. She'd always had spunk that one.

– You've done it before and no mistake. But what about him?

– Oh he can walk as well.

Joseph laughed again and pointed to Ulysses's basket.

– Not him, him. Tell you what, I'll send him on with the luggage. Good ratter is he?

For answer Ulysses rubbed his chin against the grille again.

Mr Birkett was studying a timetable pinned to the wall.

– The post van will collect the cases, Walter. We can walk. I know a short cut.

– If the gentleman isn't scared of sheep.

Mr Birkett smiled wanly. He had no power in this kingdom.

So Beatrice Lumley returned for a last time to Ecclesden by the old path up the flank of Thundersbarrow, following the sunken track of the now disused and weed-infested funicular, then turning left over the summit where Five Lords Burgh had slumped perhaps a tenth of an inch deeper from the height to which it had originally been raised in awed and superstitious tribute; past the Whispering Knights, their sponge-like heads still bobbing together in conference over the sleeping dragon, the hoard and other such intangible fairy tales. She

428

remembered that first time, when the wind had seemed to carry her along, worrying and pushing at her amazed body until she entered a new world. It made her sad now to think how she could have harboured so much exhilaration and fear. Where had it all gone? What had it all been for? Charles and Maud were both dead. Eric Wren had become a hopeless invalid. The quarry was derelict. The manor shut up. And she who had been at the centre of all these things must return now, a stranger still, bearing her secret burden of disillusion and fatigued experience. There could be no running this time, no excited encounter with the numinous spirits of the hill.

– I hadn't thought there could be such a high wild place this close to town. And you so familiar with it, Miss Lumley, so *au fait*.

Mr Birkett's voice panted a suspicion that she too belonged to this barbarous land. She hadn't the heart to disabuse him.

By now they had reached the hillocky area of flint mines. Charles's shaft had been partially filled in, while the spoil heap had collapsed outward like a mouldy soufflé, its surface furred with the greys and greens of downland grasses. The wound was no longer raw. Yet the air of age which these signs of neglect gave to the site actually served to deepen the hole and raise up the spoil. It was as if the digging were almost as old as the galleries it had sought to uncover and had been perpetrated by the same race of shadowy giants. The year war broke out suddenly seemed as remote as the last Ice Age. Mr Birkett paused, trying to make something out near the Scots pines.

– Is that a cross?

Beatrice, who remembered asking herself a similar question, nodded. Mr Birkett walked over and squatted down, squinting.

– There are letters here I think. Scratched. Yes. Two initials. E W and a word, Lod is it, no, Lob. Strange. Whatever is this Lob and this EW. It makes me shudder. It's so . . . so pagan.

She had not realised that Eric had marked the passing of his terrier. Thinking how she had come to depend on Ulysses's presence, she felt oddly moved. Then all at once was faced by something else up ahead, quite new and incomprehensible. Her companion sensed her alarm.

– What is it, Miss Lumley? What is it that you see?

– It's what I haven't seen. – She found herself laughing nervously.
– You know, I thought I knew this hill like the back of my hand and
now . . . Oh, really it's too absurd. It's . . . It's just that I don't know
where we are.

The quarry had not simply closed down. It had gone. Coming to
the perimeter of the flint mine shafts, Beatrice had expected to look
down over the jagged edge of Dragon Pit, along the scree, past the
kilns and the great cone of Lower Pit to the Bottom beyond. But it
had all disappeared. Or rather, now that her eyes had recovered from
the shock and could begin to make out detail, the quarry was still
there but only as a building sunk beneath the sea is still there,
changed utterly by the element that has enveloped it. Bushes had
invaded and drowned the quarry, ten years of hazel and ash and
thorn, of stunted oak and elder and bramble, all encroaching with a
savage luxuriance the more powerful for having endured so many
decades of slashing suppression. In summer the tide of their foliage
was a deep dusty impenetrable green, at this time of the year it had
yellowed and grown transparent. But still the bushes formed a barrier
between the observer and what lay underneath them, that structure
which, in capitulating to their invasion, had taken on a new and
mysterious identity.

– Can this be where they dug the chalk? What a ruined ugly
place. No wonder Lady Tremain was glad to let it go.

But Beatrice who had been visited by a dark joy, did not reply. It
seemed to her that the quarry and everything around it had finally
slipped free of human influence. Yet in doing so had taken on a
benign beauty which could neither be touched nor desecrated.
There had been bushes growing here before, of course, but always
on a smaller scale and always under threat of destruction. Now the
return of nature was total and irreversible. What she had once
believed was a savage place of toil and hardship, where men ripped
and blasted a recalcitrant immensity, had become a temple of silence
and calm. The old dry dustiness of lime, forever swept up, forever
created; the grit and lyddite and sweat in eyes and nostrils and

mouth; the sense of unending battle with an unvanquishable foe: all had melted away. The water from which the chalk and flint had originally been crystallised had returned at last, as a swirling sea of plantlife, a cool mere whose very presence cleansed and invigorated. Leading Mr Birkett round the lip of the quarry, Beatrice could imagine herself swimming in that cool lagoon. Beneath her the sunken city lay washed of its suffering and despair. The streets glittered white. In lancet windows seahorses bobbed. And a little terrier ran out of a doorway barking bubbles.

So in her dream, Beatrice plunged down through the waters that had come to possess the quarry, past the elders and brambles that had returned in tenfold strength to Dragon Pit, past the moss-encrusted belly of old Neb, its mouth sprouting an ash that already bore the coal-black buds of next year's leaves. Eric Wren's hovel had collapsed and become a bed for hawthorn saplings. The Bottom, where she and Charles had once driven through a squalor of humanity, was simply a V-shaped trench again, on whose short-turfed sides sheep grazed, scouring their parallel tracks.

Oh Charles you would have been happy to see all this. You who were so frightened of explosions. Who went all the way to No Man's Land and found the same quarry there with the same flint mine shafts and the same man sitting in his cave, waiting. How you panicked and ran. My poor boy. My poor lost love. Panicked and ran back to me. But now I have returned to where it all began. Returned and seen the change. And this is no longer a bad place, Charles. It is beautiful. And new. And now I know why you wanted me to come. For the last time.

– What's that you say? You want to get on? So do I. Such an ugly nasty devilish sort of a place. Quite beyond reclamation. You'd almost think a battle had been fought here.

Beatrice did not reply. She had seen what she had seen.

The sea-changed quarry was long behind them. Ahead rose the glossy green ramparts of Ecclesden's rhododendrons and camellias. Beatrice had intended passing by along the lane that led to the schoolhouse, but a flicker of curiosity inspired her to take the short cut through the rhododendron alley. From there it was only a short walk to the front of the house. Mr Birkett plucked her sleeve.

– Ought we to do this? Is it right?

Beatrice, who had once possessed the manor for one whole day, could not resist a gesture of impatience.

– You go then, Walter, if you want.

But Mr Birkett was too fascinated to heed his conscience. He followed her on to the lawn.

There was desolation here too. Neglect haunted the gardens, leaving gravel paths matted with chickweed and roses unpruned. The house was shut up, drawn curtains making every window blind. The quarry had seemed to welcome the invasion of root and branch; here everything bristled defensiveness. Mr Birkett sighed, glancing up at the now vast magnolia grandiflora which had been allowed to cover half of the wing once devoted to convalescent officers.

– Such a noble house. Look at the proportions. That fine brick Tudor front. To think it has come to this. The war was to blame. If we hadn't had the war we wouldn't have had the land taxes.

But Beatrice, who had sensed beauty at the heart of the overgrown quarry, saw in Ecclesden's decline a certain inevitable sequence. This too was a reason for coming back. To witness at first hand the collapse of a world she had once desired and feared. Only then would she be able to lay the ghosts of her memories. Glancing up at a cone of green lichen which had formed under a leaking gutter outside Charles's old bedroom window, she knew that the years when she had pretended to forget were over. Mr Birkett had climbed the grass-infested steps of the terrace, and stood respectfully, head bowed, as if before an altar.

– Look, Miss Lumley, there's a window open. That's bad. Someone might have effected an illegal entry.

The window had merely blown open in the wind. With a little start of recognition Beatrice realised that the room beyond had once contained the butterfly cabinet. As if in remembrance, a dead comma lay on the sill, its wings sogged by rainwater. Beyond, sheeted furniture rose up like pale tumuli. Beatrice recalled Charles's fascinated descriptions of the buried Roman city and turned away. Mr Birkett closed the window with a satisfied *That's fixed it.*

It was at this point that Beatrice grew almost grateful for her irritating companion. Without his presence she might have wandered on, through the walled garden to the lake and the boathouse. Then what memories would have arisen, out of the brown clumps of bullrushes, or from the wooden verandah with its sharp scent of creosote and canvas. As it was she made her companion the excuse to head straight for the side entrance to the schoolhouse grounds. Even then she had to pass through one more ordeal by fire.

– Strange. What would have been here I wonder?

The empty peacock run was choked with nettles. Behind it the classical folly rose up. Its roof had collapsed.

– Some pet animal perhaps?

Beatrice felt no desire to explain. Charles had always said his mother would release the peacocks one day. When she couldn't stand the noise any longer. As if to confirm this memory Thundersbarrow Hanger suddenly echoed to an unearthly crying as of several tormented spirits. Mr Birkett grasped her arm.

– What, what is that?

Again the stabbing three-note phrase that seemed to emerge from the very heart of the hill. Then another cry as if the word *peacock* were being attempted by a being which had either never acquired human speech or long since rejected its blandishments. Beatrice looked back over her shoulder.

– Oh ghosts of some kind. Demons of the hill.

– Molly. Are you there?

The schoolhouse snatched her voice away and held on to it as a hostage. The door had been unlocked. But there was no one. She started to call again then stopped, disliking the way her voice went so swiftly dead. Mr Birkett had long since left to go to the Limeburner's Arms where his choir would have put up. The luggage and Ulysses had not yet arrived. She was alone.

The quarry and the manor had changed; but their transformations

433

seemed to include Beatrice's return. It was different when she entered the schoolhouse, for she immediately felt that all was as it had been. The same smells, the same objects, the same feelings locked up in its rooms and cupboards. Here she had hung up her coat that blustery April night while Eric and Mrs Eddles talked in the hall. Here she had eaten in Mrs Eddles's kitchen and here looked for her boots, while Charles waited impatiently to take her up on Thundersbarrow. Everywhere she met her old girlish self and felt that what she had become since those days was as nothing. The schoolhouse did not want her as she was today. It resisted and excluded and fought against her at every turn. It only wanted the other Beatrice who had loved and been unhappy and gone away. Despairingly, Beatrice wandered more deeply into this besieged place. In her old bedroom (evidently Molly had been using Mrs Eddles's) she found the same furniture: the bed and the mattress, turned over but still bearing the bloodstain in the shape of a wing. Underneath was the same yellowed chamber pot she had been obliged to squat on during the night; and beside the bed the same bureau containing Noone's gardening journal which she had once used to record a more intimate series of events until circumspect second thoughts made her tear out the pages and burn them. Here was the same cornflower wallpaper, the same tin vent that had once sung to her its melancholy song and here the window with the view of Thundersbarrow. Below in the garden, the old mangle still stood rusting under the cherry-tree. There was the same creaking floorboard, the same slightly loose doorhandle. Oh everything always and forever the same.

Beatrice sat down on the bed, her head in her hands. How could this have happened? She was not deputy head at Chalkhampton Grammar at all. It was 1914 not 1924. The war had not begun. She had not worked as a VAD in Chalkhampton. Charles and Eric had not gone off with the Regiment to fight on the Somme. There had been no reappearance of a broken and haunted man at Artillery Row. No tense re-enactment of bombardment and cowardice. No nursing. No teaching. No time. No deaths. Nothing. She was simply the girl she had been and would have to lie here now, staring up at the slant ceiling, dreaming of the life at the manor, wondering if Charles ever thought of her, until Mrs Eddles called her down to sit in the steamy kitchen over boiled beef and a glutinous rice pudding with a skin like charred blotting paper. Nothing had changed. She was back where she had begun. What had she done to deserve such a terrible looping of years? And there, yes, she could hear her: Mrs Eddles, stumping from room to room down below.

– Nimrod. Can it be?

She had gone to the top of the stairs, her heart beating. In the hall stood Charles's half-blind retriever, panting. He was evidently deaf too, for he didn't respond. There was a movement in the kitchen.

– C'mon Nim. In here. Oh lor, Miss, how you startled me.

Molly's pale face floated in the doorway. Going down the stairs to meet her, Beatrice realised how tired she was, having made the effort to return. That was what had caused her trapped feeling. She must be strong and fight it. The past was dead.

– Molly. Weren't you to meet us at the station?

The girl, who had filled out in the intervening years and wore her dark hair short and fashionably bobbed, wrung her hands with unexpected intensity.

– I couldn't . . . that is I . . . I'm sorry, Miss. It's just that . . .

There was suffering in the eyes which Beatrice naturally attributed to the loss of her husband. Come, she thought to herself, there are others as badly off as you. Less of this self-pity. She squatted down to ruffle Nimrod's ears, in the old way. Molly grew a little calmer.

– Yes I look after him now, Miss. Poor fellow. He's on his last legs.

She snuffled again and turned away. Beatrice decided that practicality was the best solution. So she became the mistress of her own fate once again, moving through the house as if it held no memories at all, organising the unpacking of the luggage when it came and seeing that Ulysses got a meal to show him that this for the moment was home, before he wandered off to explore. But always

435

there was the suffering glint in the younger woman's eyes, suggestive of something new and raw and real. By this time they were in the classrooms, which Beatrice had asked a somewhat reluctant Molly to unlock for her. She immediately saw why. There had been much depredation. Not only had the fabric of desk and wall deteriorated, but also the stock of books and paper. After Mr Noone's retirement in the early twenties, Mrs Eddles had soldiered on alone. Then had come Molly's brief solitary interregnum. It was this probably that had done the damage. She had been expected to cope on her own. Admittedly, the classes were smaller since the demise of the quarry and she did have a regular supply teacher. But clearly, things had begun to drift. There were graffiti on the walls and a distinct smell of urine in one corner. The old world map above the blackboard was torn. The blackboard itself had lost much of its veneer. Molly's demeanour seemed to signify her unhappiness with the situation and suddenly Beatrice was reminded of a long ago evening in this very room, after the young girl had had her hair pulled. She felt a maternal tenderness.

– Never mind, Molly. You'll have a new headmistress soon. And look. I'll give you a hand. Tomorrow. Before the ceremony.

But Molly, biting her lip, would not be consoled.

– It's not that. Though I admit the place has gone to seed a bit.

– What is it then Molly?

Beatrice had not expected to have to deal so soon with another's emotional turmoil.

– It's him. He's back. And . . . and dying.

A little shiver passed through Beatrice. She realised she had dreamed something of this sort last night. She did not need to be told who was back.

There was rain on the wind by the time Beatrice and Molly reached the familiar path leading up to Old Neb. The wind was stripping the leaves from the hawthorn and elder which, untended over the intervening years, had crept out towards the centre of the way, leaving only a narrow winding track. Nimrod had followed for a short distance then lain down, head on paws. Overhead clouds moved in swift flotillas, low and grey. A flight of geese shaped like the barb of an arrow went honking past, to be answered by one of the released peacocks up in Thundersbarrow Hanger.

– How long has he been here, Molly?

Beatrice's voice was torn from her by the wind. But Molly heard.

– Only a couple of days. I've been feeding him. But he hardly eats. He's so thin, Miss. And he can hardly see. Says he walked all the way. By night. It's the face. Or what was the face. He won't be seen by daylight.

– Does he know I'm here? – Molly shook her head. – He's come back because of Charles, hasn't he? Because he knows about the memorial service.

But the wind blew harder and prevented further speech.

So for the first and only time, Beatrice entered the sea which had poured up out of the earth to engulf the quarry and all its ruined buildings. Down there amongst the tangles of branch and yellowed, scattering leaves, the sound of the wind sank to a far surf, while the air seemed to press in on all sides with a heavy underwater listlessness. Beatrice could not get her bearings. Out of the thick stagnant air the kilns rose up like three eroded reefs, their spongy walls waving ribbons of black-studded ash saplings. Then all at once the reefs seemed to float away, revealing a deep trench in which the hull of an ancient ship lay wrecked. This, she realised, must be the corrugated chapel which had been uprooted in the last landslide. Ahead Molly glimmered, a pearl fisher intimate with her suffocating underkingdom. Now they were threading through great seaweedy clumps of elder and thorn. Beatrice began to feel breathless and a little afraid. Then a dark mouth gaped. Or sea cave. They had arrived.

He lay on Sir Colin's greatcoat under the roof which had once been pierced by Charles's pickaxe. The chair was still in place and the stone with its rusty stain. He had flung his mask aside and stared up out of a disc of a face that lacked all contours. The nostrils were two holes. The mouth lipless. The skin a peculiar reddish brown, pitted and in places bearing the cords of old stitchwork. He had no eyelids to close. Nearby, on the tamped chalk floor, Beatrice noticed a little cairn of burnt-out Woodbine stubs. Molly was weeping.

– I loved my Jack and swore I'd never come back. But he, he made me.

Beatrice too was kneeling.

I am a brother to dragons, and a companion to owls.

– What's that, Miss? What's that you said to him?

But there was no need to reply. Eric Wren had returned to possess the hill at last.

On the evening of the following day an unfamiliar figure entered the church by way of the little-used north door. Sitting down at the back of the nave, she held her head in her hands for a few moments then began to cast her eyes slowly round the dim slit-windowed walls. Despite the years, despite the weight of experience and disappointment which the years had brought, Beatrice Lumley could not deny that she had hoped, albeit timidly, to find, in the ancient fragments of wall paintings, the world which she had entered as a nineteen-year-old girl one Sunday before the war. But today it was as if the deep submarine light of memory had been drained and flattened. In tableau after tableau, the figures of apostle and saint, angel and devil, had fossilised and dried out. The swelling tide of heavy submarine movement had withdrawn. Christ was no more than a wooden medieval king on a throne; Eve, her mouth ugly with weeping, a frightened woman being driven from some ignominious hiding-place. Again Beatrice put her head in her hands and saw the little ceremony of dedication in the schoolhouse garden. A child, ushered forward to cut the ribbon across the bench, had cried when the scissors did their work. Then, superimposed on this scene, she saw the schoolhouse parlour with its picture of Victoria and the ceramic pot that had once contained a brown-leaved aspidistra. Eric's coffin lay there now, waiting for tomorrow's burial. Beside it, hunched in a grief that was all the more intolerable for being wordless, sat Molly Dadger, bereaved for a second and final time. Beatrice blinked her eyes open. Soon she would go home. The tide had withdrawn. This place was no more than a windswept foreshore on which the wrack of the past lay bleaching. She had fulfilled her vow by coming here again. There was just one more thing left to do.

A MOVING COINCIDENCE. On Sunday last occurred an event in the little parish church at Ecclesden which says much about our recent history and its meaning. It was, in essence, two events, commingled, as it were, by happy chance. The first, long-planned and well-rehearsed, concerned the unveiling of a memorial plaque to the late Charles Colin Tremain, Captain in the Second Battalion, 4th –shire Regiment, the so-called 'Chalkhampton Chums', who was so tragically lost to us on the Somme eight years ago and now lies buried 'over there', in his little plot of English earth. The highlight of the service (if we except the Reverend Langridge's very apposite sermon on Nebuchadnezzar and the fiery furnace), was a performance by Dr Birkett's recently reformed Tongdean Choral Society who gave excellent renderings of 'Jesu Joy of Man's Desiring' and a traditional setting of the 'Corpus Christi Carol' which, though somewhat unseasonal, was apparently a boyhood favourite of the Captain's. The good doctor himself accompanied on the organ and many present were reminded of his extraordinary wartime concert which featured the singing of the late Miss Egerton, a much missed friend of the family. It would not be too much to claim that that particular concert did more to inspire our lads than a thousand well-meaning speeches. We have only to add that the service was a fitting tribute, the only sadness arising from the fact that Lady Tremain was herself too ill to attend.

The second event was much more low-keyed and highlighted the other darker side of that terrible but heroic conflict. For on the same afternoon occurred the short but moving burial service for one Eric Wren, a lance-corporal who served in the same battalion as the aforementioned Captain Tremain, received the DSO for conspicuous gallantry under fire on the Somme and spent his last years being treated for what, in the end, proved to be incurable injuries. Before the war Mr Wren worked in the now defunct Tremain Quarry Company, and it is a measure of the progress made in all

*areas of society that, unlike some of his forebears, the deceased left specific
instructions that he should be 'laid in parish earth'. Thus today, the casual
visitor, having mused a moment in front of Captain Tremain's modest but
dignified 'winklestone' plaque, may pass outside into the churchyard where,
under a yew-tree's enveloping shade, a humble 'other ranker' lies at rest.
Thus, these two men, though utterly divided in life by gulfs of class,
sensibility and experience, may be said to have been indissolubly united both
by their courageous willingness to give their lives for their country and,
latterly, by the peace which they both now share. As the poet hath well said:
'Age shall not weary them nor the years condemn . . .'*

She had taken the belemnite out of the locket and thrown it after
him into the grave. Maud's grave lay nearby but still she could not
bring herself to go near it. Now, walking on Thundersbarrow, she
saw how all the leaves had fallen in last night's gale and lay in their
thousands on the floor of the quarry under the naked, perpetually
swaying trees.